The Mill

By

Tracy Lamphere

Sleep Tight!

Tracy Lamphere 2004

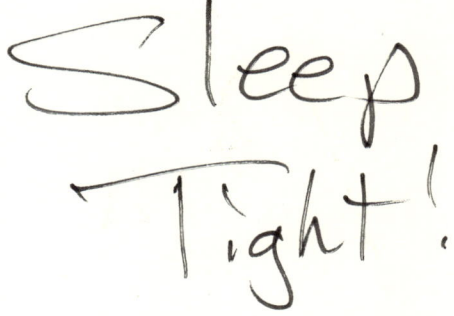

This book is a work of fiction. Places, events, and situations in this story are purely fictional. Any resemblance to actual persons, living or dead, is coincidental.

TraDon Publishing LLC
Colchester, VT 05446

ISBN: 1-4107-7335-3 (e-book)
ISBN: 1-4107-7333-7 (Paperback)
ISBN: 1-4107-7334-5 (Dust Jacket)

Library of Congress Control Number: 2003094817

This book is printed on acid free paper.

Printed in the United States of America
Bloomington, IN

1stBooks - rev. 08/19/03

In loving memory of my sister
Shari Lynne Lamphere-Sperry
With whose help and support
made this possible.

I want to thank my wife, Donna for all the support
and love she gave me while writing this book.
I Love You!

I also want to thank my mother, Judy for all her support
and help. Thanks for the push.
And, special thanks to my editor, Upton Brady. He not
only caught the mistakes—he taught me patience.

Last, but not least, I want
to thank Pete Collins for
proof reading.

Chapter 1

The night was cool despite a slight warm breeze blowing from the west. Spring was giving way to summer. He parked his truck on one of the numerous side streets and locked it. It was nine o'clock at night and the streets were empty and quiet. The town always seemed to shut down around seven each night. It took him only minutes to get to Maple Lane. In front of one of the houses located in this quiet little development on the outskirts of town, he stopped. Most of the lights in the house were off, but he saw one toward the back. He stood there a few minutes before knocking.

He reached into his duffel bag and pulled a piece of duct tape from it. With the other hand he knocked on the door, and waited there until he saw a light in the front room come on. He looked around and saw no one. His confidence rose. The door started to open slowly, exposing the chain lock on the inside. A woman peered around the side of the door. "Hi Vicki" he said, "It's me. I'm sorry it's so late."

"Its okay, come on in." She shut the door a moment to remove the chain, and as he heard the chain fall he made his move.

He pushed the door open with one foot and lunged at her, tossing his duffel bag on the floor. He grabbed her behind the neck, and, slapping the duct tape over her mouth, forced her to the floor. He pinned her arms under his knees and took off the tie from around her bathrobe. He wrapped it as tight as he could around her wrists and knotted it. Then he looked around to see if he had disturbed anyone else's sleep. Hearing nothing, he pulled her to her feet. Her robe fell open, exposing her body except for a pair of panties. She watched him as he stood there touching her breasts and then moving his hand down to the top of her panties. He reached his hand into them, rubbing her crotch until he couldn't take it anymore. She didn't resist him at all, as if she were a rag doll being played with, but she watched his every move, never taking her eyes off him. Grabbing his duffel bag, he forced her down the hall and held her tight to his body as they passed several closed doors and entered the open one at the end of it.

He pushed her onto the bed as close to the center of it as he could. Throwing his duffel bag on the bed, he got on top of her. He pulled some rope from his bag and laid it on the bed. He took her arms that were already tied together by the robe tie and placed them above her head. He replaced the tie with a piece of rope and threw the tie onto the floor. He tied another piece of rope between her wrists and the headboard. Then he tied each knee as tightly as he could to the corner posts of the headboard. Standing next to the bed, he reached into his duffel bag and pulled his knife from it. He

leaned over her and ran his tongue down her belly to the top of her panties, then dragged the tip of his knife down the same path his tongue had taken. When it reached the waistband of her panties, he cut them and ripped them from her body.

He noticed that she started to shake her head back and forth in an attempt to beg him to stop. That excited him even more. He cut the length of both sleeves of her bathrobe and pulled it from her body. He brought his face to her crotch and started to perform oral sex on her. He pulled back after only a few seconds and took his roll of duct tape and a black full-face ski mask from his bag. Putting the mask on over his head, he grabbed the duct tape, and left the room. He stopped at the first door on the right side of the hall and went in.

A few minutes later he returned to the master bedroom to find the woman in tears. He stood there staring at her little body, small breasts, and her legs spread to the point of splitting her in half while taking his clothes off. Getting on top of her, he placed one of her nipples into his mouth as if to seductively caress it. He lifted his head from her breast and in the same motion rammed himself into the opening of her backside. She arched her body as the pain from what he was doing rippled through her body. It didn't take long for him to finish what he was doing and he lay on top of her panting, after he finished. Getting off her, he sat next to her on the bed and started to caress her body. In a few minutes, he aroused himself enough to continue. Getting back on her he took himself and pushed his way into her, slamming her pelvic bone with every downward thrust.

He pulled himself out of her and reached over her head untying the rope that held her wrists to the headboard. Getting off her, he went to each side of the bed untying each knee. Weakened by his assault, she brought her legs together and he tied them together. Pulling the sheets out from the sides of the mattress, he placed them over her. He lifted her hundred pound body from the bed, placed her over his shoulder and carried her through the house to the garage, dumping her limp body on the cement floor in back of the car. He retrieved her car keys from the kitchen counter, returned to the garage, opened the trunk, and lifted her body into it.

After checking the house to make sure he left no clues to his identity, he got into the car and pushed the garage door's remote switch to open it. He pulled out as soon as it was high enough. Backing out onto the street, he pushed the remote switch again, and as the door shut he drove away. He turned down the hill that led to the canoe access for the Winooski River and stopped at a gate. Getting out of the car, he walked over and unlocked it. He drove through the gate, stopping once again inside to get out and relock it. Driving around this old brick building to the back, he

stopped the car and got out, walked around to the front door and let himself in.

He went through the building to the rear door, he pulled Vickie from the trunk and took her inside. What he didn't know was that Vickie had untied her legs. From the floor, she peered through the sheets and watched as he walked away. Realizing this might be her only opportunity, she took off running. Paul wasn't far behind and when he got close enough, he dove forward and tackled her. Vickie's head slammed against a machine—slicing the side of her head open. Paul stood up and saw her blood mixing with the machine oil in a large pan under the machine. He shrugged, then threw her lifeless body over his shoulder.

Nestled in the foothills of the Green Mountains, sitting on the outskirts of Burlington, Vermont's largest city, is the small community of Winooski. This little town changed very little through the years, Vermont's own little Mayberry RFD. The only thing it lacked was the checkerboard outside the general store. The worst that had happened is what nature threw at it in the 1927 flood. The greatest flood ever seen in the state's history had nearly destroyed everything, but the citizens of Winooski rebuilt the town and settled back into their lives with hardly a hitch.

As time went by so did the need for the old-fashioned cotton mills, and the factories that produced equipment for making war. Only one mill survived, maintaining its original purpose through the years—the machine tool mill. One of the three other mills was turned into some kind of storage facility, and another became a mall with many different kind of shops and restaurants. The third one overlooked the falls of the river and was changed into luxury apartments with a physical fitness center located on the bottom floor. The machine tool mill was managed by the same family, who handed it down from one generation to the next. Their product, like The Mill, would stand the test of time, because there was always a need for high-quality precision tool manufacturing.

The town didn't require much from its police or fire departments. A skirmish at a local pub, a traffic accident, and maybe an occasional house fire were their only challenges. The nearby Burlington police and fire departments reassured the townspeople that any greater problem could be dealt with.

Back at the turn of the century, when the mills and factories were producing at full capacity, it seemed everyone in this town worked at one or the other. Even children could be found working twelve to thirteen hours a day to help support their families. Child labor was the manufacturers' way of both cutting down on operating expenses, and of keeping up with the demands for their products. It wasn't odd to see entire families, even

numerous generations within the same family, working in the same mill. Sure the mills had their injuries, accidents, and even loss of life, but in the owners' minds nothing outweighed the profits they were making.

There are a lot of people still living here with the stories of the past, and some are the same people who grew up in those buildings working from when they were six or eight years old until they retired in their sixties. Not all the stories are good, and some of them are downright disgusting. Sweatshops they were called by some, death mills by others, and yet to most they provided a living they could not otherwise have made. One man in particular had very vivid memories of those times. He grew up in The Mill, working there his whole life. His name is Sam Lamperee, a little man weighing about a hundred and forty pounds wet. Gray hair, darkened skin, and numerous wrinkles over his entire body are all he has left from his career at The Mill. If you were to look in the books and ledgers of the past at The Mill, you would see that his surname was listed at least forty times, all the way back to the founding of The Mill. To this day he has grandchildren, and great grandchildren working there.

Let me introduce myself, my name is Larry Stone. As a freelance reporter for most of the local newspapers it is my job to try and get a story before all the other reporters do. The above brief history is taken from an article I wrote several years ago for the Colchester Centennial, and the opening story is one I made up after I knew as much about the case as anyone could. It's rare for anything interesting ever to happen in Vermont, so my job is not always easy, though I'm often helped by Nick Parker, a childhood friend who just happens to be the senior detective for the Winooski Police Department.

Growing up, I didn't have many friends, but that didn't seem to bother me much. It was during my last year in high school that I decided on my career. Nick and I had gone fishing down at the Winooski River on the Intervale when we came across a car hidden in a cornfield. When we went over to see what it was doing there, we saw a man in the front seat and a garden hose coming out of the window. We both ran to the police station to report what we had found. Since then, I always felt the need to be the first to get a story. I decided to become the best investigative reporter that Vermont, or anywhere else, had yet seen.

I have only left my hometown once in my life for any great period of time. After graduating, I left Winooski to attend college in Castleton, Vermont. Castleton State College is small, but it has one of the best media degree programs offered. While attending school I joined the school's newspaper, starting at the bottom and in my senior year becoming chief editor. My college years went by fast with numerous trips back home to

visit family and friends. Upon graduating, I accepted a job at the local newspaper in my hometown as a reporter.

The year was 2000, and Winooski had not changed much since 1979, when I went to Castleton State, with two exceptions—the population had risen and the crime level rose proportionately in both sophistication and style. The days of someone knowing everyone in town, or even knowing his neighbor by their first name were gone. Sure, there were some old timers still left like Sam and his family, but they were few and far between.

That winter was cold, and bleak. Most people stayed inside except to go to work, and to do the shopping. Getting around seemed to be harder and harder as all of the colleges started their spring semester, and students poured in from all over.

Springtime came and so did the flowers and the songbirds. Something was different on this spring day—so different that people would be talking about it for years. It wasn't the weather, flowers, or birds that would be imprinted into everyone's mind; it was the disappearance of two of its citizens. It was unbelievable to most in the community that something of this magnitude could happen to one of its own families. "This don't happen here," they said, "It happens in New York City, or California, but not here."

It was about 8:30 in the evening on May 27 that the local police department was summoned to 1239 Maple Lane in the East Mill Yard Estates development. This was one of those upper-income developments that had recently sprouted throughout the countryside to accommodate the growing population. It was just one of many.

The home belonged to Pat Lamperee, the eldest grandson of Sam. He was a salesman for The Mill and was often out of town on sales trips. This one was no different. It seems that he was out of town most of that week. When he returned Friday afternoon, instead of going to the plant he wanted to surprise his wife. He pulled into the driveway and ran through the front door yelling, "Surprise!" There was no answer from his new wife of six months, or the two children he had gained in the marriage. In the kitchen, he noticed the laundry basket with the clothes placed neatly in it, and a half full glass of ice tea on the counter. He tiptoed to the end of the hall, and threw open the door to the master bedroom, thinking that all three of them might be hiding in there to surprise him. It was empty.

He shut the master bedroom door quietly, and positioned himself in front of his children's bedroom door. He burst through the door saying, "I got you now!" He stopped in his tracks, when he saw his two daughters lying in between their beds naked, bound, and gagged. Their mouths were stuffed with something and were taped over. Duct tape around both their

necks kept them face-to-face. Their wrists were bound behind the opposite girl's back and their ankles were wrapped tightly together. As gently as he could he pulled the tape from around their necks and off their mouths.

He saw it was their panties gagging them behind the tape. They immediately started crying and screaming not only from fear, but also from the pain when he took the tape off. Trying to shut out the screams of pain as the tape pulled from their tender skin, he worried that they might have been raped. Once he got them freed, he looked into their eyes and asked, "Are you both all right? Did somebody hurt you? Where's mommy?" They couldn't stop crying enough for him to get a clear answer. All he could really understand was something about a man in a mask.

Panicked, thinking the worst, he told his daughters to stay put and ran through the rest of the house yelling for his wife. There wasn't a room or closet that he didn't look in. Nothing was out of its place. Her car was parked in the garage—the hood was even cold. Running back into the house to his daughters' bedroom, he found them exactly where he had left them, still too afraid to move. He wrapped them in their bathrobes. They were still unable to clearly tell him what happened so he went into his bedroom to call the police.

The police arrived at 8:47 PM, and entered the house with extreme caution given the baffling call they'd just received. When they found Pat, he was trying to comfort his daughters who were crying uncontrollably. Taking them out to the living room to talk to them, they called the station for a detective. It just so happened I was at the station talking to my friend Nick, the senior detective, when the call came in.

Nick Parker was an average size man who had always wanted to be a marine. After being refused by the military because of his smallish size and scrawny build, he set his sights on local law enforcement. Standing a little less than six feet tall he had the classic Marine-style buzz cut, and worked out constantly at the gym, which explained his muscular build. It was after a year of working out and studying that a position opened up on the Winooski police force. The written and physical exams were no trouble and he passed them with ease. Now, having gained acceptance to the Winooski police force, he continued studying and working as many hours as he could in order to learn all that he could. He became sergeant after just five years on the force and detective after ten years of dedication.

Terri, who was the dispatcher on duty and who had been with the force for thirteen years, told Nick he was needed at the crime scene. I asked if it would be all right to tag along. "Sure," he replied, "but don't touch anything, or get in the way." When we entered the house, I saw the two victims on the couch trying to inform the officer what happened. Officer

Steele, who was the first one at the scene said, "Sorry Nick, for ruining your Friday."

Nick said, "What's going on?" He told Nick about Pat Lamperee returning home to find his wife gone, and the condition in which he found his two little girls. Nick radioed in to have his partner Steve join him at the scene and bring the portable crime lab. Then he called for an ambulance to take the father and the two girls to the hospital.

Steve was a short, heavyset African American man who had moved to Winooski ten years ago after serving on the New York City police force for ten years. He had gotten fed up with dodging bullets in the city and came to Vermont looking for some peace and quiet. Accepting his position in Winooski, he thought his biggest problem was going to be deciding which flavor donut to purchase. Up until this day, life in Vermont had been exactly as he pictured it. Quiet and peaceful were the only words he used to describe his new life to old friends who still lived in the city.

Officer Steele greeted Steve at the door and told him where to find Nick. Nick told him what details he had gathered and explained that Lamperee and his two girls had gone to the hospital for treatment. Grabbing the lab kit from Steve's hand, Nick told Officer Steele to tape off the house. Steve began the tedious job of taking fingerprints, while Nick looked for other evidence. Nothing in the house looked out of place, as Pat had told them. Every inch of the house, both inside and out was photographed.

They started their fingerprinting in the kitchen where the clothesbasket and the half-full glass of iced tea were left because it appeared to be the last place Pat's wife had been. They found plenty of prints and, not knowing which ones belonged to the family members, they had to gather them all. The pieces of duct tape were gathered into an evidence bag along with the panties used to gag the little girls. There were some, but not many, prints found in the little girls' room. The rest of the house and the car in the garage yielded numerous prints. As the detectives were leaving the house, Officer Steele brought in one of the next-door neighbors. He told them that the neighbor had seen Mrs. Lamperee leave around 10:00 PM Thursday and then return around 11:30 PM. The two detectives asked him to meet them at the station the following morning.

They went back to the station to start processing the evidence they had gathered. Terri greeted them at the door, curious as always about what was going on. Nick replied, "We aren't sure. It's either a missing person made to look like an abduction, or an abduction." The detectives were obviously tired, but they continued on with their business, cataloguing evidence and locking it up in the safe in their office. On the way out of the office for the night, Nick handed the dispatcher the information on Mrs. Lamperee, so an all points bulletin for her could be sent to all the

surrounding communities' police departments. It was the end of a most unusual day for the detectives, and, looking beat, they left to go home. I left to go to the hospital to see if I could speak to Mr. Lamperee and his daughters.

I first approached Mr. Lamperee at the hospital introducing myself as a friend of Detective Nick from the Winooski Police Department. He looked terribly distraught over what he had come home to, just hours earlier, but seemed to have calmed down considerably. Following their arrival at the hospital, his daughters were given a thorough examination, and sedated so they would get a good night's sleep. Mr. Lamperee was also examined, and refused sedation until he could reach other family members. His first call was to his mother Jeanne, who was still living in the area about thirty miles north of Winooski. She told him that she would come in if she could get hold of his younger brother for a ride. He hung up the phone, and tried his brother's phone number. He got a busy signal, and thinking his mother might be trying it at the same time, he hung up. He waited for a few minutes before trying it again. This time his brother's phone rang, and rang. He let it ring for ten or twelve times before he hung up.

After hanging up the phone he realized that it being Friday night his brother was probably out drinking, as usual. He then called his sister Donna, who lived in Middlebury, Vermont. She married right after high school, and had lived there ever since. She told Pat that she would be there as soon as she could, but she didn't think that it would be before first thing in the morning. The doctor then returned and convinced Pat that a mild sedative would help him get a good night's rest. Before he dozed off, I was able to ask him a couple of questions. The first question I asked him was, "Are you and your wife having any marital problems?"

"Absolutely not; she's my best friend." Seeing that the medication was taking effect, I asked him only one more question, "Is there anyone you know who would do your family any harm?"

Pat answered very softly, "No."

Saturday morning came fast enough with the alarm clock sounding off at 5:30 AM. I wanted to get to the police station no later than 6:30 AM, to be there when Nick and Steve arrived. I entered the police station carrying donuts in one hand and coffee in the other. Terri giggled as she greeted me, "Up early this morning?"

I laughingly replied, "Aren't we all." She pointed back into the office area where Nick and Steve were already hard at work. When they saw that I had brought donuts, Nick shouted, "Break!"

Steve asked, "Were you able to get any useful information from Pat last night?"

"Just that his wife was his best friend, they had no marital problems, and that he didn't know of anybody that would want to harm his family."

It was about 7:30 AM when the Lamperee's neighbor walked in. We all told him to come in, have a seat, and to help himself to the donuts. He'd come prepared with his own travel mug of coffee.

Sitting down in a chair, he took a donut and leaned back to relax. Nick said, "I know we met last night, but I don't recall your name."

"It's Russ Wilcott, and I don't know if what I can tell you will help."

"Just tell us what you know, and don't worry, anything you can tell us will be a big help."

He started out by saying that he usually didn't snoop into his neighbor's business, because he felt that he wouldn't want them to snoop in his. Russ continued, "When I saw the police over at their house, I thought I had better tell you what I had seen."

"You're absolutely right, any little bit of information can be helpful."

That's when I introduced myself, and said, "You told us that you saw Mrs. Lamperee leave the house Friday at 10:30 PM, and return at approximately 11:30 PM."

Mr. Wilcott leaned forward, and replied, "It wasn't Friday, it was Thursday night, and 10:00, not 10:30. The only reason I found it particular was that I didn't notice the children with her either time, and they never go out leaving their children alone."

Nick looked at Steve and me, and said, "Well I guess we had better go back for another look, and this time let's get the boys to impound the vehicle." He then asked Russ, "Is there was anything else that you might have seen that night?"

"No." The two detectives thanked Mr. Wilcott for coming down to the station and told him that if they needed to they would call him. Mr. Wilcott then stood up to put on his coat, taking with him his coffee and a donut as he was walked out of the office. The two detectives were headed out the door with me right behind them.

We made it to the Lamperees' house within fifteen minutes. The tape from the night before had been removed and everything appeared to be normal. Nick and I went around back to investigate the area around the clothesline, and Steve headed into the garage through the side door. Steve turned the doorknob and to his surprise he found it unlocked. Nick and I couldn't find anything outside around the clothesline, so we went in the garage to join Steve. Steve was on the driver's side of the vehicle squatting down with the door open looking in at the floorboards. Nick opened the passenger side to inspect it. Steve said, "The only thing I see is that it looks

as though somebody might have dropped some ashes from a cigarette." Nick told him that the Lamperees weren't smokers and asked him if it could be something else.

Steve replied, "It sure looks like cigarette ashes to me, but I could be wrong." The patrolmen with the wrecker pulled up to the driveway at that moment, so both of them shut the car doors to go out and meet them. The detectives told them to tow it down to the station's garage and to wrap crime scene tape around it so as to prevent anyone from going into it. From there the three of us went to the hospital to talk to Mr. Lamperee. They wanted to ask him not to return to the house as he might unknowingly damage evidence.

When we arrived at Mr. Lamperee's hospital room he was just finishing his breakfast. He asked if the police were able to find out anything about what happened to his wife and children. The two detectives assured him they were still working on it and that they were waiting for results to come back from the state police lab. They asked Pat not to return to the house and if the three of them had another place they could stay. If not, the police department would supply them a place. A woman came in without announcing herself and went directly over to the bed, grabbing Pat in a hug and saying, "Where are the girls? Are they all right?"

He replied, "Yes they are. They're down the hall. They're in shock over what happened to them, but are more worried about their mother."

"I won't take no for an answer. You three should stay at my house. Pat, if you don't want to come, I can take the girls home with me until you send for them. I don't want you to worry about anything."

Patrick leaned over to the side of the bed to hug her, saying, "Thanks, I love you Sis."

She then left the room to go say hello to the two girls and to see how they were doing. Pat looked at the detectives, shrugged his shoulders, and said, "Now that's a great sister, uh? Wish I could say that about the rest of my family."

Nick asked, "What do you mean Mr. Lamperee?"

Angrily he answered, "My mother can't even come here to see how her grand-daughters are doing, let alone her own son. My lousy brother is nowhere to be found and is probably passed out somewhere with no worries in the world."

Steve replied, "That's tough. I'm sorry. If there is anything we can do, please let us know."

Feeling bad for the guy, I asked, "Do you need a ride somewhere?"

His reply was quick, "Sure, give me a couple of hours to get ready, and to make sure my girls are taken care of."

"Sure, no problem." I looked at my watch and told Pat that I would meet him down in the lobby in two hours. When I left, I wasn't sure where Pat had in mind for me to take him, but I figured that given what he and his two little girls had just gone through the least I could do for him was to give him a ride to where he would be staying.

I got back to the hospital with a few minutes to spare, so when I pulled up to the front door, I parked and lit a cigarette. By the time I had finished smoking it had been exactly two hours from the time we agreed to meet. Just as I got through the inside set of doors I heard a man yell, "Larry I'm over here." Looking around, I saw Pat standing there with his sister. He explained that he was sorry for keeping me waiting, but he had to let his sister know where he would be staying and that he would call her later that day. I told him not to worry about it and we turned to leave. We got into the car at about the same time and looking at him, I asked, "Where to, Pat?"

"If you don't mind I would like to run by my brother's house to see if he is there and if he is I'll just get out there. If he isn't I'll need a ride to my mom's—if that's okay?"

"Sure, anything that I can do to make it easier for you." We drove by his brother's apartment in Winooski and Pat didn't see his pickup anywhere around outside the building. He explained that his brother owned a black Toyota 4 X 4 pickup truck. Pat asked, "Would you mind me running in to see if he's home even if his car's not? I'd appreciate it very much."

"Sure." It was only a couple of minutes before Pat came back out shaking his head.

"Well I knew it was a long shot, but you never know. It's strange for Fred not to be home. He always goes to the bars, but he always makes it home."

"You never know. He probably met the girl of his dreams, or at least the girl of last nights' dreams."

With that we both let out a chuckle. I looked at him, and asked, "Mom's?"

"Please. Do you know where Fletcher is? If you can get us there, I'll get you the rest of the way."

"No problem." Within forty-five minutes I had Pat at his mother's house and was headed back to town. I returned home so I could start to write my story about what had been going on the past couple of days.

The rest of my day was uneventful, with only a few phone calls to the police station to see if Nick and Steve had come up with anything new. Nick told me that because of the weekend the process was a lot slower and they hadn't heard anything from the lab. They also hadn't received any word on Pat's wife's whereabouts. I settled into finishing my story while

waiting on my dinner to finish cooking. I went as far as I could with my story, finished eating, and went to bed hoping that Sunday would bring some news about the case, or Pat's wife.

Chapter 2

Sunday was usually very quiet and boring. Only the malls in Burlington and grocery stores were open, but not until eleven or so. At The Mill, as it was called, where Pat worked, the manager, Rob Blodder, came in generally around 8:30 AM, on his way to church to do a general walk around to see if everything was okay. I knew this because we attended the same church, and occasionally he would get there late if something was wrong at the plant. At church, I noticed neither Rob nor his wife showed up at all. I decided they both must be sick.

Just as I was getting into my car, after mass, I heard the sound of emergency vehicles off in the distance. When I hear sirens my reporter's adrenaline starts running. As I pulled out of the parking lot, a police cruiser went speeding by with its lights on and siren blaring. It was headed in the direction I take to go home, so I figured I would try to see what was going on. To my surprise they were headed down over the hill in the direction of The Mill.

I parked my car at the top of the hill to see if I could see anything going on, but I couldn't. I got out of the car, locked it up and walked down the hill to The Mill. By now my adrenaline was racing full tilt. At The Mill, I saw the gate was open and the yard full of emergency vehicles with hectically flashing lights. Rob's truck was parked just outside the gate as usual. Approaching his truck, I noticed Mrs. Blodder was in it. I went around to the driver's side, and, with a smile on my face, spoke through the open window.

"Hi, Lisa. What's going on? A false alarm or something?"

She had a worried look on her face and replied, "I don't know. Rob came running out of The Mill after being in there for a while, yelling to me to stay in the truck. The next thing I knew there were police cars coming down over the hill with the ambulance following."

I told her that I would try to find out what was going on. At the front door, I was stopped by one of Winooski's finest.

"You're going to have to stay back outside of the fence until further notice." I reluctantly obeyed, returned to the truck to tell Lisa that I couldn't get in, and ran up to my car to get my camera. Coming back down the hill with camera in hand, I had to step to the side because the ambulance was racing up the hill with its lights and sirens going.

When I got back to The Mill, I saw Nick and Rob standing beside Rob's truck, talking with Lisa. I reached them just as they were finishing their conversation and Lisa was rolling up the window. They didn't see me,

and headed back through the gate. At the same time, Rob's truck started up with the back up lights coming on. Lisa was taking off with the truck and leaving Rob here. As she passed me, the look on her face made it hard to determine what might have been said, so I just gave a smile and a wave as she drove by. Rob and Nick were almost at the front door when I yelled to them, they saw then and waved me over to them.

"Nick, Rob what's going on? Is everything all right?"

Nick said, "I'm afraid it's one of those weekends. You can come in, but I don't want you to touch anything and you have to stay on my heels, okay?"

"Yeah, sure." Rob didn't look good at all. His face was all white, as if he had seen a ghost or something. We went into the plant where I heard Nick say, "Rob, it would probably be better for you if you stayed in your office until we get done." We stopped to make sure that he made it to his office okay, and then Nick turned to me with a look on his face that I had never seen in all the years we'd known each other. I asked, "What's up?"

"You're not going to believe this one. Just remember I don't want you to touch anything."

"No problem."

We went down a stairway that led to the lower floor where the production was done at The Mill. We got halfway down and stopped at a doorway on a landing. Nick opened the door and we entered a small room where steel rods were stacked up against the wall. We maneuvered around a couple of worktables, and got to another doorway. Nick turned to me, and said, "I hope you're ready for this, because it seems like this is your lucky weekend as far as weird stories go."

I followed him down a small staircase into a room that looked as if it had five big ovens in it. We took a few steps toward these oven-looking devices and stopped. There was crime scene tape all around the ovens, and other areas of the room.

This room was dark and dreary even when lit. Even in the dimness I could see the large oven-like machines weren't like the conventional ovens in a kitchen, but rather they resembled a large pot that held a lava-like substance. The two in front of me were square, whereas the other three were round. A rail system of sorts hung from the ceiling. Positioned above one of the square vats on this rail was a hoist that operated electrically by a hand-held control box. I asked Nick, "What am I supposed to be seeing, or did I miss something?" Nick then pointed down in front of us toward the vat with the hoist over it at what appeared to be the remnants of a burnt human hand, a right hand with some kind of ring on it. "From what Rob told me, this is called the heat-treat area. It is here they take raw steel and harden it to be used to make their final product."

I asked, "Is that what I think it is?"

"Yep, it sure is. Whose we aren't quiet sure yet. Come on, there's more."

Turning around in the opposite direction, we headed down a small incline, a ramp through a small corridor where there was a workbench and then into a larger room with all kinds of machines, as far as your eyes could see. I thought this must be the main production area. Lining the outside wall was a row of very large machines. I then saw one of them had that all-to-familiar yellow crime-scene tape around it. Steve was taking crime-scene photographs before anyone disturbed the area.

While I waited for Steve to finish, I quickly jotted down the information that I had already been given and all that I had seen so far.

Steve finished and we went over to the front of the machine. It appeared to have two really huge grinding wheels shrouded by metal covers. The whole machine was sitting in what looked like a very large metal drip pan. Getting closer, I noticed that the fluid that was lying in this large drip pan was a dark reddish brown color.

"First of all what kind of machine are we looking at?" I asked Nick.

"Rob said that the area of The Mill we are in is called the centerless department, and this is what they call a rougher. It's used to take the steel after being heat-treated down to a diameter within five thousandths of an inch of the finished tool's diameter."

I asked Nick if he knew what the strange-colored fluid was. Nick's reply left my mouth hanging open.

"It appears to be human blood mixed with oil." Nick then left my side to get a closer look at the front of the machine. He put on thin latex gloves and gave a yell to Steve to bring him a plastic evidence bag and a specimen vial. Leaning down, Nick took the little glass vial and used it to scoop up some of the liquid that so entranced me when we first walked up to the machine. He handed it to Steve, who capped it and then put it into a bag for safekeeping. Nick then turned and headed back toward the little room where the ovens were.

"Well" he said, "are you coming, or are you just going to stand there?" It took me a few seconds, but I replied, "Yeah, I'm right behind you." I was thinking to myself that this was something you see in the movies, not in Winooski, VT. We got back to the heat-treat area where a patrolman was standing guard. Steve handed Nick another evidence bag, and told him that he was going to take a look through the rest of the building. Nick told him when he got done to give a call to the State Police and tell them to send over their crime scene technicians.

"I want this whole lower floor gone over for prints and anything else they can think of before the end of the day. Make sure you emphasize

that they have to be done *before* tomorrow morning, when the place opens. We don't want any of the employees ruining any evidence that hasn't shown itself yet."

"Sure, no problem," Steve said. "I'll also tell them to process it quickly, and get the results back to us ASAP." Nick bent down to pick up what remained of the hand lying on the floor.

"I bet you thought you had seen it all, didn't you?" I was swallowing repeatedly, trying not to gag, and Nick pretended not to notice.

"I just have a couple of questions for Rob," he said.

When we got to Rob's office door, I heard him on the phone telling someone about what was going on. Seeing us in the doorway, he hung up the phone and told us to have a seat. I took a seat and Nick just leaned up against the doorjamb. Nick told Rob that he had a couple of questions, and explained that the State Police crime scene technicians were on their way.

"Why them?" Rob asked.

Nick replied, "They have more people that are specialized in going over these types of situations, not missing anything, and having good results. I also thought that you would want this taken care of quickly so your production would not be interfered with when the employees come in tomorrow."

"So they will be done by tomorrow and I won't have to shut the plant down?"

"That's right, and when they're done, I'll give you a call so you can come down to lock it back up."

"Here's my phone number, but if all you want is someone to lock the door give, Fred Lamperee a call. He lives right around the corner, and can be here within minutes. Here's his number."

"He has the keys, and the alarm combination?"

"Yes."

"Are you and Fred the only ones with the keys and combination to this place? And was there anyone working here on Saturday?"

"Fred, myself, the upstairs office manager, and the owner of the company are the only ones with access to The Mill's lower floor's alarm combination. I was just talking to the owner, Ron Lackly, on the phone. Seeing he owns the place, I figured he ought to know what was going on and no the plant was shut down for the weekend." He further explained that he came in every Sunday on his way to church just to make sure everything was all right, and as soon as he saw the hand on the floor, he bolted up to his office to call 911.

Nicked asked, "Did you see anything out of place other than the obvious, prior to going downstairs?"

"Nothing seemed wrong. When I entered my code to shut the alarm off, the screen told me that a few of the sensing beams had to be bypassed. They sometimes have to be bypassed in order for the alarm to be set. Sometimes things get in the way of a beam that prevents the alarm being set, and the individual has to check the area that is having a problem. Seeing that everything is secure, they try setting it again. If it shows that it can't be set because of those beams being interrupted, they can then just bypass the area, allowing them to set the alarm. In this old Mill it isn't uncommon for that to be done."

"Who set the alarm on Friday?"

"It should have been the people who work on the third floor because they work till five, but we can go see."

We all walked over to the alarm control panel at the entrance of The Mill. Rob said, "All I have to do is put in my code, and run an inquiry for that date. Let's see. I was right. I thought I had asked Fred to work late that night to get things set up for Monday's work."

"Is that unusual?"

"Thinking about it, I did ask him to make sure that his work got done so the rest of the plant would have enough work to stay busy on Monday. I'll check to see if they had to bypass any alarms. Well, it says here they had a problem with the one in the heat-treat area, the little room off the stairway, and this main hallway. They're the ones that usually give me problems."

Nick thanked him for all his cooperation, told him he could leave, and that if he needed him for anything he would call.

Nick and I followed Rob outside where I told him that I was going to leave so that I could get my story done, hopefully before any of the other reporters got it. As I walked through the gate, Nick asked, "Would you please keep it as general as possible, not mentioning details of any kind unless you run it through me first, Larry?" I told him that I would keep it very vague, as long as Nick promised to give me first call if anything new came up.

"I promise," he said.

I shot a picture of The Mill, and I walked up the hill as the State Police Crime Lab truck turned the corner followed by Lisa who came to pick up Rob. When I got home, I sat down to compose my article. It wasn't hard for me to write a brief article about Friday's situation, because so far it was just a simple break in / missing person. I did find it hard to be vague about what happened today, but I had promised Nick that I would. My deadline for any story was four o'clock. I finished quickly, and jumped into my car to deliver copies to both papers.

I went to the *Colchester Centennial* first because it was right down the road from my house, on the way into Burlington. I told them I had a great story that no other reporter had gotten wind of yet. They took my copies and told me they would run it in Monday's paper, upon review.

I high-tailed it to the Burlington paper's downtown office. On my way, I ran over the details of the whole weekend in my mind and something just didn't seem right. I had to go by Fred Lamperee's apartment building, and then it hit me. Fred's car still wasn't there. At the Burlington paper's office, I explained what I had to the editor on duty. The editor told me it sounded like real good stuff. I told him I would be back to get my check next week. As I headed back to Winooski, I picked up my cell phone to call Nick at the station, hoping he would still be there. When Teri answered the phone, I told her to tell Nick that I would be there in ten minutes.

I found Nick and Steve in the back attempting to fingerprint the hand that was found at The Mill. When they finished Steve took out a little scalpel-like knife, removed a tissue sample from where it was torn from the arm, and smeared it onto a glass slide. I watched as Steve did his sampling, curious to why he was doing it. He noticed me watching him, and said, "We might be able to get a DNA sample from it." When they were done with their work, we sat down in Nick's office. I told them that something seemed weird to me, so I thought I'd stop by to tell them. "What do you have that's so important, Larry?" Nick asked. That's when I leaned forward in my chair and explained that I gave Pat a ride home from the hospital on Saturday.

"He wanted to go to his brother Fred's house, so we drove by. Pat didn't see Fred's truck, but we stopped anyway. Pat ran in to see if he might be there. When he came out, he got back into the car, and said Fred wasn't home. He also said that he asked a few of his neighbors if they had seen him. That's when I took him out to his mother's house to stay. On the way out, I remember him saying that he was unable to get in touch with Fred Friday night from the hospital. So, when I left The Mill today to go home I was thinking that it sounded strange that Fred worked late Friday night, Pat couldn't reach him from the hospital that night, and he still wasn't home on Saturday. To top everything off, he had access to The Mill and when I drove by just a few minutes ago his truck still wasn't at his apartment."

Nick and Steve both looked at me with a strange half comprehending look. Nick broke the silence by saying, "Quite a bit of detective work, Larry. Thanks for stopping in to let us know all of this. Give us some time to look into it, get some of the results back, and if we find out anything you will be the first we call." I left the station knowing what they might be thinking, but what I didn't know was if, or how it tied into the disappearance of Pat's wife.

I decided to go home to relax from the longest weekend that I'd had in a long time. When I got home, I put on my sweats, fixed something to eat, and lay back on the bed to watch television till I fell asleep.

It seemed as if I'd had about fifteen minutes of sleep before I was woken by my telephone ringing. Picking it up to answer, I looked at the alarm clock and saw that it was 1:00 AM. Still half asleep, I mumbled, "Hello, who is this?"

"Larry, get down to the station as soon as possible," Nick said.

"Nick, what's going on? Do you know that it's 1:00 AM?"

"Yeah, I know what time it is. Just get your ass down here now!" I told Nick I would be there as quick as I could, and hung up the phone. I was there in twenty minutes. "I hope you people have coffee, because I couldn't find anyplace open on the way in," I groaned.

Steve replied, "We got two pots just brewed, help yourself." Thanking him, I poured myself a large cup, and sat down with the obvious question on my face.

Nick and Steve both said they were sorry for me having to come to the station at such an hour, but told me they had their reasons. I relaxed a little as the coffee started to kick in, and they explained that the Vermont State Police crime scene unit retrieved numerous prints from both areas of The Mill and had brought the prints to them so they could look in their files here at the office for a possible match. They went further to explain that they were unable to get in touch with Fred Lamperee to lock The Mill. Nick said, "We were hoping that you would show us how to get to his apartment since you have already been there with his brother." I told them that I would be glad to take them there.

We left in the same car, hoping that it was going to be a quick trip. When we got there Steve knocked on the door, and got no response. He tried again several times, but got nowhere. One of the neighbors stuck his head out of his door and told him Fred hadn't been home all weekend. Not knowing really what to do, we left the apartment building and returned to the station.

When we arrived back at the station, Nick turned to Steve and asked, "Why don't you check the computer to see if we have anything on Fred Lamperee, and I'll go ahead and call Rob Blodder to let him know that he needs to come in to lock up The Mill."

While Nick talked to Rob, Steve said to himself, loud enough to be heard, "I found you." It was then the printer started buzzing and humming. He tore the copies off the printer, came over to the desk, and placed the report in front of Nick. It appeared that Fred had been picked up six years

ago shoplifting from a local grocery store. They even had a set of prints that were taken by the arresting officer.

Steve said, "Out of curiosity I'm going to check them against the prints we have available."

There must have been some thirty sets of prints collected at The Mill to compare with the ones they made from the hand they had found. Rob showed up to tell us that he had locked The Mill. He also thanked them for everything the police department had done in order not to interrupt his production on Monday.

As Rob left, Steve came running into the room from the back saying, "Nick you're not going to believe this."

"What do you have Steve?"

"I think I got a match on Fred's prints."

"NO! Was it out of one of the prints taken at the plant, or what?"

"No, it actually came from the print of the hand that we made earlier, but we should send it out to be verified. Along with both samples of tissue from the hand, and the fluid taken from the machine for a DNA test."

Nick agreed, saying, "It will take at least two to three weeks for the DNA to come back, but at least we can get the print results back within a day or so. You'll take care of that, Steve?"

"I'm on it, boss."

Chapter 3

Nick told Steve that he was going to the Chief, and ask for a search warrant for Fred Lamperee's apartment, based on the print match they had. Laughing, I said, "I'll meet you here at six o'clock sharp." It was 2:55 AM.

To my surprise Nick answered, "Sure, but you know the rules. If it wasn't for you and the little detective work you did we wouldn't be this far. Don't let the Chief see you though, you know how he feels."

"I know, don't touch or say anything. Don't worry, I'll stay home until you call me and then I'll meet you over there within fifteen minutes."

I woke up around noon, wondering if I might have missed Nick's call, or why he hadn't called with half the day gone by. About thirty minutes later the phone rang. The Chief had wanted Nick to wait on the warrant until the print confirmation came back, but as luck would have it the phone rang in the middle of their meeting. It turned out to be Rob Blodder, wanting to tell them that Fred hadn't shown for work. They were waiting for the warrant to be signed, and it should be ready within a few minutes. I told him I'd get dressed and would be waiting to hear from him.

While the coffee brewed, I jumped in the shower to wash the weekend away. I wouldn't forget this past weekend for a long time. As I pulled on my clothes the smell of fresh brewed coffee filled the house. Just as I started pouring a cup, the phone rang.

"We'll meet you there in fifteen minutes," Nick said. I told him I was on my way. I made it there with about five minutes to spare.

Nick and Steve arrived together with all their equipment loaded in the back seat and trunk. They both looked as tired as I felt. Steve said, "Larry, long time no see."

I laughed dutifully. Nick told me that while they were waiting on the warrant they checked the prints some more, and found the print that they made from the hand also matched a print that the State police crime scene people pulled off the electrical control box in the heat-treat area. I asked, "How can that be his hand on the floor, and his print on the control box?"

Steve said, "If you come up with the answer to that please let us know, because we haven't figured it out either." Nick was already at a door with a sign that read OFFICE, and as he knocked on it Steve and I came up behind him. A little old man answered the door. Nick explained very slowly to make sure he understood. Nick said, "We have a warrant to search Fred Lamperee's apartment, which is number six. We would

appreciate it very much if you would accompany us. In case Mr. Lamperee isn't home, you could let us in."

The little man said, "Yeah, Yeah. I don't want you kicking in the door just so I can fix it, especially when I know he isn't home."

I asked, "He isn't home?"

"No, and he hasn't been home all weekend", the man replied.

Steve knocked on his door just in case, but got no response. We all backed up so the manager could get to the door and unlock it. He opened the door, stepped aside, and said, "Help yourself and let me know when you leave, so I can lock it back up." Nick was the first in. He reached around with his hand searching for a light switch. It took a few seconds, but he finally found it on the left side of the entrance. Nick and Steve pulled pistols out from under their coats, released the safeties, and proceeded to enter the apartment. I went in last. As a matter of fact, I didn't enter until they told me the place was clear.

The first thought I had was that this person would never win the Good Housekeeping Award. It actually looked as if it was either being used for a garbage drop-off, or nobody had lived there for months. The detectives came back from the bedroom area and put on latex gloves. Steve handed me a pair of gloves. Nick said, "Remember Larry, before you actually move anything give me or Steve a yell."

"No problem, Nick." I didn't exactly know what they were looking for. I stood there for a few moments to observe the two detectives doing their job. They were picking up old magazines to see if they were covering up anything, and then placing them back where they found them. Steve went over to one of the corners to check out a pile of clothing that looked like it may have never seen water, but for an occasional rain.

I was dumbfounded that any human being could live like this on a daily basis. I looked all around. The number of cobwebs amazed me, and it looked like one giant spider web because there were so many of them intertwined. I noticed that there were stains of different colors over most of the walls. Besides the dirt and filth, what struck me was that there weren't any pictures or mirrors on the walls. Nothing. There was a little thirteen-inch television in one corner of the room, and across from that was what looked like a reclining office armchair. The television was perched on an old wooden chair. There were no tables or lamps of any kind. Half of this room was a living room and the other half was a kitchen.

In the kitchen side of the room, I flipped a switch that was located near the refrigerator, which turned on a light above the sink. I opened the refrigerator to find a couple of unopened beers and a moldy piece of blueberry cheesecake. The freezer contained a few small animal carcasses. I yelled to Nick to come and take a look. He reached in and pulled out two

undressed squirrels and three undressed chickens. It appeared Fred actually intended to eat them.

The floor in every part of the apartment was littered with old books and magazines, as if this person were using them as a floor covering instead of carpet. Nick pointed out the numerous torn out pages of road atlases. The maps mainly covered Massachusetts, New York, and Vermont. They seemed to be only in the living room. These magazines, and books didn't stop in the front rooms; they were all over the bedroom and bathroom, too. The bedroom had one thing that the rest of the place didn't have, a picture, and, no, it wasn't a family picture. It was an adult magazine's centerfold ripped out of the book, and put up on the ceiling above the bed. I thought this wouldn't have been so bad except it had been mangled to some extent. The picture itself was intact, but the strange thing was that the picture had slashes in the area of the girl's genitals. I stepped into the bathroom and saw the same kind of pictures on the walls. The bathtub and toilet were no worse than the rest of the house. What was amazing was that the stench in the house didn't get stronger in any one part of the house; it was pretty much equally disgusting throughout.

Back in the bedroom, I noticed a book on the floor just behind and underneath the headboard. I picked it up and to my surprise saw on the cover DIARY. Thumbing through, reading quickly, I was surprised to see that Fred had apparently written in it regularly. I joined Nick in the living room. I carried it out to the living room to let Nick know about it. "Man did you see those bedroom walls?"

"Sure did. I guess he has a problem with women, especially the one above the bed." We both had a nervous laugh at that one. What else could you do when a place was so disgusting? Nick asked me what I had in my hands.

"It appears to be his diary. I didn't read it, but that's what is on the cover. Do you mind if I take it home to read? I wouldn't mind finding out what kind of person lives this way."

"No, I don't have a problem with it, but none of it becomes public until this is all over. Just remember the only reason I'm allowing it is because you're my friend. If the chief finds out—it's all on you."

"Sure," I replied.

Steve went down to get the manager and I went back into the bedroom to see if maybe I had missed anything. There wasn't anything on the same side of the bed, but on the other side there was another book of the same style. When I leaned over to get it I had to reach blind for it, because there wasn't enough room for me to get down on all fours to grab it properly. When I finally reached it, I felt a sharp prick, so I repositioned my hand, and got it. It was another diary. What stuck me was a little penknife

sticking out of the book, like a bookmark. I figured it would be okay to take this one too since Nick said I could read the other one. I tucked the second diary under the first, and went toward the front door where Nick was still looking around. “Larry you know it’s a strange place this guy lives in. What are we in for?”

“I don’t know Nick, but if I find anything in the diary I’ll let you know.”

“Let’s go, I’ll buy the beer.” Just when we were stepping out into the hall we met Steve and the manager.

Nick said, “Steve, I want this door sealed, and police locked. Make sure someone does it ASAP.”

“No problem. I radioed for a patrolman to come down to stand watch.”

The detectives went back to the station with me following behind in my car.

While Steve took care of the paperwork, Nick and I headed down the street to a local pub by the name of Champions, a nice quiet little place where you could drop in for a beer and not be squeezed shoulder to shoulder with other people. After we ordered, we sat across from each other staring blankly into space as if the other person wasn’t there. I finally broke the silence.

“Can you believe these past few days? That place we just came from was definitely weird. Furthermore, if both prints do match, how did the print from the hand get on the control box?”

“No, I can’t believe it. This shit doesn’t happen in Winooski. Or at least it’s the first I’ve seen. Weird wasn’t the term I was thinking of to describe Fred’s apartment; it was more like bizarre. As for the prints, I have no clue, but I’m going to wait to see if they do indeed match before I start thinking about that. The other piece of this puzzle was Friday night and how it tied into everything else that went on, or was it a separate incident? I guess I need to go home, relax, and think about it for a while. It’s all just too Bee-Zar!”

I got home to a chilly house. I immediately turned up the heat. I changed into sweats, a tee shirt, turned the radio on to my favorite easy-listening channel, and got a soda. I took the two diaries and placed them on the nightstand, fixed the pillows so I could be propped up while reading them. I picked up the top one, and, seeing that it was the first one I found with more recent entries, I decided to look at the other one to see where it started. I opened the front cover and saw that the first entry was dated June 11, 1996. I removed the penknife and placed it on the nightstand marking the page it was stuck in by folding down the corner. Fred had placed the knife there for a reason, so when I got to that spot in the diary I wanted to

try and figure out why. Before I started reading I got my tape recorder and some blank tapes. I wanted to make sure that if I came across something interesting I would be able to remember it.

Now it was time to get started. I climbed onto my bed, picked the diary up, took a drink of soda, lit a cigarette, and got comfortable in anticipation of what I was about to read.

The first entry was made on June 11, 1996. Fred is nineteen, so that made him fifteen at the time of his first entry. He wrote about how he was getting bored during that summer, and that living at his mom's house out in Fletcher was not where he wanted to be. He also stated that his brother Pat had set up an interview with The Mill's manager, so maybe he could get a summer job there. The interview was set for the fourteenth. The twelfth and thirteenth didn't have much to say other than he was getting excited about his interview. Fred did mention that living out in Fletcher gained him a liking for eating squirrel meat, but only if his mom fixed gravy and biscuits with it. I guess that explains the squirrels in the freezer at his apartment. At this point I thought that it had to get better than this, and continued on.

June 14, 1996. My brother came to pick me up for my interview today at The Mill. Pat told me to grab a change of clothes in case he couldn't get me back out to mom's afterward. I met with the manager about the position as a custodian. The responsibilities weren't much, but that doesn't bother me. I'm really nervous about the thought of having a job. Up till now the only responsibilities I have had were to take the garbage out, and to clean my room. It was out of boredom that I started writing in this diary. Rob Blodder, the manager, explained my duties and pay. Rob asked me if I wanted the job, and I told him, I sure did; when do I start? He told me to be there first thing tomorrow, the fifteenth. Rob then paged Pat to his office and explained everything to him.

Pat, according to Fred's diary, told him he could stay with him. Pat had just gotten a new apartment that would be large enough for the both of them. This entry ended that night with Fred writing, *I can't believe I got the job. Before I go to bed Pat is making me call mom to tell her the good news and explain that I was staying with him.*

June 15, 1996. Today Pat woke me up at 5:30 in the morning so I could get ready for my first day of work. I was getting ready as Pat explained to me, even though this was a summer job, if I did well they would ask me back on all my summer breaks from school. I went into work with the best attitude anyone could have. I knew that practically everyone in my family had worked in The Mill, and I wasn't going to let anyone down. When I got there, a coworker by the name of Joe, took me through the plant and explained the details of my job. Of course, everyone wanted to get a look at the new person, but this didn't bother me. I met some people, and

was told that I probably would get to know everyone there because my job took me to all areas in the plant.

He wrote in his diary that night. *I love it at The Mill along with the opportunity to live at Pat's place like an adult. Being that it was my first day and being exhausted I'm going to say good night.*

Soon Fred was getting up on his own, because his brother was going to the other plant in Riverside, Massachusetts, training in the sales department. He would be gone for two or three days at a time, so if Fred wanted his job it was his responsibility to make sure he got to work on time. He wrote, *Being new to this having to get up to go to work, I better call mom to ask her if she could call in the morning to make sure I was up.* In Fred's mind it was all worked out, even knowing that he couldn't rely on his mother. Even though Fred worked eight hours a day, when his brother was gone he wrote how great it felt being out on his own and it was getting easier by the day to get up on his own for work. After a while waking up wasn't a problem. Work became routine, and, according to Rob, he was doing a fine job. His first week ended with him writing, *I'm going to see grandpa tomorrow because I don't have to go to work.*

Fred knew where his grandfather lived and it wasn't that far from Pat's place. He slept in, according to his entry, that Saturday, because it was his first day off in a week. He wrote, *June 19, 1996. Getting up at ten o'clock, I had a couple of eggs with toast, and got dressed to leave. It only took me twenty minutes or so to get to grandpa's house, which is located near the center of town, along the river.* His entry stated that he had lived there nearly forty years, staying on even after grandma's death. *Knocking on the door I didn't get an answer right off, so I knocked again. I heard a voice coming from inside the house telling me to hold my horses. I didn't tell him I was coming over, because I wanted to surprise him. I grew up without a dad and I always treated my grandpa with the same respect that I'd have treated my father; if I had one.* The rickety old man answered the door and stated what a pleasant surprise it was to see that his grandson, or at least one of them, hadn't forgotten him. *I take it by his comment that Pat didn't see him much.*

Although the old man went into the kitchen to fix something for lunch, he hadn't lost his hearing, and wanted to know if Fred was hungry. *I explained that I was working down at The Mill. Grandpa couldn't believe his ears and made me repeat myself.* His grandfather was excited, telling him how he worked there from the time he was eight years old until he retired fifty-some-odd years later. Fred wrote, *Grandpa went on the entire time I was there with stories of the old days, and how great it was that I was following in his footsteps. When he asked me what position I had at The Mill, I told him I was a custodian. Apparently that didn't go over well with*

grandpa, because all he said was, "Is that right?" Quickly changing his tone, grandpa, told me, "We all got to start somewhere." That made me feel a little better especially when he told me he started picking up metal shavings there. Not wanting to leave, according to his diary, Fred nevertheless said his good-byes and headed home for it was getting close to ten o'clock at night. *I knew my way home all right, but Pat had told me that it could get rough on the weekends downtown near the bars. When that thought came to mind, I started to run."*

Fred stayed in Sunday watching movies all day. He mentioned how the weekend seemed to go by so fast to his brother, who got home early Sunday afternoon, and his brother gave a friendly laugh. He also explained that, the more that you work, the longer the weekdays seemed. As Fred's brother explained, the weeks seem to get longer and the weekends, well, were never long enough for anyone. The entries in his diary were short and they consisted mainly of what he did that day, or maybe a new person he had met. Fred seemed to keep pretty much to himself while he was at work, offering the occasional hello and how are you exchanges.

Reading his diary, I decided that he wanted it this way. He had made several entries about how he was trying to keep his mind on his job and his eyes open to everything that was going on around him in the different areas his job took him. Fred didn't want to stay a janitor, but realized this was just a trial period for the summer. He really wanted to concentrate on being the best that he could so they would ask him back. Joe seemed to be one of the people that Fred enjoyed being around at work. When Fred had a problem, or didn't understand how to do something, Joe was always helpful. In one of his entries dated July 2,1996, he mentioned, *The more Joe is helpful the more it seems he has an ulterior motive. The less Joe has to do, the happier he is. Thinking about it, that's the way most people are when they have been at the same job year after year.*

July 4, 1996, I have today off. It's not paid, but once I get a full time job here it will be. I think mom is coming into town to go watch the fireworks with us. If she does come in, I hope she behaves herself and watches how much she drinks. Pat is going out to get her in a couple of hours. He asked if I wanted to ride out with him to get her, but I told him that I was going to run over to grandpa's house to say, "HI." Got to go, will write later before I go to sleep to let you know how it goes with mom.

Fred finished getting dressed and left to see his grandpa. He later indicated that his grandpa was proud of him working as hard as he was at The Mill. His grandpa also emphasized that Fred needed to try and get into the centerless department where they grind down the steel to the finish size of the tool before the cutting edges are ground into it. At least there he could use his smarts and abilities to the best of their potential. Fred's

response was that this was only a summer job, and that when it became a full-time job he would look into changing his job title. They said their good-byes and Fred went running home to wait on his brother, and mother.

Their mother made them something to eat for a late lunch and they all piled into Pat's car to go to Burlington for the festivities and fireworks. When they got there they parked near the waterfront, got out, and started walking down to the boathouse area. The boathouse was a local attraction in Burlington where many out of towners went to view the lake. They found an area to sit so that they could see the fireworks and that is when their mother opened the cooler to pull out a beer. By the time the fireworks were over Fred's mother was becoming obnoxious, slurring her speech, and drifting in and out with her thoughts. This is exactly what Fred didn't want to be around, but it was his mother, so he just dealt with it as it came. Fred couldn't wait to leave Burlington, so that Pat would bring their mother home. When Pat did arrive home from taking their mother back, Fred asked, "Pat, doesn't it bother you to see mom like that?"

Pat answered, "Sure, but what I don't see living away from home I don't think about." When Fred got ready for bed he concluded the entry for the fourth of July. He wrote, *I see why Pat moved out when he turned eighteen. He didn't want to be around mom drinking the way she was. Talking to him tonight, I know he knows what it is like for me still having to live there, so why doesn't he do something, anything? It's okay if he doesn't want to deal with mom, but he knows what I'm going through, doesn't he care?*

The rest of that month, entries weren't anything that was too interesting, or that gave even a bit of light into the mind of the individual we had come across this weekend. The August entries were very short. They talked mainly about Fred's work and how much he wished that he could stay there working full-time.

In the August 17, 1996, entry he wrote that he had a week left and was going to ask his brother if he could move in with him, so he could get away from his mother, and go to school in Winooski. The month ended with his job coming to an end. Rob the plant supervisor told Fred when he was leaving that he did a great job, and that he was more than welcome to come back next summer to work. *When I got home I saw that I had about an hour and a half before my brother got out of work; because the production people got out at 3:30 PM, and the office people got out at 5:00 PM.* He waited anxiously for the confrontation with his brother telling himself how much he loved Pat, and that Pat loved him the same in return. *In my eyes there is no reason in hell why he wouldn't take me in, so I could get away from the situation with mom.*

When Pat got home he wasn't in the best of moods after a long day on the phone dealing with irate customers. I waited for the right opportunity and asked Pat, "Would it be all right if I stayed with you, and went to school here in Winooski?"

Pat's response was, "No. What are you, stupid? Mom would never go for that, and you know it, besides if I can do it, so can you. So get your stuff together, get in the car, and let's go. I'm beat, and just want to come home to go to sleep."

Turning around in disappointment, I got my stuff together, threw it into Pat's car, and sat there waiting till Pat came out to give me a ride home. Pat came out, got into the car, and started it as he looked at me, and said, "It isn't all that bad at mom's." The rest of the ride was silent.

I don't want to go back to live with her; I wanted to stay at my brother's where there was a sort of peace for me. We arrived at moms and Pat didn't even get out of the car. Saying our good-byes, Pat told me that he loved me and that Rob told him that he had a hard working brother. I grabbed my stuff from the back seat leaned into the front passenger side window to say, "The hell with you, and your love. This September I turn sixteen, and I can drop out of school if I want, live where I want, and work full time, so again, the hell with you." That was about the extent of his August twenty-forth entry except for the words, *MY BROTHER SUCKS!!!!*

Chapter 4

As I read further on in the diary, it was becoming clear that Fred was uneasy with his mother's drinking, and not having any money coming in. It started to eat at him little by little. Fred also mentioned that he missed being able to see his grandpa when and if he wanted to. Having to live where he wasn't happy was just another thorn in his side. I did find some interesting things toward the middle of the month. It was September seventeenth, Fred's birthday. When he got home from school, Fred found his mother in the living room sitting there watching television in nothing but her panties. He was startled to find his mother that way, but seeing all the empty beer bottles on the floor explained her condition.

He wrote, *Walking up to her, I asked, "Mom what are doing? Do you realize you are in the living room with just your panties on?" She turned to me to reply, and before she could, tears started to swell up in her eyes. Gaining a little bit of composure, she said, "I realized it had slipped my mind that it was your birthday. I didn't get you a present or a card. That's when I lost it. My baby boy—how could I forget?" I helped her to her bedroom trying to be the good son. I didn't know at the time I was looking at my mother's breast, and it wasn't until she said something to me about my birthday that I realized that I was. I thought to myself there was no harm; it's mom. I'm sixteen, and this is my first time ever seeing a naked woman in person. As quickly as I could, I took her to her bedroom, and put her to bed just before she passed out.*

Leaving her there I shut the door and went back into the living room to clean up the mess she had made with the empty beer bottles, and cigarette butts that had fallen on the floor when she went to put them out. While I was doing this, I was thinking how lucky she was that I had come home from school, because she might have accidentally burned down the house. My hands were full of empty beer bottles, and the ashtray she was using. Walking to the kitchen to dispose of them I tripped, spilling beer from one of the bottles on the floor and myself. Getting rid of the bottles and ashtray on one of the kitchen counters, I went back to wipe the beer up off the floor. The smell of stale beer covered me, and my clothes, so I went to my room to get a change of clothes I could put on after I took a shower. As I was taking a shower, I thought to myself that I didn't want to deal with this anymore. If I couldn't stay at Pat's, I would stay at grandpa's house. School is boring and with the thought of having no money I liked the idea of just quitting school.

The shower curtain flew open. My mother was standing in front of me completely nude. I realized that I was also totally nude, and as I watched my mother's eyes checking me out I felt her hands starting to rub my penis. I leaped from the shower to grab a towel, and ran out of the bathroom, screaming and swearing at her. She just proved how sick she was, and I wanted her to stay away from me. I stayed in my room the rest of the night with my door locked. How could she have done that? What was she trying to do? That's it, I got to get out.

The next day he dressed in his room instead of the bathroom and came out only when it was time to leave to catch the bus to go to school. *I heard my mother saying something from her bedroom, but completely ignored it until the front door shut, silencing her.*

A couple of days went by before he wrote anything else in his diary. September 20th. *Instead of going to school, when the bus dropped me off, I turned around and started walking away. I went back to the road where we lived to a spot in the woods where I could see my house but no one could see me. A car pulled up to the house a few hours later. It was the neighbor who lived down the road. As I watched, she went into the house and within a few moments the door opened and my mother came out and left with her. The neighbor must have been coming to give her a ride to the store I thought to myself, probably to get more beer. I waited as the car drove away and until they were completely out of sight to come out of my hiding spot. I ran to the house as fast as I could. Getting to my room I grabbed my duffel bag from the closet and started filling it with my clothes, personal belongings, and shoes I would need to get by on. I didn't want to leave a note, but I did.* In his entry he said the note read, *"Mom can't live like this no more, don't worry, and just take care of yourself." I placed the note on the refrigerator knowing when she got back she would see it when she put her beer away. I also thought that I would have a good enough head start that she wouldn't be able to find me.*

With my duffel bag thrown over my shoulder I headed back to the woods. I knew a shortcut, or at least it was a route I could take to the interstate without anyone seeing me. The hike through the woods took me longer than I thought it would. When I emerged from the woods, I saw the road. Walking over to it, I set my duffel bag down and stood there waiting for a car to go by. I had never hitchhiked before, so I was doing the best that I knew how. Seeing it a million times in movies and on television, I figured I would get a ride from the first car that went by. It didn't happen that way for me, and, as a matter of fact, it wasn't until the twelfth or thirteenth car had gone by before someone stopped. The car pulled over just ahead of where I was standing. I ran to the passenger side front door and opened it. The guy driving explained he was headed for Burlington if I

wanted a ride. I told him sure and throwing my duffel bag in the back seat, I got in the front. When the car pulled away from the side of the road I felt such a feeling of relief and that freedom had finally come for me. It was almost like a thousand pounds had been lifted from my shoulders, I was free. My thoughts were broken up, when I smelled a strange odor in the car. It reminded me of what the boys' bathroom smelled like at school.

I asked the driver if that was marijuana. I was caught off guard when he handed it to me saying, "It sure is, and it's the best around. Help yourself." I didn't want him to think that I was a nerd or anything, or even maybe that I might be a rat, so I took it from him, put it to my mouth, and took my very first hit off a marijuana cigarette. He said in his diary that at first he coughed, and choked on it like he assumed everyone did. The more the stranger passed it to him the easier it became to hold it in. Fred's feeling of freedom was intensified by his introduction to pot. The feeling was so overwhelming that he wrote, *Nothing in my life had ever made me feel this great. The rest of my ride was very relaxing and consisted of light conversation, laughter, and just sitting back listening to the music as the miles were put between my nightmare and me. The man asked me where I wanted to get out and I told him Winooski would be great. The car pulled over right before the exit to Winooski and stopped. I got my stuff from the back seat as I thanked him for the ride. I looked at the guy to say my good-byes, and noticed he was handing me a marijuana cigarette, telling me I looked like I could use it. I grabbed it, saying thanks as I shut the door, and threw my duffel bag over my back. I started to walk down the ramp towards Winooski.*

Fred explained that his grandpa greeted him with open arms. He told his grandpa he couldn't stay any longer with his mother; her drinking and "mental head-trips" were too much for him to deal with. Fred went on further to explain that school no longer interested him and that he'd rather earn his way than live in purgatory. They talked all day and into the night, stopping only to eat something for dinner. Fred started to doze off in the living room chair, so his grandpa told him he ought to go to bed, and that he could use the spare room. As his last line in the entry for September 20th he wrote, *I'M FREE!!!*

Apparently that night his grandpa had betrayed him by calling his older brother to let him know where he was. Fred realized what his grandpa had done when he read the note the next day that Pat had left for him. It said, *"Fred, when you get this please come to The Mill and don't worry mom doesn't know."*

It was a long day for me and I didn't get up until eleven that morning. Seeing Pat's message on the table I asked how my brother found out, and grandpa told me that he had called. He explained that Pat had

called out to my mother's house earlier in the day, but didn't get an answer. Pat tried a couple of hours later. Mom answered the phone and told him she hadn't seen me. He called grandpa's taking a chance that he might have seen me. He sounded concerned to Sam, and he went on to tell him the conversation that I had with him about staying there, and what his reply was. Pat wanted to apologize for his part of the conversation we had when he dropped me off.

I sat down at the table, while listening to grandpa and ate my cereal. I think I finally understood why he told Pat that I was there. Thanking him for his honesty, I got up, rinsed my bowl, and went off to take a shower. By the time I got dressed it was about 11:45 AM, and not really knowing my brother's schedule, I called The Mill to see what he wanted. I said, "I heard that you wanted me to call, so I am." Pat told me that his lunch started at noon and that he wanted to come over to pick me up. I told him that I wouldn't go with him if he were planning to take me home, so Pat agreed that he wouldn't.

Pat arrived at the house to find me sitting on the front porch. As soon as Pat stopped the car I got up, went over to the passenger door, opened it, and got in. I explained to Pat what drove me to leave mom's house and when I got done I added that there was nothing to say that would change my mind. Pat asked, "What do you plan to do?" My response was that I was hoping to start working full-time at The Mill. I told Pat that my desire for schoolwork was gone. Grandpa had told me that I could stay there until I got my own place and all I needed was a job. We drove up to McDonalds to get a bite to eat before we returned to The Mill. When we got back, Pat told me he wanted to go in first to tell Rob what was going on and that he would come out to get me when they were ready. Within minutes, Pat was at the door waving to me to come in. I went in to see Rob about getting the job back that I had that past summer, but Rob explained that he had filled that spot with a part-time employee. He told me the only position available, if I were interested, was in the centerless department. I told him any job there would be appreciated.

Rob said, "You come in tomorrow at seven o'clock, we'll fill out the paperwork, and I'll introduce you to your new lead man." Pat thanked Rob as we were leaving, as did I, adding that Rob wouldn't be sorry with his decision. I, the whole time, was thinking to myself, "Wait till grandpa hears this." Outside I turned to Pat to give him a hug and to thank him for what he had done. As I walked away, Pat yelled to me, "We'll see you bright and early tomorrow morning."

I went through the gate and I looked down the hill to the river where the town had a canoe access. I walked down there to take a look and decided to take a break and smoke a cigarette. Reaching into my pocket, I

found that marijuana cigarette the guy who picked me up the other day had given me. Looking around to make sure that no one could see me, I lit it up. I smoked almost half of it before things were getting altered with my senses and decided to save the rest. Putting it out, I lit up a cigarette and sat back trying to forget the awful scene I had in my mind from my birthday. While I was sitting there I noticed that being high was really neat and I didn't know why I hadn't tried it before. I thought how grandpa was going to be excited when he found out that I got a full time job in the centerless department. I headed up the hill on my way back to grandpa's.

It was at this point that I had to put down the diary, so I could go to the bathroom. I was standing there in the bathroom taking care of business and thinking how odd it was that other than the episode with Fred's mother and the couple of times he smoked pot there wasn't anything unusual about this kid. I wasn't going to give up. Finishing, I lit a cigarette, got on the bed in a relaxing position, and picked up the diary to read on. Before I got started though, I did note that the entries skipped days and sometimes even weeks. I opened it back to the day of the twenty-first to find out what Fred's grandpa said to him when he found out about his new job.

I told him my new job was in the centerless department. Grandpa's eyes opened up as wide as they could go and he had a smile from ear to ear. Grandpa told me that this was such a special occasion that he was going to pull some venison steaks out of the freezer and make me a special dinner. He wanted to hear the whole story. I sat down at the kitchen table and started to tell him about my day when grandpa said, "Wait, before you get too far, why don't you grab a beer out of the refrigerator." Not sure if he meant for me to get him one, or both of us one, I grabbed just one and put it on the table in front of him. Grandpa asked, "What, you don't want to have one with me?"

I, of course, told him sure. Grandpa took the venison out of the freezer to thaw it out in the microwave, so that he could put it in a frying pan to cook it his own special way. Grandpa then turned to me to tell me now that I'm living here, breaking bread, and sharing a beer he thought that I was old enough to start calling him Sam. I told him okay, and that it would be a lot easier than saying grandpa all the time. We both laughed, took a drink off our bottles, and continued to talk.

Fred helped cut the onions, mushrooms, and green peppers that Sam was going to add in the pan. Reaching into the refrigerator, Sam grabbed another two beers for them saying how proud he was of Fred for his new job. By the time dinner was over, the two of them had put a good dent in the twelve pack that was in the refrigerator, and said their good nights at about the same time. Sam reminded Fred to set his alarm, and as a back up he would, too. Fred wrote, *It's September 21st the second best day of my*

life. I got a full time job at The Mill thanks to my brother's help; maybe he does love me. Sam and I just finished a venison dinner, and I got drunk for the first time. Life couldn't be better. With that I'll finish writing, so as I can go to sleep.

Fred wrote in his diary on September 22nd: *This was the beginning of a whole new life for me.* Fred arrived on time to begin his workday and reported to Rob Blodder's office to fill out paper work and meet up with his new supervisor. Fred completed the paperwork by the time that Donny showed up at Rob's office.

Rob told me that he wanted me to meet my new supervisor, Donny. I thought to myself that he looked familiar from when I worked there in the summer, but I wasn't sure. I said that it was nice to meet him.

Donny shook my hand, and then told me to follow him, so he could introduce me to some of my coworkers in the department and the person I'm going to train with. He explained to me that he was one of his best workers he had in centerless, although he's young. I told him if he's the best, then that's who I want to train with. I asked him if he knew my grandpa who had worked there years ago and told him his name. Donny told me that the name sounded familiar, but he didn't know him personally. I proceeded to follow Donny to the stairway that led down to the production floor.

When we got to the first floor Donny handed me a pair of safety glasses, and ear plugs. Going over to the centerless department I saw a lot of familiar looking people that said hi to me as we walked by. Donny yelled to the worker that was going to train me. He then introduced us to each other—telling him my name and telling me his. I shook Andy's hand and said hello.

Andy took him over to the machine that he would be working on. Fred said that Andy had bright red hair, pierced ears, and tattoos. At the same time he was thinking that this guy was pretty cool, he was also worried about the machine's size and wondered if he would be able to do the job. Fred told himself that it wouldn't be a problem, because he knew that he was a quick learner. The morning flew by fast and the next thing that Fred heard was the break buzzer sounding over the noise of his machine. He wrote, *When the buzzer went off, Andy said, "Come on dude its break time. I'll show you where we hang out." Andy then asked me if I smoke? I told him I did and he told me to follow him.*

It was here that Fred would meet the new clique of friends he would be hanging out with while at work, and sometimes after work. Fred pulled out his pack of cigarettes while talking to his new friends. When he went to take one out, he accidentally grabbed what was left of the one that the guy gave him when he was hitchhiking. The only person who noticed it before Fred realized which one he had in his hand was Andy. He wrote, *Andy told*

me that I had better put it away and save it for lunch. That's when Fred noticed what he was talking about, and quickly stashed it back in his cigarette pack. Reaching in for another one, he looked at Andy to see that he had a grin from ear to ear. On the way back into work, Andy told him that he could do lunch with him if he didn't have any other plans. Fred nodded, and hurried back to his machine to show he was eager to work.

The lunch buzzer went off just as he finished with a job and was asking Andy what to do with it. Andy told him to leave it there until after lunch. Both of them went to wash up. The guys all jumped into a car and left the company property as they did every day. As soon as the car started up the hill, they lit up. Fred, not being a pot smoker for very long, had only taken a few hits off the pipe when he started to feel the effects, and stopped. They returned to The Mill with a few minutes to spare, so they all got out to smoke a cigarette. When the buzzer sounded they put them out and returned to work. On the way into The Mill, Fred asked Andy if they did that every lunch. Andy said that they sure do. Laughing, they went back to their department to finish the day.

The last half of the day went quickly for Fred, or at least it seemed to. He picked up the operation of the machine faster than he thought he would. When Fred tallied up the numbers from the jobs he'd completed he was surprised to see the number of tools that he ran through his machine, and so were Donny and Andy. Donny said, "It looks like he's going to work out if he can keep these numbers up." Andy agreed, and proceeded over to Fred to tell him what a good job he had done, and that he could wash up. Fred went home to tell Sam how his day went. No sooner had he got on the porch than the door flew open. Sam was so excited to hear about his day that he couldn't even wait for Fred to come through the door. Explaining how his day went over a couple of beers and then dinner, Fred retired early to his bedroom. He went in, shut the door, changed into something more comfortable, and relaxed on his bed. He turned on his radio. Taking out his diary he began to write—recounting his day, and finished with, *Good Night.*

The entries in his diary went on from day to day, missing some days, and even skipping a week, or two. The entries that he did make all seemed to be the same, repetitiously recounting how he enjoyed his job, how easy it was becoming, and how he became closer to Andy in their friendship. He went on to say that he was even invited to Andy's apartment one day after work to drink a couple of beers, and to get high. Fred's use of drugs and alcohol became more intensified as the days, and weeks went by. In his entry on October thirtieth he mentioned that he even noticed that he was into it more than he thought he would ever be. He rationalized that his use was out of boredom with the job, and his personal life. He didn't have a girlfriend to share that side of life with. All he had were male friends. In

this entry he even mentioned how there were a couple of cute girls at work, but nothing to brag about. If he kept his mind on his machine and job, he figured he would be all right. He ended the entry by writing, *Maybe some day I'll have a girlfriend, but I'm not going to worry about it now.*

I started to lose interest. But I figured that I had better continue without skipping any pages if I was going to learn about Fred and what made him tick. It seemed the fall months were boring with Fred just going to work every day, having a few beers with his friends, and then going home for the evenings.

November 13th entry. *It was to cold outside to be doing anything, but I had to go to work. Thank God for pot. It's easy for me to get it from my friends at work and with the beer that Sam made sure he kept in the house; I'll make it through the winter.*

Sam didn't ask for much money from Fred. He had to help out with the food, beer, and the electric bill. On top of this, Sam charged him fifty dollars a week, which he put into a bank account, so that Fred could save enough to get a place of his own. Not that he wanted his grandson out; as a matter of fact, he enjoyed his company. Having someone else in the house gave Sam a sense of being and purpose, whereas alone it seemed that he was just maintaining his existence.

Chapter 5

Spring started out with a break in the cold weather, and a newfound drive in Fred. Fred wrote throughout the winter months that his progression in the centerless department was at its peak. He felt that he couldn't expand himself anymore in the position that he started last September. He went on to write that he was becoming complacent, and bored. Although he had these feelings he never let his production level go down to the point that his superiors had to talk to him. They really didn't even notice a change in his attitude, he wrote. The one annotation he made was in March where he wrote on the tenth day that work was really beginning to bother him and that something had to change. The thought of standing behind this one machine for the next twenty-five years didn't seem too appealing. Still, at the end of every day he would come home, sit with Sam to have a few beers and talk about how his day went.

It was in the April 1, 1997 entry that he wrote about an opening in the heat-treat department. He saw it one day posted on the bulletin board near the lunchroom where he would go after smoking a cigarette at lunchtime, if he didn't go out with Andy and the rest of them. Going out every day, getting wasted, and coming back to the same machine didn't always interest him. Fred's tolerance for marijuana did increase as did his beer consumption, but as he put it one time to Sam, he wrote, *I don't have a problem grandpa. I go to work every day, I'm never late, and I don't do it at work.* As Fred wrote this he must have thought to himself that ever since he had been at Sam's he hadn't ever lied to him, but he just had. It was only a little lie, he thought to himself, and as long as it doesn't affect his work, Sam would never know the difference. He ended his entry by writing, *I made my mind up to go in tomorrow and ask to be considered for the heat-treat department. If that became routine to me after a while, at least I would be learning something new. The more I know, the better off. I am.*

He got to work a little bit earlier that day to speak to Rob about the position. He explained how he would be willing to go out to the centerless department if they needed the help, and if things were under control in heat-treat. Rob said, "Let me think about it for a little bit, talk to Donny, talk to Jimmy who runs the heat-treat department, and I will let you know by the end of the day." It was about a quarter of three when he heard a page for him to go to Rob's office. When he got there he found Donny, Jimmy, and Rob all waiting for him. They explained how he would be missed for his production in the centerless department, but they also told him that his great work attitude would be beneficial to the heat-treat department. Rob told

Fred he had the position in heat-treat. He also went on to explain to him how they were going to work it out, so hopefully he would be somewhat a benefit in both departments until he could be replaced in centerless. Fred was smiling from ear to ear when he heard the news, and guaranteed them all that they had made the right decision, and he wouldn't let any of them down.

With that he left the office to go downstairs, finish up what he was doing, and to clean up. He left The Mill with an inner feeling of delight because they saw enough potential in him to give him this chance.

Fred got home at the usual time, went to his room, smoked a pipe full of pot, and went down to have some beers with Sam. They ordered out that night for pizza and while waiting for it they walked over to the nearest store for another twelve pack. By the time they got home the pizza delivery was just coming around the corner at the end of their street. They sat down in the living room watching the local news while they ate, and started on their next twelve pack. Laughing, and joking about how the news station's weather person was hardly ever right, Fred told Sam that he had some great news to tell him. Fred didn't stop to think about whether or not Sam would be upset. He told Sam that he would be working in both departments at first, but would eventually end up working full time in the heat-treat department. Sam looked pleased, but as Fred wrote later that night, *It was a look of forced emotion.* Fred knew that Sam wanted him to stay in the centerless department as he had. Finishing his entry he wrote, *Everyone is different, and I hope grandpa understands that.*

I went to the kitchen to get something to munch on and lay back down to continue reading. It seemed Fred was sincerely concerned over his grandfather's feelings, but was finding his own identity at the same time. I was anxious to find out if he had indeed made the right decision, or at least if he felt that he had made the right one.

April 3rd was actually his first taste of heat-treat, and at the end of the day Fred came out of The Mill like a new person.

There were so many new things to learn and remember. I'm amazed that the steel could be put into these things they called ovens and not melt. The substance in the ovens looked like molten lava. The safety issues involved were more severe, as Jimmy put it, "That lava looking stuff could peel the hide right off a person." For an example of this, Jimmy threw a cigarette into the open mouth of the oven; I just stood there in amazement as it disappeared into nothing. It didn't even leave any ash on the top of it—it was completely gone. Jimmy went on to explain to me that because I was still working in centerless I would first learn the simpler things and that I wouldn't have to deal with the ovens at first.

Fred wrote later that week that it was really tiring to him going back and forth, but he was going to do it because he knew he could, and that it wasn't always going to be like this. Fred figured that it was as much mental exhaustion as it was physical. He wrote, *I had to learn all the temperatures, steel styles, and new safety requirements essential to avoid injury.*

He was out at his centerless machine for the whole next day. Talking and joking around with Andy throughout the day made him realize he missed it. Andy asked how he liked it out in heat-treat, and if it was everything he thought it was going to be. Fred tried to make him understand how bored he had become standing behind one machine, while at the same time trying not to put Andy down for his liking to do just that. Andy replied, "Don't worry, dude, it's not for everyone. Are you doing lunch with us?"

Fred answered, "Of course I'll be doing lunch with you and the other guys." It was at lunch, while getting high with the guys, that he started to tell them what he had been told by Jimmy: "Yeah, if you wanted to kill someone all you would have to do is dump them into those ovens in heat-treat, and nobody would know." They all laughed, and went on talking shop gossip. Before they knew it, it was time to go back to work. When they arrived Donny called Fred aside to tell him that they found someone to replace him, and that this would be his last full day in centerless. With a smile, Fred said, "Thanks Donny. If you ever need the help let me know." They shook hands and Fred went back to his machine to finish the day.

When Fred left he knew that this wasn't going to be a good night with Sam. Even though Sam said he was happy for Fred and wanted the best for him, Fred knew different. Fred decided not to change anything about his routine. After their ritual bull session over a few beers, Fred said he was going out for a bit. After walking around the block a few times he went back inside and sat with Sam in the living room. Sam looked at him, and asked, "Now what?"

"What do you mean?" Sam explained the last time he sat with him in the living room he told him he was switching departments, so he figured something was up. Fred said, "Today was my last day in centerless. I start full-time in heat-treat tomorrow." Sam glanced at him and then focused back on the television.

Fred went to his room a little upset knowing that Sam was upset with his choice. All Fred wanted to do was to lie on his bed. Lying there smoking a joint, Fred reached down under his bed to grab his recent edition of *Playboy Magazine*. Thumbing through it, while smoking his pot, he found that he was getting an erection. He went on to look at the pictures as he finished his joint. Putting it out, he reached down and began rubbing himself to the point that he ejaculated in his pants. He smiled, as the

immense feeling of relief overcame his body and mind. He wrote, *I don't feel bad at all about masturbating. I'm not hurting anyone, and it feels good.*

Going to work the next day marked the beginning of Fred's new career, and when this thought entered his mind a smile came to his face for the rest of his walk to The Mill. He went down to the heat-treat area where he met Jimmy who told him it was going to be a long day. He explained that they had a lot of steel to cook, and then it had to be sorted, and sent out to the next department. He also asked Fred if he would work overtime to try and get it done by the end of the day. Fred only worked to three-thirty normally and knew that the upper floors worked until five, so he figured at the latest he would be getting out at five. Fred's day ended at seven o'clock that evening, and when he got home he barely felt like taking the time to visit and have a few beers with Sam. "I got to go to bed, Sam. I'm beat. This was the longest day I ever put in at The Mill since I've been there," Fred explained as he headed for his bedroom.

He went into his room, shutting the door behind him. Fred lay on his bed as he did the night before, smoking and pleasuring himself. He then turned off the light and went to sleep. Fred didn't write about this day until his next entry on April 7th.

As during the winter months, Fred's entries became sporadic. There was no systematic entering on his part except that he seemed to write less as his hours at work increased. Fred would then cram a lot of days into a page or so of writing. His next entry was on May 6th, where he started to explain that his department had been working overtime for the past month or more. It didn't really seem to bother him though, because he wrote that he was able to save some money, and learn the job quicker. Fred wrote about how Jimmy was preparing him for when he went on vacation, so he would be able to do the job while he was gone. He also wrote that there was a new girl working on the third floor who was really cute, they would talk occasionally, and in his bedroom he would fantasize about her while masturbating. Fred didn't write much about his self-enjoyment except that it was such a great feeling and that he was getting anxious for the real thing.

By the end of May, Fred found out that he was going to have a weekend off, so he would be able to go out without having to wake up early the next day and go to work. Fred wrote, *I found the nerve to ask Diane—the girl on the third floor, out to a movie and for something to eat. She told me she would really like that.*

Diane, having just turned eighteen, was able to purchase a good, used car, and offered to pick Fred up at his house Friday night at about six o'clock. From the time he got home until the time that she actually picked him up was only a couple of hours, but it seemed like days. Fred almost

busted the front door down when he got home. Sam, alarmed, asked him what was going on and Fred explained that he had to get ready for a date. Sam asked, "A date? What's her name? Where are you two going? How old is this girl?" Fred replied in broken sentences as he passed Sam going back and forth between his bedroom and the bathroom. Fred said, "Her name is Diane…she's eighteen…has her own car…to get a bite to eat, and then to a movie." Sam went to the kitchen to grab them both a beer.

Sam raised his beer to toast Fred saying, "To you, son, and your first date."

"Thanks grandpa." Taking a quick shower to get the smell of The Mill off him, he got dressed in a somewhat new pair of jeans, and a nice tee shirt. He put on some music as he sat on his bed waiting for the time to pass and decided to fill his pipe so he could get a quick high before she came. When he finished, he went out onto the front porch, lit a cigarette, took a deep breath, leaned up against one of the porch rails and relaxed with his eyes closed, enjoying a slightly cool spring breeze. Looking at his watch, he saw that it was still only 5:40 PM. His heart started to race thinking about what to do, what to say…this being his very first date. He lit another cigarette. No more than thirty seconds could have passed when he heard a car horn, and a girl's voice asking, "Hey good looking, looking for a date?" Opening his eyes, he saw that it was her, she was early; a good sign, he thought to himself as he approached the car, and got in.

As the car pulled away from the curb they started to talk about where they would go to eat. They finally decided that they would go to an Italian restaurant, because both liked Italian food. Fred, of course, was a gentlemen opening doors and pulling out chairs. The conversation was light over dinner because they really didn't know each other, but they were diligently working on it. She told Fred that she and her best friend were sharing an apartment in Burlington, and so forth. The subject of what movie they were going to go to after they finished eating came up. Agreeing that they both liked scary movies, they decided to go to one. When they were finished with dinner Fred grabbed the check so that he could take care of the bill. Diane told him it wasn't necessary for him to do that, but he said that he wanted to. On the way to the movies Diane pulled her cigarette pack out of her pocket book, reached into it, and pulled out a joint. She asked, "Do you smoke pot? If not, do you mind if I do? I like going to the movies high."

Fred said, "I sure do smoke, no I don't mind, and if you hadn't pulled one out I was going to." By the time they got to the movie they were both comfortably high. The littlest thing made them laugh. They got out of the car and started walking toward the theater when Diane grabbed Fred's hand to hold on to. Fred wrote in his diary that this movie was the best

movie he had ever gone to, and not watched. He wrote that he just kept looking at Diane throughout the whole movie. After the movie it was about 9:30 PM, so Fred said, "If you want, we can go to my house, hang out, listen to music, and have a couple beers. The night is still young."

"Sure, that sounds great."

When they arrived at Fred's house, he yelled out to Sam, so he could introduce Diane. Fred found him in the kitchen putting some beer in the refrigerator, and said, "Grandpa this is Diane. She works at The Mill, too. Since you are right there would you hand us a couple of beers?"

Handing the beer to Fred, he looked at Diane and said, "It's very nice to meet you. You can call me Sam, and you're right, Fred, she is pretty." With the introductions behind them, and embarrassment flushing Fred's cheeks, they went to Fred's room so they could listen to music, and get to know each other better. They finished their first beers rather quickly, and Fred went to get two more. It seemed they had a lot in common—television shows, food, bad habits, and music. It was at this point that Fred pulled out his marijuana. Filling his pipe, he handed it to Diane. She set it down in the ashtray. Fred, not knowing what she was doing thought to himself that she had had enough, and she wanted to take a break. Sitting back on the bed, she took Fred by surprise, leaning over to give him a kiss—a tongue kiss.

Fred started to wonder if this was really happening, or if he was just dreaming. His hand worked its way up to her breasts, and that is when he decided this was real. They were firm and just the right size, not too big and not too small. They continued to kiss and Fred felt what he believed to be her nipples becoming erect. Going by what he read in his Playboy magazines, he reached under her tank top to caress them. He couldn't believe that he was doing this on the first date. All of a sudden he felt her hand on his thigh rubbing it, and working her way up to his crotch. The feeling was unbelievable. Even though he had done this himself before, it was a completely different sensation. She leaned back on his bed, at the same time kicking her sandals off onto the floor. He started to take her shirt off as she pulled his off. She then started to unzip his pants to feel him better, and as she was doing this, Fred worked on her pants. Finally getting them unzipped, he reached into them to feel her crotch. It was his first time actually touching a real breast, or a girl's pussy.

She stood up and grabbed her pants at the waistband to slip them off. Standing there within two feet of Fred, she bent over to pull them off her ankles. With her ass in his face Fred started to pull his pants off, too. She pushed him back onto the bed until he was lying face up looking at her. He explained that it was his first time.

"It's not mine, don't worry about anything, I'll be gentle. Do you have a condom? If not, don't worry, I got one."

"No I don't." She picked up her purse, got it out, and laid it on the bed next to them. She then proceeded to rub him at the same time she was kissing him on the chest, working her way up to his mouth. She got on top of him, started to grind their crotches together to the point that Fred was having trouble holding back. When they both got to the point that they couldn't deal with it, she reached over for the condom. She put it on Fred and moved herself over the top of him. As Fred felt himself entering her, his thoughts ran wild. She moved her hips up and down, and the feeling became more pleasurable than Fred ever imagined. She leaned over to kiss him, and while they were kissing Fred ejaculated. In the middle of his orgasm his mother's face flashed numerous times in his mind, which, in turn, put an end to his orgasm. She finished with her orgasm shortly after Fred did. Raising herself off his sweaty body, she lay down beside him and lit a cigarette. Feeling uncomfortable lying naked next to her after having that flash of his mother's face, he got up, took off the condom, threw it away, put on a pair of boxers, and said he was going to the bathroom. Diane had no objection because she was still smoking her cigarette and resting. When he returned from the bathroom Diane was asleep, so he stood looking at her as though he was doing a scientific exam. Not wanting her to wake up and find him standing over her, he covered her up with a sheet, and went to the kitchen to get a beer.

When Fred got to the kitchen, Sam was sitting at the table having a beer. Fred went to the refrigerator, got a beer, and sat down across from him. Sam had a big smile on his face when he asked, "Was she good?"

"I guess she was okay, but what do I know? She was my first. Lets' put it this way. I don't see what the big deal of having sex is all about. It was okay. Sure it felt good, but that's about it."

Sam looked at Fred, shook his head, and said, "Someday you will understand, don't worry." Fred finished his beer and went back to his room to check on Diane.

The door opening aroused her from her sleep and she asked what time it was. Fred answered, "It's one o'clock in the morning, why?" She wrestled with the sheet as she got up and standing there for a moment, as she located her clothes, she told Fred she had to go because she had to be at her parents' by nine. Fred just sort of stood there staring at her naked body, which he thought looked very nice—firm breasts, slender hips, and a nice round cute little ass. Fred told her where her clothes were, and as she turned around to thank him, he didn't see her beautiful young face; it was that of his middle-aged mother. The same one he saw when they were having sex. Wondering if he was going crazy or something, he closed his eyes and

rubbed them. He opened them to look one more time, and this time he saw Diane's face on Diane's body. She came up to him and gave him a kiss good-bye. She told him he could call her tonight if he wanted to go out again. He told her he was going to be busy helping Sam, but thanked her anyway. She told him that she would see him at work and then left. Fred followed her to the porch, stood there as she got in the car, and waved as she was leaving.

He returned to his room to go to bed, writing in his diary that he had just gotten laid for the first time. He also wrote that he thought that he might be going crazy with those images of his mother he was seeing while he and Diane were having sex. He hated his mother. He couldn't understand why he was seeing her. All he knew was that if it happened once, then it might happen again. So he decided that night to stay away from women for a while. Saturday came quick, and so did Sunday. He didn't call Diane that weekend for fear that they would end up having sex, and he didn't want that. When Sunday night arrived, Sam and Fred were having some beers in the living room when Sam asked him how come he hadn't called Diane. He said, "I decided to stay away from dating for a little bit until I get more on my feet at work and maybe a place of my own." It was then that Sam explained to him that he had been putting money away for him a little each week. Fred asked, "How much money?"

"Well let's put it this way. You probably have enough to get your own place."

On that Monday, which was June 8th, Fred got to work early so he would be able to socialize a little with his friends before he had to start working. It was always too busy in heat-treat to stop and socialize as he had in the centerless department. Fred went into the shop after saying bye to his friends and went down to his department where Jimmy was already waiting for him. Jimmy told him that he was going on vacation the next week and that Fred would be there alone.

"Can you handle it?"

"Hell, yeah, I can. You just watch and I'll make you proud." Jimmy told him that Friday was going to be like a test day. Jimmy wouldn't come down the whole day unless there was an emergency.

That Friday started off like any other Friday. Jimmy met Fred down in their department and wished him good luck. This was Fred's chance to prove to everyone how good a worker he was and to show how quick he picked it up. He was finishing up some work that was left from the day before when he heard someone say, *"Freddie."* It wasn't at a normal volume level; it was more like a whisper. He turned around, but saw that no one was in the room with him. He heard it numerous times throughout the day, but couldn't figure out where it was coming from, or who was doing it.

The last time he heard it just before his day ended, he made up his mind to do something about it. He ran up the stairs to find Jimmy. When he did, Jimmy asked him how he made out down there, and if everything went all right. Fred told him everything went fine except when he came down and messed with him. Jimmy asked him what he was talking about, and when Fred explained, Jimmy just laughed. He told Fred that he didn't do anything, and that he must have been hearing things.

Fred went downstairs to get his coat and found Andy waiting for him at the time clock. He heard it once again, but this time someone else was there. He asked Andy if he had just heard someone call his name. Andy looked at him laughing, asking, "What have you been smoking down here? I didn't hear anything, dude." They punched out just as the buzzer was going off. On his way out, Jimmy told him that he had done a great job, and handed him his keys.

"You're going to need these keys next week if you have to come in early, and here is my code to the alarm at the front door. I talked to Rob", he added, "and he said that if everything goes well while I'm on vacation he will give you your own key."

When Fred got home he ran into the house, telling Sam everything about his day, how well he did, and that The Mill's manager was going to give him his own key.

Then he went to the refrigerator, grabbed a beer, and went to his room. He got his diary out and dated it June 12th 1997.

I think I'm going crazy little by little. First, I was seeing my mother's face in the girl's face I was having sex with and now I'm hearing voices calling my name at work. It was like a whisper, but in the heat-treat area you wouldn't be able to hear a whisper and that's why I think I'm going nuts. If it was as low as a whisper it must be coming from within my mind. I stopped having sex so I wouldn't have that happen to me again and am I supposed to stop working to stop the voices? I got to go to sleep.

Chapter 6

The morning of Saturday, June 13, 1997 came quickly for one reason or another. It might have been because this was his first day in his department alone without Jimmy making sure everything was done properly, or it might have been because he stayed up late trying to figure out what was going on in his head. It was hard for me to put the diary down even to go to the bathroom, but some things can't wait. I was even trying to figure out what was going to happen before I read it. There was nothing about this guy that was normal. It seemed things would go bad or weird for him no matter how hard he tried. Finishing the call from Mother Nature, I made my way back to the bed. I was obsessed. Lighting a cigarette, I settled back onto my bed and picked up the diary. I noticed that I was getting close to the folded-down corner where Fred had placed the penknife.

I got to work at about 4:30 AM, where I met Rob opening the gate. He told me that he wanted me to walk around with him, so I could see what was done when opening up The Mill. I mentioned to Rob that Jimmy had said that as time went by I might be opening the plant when necessary. Rob said, "You might have to, but for now I want you to concentrate on doing your job. It's not going to be easy down there by yourself. We'll deal with the other as the need arises." Rob showed me how to enter the code into the alarm box, what lights needed to be turned on, how to turn on the air compressor, and of course he showed me what I didn't have to worry about, too. I thought to myself that opening The Mill would be more difficult until Rob showed me. There's nothing to it.

They returned to the break room on the second floor to get a coffee out of the vending machine. Fred noticed that Rob was a different and more relaxed guy when there weren't a lot of people around. He thought to himself that he isn't all that bad, but he wouldn't say that to Andy, or anyone else. Rob asked Fred if Jimmy left him a list of priorities for him to work from. Fred told him not to worry, he had a list, and he would do as much as he could by doing the best that he could. As Fred started to walk away, Rob said, "I know you will, or Jimmy wouldn't have gone on vacation." Fred started to go down the stairs, taking his time because no one else had arrived yet. He thought that this would be a good time to sneak out back to take a couple of hits off his pipe. When the door to the heat-treat area had shut behind him and as he started toward his work area he heard a faint clanking noise. Spinning around, he didn't see anything at first. Then he saw a little mouse that had evaded the mousetraps placed all around the building. "Paranoid or what?" he thought.

Fred had a few tokes from his pipe, smoked a cigarette, and returned inside. He took off his jacket, picked up his coffee for a drink, and noticed that the ovens' smoke was thicker when they were first turned up in the morning. Taking another drink, he heard, *"Fred, kill. Fred, kill."* He noticed that the smoke coming off one of the ovens had taken an almost human form. He could barely make it out, but he swore to himself he saw what he saw. Then he heard it: *"Fred, Kill. Fred, Kill."* He didn't really get a good look at whatever it was because he was running out of the area as fast as he could. The voice was the same one he'd heard on Friday, but he had never seen anything before.

Gathering his composure, he went to the break room. As he was getting his coffee he said hi to everyone, looked at the clock on the wall. Then he went outside and lit a cigarette to calm himself, and noticed that his hands were shaking. Donny came up to him from his truck and asked if he was going to be all right. Fred snapped back, "What do you mean all right? Of course I'm all right."

"Hey, take it easy! I was just wondering since you will be by yourself. I'll come down to see how you're doing periodically to make sure you're all right."

"Thanks."

Donny went inside to get a coffee. Fred sat down on the cement stairs talking to himself out loud, telling himself that there was nothing in the smoke but smoke. Rob noticed him outside and sticking his head out the door told him it was time to go to work. He put out his cigarette and went inside.

When Fred went through the door he was very cautious. He made it all the way to his worktable where he put his coffee down and took a thorough look around. He didn't see anything that looked out of place, or even the least bit strange. He thought to himself that maybe he was just letting his imagination run wild on him and nobody would believe him if he told them. He also couldn't figure out why on Friday he could hear the voice and Andy couldn't. *It must be all in my head, working too many hours, or something like that,* he wrote.

From that point on Fred's day went as normal as normal could be. His workload was, of course, doubled since Jimmy wasn't with him. It wasn't until the end of the workday—10:00 AM because it was Saturday—when Fred was standing at the time clock waiting for that last minute to go by, that he heard a voice again. *"Fred, help. Fred, help."* Fred's eyes got as large as silver dollars at the same time the hair on the back of his neck stood on end and he could feel a cold draft. Looking to see if all the doors and windows were shut, he thought to himself that this time it was different;

it was a little girl's voice that he heard. Punching the time clock, Fred ran up the stairs and left the building at the first exit door he came to.

When Fred got home he didn't mention any of this to Sam, because he feared that even Sam would think he was going nuts. He went to his room and stayed there the rest of the day, not even coming out for food or beer.

Because of all that has been going on I really think I might be going nuts. Voices, only crazy people hear voices. The third time that I heard them it was a different voice. But what about the human shape I saw in the smoke? Was it that I'm overtired, or did it really happen? I don't know what's going on, but I sure would like to find out. I'm going to sleep now, so maybe when I wake up it will all be just a bad memory.

The next morning when Fred woke up he just sat there in his bed for a moment thinking that if they were real, why him? He decided to go to the kitchen, grab some coffee, and see what Sam was up to. Sam was there at the stove cooking bacon for their breakfast.

"Good, I'm glad to see you haven't lost your appetite. For a moment you had me worried. When you got home yesterday you didn't say maybe two words to me and you didn't even have a beer with me. I thought maybe you were sick or something."

Fred told him that he was sorry, he had a lot on his mind, and he just wanted to try and figure it out. Sam said, "No problem. Did you figure it out, whatever it was?"

"Nope, not yet."

Finishing the gourmet breakfast that Sam had cooked, Fred went to his room to smoke a little pot, and to take a shower. In the shower, he got aroused. He closed his eyes and stroked himself. He envisioned Diane's young, tight body. Just as he was coming to the peak Diane's face turned to him, and said, *"Fred help, Fred help."* He exploded inside and outside, for it had been a while since he had done this. When he opened his eyes the shower curtain flew open and his mother was standing there naked in front of him. He shut his eyes again, opened them, and saw that there was nobody there. It all had been in his mind, then it hit him that what Diane said in his fantasy were the same words, and voice he heard the other day at work.

He returned to his room to get dressed, and to smoke some pot. These things can't be happening, he thought, but they were happening and he didn't know why. He left his room, went into the kitchen to get a beer, and to see if Sam wanted one. When Fred brought a beer to Sam in the living room Sam asked if he was all right. Fred looked at him and told him sure. They sat and talked about how Fred's new position was going. Fred said that he really enjoyed it and the responsibility that went with it. After

having three beers and watching an old rerun on the television with Sam, Fred decided to go for a walk to see what was going on in the neighborhood. It was a bright sunny day out and the warmest that it had been for a long time. He took a few hits off his pot pipe, put on his sneakers, and headed out the door. Sam asked, "When you get back we'll go to the store for some beer, okay?"

"Sure Sam, anything you want." Just as he finished saying that the door shut behind him.

Fred headed in the direction of The Mill for no particular reason, but sub-consciously, as he wrote later that night, he wanted to see if he'd have any more episodes. *This has to be my imagination and just my mind playing tricks on me. It was as if there was a magnet drawing me toward The Mill.*

Was it his imagination, or was there something there?

At the top of the hill that led down to The Mill, he paused. The feeling that brought him this far was far too strong to resist. The gate was locked, so he turned onto the roadway that went around The Mill. As he rounded the corner at the far end of the road that led back to the main road, he felt relieved. "So far, so good." But just then he heard, *"Fred help us, Freddie come back, we need you."* The voice was different this time from the first three times. This time it sounded like a small crowd of people that had mixed voices of old, young, male, and female. He took off running toward the main road. Turning around to take one last look at The Mill, he noticed a group of figures that had been formed in the smoke coming out of the exhaust of the heat-treat area. He stopped to rub his eyes to make sure he was seeing what he saw, and as he opened his eyes the figures seemed to be drawn back into the building, disappearing at the same time.

When he got home, he went to the store with Sam as he said he would. When they got back, he took a beer to his room. He sat on his bed holding his head in his hands, shaking it back and forth not knowing what to do. He decided to smoke some pot. I thought to myself as I read, Fred depended on beer and pot to make everything all right. Sunday ended with Fred staying in his room, only coming out for a beer and to use the bathroom.

June 14, 1997, This has to stop one way, or the other.

Sam woke Fred up the next morning after he hadn't heard Fred's alarm go off. Sam had already made the coffee when Fred came out, so all he had to do was grab a cup and run out the door, so he wouldn't be late. All the way to The Mill, Fred was thinking that he had to concentrate—he was there by himself, and if he let this stuff get to him he wouldn't be able to perform. He made it to the time clock with only two minutes to spare. He was headed down the stairs to the heat-treat area when he heard, "Fred, Fred," in almost the same tone as the voices he had been hearing. Turning

around quickly, he shouted, "Leave me alone!" He was surprised to see Andy sneaking a few drags off a cigarette and realized that it must have been him he had heard. Andy wanted to know if Fred wanted any, but Fred shook his head and hurried to his area.

"See ya at break, dude," Andy yelled after him.

In heat-treat, Fred couldn't concentrate at all. The voices kept asking for his help, for him not to leave, and for him to kill. Over and over again the same phrases—the only thing that changed was the tone. Sometimes it was a female; mostly they were males, young and old. There was no place that he could go to escape them. They seemed to follow him—never letting up, always persistent. He started to see more and more human faces and figures coming from all five ovens. He would turn his head away from them, and when he turned back they would be gone. Somehow he managed to do his job and do it well enough that no one noticed his conversations with the voices he was hearing. If they did, he would surely be called crazy and probably lose his job. At the end of the day, as he headed for the time clock, all of a sudden he felt a draft that gave him a huge whiff of the smoke from the ovens.

This time that smoke from all the ovens formed into the figures he had seen before. They appeared to surround him as he spun in all directions looking for a way to escape. His movement was stopped abruptly, as if something had frozen him in place. Panic set in and before Fred knew it he felt something engulf his whole being. Looking down, he saw one of the cloudy figures moving up his body. This entire cloud entered his nose and mouth until it vanished completely. He immediately started to choke violently and fell to the floor.

He searched around as he tried to get his breath to find someone to help him. But then the large cloud was gone and he could now move freely. The end of the day buzzer sounded, and as he punched out he looked around and saw that everything appeared normal near the ovens. He turned and ran up the stairs to get out of there as fast as he could. He looked back once more and saw nothing unusual. He continued to hear the voices until he left the building, but now they seemed more intense and much clearer to him.

On his way home, he decided to go a different way in order to get a pack of cigarettes. He was running low and didn't want to have to go out after he got home. The dark was becoming an eerie place and time for Fred. He wrote that night that he didn't even like closing his eyes for fear that the voices would come back. He walked into the store and asked the clerk for two packs of Camel non-filter, but then he said Marlboro Red, which was his regular brand. The clerk told him to make up his mind because he didn't have all day. Fred said, "I'll take two of each," not knowing why he asked for Camel non-filters.

On the way home he saw a sign in a window of an apartment building, "Apartment for Rent." Fred thought to himself for a minute, decided it couldn't hurt to check it out, and knocked on the door marked, "Manager." A short little old man with bifocal glasses and a receding hairline came to the door. Fred told him he was interested in the apartment for rent. "All right," he said, "Give me a second to get my shoes on and I'll take you to it. I need first and last months rent up front."

Fred said, "Okay." They got to the apartment with the number six on the door and went in. It wasn't that big a place, but it did have a separate bedroom. Fred asked the manager exactly how much would he need to give him. The old man told him seven hundred, not including the lights, but the hot water was included, cash—no checks accepted. With that Fred thanked the man and started on his way home. He lit a cigarette, and after he lit it he noticed that it was a Camel non-filter. He continued to smoke it and found he liked it. Fred shrugged. It was only a cigarette.

When he got home he said hello to his grandpa and asked him if he wanted a beer. Sam said, "Sure." Fred told Sam about finding an apartment that he could afford. It was on Spring Street, just around the corner from the house. Sam asked him all about it, and how much it was going to cost. Fred told him that the heat was included, and it was perfect for him, being so close to The Mill. He would still be able to walk to work. Sam was all excited for him, but Fred could tell that he was a little upset that he would be moving out. Sam told him that he would get his money from the bank tomorrow. Fred thanked him for understanding and went to his room.

On his way out the door the next morning, he asked Sam to remember about going to the bank. Sam said he would have the money by the end of the day. All the way to work Fred was thinking that he shouldn't trust Sam to get it and if he did he probably would spend it. At the same time he was telling himself that this was his grandpa and that he wouldn't steal from him. This conversation in his head felt like there was somebody else inside him telling him what to do.

Ever since I started hearing those voices and seeing what I've seen in the heat-treat area, I've started buying the wrong cigarettes, smoking them, liking them, and not understanding any of it. I was perfectly happy living at Sam's, but something made me go into that apartment house and ask those questions. The next thing I know I'm telling Sam to get my money out of the bank.

When Fred got down to heat-treat he found that it was all messed up. Things had been moved around and put out of place. He started to put them all back where they belonged. Just then Rob came down to see how he was doing.

"I see you've changed your mind on how you want things set up," Rob said.

"What are you talking about? I came in this morning and found it this way."

"Sure you did. You must have took time out on Saturday at the end of the shift to move things around to make it easier for yourself."

Fred looked at him, puzzled by what he had just said. He didn't remember moving anything—why was he starting to do things and not remember them? "Yeah, I forgot I did, but when I came in I thought that Jimmy wouldn't want it this way."

"I take it that you didn't hear the news."

"What news?"

"Jimmy isn't coming back. He found another job that paid more money. So you're in charge down here now. You can put things where you want. Just make sure the work gets done."

Fred told him that the work would be no problem and that he would work whatever hours were needed.

Fred couldn't believe that he was actually a lead man. He was only in charge of himself, but that didn't matter. He had a title and the pay that went with it. He couldn't wait to get home and tell Sam. When he got in the door Sam handed him his money. Fred asked, "What's this?"

"It's the seven hundred dollars you asked me to get out of the bank for your apartment over on Spring Street."

Fred had forgotten all about it, but to keep Sam from thinking he was weird he took the money and stashed it in his pocket. Fred said, "I have great news to tell you. Rob the production supervisor put me in charge of the heat-treat department." He went on to tell him the details on how he would be included in all the lead meetings, he'd get his own code for the alarm, and the key that Jimmy gave him was now his. Sam told him that he was proud of him and that it looked like he had a promising future there. Sam went on to say that Fred better get going if he didn't want to take a chance on losing that apartment.

He left the house with the money in his pocket, but he didn't really remember where the apartment was. Sam said it was on Spring Street, so he thought he would start there. As soon as he turned the corner it was as if he knew exactly where to go—almost like an inner force was guiding him there. Fred knocked on the manager's door. When the little old man answered the door Fred said, "Here's the money. Where are my keys?" The manager went back inside, and, shortly, returned with two keys. One was for the mailbox and the other was for the apartment door.

"Rent is due by the first of every month and no later than the fifth." Fred told him not to worry about getting his money because he didn't have

any other bills to pay. He turned to go up to his apartment, somehow knowing which one it was. It was as if he had been here before, and he knew he hadn't. It was the perfect size, and the price wasn't bad. He wrote later that night he didn't really know how he came to find this place, but it was close to work and it was about time that he got out on his own. He felt proud of himself. He'd gotten a promotion, a raise, and a new apartment. What was going on in his head, however, was a whole other matter.

On his way back to Sam's house Fred found himself stopping at The Mill, not knowing why. Then he heard those voices coming out of The Mill, sounding as if they were right next to him. They weren't saying "Fred." This time they were saying Paul. He thought he heard them say, *"Paul, you know what to do. Don't forget us, Paul."* He didn't pay much attention to them this time, because he was in a hurry to move to his new apartment. He called Pat at work to see if he would help him move, because he had a car. Pat told him that he would be glad to help him, but it had to be after five o'clock.

When Pat came over, Fred couldn't wait to tell him about the good things that had been happening to him since he started working at The Mill. He told him, everything. Pat knew about everything that had gone on at The Mill, but he didn't know about the apartment. Pat asked, "You're my little brother. Do you actually think that I'm not going to check on how you're doing? Come on now, we need to get going in order to be done before dark." Sam asked if they had any rope, so they could tie the stuff down. Fred told him it was all in the back seat and some was in the trunk. Sam asked, "Well, where are you going to put the bed?"

Fred looked at him in surprise. "What bed?"

Sam explained that he was going to need a bed at his new place, so he could have the one he was using and along with it Sam gave him the thirteen-inch television. Fred, not knowing what to say, went over to Sam and gave him a big hug of thanks. They put the television in the back seat and tied the box spring, with the mattress and frame pieces, to the top of the car.

After unloading the car at his new apartment Fred gave Pat a beer and they toasted his new apartment. Pat asked, "When did you start drinking?"

Fred answered, "Drinking? I'm not drinking. I have a couple of beers every now and then." Pat looked the place over and gave his approval. When Pat left, Fred pulled the rest of the beer out of a box, so he could put it in the refrigerator. He set up his bed to have something to sleep on and put the television in the living room. There was really no place to put it. He just sat it up on a box. *The phone, cable, and lights are going to be turned on June twenty-first, tomorrow, but I can rough it one night.* His

new apartment had all sorts of strange noises, but eventually he did fall asleep.

In the middle of the night Fred woke up screaming. The clock said 2:00 AM. Getting up, he went to the refrigerator to get a beer and lit a cigarette. He was thinking how real his dream seemed and how it happened right here in his new apartment. In the dream, he had sex with some girl and ended up killing her. He not only killed her, he dismembered her. The beer and cigarette calmed him down enough so that he was able to go back to asleep.

Surprisingly, Fred got up with his alarm the next morning and rushed off to work. He wasn't running late, but he did want to see how long it took him to get there from his apartment. When he arrived, Rob stopped him as he came in the door to hand him a list of things in the order they needed to be done. Rob knew that Fred knew what to do, but he wanted to be on the safe side until Fred had time to get a routine down. Fred didn't mind the list at all and agreed that it would be helpful. He was heading toward his department when Rob yelled to him to stop. He told Fred that he wanted to go over setting the alarm and disarming it with him.

Fred couldn't believe that in just a little more than nine months he was a lead man, locking up the building, and going to be opening the building, too. Everything went well, so Fred headed down to his area. A couple of minutes later, the voices started. He could basically understand them except that they were saying, *"Paul."* He sort of let it go in one ear and out the other, so he was able to get something done.

"Fred, who you talking to?" Fred turned around and saw Donny standing there watching him.

"What do you mean? Who am I talking to? I wasn't talking to anyone. Do you see anyone out here?"

"No, that's why I'm asking." Fred shrugged and went back to work, but he was scared—for his sanity, for his job.

It was June 21st, and the day went by fast for Fred. He couldn't wait to get home, because he knew that his television and lights would be working when he got home. At home, he opened a beer, lit a cigarette, and sat down in front of his television. He was about to turn it on when there was a knock at his door. He opened it to find Andy and Donny there, Andy holding a half-gallon of some kind of liquor. Fred told them to come in and went to the kitchen for glasses. Donny told Fred that Andy and he just wanted to see his new place, so they decided to come over with an apartment-warming gift. They stayed for a few hours, ordering pizza, and drinking at least half of the tequila before Donny said that he had to leave. Fred told them thanks and that he would see them in the morning. He'd just barely made it to the bed before he passed out. Within a few hours he was

awake screaming again with sweat running down his face. It was the same dream he had the night before.

It was here that I put down the diary, so that I could go to sleep myself. It was 10:00 AM before I woke up. After a quick breakfast, I started right in again on Fred's diary.

After the June 22nd entry, Fred made single line entries most of the time. Sentences like, *My dreams are the same over and over again and those voices have got to stop.* On July 15th, Fred wrote, *I noticed the more I heard the voices the more I would dream; like they were somehow connected. The lack of sleep from the long hours at work and my dreams waking me up during the night are going to kill me.*

At work the next day Rob informed him that he would have to work overtime starting next week, and that he could work it any way he wanted to, just as long as the work got done. Fred's first thought was about being locked up in The Mill by himself and whatever was making those voices. He started to ask Rob for some help, but just before the words came out he decided he'd better not ask, so Rob wouldn't think he couldn't handle it.

The following Monday, he headed down to his area, and expecting to hear the voices, Fred said, "Morning everyone, I'm here." No answer. He repeated himself. Still not getting an answer he hung up his coat and got to work. The end of the day came and all his friends said good-bye to him as they passed through his area. About fifteen minutes later, his phone rang. Rob was on the other end telling him that he was just about to leave and wanted to know if he needed anything. Fred told him that he was fine and asked him when the third floor was leaving. Rob replied, "They leave at five o'clock and I'll have them lock the gate, so no one can get onto the property. Have a good night and be careful."

"Thanks and I will. My whole day went great, so I don't expect to have any trouble." With that, Fred got back to work.

His night finished around seven o'clock. On his way out he stopped in the lunchroom to get a soda. As he unlocked the main gate, he looked back at The Mill and saw an older man walking toward him. He didn't look real to Fred; he looked sort of cloudy like the ones he had seen in his work area. He heard, *"Fred, wait for me,"* coming from the direction of the man. Rubbing his eyes, not believing what he was seeing, he looked again. The figure was gone. Locking the gate as quickly as he could, he ran up the hill and most of the way back to his apartment. Once there, he grabbed for the tequila bottle that Andy had left him, took a big swallow, and then another one. At the same time he was reaching for a beer. He filled his pipe with some pot, and took a long toke. He tried to convince himself that he hadn't seen what he had just seen. He went into the other room, where he sat

drinking tequila and smoking pot until around midnight, when he called it a day.

He had no problem getting to sleep, and in fact he passed out still dressed in his clothes. It must have been about three hours later when Fred woke up with the strangest memories of a dream he'd had. In the dream, he walked down to The Mill and tried to open the main gate. When he couldn't open it he turned around, and walked back home and climbed back into bed. That's when Fred woke up in a sweat. When he went to the bathroom, he noticed that his sneakers were still on. He thought that he had taken them off before he started to drink, but did he or didn't he? Instead of thinking about it he just got back into bed to get some sleep. The alarm went off right on schedule. He got up, opened a beer, sat down in the living room, filled his pipe, and got ready for work.

Chapter 7

Fred's life seemed to be deteriorating, as were the entries in his diary. I couldn't really determine whether it was the effect of long work hours, or the strange things that seemed to be going on. The one thing I did see was Fred's dependency on alcohol and drugs. He needed them before going to work in the morning, he used them with the guys at lunch, and now he was using them to help him sleep. Didn't anyone see this pattern with Fred? It must not have affected his work ability: however, what did seem to be affecting his work were the hallucinations he suffered in his work area. Every time he saw an apparition, or heard a voice, it would startle him. He'd drop something or even stop, unable to move. His friends heard him talking back to these voices, but no one else saw or heard what Fred was seeing and hearing. If anyone else had heard or seen these things I was sure that Fred would have written about it in his diary.

He was working twelve-hour days, every day except Sunday. At the end of the first week he asked Rob for some help in his area, because it was getting backed up. Rob told him they were looking for someone to hire and that during the regular workweek he would send Andy out to help him until they did. Fred thought the voices would stop, having Andy, or someone else out there working with him, but they didn't. Every time he answered them, Andy would just sort of look at him as though he was really strange, as of course would anyone who saw him talking to someone who wasn't there. Andy would simply ask, "Dude, who are you talking to?" Fred replied, "No one." That was all that was ever said about it.

Fred wrote in his August 1st entry that Andy was the only one he felt comfortable around because everyone else thought he was a little strange.

Andy is really my only friend. All he wants to do is party and have a good time. He also didn't mind when I asked him to go to the liquor store for me. He is my only true friend.

The month of August brought more one-line entries until about the tenth of the month. It was then that Fred mentioned sleepwalking again and this time he was more detailed about it. *I remembered this time putting my sneakers on and leaving my apartment. I can remember most of what happened. I recalled going down to The Mill, this time I entered the property using my own key to get through the gate, and locking it after going through. A few people greeted me outside The Mill. The people,* he wrote, *who were waiting, included a woman who looked to be in her twenties, an older man in his thirties, and two children around the ages of ten or twelve. They seemed to be on a break, because the man and woman*

were smoking cigarettes, and the children were playing toss with a little, blue ball. I knew that it was blue; that was the only thing I saw in color. The rest of the time everything was in black and white. Opening the door with my key, I proceeded to turn off the alarm.

They seemed to be following me down to the heat-treat area where they all said, "Thanks Paul for letting us in." I turned around, went back to the alarm, reset it, and left the building. I got back to the main gate and unlocked it again to get through, and of course relocked it before I left. I returned to my apartment and went straight to bed.

He awakened a couple of hours later screaming and sweating like a pig. Sitting there in bed he saw that he really did have his sneakers on and that's when he decided to write down what he remembered about his dream.

The next morning, he decided to add some more to the same entry. He wrote that it was his second dream that actually woke him up. He was dreaming that he was back at his mom's house on his last birthday. When he went through the door she was drunk and naked except for her panties. It was the same scene that he really did see on his birthday, except this time she was rubbing her crotch, telling him how much she wanted him. Not being able to take it anymore, he snapped. He grabbed his mother by the neck, and began to strangle her. It was at this point that he awakened in a sweat, screaming. He wrote, *I really did feel like killing her that day. How could she do that to me on my Birthday*?

The next day was August 11, 1997, and according to the little bit he wrote he got up, had a beer and a little to smoke before leaving for work. He arrived at The Mill a little early and there were a few people standing at the front door smoking cigarettes. They all said hello to him and followed him inside. On his way down to his area, he was thinking how much this was like the dream that he'd had last night. He thought to himself that if he tried to figure everything out, he wouldn't have any time for work.

He got down to his work area and at the bottom of the stairway he took off his coat. When he walked over to his worktable, he couldn't believe what he saw sitting on it. On it was the little blue ball the children from his dream had been playing with. He wrote in his diary, *The ball was real, but what happened last night when I slept couldn't have really happened.*

Even though each entry was short the dream he had of his mother was haunting him every night, as was the sleepwalking dream.

I noticed in the September 15, 1997, entry all Fred wrote was, *Happy Birthday Paul,* and Paul had a line through it with Fred written next to it. That's when I first began to wonder if Fred was struggling with this person he called Paul for possession of his own mind. Could that be true?

On September 30, 1997, Fred mentioned that his work was piling up, but thought he had a pretty good handle on things. He wrote that his brother must have been out of town on a sales trip on his birthday because he had never missed one before. He did come down today at work to say, "Happy Birthday." He wrote, *My seventeenth birthday, big deal.* Reading this, I thought that maybe Fred was getting a handle on his mental state, too. He didn't mention his sleepwalking, or the dream about his mother. There wasn't anything abnormal in his entry at all. It actually brought a smile to my face thinking that things might be turning around for Fred. I knew he was still drinking and smoking though, because he mentioned that he had to go so he could get high before he went to bed.

A month later, he wrote, *I was on my way to The Mill when I ran into that girl that I dated once from the third floor. She had stopped working at The Mill for another job. I was near the top of the hill that led down to the building when I saw her car drive by. I went down to the same group of people that were always down there waiting for me to let them into the building. This time I only let them in; I turned around to set the alarm when one of the little boys asked, "Where are you going, Paul?" I told him that I would be right back.*

I set the alarm, then locked the main door, and after locking the gate I walked up the hill and as I did this I heard the sound of a car motor running. Before I had actually reached the top of the hill, I saw Diane's car sitting there. I went up to the passenger side, opened the door, and asked, "What's up?" She replied, "All my friends are sleeping, and I was looking to party. You know I like to drink a little, and smoke some." I replied, "Well, I'm not doing anything." She told me to get in, I told her about my new apartment and instead of driving around we decided to go there. I remembered why I stopped seeing her, but got in anyway.

We decide to park her car in a parking lot at the top of The Mill's hill. It was a public parking lot, and walked to my apartment, which was only two blocks away. She carried her fifth of rum in her purse along with her pot. When we got there she couldn't believe that I really did have my own place. She walked around with me as I gave her the grand tour and then we went back into the living room. We sat getting drunk and stoned. A lot of time had gone by so we had a lot to talk about. I could see she didn't really want to continue talking by her occasional touching of my body. Then she leaned over and as she kissed me, I felt her hand on my crotch.

While we kissed, I placed one of my hands under her shirt on her breast while I worked on her pant's button-fly with my other one. I proceeded to pull her pants apart until I could see her lacy, white panties. I then reached down inside them placing my hand on her crotch. It was then I realized exactly how horny she was. As I continued to rub her moist crotch,

I felt my zipper open and as she pulled me out of my pants, she leaned over and put me in her mouth. My first thought as Diane's lips were going up and down on me was that this was my first time getting oral sex. It was at that point that I exploded in her mouth.

She then stood up and finished undressing while I did the same. Lying back down on the floor, I got on top of her. She reached down in between us and guided me into her. So far it seemed everything was going to be all right this time as I slid in and out of her. We were pounding our crotches together and as I got close to having an orgasm, I started seeing my mother's face instead of hers. I tried to close my eyes, but it was too difficult. Every time I opened them I saw her, so I stopped for a minute still inside of her just lying there. She asked, "Not this again?" That must have been when I snapped.

I got off her and went over to the chair in front of the television. She stood up and started cussing me. Looking around, I saw some duct tape lying on the floor. I tore a piece from the roll. I got up from the chair and walked up behind her and before she realized it, I was there; I threw her to the floor. I got on her to pin her down and took the piece of tape and slapped it over her mouth. I grabbed my belt from my pants to tie her hands together and I used her shirt on her ankles. Seeing that she was moving around trying to get loose, I hit her with one hard blow from my fist to the side of her head knocking her out. Making sure that I tied her tight, I grabbed her pocketbook to get her car keys, and after getting dressed I left to go get her car.

I was gone only ten minutes, and when I returned I parked the car near the back door of the apartment building. I looked to see if there were lights on in the building and saw that there weren't. I got some rope and replaced my belt and her shirt, making sure that she wouldn't be able to get away. I rolled her up into a throw carpet that I had in my living room, threw her over my shoulder, and put her in the trunk of her car. Looking all around to make sure nobody had seen me, I got into the car and headed to The Mill.

At The Mill, I got out to open the gate and after driving through, I got back out to lock it. I drove the car around to the back of the building where the heat-treat department was and turned off the motor. Getting out, I went back up to the front door, went in, turned the alarm off, and proceeded to the heat-treat area.

As soon as I got to the bottom of the stairs I saw the people there that I had let in earlier that evening. They all greeted me, saying, "Hi, Paul." I said, "Hey there." Going over to the back door, I unlocked it and went out to the car to get her out of the trunk. I threw her over my shoulder and placed her on the floor in front of the ovens. After removing the carpet,

I stopped to take another look at her young breasts, and her natural blonde pubic hair. By this time Diane started to come around and as she looked around to see where she was she started to panic.

She struggled to get free, but I placed my foot on her chest to hold her down on the floor. Grabbing the electric hoist control box, I looked down at her, and said, "This is what happens when you piss Paul off." I was holding the down button on the control box with my thumb until the hook was on the floor near her hands. I then reached down and hooked it to the rope in between her wrists and pushed the up button.

During this time the two children were begging me to stop while the two adults were saying the same thing. I told them to mind their own business, that I'm doing what I had to do, and that they needed to get back to work. As she was being lifted up to a sitting position she was still looking around to see who I was talking to. As I continued to lift her up, I said, "Paul has to do this, and Paul has to do that. Well I'll show you what Paul wants to do." I could hear her trying to say something—maybe begging me to stop—through her taped mouth. It fell on deaf ears. I had her as high as I needed her. I paused to take one last look at her as she looked down at me with those beautiful, scared blue eyes, then I pushed her back over the oven.

She started to shake her head frantically and the sounds were getting louder from underneath the tape. She spread her legs at the knee in a last ditch effort to change my mind, and stop what I was doing. I leaned over to the left of the oven where I saw some old rope lying on the floor. I picked it up and lashed her knees together; laughing the whole time I was doing it.

They all stopped working to see what I was going to do. That's when I reminded them that it was Paul who opened the door for them, and if it weren't for Paul they would all still be out in the cold. They all quickly turned their backs to me. As I stood there taking my last look, I saw blood running down her wrist from underneath the ropes, and then it happened. My mother's face started flashing in and out of my mind as I looked up at her face. I couldn't take it anymore and I had to stop this from happening. I pushed the down button and held my thumb there.

I had to guide her feet a little to get her lined up, but as soon as her feet hit the molten liquid, I watched in amazement as she disappeared little by little into the oven. It went pretty smooth for the first time, except I had misjudged her breasts getting in the way. I picked up a metal rod that was lying on the floor. She was already dead at this point, so anything I had to do to finish up couldn't hurt her. I took the rod, placing it in between her breasts, and pushed her back a little so that I could get the rest of her in. Taking a knife off my worktable, I stopped lowering her to cut the ropes on her wrists, allowing her arms to fall in, and then she was gone.

I told the others that I would see them tomorrow. On my way out of The Mill I grabbed a three-gallon gasoline container. Setting the alarm and locking the front door, I went around back to get her car. I shut the trunk, got in and drove through the gate, stopping only for a minute to get out and lock it. I needed to fill the gas container I had taken from The Mill and decided to go to one of the local all-night gas stations in Burlington. After getting the gas, I drove to a secluded field on the outskirts of Winooski, but near the Burlington and Colchester town lines.

When I got there I took out her registration, insurance paperwork, and removed both her plates. The Vehicle Identification Number tag on the dashboard was a different story. I took the screwdriver that I used to remove the license plates, and tried to pry it off the dash. After a few tries it hadn't budged and I thought I had been there too long as it was. I gave up and started pouring gasoline over the inside of the car, making sure to soak the dash area. I poured the rest over the outside of the vehicle and threw the empty container inside the car. Lighting a match, I lit the corners of her paperwork, and threw them into the car, which started a raging fire. As I walked toward Winooski and before I disappeared into the woods I looked back once more to see if anyone had noticed the fire. I didn't see any headlights on the main road or on the road that led to the car, so I took off.

I had left the car closer to Burlington, so that the cops would think that it was just another local gang's stunt. I made it home and collapsed in the chair when I noticed Diane's clothes were still on the floor of the living room. I got up and threw her clothes behind my chair in the living room, along with her purse. At this point I was beat, so I went to bed.

The alarm went off, which woke him up. When he finished writing his entry, he got up to make some coffee before he had to go to work. Returning to his bed and reading his entry, he wrote that the dream he had had last night was the worst ever. He finished the entry with the sentence, *At least I'm getting pussy in my dreams.*

When he got to work he went in to see if Rob had found him any help yet. Rob told him no, but they were still trying. He also told him to keep up the good work. Fred said, "I'll do my best." When he passed the lunchroom he saw a copy of that day's newspaper. He grabbed it on his way by and went down to get started working, thinking that if what he wrote in his diary were true he would see something about it in the newspaper.

He looked everywhere in the paper, but couldn't find anything about a murdered girl, let alone a missing girl, and nothing about a car fire. Fred started work, and then remembered the police log in the newspaper. When he opened the paper, he scanned through the police log and there at the bottom the last entry stated there had been a response to a vehicle fire. It

went on to say that it appeared to be an abandoned vehicle driven there for the sole purpose of burning it.

That day, the voices became one voice—that of the older man in his dream. He said, *"You need to be more careful, stick with what we had talked about, and we want to see you tonight. Do you hear me, Paul?"* Without thinking, Fred answered back, "Yeah sure, I hear you." Catching himself answering to the name Paul scared him. The only time he had answered to the name Paul that he was aware of was in his sleepwalking dreams. As he was leaving that afternoon, he heard the man's voice again. He saw nobody, but the voice repeated, *"Don't forget to come tonight."* Fred, seriously thinking that he really might be losing it, turned, set the alarm, locked the door, and went home.

On the walk home a car drove by and honked at him. It stopped at the side of the road just ahead of him, and he saw that it was Andy and a couple of his friends. They wanted to know if he needed a store run, or just maybe a ride home. Fred told him he sure could use a half gallon, if they didn't mind running him to the store. No problem, they said. Fred got in the car, pulled out his pipe, filled it, and handed it to Andy. He thought that it was only right to get them high in exchange for them giving him a ride. Andy ran into the store for Fred, and as he got back into the car he handed the bottle of whiskey to Fred. Andy then took out his pipe and filled it. They all were really high by the time they got him back to his apartment. Getting out of the car, he turned to say thanks again. Andy smiled and told him that he would see him tomorrow at work. Fred turned away and walked into his building and entered his apartment to end his day by finishing the entry from November 1, 1997.

That night when he went to bed he did his usual two shots of tequila with a beer chaser, and a pipe full to help him sleep. It wasn't long after Fred had fallen asleep that he was off on his routine walk to The Mill, remembering that he was told he had better show up as he was leaving work that day. It was as if his subconscious was hearing what his conscious was hearing during the day. When he got to the gate, he saw that they were all there waiting for him. Fred went to the door, turned off the alarm, and let the others in. The older man stayed behind so he could talk to Fred alone. When their conversation was done the older man joined the others downstairs. Fred then set the alarm and left. After Fred locked the gate he returned to his apartment and got back into bed.

The next morning he wrote in his November 2, 1997, entry:

The older man told me to only do what they discussed and only what they had discussed. I don't like being told by anybody what to do, and not to do. In my dreams they were calling me Paul, but if I'm Paul in my dreams then Paul don't like being told what to do, either. I really don't

understand what is going on, but it seems harmless so far. It was just a coincidence about that car being found burning the other night by the police. Heck, I haven't seen Diane since she stopped working at The Mill. I must have been horny that night, and her being the only girl I had sex with, she appeared in my dream. I wonder how she is doing? I have to look her up sometime and tell her about this little dream I had with her in it. I think that I still have her telephone number. When I get to work I'll try calling her on one of my breaks.

Fred went in to work that day with almost a changed attitude. He thought to himself that all the stuff he was experiencing was just his imagination and dreams, and he wasn't going to allow them to control his life. All morning, he was thinking to himself about giving Diane a call during his first break and all morning long those voices were telling him not to. He couldn't figure out why they didn't want him to call and when he got the chance he did. Her roommate told Fred that she hadn't heard anything from her in a couple of days and she would tell her that he had called when she saw her.

He went outside to smoke a cigarette, and to talk with Andy for the rest of their break. The buzzer went off for everyone to return to work, but Fred stayed there to finish his cigarette. While he was standing there he heard the older man's voice telling him that's why he needs to listen to them, because he may find out things that he didn't want to find out. Fred went back to work. It wasn't until the end of the day that it came to him that the last time he had heard a voice was at break time. In one way he missed them and wondered why. He wrote in his diary at the end of the day how boring his day had been.

Chapter 8

From November 2nd until the end of December there were only one-line entries. If he had the sleepwalking dreams, or the dreams of his mother, he didn't write about them. He generally wrote when he was high, or drunk. I guessed this is when he felt the least inhibited and was able to express himself most easily. I took this opportunity to write down the dates of the dream Fred had had about that girl named Diane, to go to the bathroom, stretch my legs, and to figure out what to do next. I decided to wait to tell Nick about Diane until I had finished both diaries. I went back to the bed and, getting comfortable for now, or until the bathroom or my stomach called me away again, I picked up the diary, and began to read.

Fred's next entry was January 1, 1998, and as I finished turning the page I noticed that this was the page where the knife had been placed. Fred wrote that it had rained all last night and then everything froze up. The electricity went out, cable was out, and telephone service was dead. He wrote that he went out his front door to see how bad it really was. He saw trees bent double, telephone and electric wires on the ground snapped by the weight of the ice. Everything he looked at was covered with ice; he didn't see any cars out and about, the sidewalks were bare, and glazed with ice. He went to work anyway, because all he had to do was walk down the hill.

But with practically every other step he took he fell down on his ass. The Mill had no electricity either and he was one of the few who did go in to work. Rob came out to the lunchroom, where they were all gathered, to tell them to go home; he would pay the ones who showed up for the day. Fred turned to leave when he saw Rob coming back out of his office saying, "Fred, I'm glad you haven't left. I need to talk to you before you leave."

"Sure, what do you want?"

Rob explained that he was going to have to stay until electricity came back on, and that he wanted Fred to spend the night there if it didn't come on by 4:00 that afternoon. Fred accepted the job thinking that Rob would see how dedicated he really was. Rob gave him the company beeper and told him that if he needed him he would use his cell phone and beep him at four o'clock. Fred went home. At 3:45 PM, the beeper went off. Fred wrote that he would finish the story about the ice storm of '98, in his next entry. Then he decided his diary would be a perfect way for him to pass time away. He could write down everything that happened during the night, and that way he wouldn't have to remember it all. He placed it in his backpack with his alarm clock, and a few other necessary supplies to get him through the night.

Fred got to The Mill at 4:25 PM, because the public works department still hadn't cleared off the sidewalks.

I've walked this route while both awake and asleep, this must have been the eeriest time of all. Nobody had electricity, everyone's lights were off in their house, the streetlights were all out, and the whole town seemed to be extra quiet. With no one on the roads the only thing that broke the silence was the siren of an emergency vehicle in the distance.

He went to Rob's office. Rob gave him three flashlights and some instructions for things he wanted done while Fred was there. Rob said, "It's all yours. Have fun, do the stuff on the list every other hour, and don't be too afraid." With this, Rob left the building and Fred locked the door behind him. Fred wrote that he watched as Rob drove out the gate to make sure that Rob locked it. He looked around at the inside of The Mill thinking that with the lights out it was a pretty eerie place.

Trying to put this last thought out of his mind, Fred looked at the list and started at number one. He went to the third floor thinking that it would take him the longest because it was an area unfamiliar to him. The third floor was so quiet that he started to get goose bumps on his arm. He saw that everything was all right and started down the stairs to the second floor. There were only a few items that he had to check there, mainly doors and windows.

When Fred finished the second and third floors he went down to the first floor where he felt confident and secure. He started on the opposite end of the building from his department, an add-on to the original building. He wasn't sure exactly what they did out there, but he thought that they worked mainly on special orders, he wrote in his journal later that evening. He also wrote that he didn't really know anyone who worked in that department.

He continued to work his way through the first floor checking the list off as he went along. At this point Fred heard a loud metallic noise, almost like a steel hammer hitting a piece of steel. Spinning around, moving toward the direction that the noise came from, Fred shone the light in front of him searching and looking for a reasonable answer for what made that noise. He knew that he was the only one in the building, unless someone had broken into the second floor while he was down on the first. Adrenaline was pumping through his veins. Then he found what he thought might be the source of the noise. It was a large steel pipe that had fallen from the wall and was leaning against the machine it had fallen on.

Since I'm the only one who will ever be reading this, I guess I can be truthful in the entries I write. That pipe had me real scared, although I knew that nobody could be in the building, I still thought...I don't know what I thought. With those damn voices I've been hearing who knows what anything can really be. I know for a fact that I heard those voices and now I

wasn't hearing them. How come Andy didn't hear them that time he was down there when they were speaking?

He made his way to his own work area. It was normally the warmest place in the building, but Fred found it just as chilly, eerie, and quiet. He was expecting to hear the voices, but they were silent. He went around the backside of all the ovens and checked the gas supply lines to make sure they hadn't frozen. He then went to the second floor lunchroom, where he made himself a bed by putting three benches together and covering them with the blankets that Rob left him. He lit a cigarette. Under normal circumstances he'd never be able to smoke in the lunchroom, and the thought made him laugh out loud. He finished his cigarette, flushing it down the toilet, and made his way back to his makeshift bed.

With the flashlight lying on the top of the blankets, he finished writing in his diary. He wrote that it was a strange quiet, not like that of being home in bed waiting to go to sleep, but a quieter, eerie quiet. He set his alarm clock for two hours later, so he could make his rounds again. When it woke him, he thought that the feeling that somebody else was in the building, or that he was being watched would subside as he made more and more rounds. Nevertheless he brought a full pipe of marijuana with him. He smoked it while he did his last security check before midnight. Getting back to the second floor lunchroom and going to his bed, he looked at his alarm clock; seeing that he had a few minutes to go before midnight he finished his entry for January 1st. He then turned the page, dating the top right-hand side January 2, 1998.

The next time that Fred was awakened was not by his alarm clock, but by someone shaking him by his shoulder saying, *"Paul, wake up, Paul, wake up."*

Not really being fully awake Fred asked, "What? What do you want?"

A man's voice replied, *"Paul, you forgot to let us in. Why, Paul, did you forget?"* Fred's response was, "I must have fallen asleep." Fred sat up on his bed and found them all there sitting across from him just staring, not saying a word. Fred said, "The Mill is shut down because of the ice storm. You don't need to be here tonight."

The older man answered back, *"You're wrong, Paul, we always have to be here."* They all started to go down to the first floor, by way of the main staircase and Fred followed. When they got to the first floor, the woman who was the second oldest started to weep. Fred reached down to take one of her hands in comfort, and asked, "What's wrong, Ruth?" Instantly an image flashed in Fred's mind. It was of a woman who was lying on the floor bleeding from her head and neck. It looked as if one of

the grinding wheels might have fallen on her during installation, crushing her skull. Paul took her away from that area by pulling her by the hand.

The group of them continued to walk toward the heat-treat department, and as soon as they were out of the area the woman stopped weeping. It was at that moment, almost to the second, that the two children started to cry. They were at the bottom of the built-in floor ramp just before the entry to the heat-treat area. Fred went over to see what was troubling the children.

Putting his arms around both of them he asked what was making them cry. More flashes hit Fred; it looked like this might have been a loading area at one time or another. There was a truck with its back door open and a man on a forklift leaning over the steering wheel and crying. One fork looked like it was snapped off, and a machine had come down on top of the two children that Fred had his arms around. One boy was crushed completely with only his head being spared; the other boy was leaning up against the wall with both of his legs severed at mid-thigh. Fred thought that he must have pulled himself clear after the machine had fallen. People came running to the child, but before they got to him he had breathed his last breath. Starting to cry himself, Fred stood up and started walking with the children toward the older man who had continued to walk out to the heat-treat area.

In the heat-treat area where they all gathered as they usually did, the older man told the woman and children what he wanted them to do. Fred stood there for a moment watching them. They appeared to be sorting something out on a small table. The older man then looked at Fred, put his hand on his shoulder and said, *"We didn't want you to forget what your purpose was, Paul. You said that you would handle it for all of us. You told us that you wouldn't let them get away with it. All those people, all those years gone by, and still nobody has done anything. Don't let us down, Paul."*

Feeling somewhat puzzled, Fred answered him, "I haven't forgotten, and I will make them pay for what they have done. To the best of my ability, the ones who have done this will never forget." Fred headed to the lunchroom. He was almost at the top of the stairs when the older man said, *"Thanks, Paul."* Fred had returned to the bed that he created out of the three benches, and the next sound he heard was that of the alarm clock. He sat up and noticed he was sweating. Bits and pieces of his dream started coming to his mind clearly as if he had actually done them. That's when Fred decided to get his diary out, so he could record as much as he could remember.

2:00 AM came quickly, but Fred delayed making his rounds until he finished writing in his diary. It took Fred about an hour to finish up and start his walk-around.

He started to head down to the opposite end of the building as he had done before. He slipped on something, and when he squatted down to get a closer look, his flashlight dropped from his hand to the floor. It appeared that Fred was standing in the middle of a pool of blood. He retrieved the flashlight, but got blood all over his hand. He shone the light around, and saw that the whole area was splattered with blood. Fred had a flash of the women being crushed to death right where he was standing. He tried to convince himself that this wasn't really happening and that he needed to finish his walk-around. He started out again and noticed that his hands didn't feel wet anymore. He shone his flashlight back where he'd just come from and saw nothing out of place.

Laughing to himself, thinking how immature he was to let his imagination get to him like that, he shook his head and continued on with his inspection, though mentally he prepared himself for anything. But he found nothing out of the ordinary.

As he headed back to the lunchroom, he heard a man say, *"Don't forget"*, or at least that is what it sounded like. Stopping in his tracks, he had to laugh because he knew that it was totally impossible. He was the only one in the place. He wrote the whole experience down so he wouldn't ever forget this night. When he finished, it was almost five o'clock. He figured he wouldn't have to do another walk-around, because Rob was coming back around seven that morning. He set his alarm for 6:30 AM, lay back down and quickly fell off to sleep.

The next thing he knew was that he was being awakened, as he had been the last time, by someone tapping his shoulder, telling him to get up. Half awake, Fred grabbed the person's arm at about the same time he heard the alarm blaring, bringing him completely awake to find himself holding onto Rob. "Hey, Hey Fred it's just me! Fred, it's me!"

"Yeah, I know, Rob", he replied. "You caught me in the middle of a dream and startled me."

Fred got his stuff together and followed Rob to his office. Fred told him that everything went great. Rob thanked him and repeated that he would pay Fred for his night's work. At home, Fred put one last entry in his diary.

Well, this is the last page. I guess I'll get another one because I sure as hell can't tell anyone else about the dreams I've been having they might think I'm crazy or something. Ha, Ha.

I closed the diary and shook my head in wonder. Was Fred crazy? I just lay there a few minutes thinking about how weird it all sounded. I must have dozed off, because the next thing I knew my phone was ringing. I looked at the clock as I reached for the phone and saw that it was quarter of eleven. Putting the phone to my ear, I heard a voice saying, "Larry wake up, or is this your stupid answering machine?"

"No it's me. What's up, Nick?"

Nick said he was just giving me a call to see if I might be done with Fred's diary, and if I were, would it be possible to bring it into the station. I told him that I was finished, but I was just waking up so it would be a little bit before I could get to the station. I had to take a shower to wake the rest of me up. Nick laughed, and told me just to call him before I left so that I wouldn't waste his time coming in just to find that he had to step out for something.

In the shower I started to think about what I was going to say to Nick and if I should say anything yet about the second diary. If I did tell him, Nick would probably wonder how come I didn't say anything about it before now. I decided not to tell him, or at least not until I'd had a chance to read it and make my notes.

As I poured my coffee at the kitchen table, I figured that I would just tell him what I had read, and emphasize that he would need to read it and make his own judgment. If and when he took the time to do that, if that is what he decided to do, and then wanted my opinion, I would give it to him.

I called the police station and told Nick I was on my way.

At the station Nick seemed worried, as if I might have forgotten the diary in my haste to get to the station. I looked at him, put my briefcase up on his desk, and opened it. I handed him the diary and asked, "Did you really think that I wouldn't bring it?"

"You're pretty slick, Larry." Nick smiled. I was waiting for him to ask about what I had read, or what I might have thought, but all he did was take it from me and put it in his top right-hand drawer. He thanked me for returning it.

"Aren't you the least bit concerned about what's in it?"

Nick looked at me with a somewhat puzzled look, and replied, "Yeah, sure I am, but right now Steve and I are working on something that is stumping us." He handed me some documents. The first one confirmed that the fingerprints from the electric hoist control box were Fred Lamperee's and matched those of the severed hand.

"So, I thought you already knew that?"

Nick leaned forward, took the top sheet and pointed to the one underneath, which I had mistaken for a duplicate copy.

I read that the liquid found at the base of the machine was in fact human blood mixed with machine oil, but the blood type from tissue off the hand was not the same blood type. The sample from the hand was AB positive, and the sample from the drip pan was B negative. The only other prints found in both areas besides Fred's were those of people who worked there. I placed both documents back on the desk, sat back in my chair, and said, "Well it seems as though you have two dead people, but no bodies."

Chapter 9

On the way home I again had to pass Fred's apartment building, and the street that led up to the Lamperees' house. When the events of this weekend first started, going by Fred's apartment gave me the chills, but as the weekend progressed it seemed as though I was becoming more accustomed to what was unraveling. As I approached my driveway I became excited. I felt my heart rate increase as my footsteps drew me closer to my front door. I went through my routine of going to the bathroom, placing my cigarettes and lighter next to the ashtray on the nightstand, and checking the status of the batteries in the tape recorder. I couldn't wait to get started on the second diary, which I hoped would lead me to an understanding of this man, and what or how his character had to do with this past weekend.

As I sat on the bed my stomach let me know that it had been long enough without food. I went into the kitchen and got a package of microwave popcorn from the cupboard. I put it in the microwave, set the timer and went to the refrigerator for a beer. Not exactly a meal fit for a king, but at least it was something. It would hold me for a while.

The first entry was dated January 3rd, which led me to believe that Fred finished the second day of the New Year sleeping. The building was reopened on the third with business returning to normal, whatever that meant within the walls of The Mill. Fred got to work on time, and started by filling the ovens with salt, so that they could start melting it down and he could get on with his work. The whole time he was doing this he noted in his diary that he didn't hear any voices, or see any apparitions. He thought maybe they had a connection to the salt, or maybe even something to do with the hot molten liquid, but remembered they appeared when the ovens were down during the ice storm. After all five ovens were filled with the salt he heard his name being called over the intercom. Someone wanted him to report to Rob's office. He checked to make sure that all was okay with the ovens and everything else in his area.

When he got up to Rob's office, Donny and Rob were standing there waiting for him. He quickly wondered what, if anything, he had done to piss them off. Nevertheless, he put on a smile and said, "Hey Rob, Donny what's up?"

Donny didn't say much except hi, but Rob said, "Hey, how are you feeling after your long night?" Fred answered that he was doing fine; maybe a little bit tired, and with the ovens being down the past two days things might back up a little. Rob explained that he and everyone else

understood exactly what the ovens going down meant to the business, and told him that somebody else wanted to see him. Fred was puzzled. Rob told him to come with him, and he saw that Donny was following them. What was going on, what did they want? On the third floor, they came to a stop at a closed door and Rob knocked.

The door opened and they were greeted by a very nice-looking woman who invited them all to come in and have a seat. They sat on a couch and waited for the person on the telephone to finish his conversation. When he hung up, the man turned to them with a big smile on his face. He introduced himself as the owner and told Fred that he could call him Ron. Rob explained what had been necessary for him and Fred to do to guard the building during the ice storm. He went on further to explain that the ice storm not only left the building without phone and electricity, but it also shut down the fire and security alarms.

Ron, shaking his head, looked at Fred, saying, "You wouldn't find me sleeping here alone." They all had a good laugh. Ron told Fred it would be at least time and a half for the hours he spent there during the ice storm. Fred told him that Rob had already explained that he would be paid for it, and that it was the least he could do for Rob and The Mill. All three of them got up to go, but Ron stopped them just before they were out the door.

"Before you leave, let me introduce my wife to you, Fred. Rob, you and Donny already know her, but Fred doesn't. Fred, this is Kris, my wife."

Fred said, "It's nice to meet you, ma'am," and extended his hand.

"I'm pleased to meet you," she said, "and I want to thank you for all that you did for us."

Back on the second floor Donny grabbed Fred by the shoulder saying, "Hey buddy, I want you to know that it took me three years to meet the owner face-to-face, and another two years to meet his wife. You did it all in under two years."

Fred smiled and said, "I didn't really do anything special, and heck, I'm getting paid for it, so what's the big deal?"

Rob turned to say, "Don't cut yourself down. What you did was over and above, and there aren't many down on the production floor that would have done it. Thanks. Thanks a whole lot. I owe you." Shaking his hand Fred told them that he had to get back down to his department to make sure everything was okay. He walked away from them with a ballooning sense of pride in himself, something that he hadn't felt too often.

The end of the day came quickly for Fred. The jobs had piled up during the shutdown. With about half an hour to go before the day's end Fred was getting set up for the next day when he heard, "Fred."

"Don't start with me now," he said angrily. "Just leave me alone to finish the day."

Donny came up alongside him and answered, "What do you mean, leave you alone? I just wanted to come out and tell you that Rob told Ron he wanted to give you a raise, and Ron okayed it. If you need any help tomorrow, let me know early and I'll try to get Andy out here to give you a hand."

"Sorry Donny, my mind is elsewhere. Thanks for the offer to help, and for telling me about the raise. How come you never told me that the owner had such a hot-looking wife?"

Donny said, "She sure is nice, but I never really looked at her that way. That's right, I forget, you're young, single, and any halfway good-looking girl would get your dick hard."

They both broke out laughing as the buzzer went off signaling the end of the day. No sooner had they both punched out for the day than Andy came out to see what was going on after work.

"Why don't we go over to Fred's place and have a few," Andy blurted out.

Donny and Fred looked at each other.

"Sure," they said.

Fred got back to his place before the two of them, which gave him some time to straighten up a little. About fifteen minutes later Donny appeared with a twelve-pack of beer. Andy came right after with a fifth of tequila. Andy lifted the bottle and said, "Let's party, dude." Donny took the only chair, and Andy and Fred sat on the floor. Donny passed out the beer as Andy opened the bottle of tequila and handed it to Fred. Andy and Fred smoked some pot, but Donny passed, telling them he was too old for that shit. A few hours later Fred started on the subject of Ron's wife.

Donny sat back in the chair laughing at Fred and explained that she had to be at least 48 years old. Andy couldn't believe that she was that nice looking. He hadn't seen or met the owner yet, let alone his wife, so he didn't really know what to believe. Pretty soon Donny got up, telling them that he had enough, and had to leave. Andy in turn asked Donny for a ride home. They said their good-byes, telling Fred to keep the leftovers as Fred shut the door.

Fred put away the beer, but then changed his mind. He took a beer and the bottle of tequila and went into his bedroom. He reached down to get his diary out to finish that day's entry. It had been the second longest entry in awhile for Fred except, of course, for the ice storm. He went on to say how he couldn't get Kris out of his mind. *She has a beautiful smile, a nice ass, and really nice breasts. I can't help wanting to touch myself thinking about her, she is so fine-looking, and not only that, but as I write about her it gives me a hard on.* Saying good night in his diary, he took out one of his Playboy magazines, thumbing through it to try and find a resemblance of

Kris he could masturbate to. When he finished he tore the picture out of the magazine to save.

Fred fell asleep with his diary on one side of him and the picture of the nude girl on the other. He did manage to roll over to turn out the lights.

But his night had just begun. He rose up in his bed looking at the picture of the naked girl. He crumpled it up and threw it on the floor, and then went out to the living room to put on his boots. He got his cigarettes out of the kitchen drawer where he kept them, grabbed his jeans jacket, and left for The Mill. He got to the gate, unlocked it, looked into the yard and saw that everyone had showed up on time. Going through the gate, he turned around to lock it, and headed over to the people waiting at the front door.

They all greeted him with smiles. Knowing that they were going to have a somewhat normal night seemed to make them happy. The two children and young woman went on down to the heat-treat area as usual, but the older man said that he wanted to talk to him away from the others. He stayed with him to see what he wanted. He asked Paul if he had made any decisions about the first one and Paul thought Kris would be a good choice. A few minutes passed and both of them headed down to the work area behind the others. Paul saw that they were all busy doing their work; he turned and went up the stairs, armed the alarm and locked the door, then went out the gate and locked it.

On the way home he smiled from ear to ear thinking about how the older man agreed about the owner's wife as his first choice. Returning home, he found the owner's wife lying in his bed naked, waiting for him. He stripped down to nothing and climbed into bed next to her. Without a word, she climbed on top of him and started to rub her crotch against his. Closing his eyes to enjoy the moment, he told himself that he just needed one more look. When he opened them, the first thing he saw was his mother's face on the woman who was on top of him. Throwing her off, he went out to the refrigerator, got a beer and a bowl of pot, and went back into his bedroom to find that no one was there. He straightened out the picture of the woman who looked like Kris and tacked it up on the ceiling above his bed.

When he woke, he realized that it was just another one of his dreams. He thought about it for a while and started to write in his diary. He kept trying to analyze why his mother's face would appear in his dreams about sex and while he was having sex. Did it mean that subconsciously he wanted to have sex with his mother, or was it that he couldn't shake the image of her standing naked in front of him while he was in the shower on his sixteenth birthday? Not really wanting to think about it anymore, he

paused in his writing to take a hit off his pot pipe, and a swallow of beer. He finished up by writing that he really wanted to try and get his driver's license, and that he was going to ask his brother what he needed to do to get it.

The entries went back to being very short. It wasn't until January 15, 1998, that there was an entry of any substance. He wrote, *I went up to my brother's office on my break to find out what I had to do to get a driver's license.* His brother was pleasantly surprised to see him, because it had been a while since they had gotten together for any reason. Pat said he had met a real nice girl he was really interested in—who had two little girls. He added that they had been seeing each other for a couple of months now. Fred asked, "Are you considering getting married or something?" Pat replied, "It definitely is a consideration. She is the nicest girl I've ever gone out with, and her two little girls love me to death. Enough about me, what was it you wanted to see me about?" Fred explained to him how he felt about where he was in life. He stated that he had a good job, was saving money, and had a place of his own, but there was one thing missing. Pat asked, "What's that?"

"I want my driver's license, and thought you would be able to tell me what I needed to do to get it." He told Fred that the first thing he had to do was to study the manual, and the second thing was to take his permit test. Then he needed to find a car, or someone to take him out to practice driving around. Pat went one step further and said, "On lunch break, I'll stop by the police station and get a manual for you."

"You don't mind doing that? Thanks Pat. I'll stop up when my shift ends to get it from you."

"I don't mind at all, that's what family is for. I'll even take you out a couple times to practice."

Fred looked at Pat, and said, "Thanks, I love you, Pat." Just as he was turning to go down to the production floor, he heard someone say, "Hi Fred." Looking around, he saw Kris, the owner's wife, smiling and waving at him. He returned the smile, giving a quick glance at her body as he said hi back to her, and went back to work.

He was plugging along when he heard the older man's voice telling him not to forget what they had talked about. He told him that he hadn't, as he kept on with his work. About that time Andy came out to see if he needed any help, explaining that he didn't have much going on until more work was sent out to his area. Fred told him that he could use all the help that he could get, so Andy sat at the table and began sorting and racking the raw stock. As the time went by, Fred told him that his brother was getting a driver's manual so he could study it to take the test to get his license. Andy

replied, "Dude, if you get your license we can go out cruising. I think I heard Donny saying that he wanted to sell his black Toyota pickup truck."

"Really? That would be awesome. I love those pickup trucks. How much does he want for it?" Andy didn't know, but told Fred that he would ask Donny after lunch.

When they returned from lunch they were pretty high on pot. Fred got to work and Andy went to see if Donny would come out to the heat-treat area to talk to Fred about his truck.

Donny returned with Andy. He told Fred that it was in great running condition, and the only reason he wanted to get rid of it was because he had just gotten a new one. He went on to say that if Fred was really interested, he would bring it to work the next day, so he could take a look at it. "Sure, I'd like to take a look at it. How much do you want for it?"

"All I want is twenty-two hundred dollars. As is." Fred knew he already had fifteen hundred in the bank. Maybe he and Donny could work out payments for the rest. When the buzzer went off, Fred went up to his brother's office to get the manual. He told him about the deal that Donny offered him for his truck.

Pat handed him the manual saying, "You better get studying then. It sounds like an awesome deal. I'll do what I can to help you out, just let me know."

"Thanks, Pat." He stuffed the manual in his pocket and left The Mill to go home. When he got there, he called the Department of Motor Vehicles to see what he needed to do to take the test. He was informed that he needed to make an appointment, and that the first one available was for Thursday of the following week at 2:30. He asked to be scheduled for that one and after confirming it, he hung up. He ended his entry writing, *I would try to write some, but I'm going to study as much as I can. Unless something new comes up in my dreams there won't be a need to write until I pass the test.*

Fred wrote occasionally in his diary saying he was studying real hard to pass the test, Donny took his fifteen hundred, they worked out payments for the rest, and he was still having the same sleepwalking dreams. But on January 22nd, he wrote, *I'm taking my driver's permit test tomorrow, and I can't believe how nervous I am. I'm through studying. I need to get high, and have a couple of beers, so I can calm down a little.* That night, Fred dreamed he got up to leave on his walk to The Mill to let the others in to work, when he felt a hand push him back down onto his bed. Fred had fallen asleep that night totally naked, which was unusual for him. When his head hit the pillow he felt a mouth kissing his upper thighs, and eventually he felt someone's mouth wrapped around his erect penis. Looking down he saw that it was Kris. He put both of his hands on the back

of her head until he felt himself exploding in her mouth. He brought his hands back up to his face rubbing his eyes. He looked down in time to see her lift up her head, but it wasn't Kris he was looking at—it was his mother.

Jumping out of bed, he got dressed, threw his boots on, and left for The Mill. As he walked toward the building the thought of him getting oral sex from his mother wouldn't leave his thoughts. He couldn't believe that it might be possible that this could be happening, real or not. The thought of how nice it felt kept overpowering any other thought that he had about it. He let himself into The Mill's yard, locked the gate behind him and went over to the people waiting for him.

He let them all in, locked the door behind him, and followed them down to the heat-treat area. The children started to work, and the woman along with the older man came over to him to see if he wanted anything. Fred usually just let them in and then left. The woman asked, *"What's wrong, Paul?"* The older man just stood there listening as he tried to explain.

"It's getting rough keeping my concentration level strong on our purpose."

"What do you mean," the older man asked. Paul went on to say, "Sometimes right before heading out to come here Fred starts having dreams in which he is having sex, and then it always turns out to be his mother he's dreaming of. That, of course, throws him off, and it is hard to get him back on track. We have that test to take tomorrow and he bought his friend's truck, which means our plans are moving right along. I just got to figure out how to block him from those other dreams." The woman looked at Paul saying, *"Don't worry about those dreams. Just keep the plans we made in your mind, and he won't have any control over his."* The older man added that Fred's dreams were trying to confuse him about their purpose. Paul agreed and turned to leave, saying good night to them all. When he got home he lay back down to resume sleeping. He thought that he was just at the point of falling off, when his eyes opened wide.

Fred got out of bed wondering when these dreams would stop. He didn't stop to wonder how he got dressed; he just started to take his shoes and clothes off. He went to the refrigerator for a beer, and sat down to write in his diary. He wrote that it wasn't bothering him as much seeing his mother's face in his erotic dreams. After the numerous times her face appeared it was becoming commonplace to see it. He just didn't know how to remove her face from his dreams. He wrote, *As long as nobody else knows, who cares? I don't.* He went on to finish describing the sleepwalking dream he had just emerged from. The last sentence he wrote was, *I guess I'll stay up a little to study for my test.*

Fred got to The Mill earlier than normal, meeting Rob as he was disarming the alarm at the front door. Rob said, "You're here early this morning. Dedicated or what?"

"Or what. I wanted to ask you if it would be possible to leave at the two o'clock break, so I could go take my permit test?"

"Sure. Just let me know when you leave." Fred thanked him and went down to his work area to get started. He decided to work through his breaks that day, only stopping long enough to smoke a cigarette. On his way out Donny and Andy wished him luck on the test. At the time clock, the voices whispered, *"Good Luck."* Ignoring them, he punched out, and went up the stairs to leave. Rob met him at the front door and also wished him good luck.

"Thanks Rob, and I'll try to get back before the end of the day if possible."

"Don't worry about it, we'll see you tomorrow."

On the bus to the police barracks, Fred began worrying again that he might fail the test. As he walked from the bus stop, Paul started to reassure him about the test. These thoughts, as Fred put it in his entry, were so forceful that he let go of his negative thinking and got his confidence back. When he entered the building he went up to the counter and leaned on it, waiting to be noticed. A feeling of familiarity overwhelmed him. He muttered to himself, "This place hasn't changed much."

He heard a man's voice question, "Excuse me?"

"I'm sorry I was just mentioning that this place hasn't changed much over the years."

"It sure hasn't, but according to your application this is your first time here."

Caught off guard, Fred said, "That's right, never mind me. I guess I'm just nervous." The man handed Fred the test and pointed where he should sit and take it.

Writing down his name, his birth date, and social security number Fred settled in to take the test. The questions appeared to be easy. It was as if he had the whole manual in his head. As he was answering the last question Fred looked at the time. He couldn't believe it; according to the clock on the wall it had only taken fifteen minutes.

He went over to the counter to hand in his test. The man behind it looked at him, gave him a smile, and said, "That didn't take long. You can sit over there while I correct it." For some reason Fred had no doubt about the results.

It didn't take long for the man to finish correcting it, and to call Fred over to the counter.

"There's something wrong with your test."

Fred asked, “What’s wrong, did I fail?”

“It appears that you got all the answers right, but the information at the top is different than what you wrote on the application. You wrote down a different birth date and social security number.

“What do you mean?” The man turned the test paper and application around so Fred could see it.

“I’m sorry sir. I just must have been nervous. I’ll change it now, if that’ll be okay?” He then wrote in the correct information, and handed it back to the man behind the counter. Looking at both pieces of paper the man said, “Now that’s better. Step over here to this machine, and tell me the numbers that you see.”

Fred answered all of them correctly, and with that the man said, “Congratulations son, here’s your permit.”

Fred was smiling ear-to-ear. “How long do I have to wait before I can take my road test?”

The man said, “Don’t rush it, son. There is plenty of time, but the minimum time is one month.”

“Thanks.”

The thought came to him that he should stop and tell Sam. The bus took him to within two blocks of Sam’s house. It was already 3:30 in the afternoon, and all of his friends would be getting off work and driving by on their way home. Just before he got to Sam’s house Donny and Andy went by. They saw him walking and pulled over to ask how he had done. When they found out he passed his test they told him that they would stop by in an hour or so.

When he went into the house, Sam scolded him about how long it had been since he had seen Fred. Fred explained that he had been busy at The Mill, with the ice storm and everything. Sam told him to come into the kitchen so that they could talk, and so he wouldn’t burn the supper he was in the middle of cooking.

Fred said, “How about a beer, Sam?”

“I’m sorry, son, I clean forgot to offer you one. As a matter of fact I think I’ll join you.” Fred told him about his raise, how he slept there all night by himself, and how he had been introduced to the owner and his wife. He then topped it off with the news of him buying a truck, and how he had passed his permit test. Sam couldn’t believe his ears.

“I never had the opportunity to meet the owner in all the years that I worked at The Mill. You’re telling me now that you have your permit to drive a car, and that you also bought yourself a truck? Well, that deserves another beer, drink up.”

“I’ll take another one, grandpa, but I got some friends who are going to meet me at my place in a half an hour.” Sam toasted his youngest

grandson, and they both proceeded to chug down their beer. Fred stood up, gave Sam a hug and kiss telling him that he loved him, and said he had to leave. Sam yelled, "Don't be no stranger, and stop by sooner, you hear?"

At home Fred noticed that he only had three beers in the refrigerator, and a couple of shots of tequila left. He was almost out of pot, too. He figured that he would get Donny to give him a ride to get some beer, and that the guys would bring some more pot.

Fred had just settled down to light his pipe, not wanting to wait for his friends, when he heard a knock at the door. Fred set his pipe under his chair, and answered the door. Fred was glad to see them, but asked Donny before he took off his coat if he could take him to the store to get a twelve-pack. Donny answered, "Sure, let's go." On their way out to the truck Donny told Fred to get in the driver's side.

"What do you mean?"

"Didn't you get your permit?"

"I sure did."

"Well then, you're driving", Donny replied, and handed the keys to him.

Fred didn't have to ask where to put them, or how anything else in the truck worked. Starting the truck and putting it into gear, he put on the blinker, and pulled away from the curb. It didn't take him any time at all to get to the store. Fred drove the truck as if he had driven it before. Donny looked at him, and asked, "Where did you learn how to drive?"

"I'm not sure. When I got in the truck it felt as though I had done this before. I can't remember ever driving, but it sure seemed like I knew what I was doing."

"It sure did. I don't think that you did anything wrong. How long is it before you can get your license?"

"Thirty days."

They got out of the truck, Fred handed Donny some money, and they both went into the store. When they left the store Fred got in the driver's seat again. Donny laughingly said, "Make yourself at home." When they got home, they found that Andy had already started without them. He had done at least three or four shots, took some hits off Fred's pipe, and was watching cartoons on television. Looking up, Andy said, "Dude."

"Dude, Donny let me drive his truck to and from the store."

"Dude, how many things did you hit?"

Donny said, "None, he did awesome, as if he had been driving for years." Donny and Andy had to leave in less than thirty minutes, so Donny's wife wouldn't get pissed at him. They sat down to do some quick, hard partying to celebrate Fred passing his permit test.

His buddies left earlier than he had wanted and he looked around his apartment not sure what to do with himself. He went into his bedroom to write in his diary what he had accomplished this day. He ended his entry by stating that out of next week's paycheck he was going to have his truck registered, inspected, and insured. This way he could practice his driving in his own vehicle. Leaning forward, he turned the television back on, but found himself dozing off to sleep as he heard his diary fall to the floor. He adjusted himself in his chair, but within minutes was sound asleep.

It wasn't long before he was up and on his way to The Mill. He found the people waiting near the gate instead of by the door. He asked them what was so different about tonight that they were waiting here. Together they said, *"Congratulations Paul."*

"Oh, the permit thing," he said.

As he walked to the front door, he felt a hand on his shoulder. The older man smiled, and put his arm around him, saying, *"I'm proud of you Paul. Now it's time to get busy."* He opened the front door, then disarmed the alarm and let the others in. After everyone was in he locked the front door, and reset the alarm. Turning to go downstairs to see the others, he found the older man sitting in the lunchroom. He asked Paul to sit down.

As Paul sat down on the bench, the older man rose and stood in front of him like a teacher might in front of a class. He again told Paul that he was proud of him, but that the time was running short.

"Look, Paul, you know why we are here and what we have to do. You're the one who guaranteed us that you were the best choice. The time was right; you being close in age, but it just seems that things aren't getting done."

"Look, it takes time. We discussed that it has to go this way—to work it in slow so that Fred wouldn't notice."

Paul told him what Fred had written at the top of his test paper. "He wrote all my information first, and let's get real, I knew how to drive a vehicle fifty or so years ago. I don't need a license, but Fred does. If this is going to work it has to go step by step."

"I'm sorry, Paul, you're right. As far as I'm concerned if it wasn't for people like him, we wouldn't even have the opportunity to make it right. You are doing a good job. I've been watching your progress, and I think that Fred really thinks he's going crazy. Nobody around him has noticed, and that's good."

Paul reassured him that he would try to pick up the pace, and that the end wasn't too far off. The older man gave Paul a hug and told him he'd better get back so that Fred would be able to get up and go to work. Paul went through his usual routine to exit the building, but this time he had a feeling that someone was watching him from behind. Turning around, he

noticed one of the children watching him leave the gate and waving good-bye. He locked the gate, turning to head up the hill so he could put Fred's body to rest for the night.

Chapter 10

Back in the apartment he returned to the chair where Fred passed out, and then changed his mind. Paul picked up the diary and Fred's pen, and started to write where Fred had left off. He wrote, *I need to locate a road atlas. The time is right; I don't need a license. I have to bring this to an end for everyone concerned. That bitch is the FIRST.*

He finished and lay the diary down on the floor. He then went into the bedroom, took Fred's hunting knife out, and drove it into the picture Fred had put up of the girl in the magazine who reminded him of Kris. He lay down on the bed staring at the picture on the ceiling, and fell off to sleep. When his alarm went off he got up without hesitation. Sitting on the edge of his bed, he paused for a moment remembering that he thought he had passed out in the chair in the living room. He looked down at the side of his bed for his diary to write what he had just dreamt, and saw that it wasn't there. Wiping the sleep out of his eyes, he got up and went out to make his coffee. With this done he turned to go into the bathroom, and saw his diary sitting open on the floor next to the chair in the living room. He reached for a cigarette and lit it.

Sitting in the chair, he grabbed the ashtray off the floor so he could rest his cigarette in it while he was reading. He looked to make sure that he had placed it firmly in the ashtray and realized that it wasn't his brand; it was one of those Camel non-filters. At this point he was more concerned about why his diary was out in the living room and not by his bed. He started to read his last entry. He read it, got down to the part where Paul had written in it, and that is when it hit him. Recalling his dream, writing as he went along in his mind, he recalled that in part of it he sat down and wrote in the diary. Other than smoking different cigarette brands, knowing how to drive when he never had before, and waking to find himself covered with mud or still dressed in bed, he had never had any other proof of his dreams. This was the first time he had seen something Paul had done during his sleepwalk dreams that was there in front of him and that he couldn't deny. He lay down his diary to get a cup of coffee, and returned to finish up his entry before work.

When he finished the entry, he added that it was taking too long. *I need to get the atlas to know how to get there. There won't be any problems taking care of business, but before I do I have to know where to go.* He closed his diary, sat his coffee on the counter, took a drag off his cigarette, then put it out in the sink, and went in to take a shower. He noticed that he had only fifteen minutes to get dressed, and get to work on time. He was on

a dead run as he left his apartment door. He had never been late, and he wasn't planning on being late today. Going down the hill he slowed to a walk, lit a cigarette, and thought about what he would give as an excuse if he was ever late. He couldn't tell anyone that he was hanging out at The Mill and getting very little sleep. He could tell them that it wasn't him; it was Paul's fault.

Laughing to himself, he threw his cigarette on the ground, and went in the building to punch in. He got to the time clock just inside the door as the buzzer went off. He heard a voice say, "Almost didn't make it today, Fred?" Turning around to see if it was one of the voices or someone else, he hesitated to answer until he was sure. It was Donny. He shook his head and said, "It sure was close this time, Donny. Those late-night parties are killing me."

Donny held out a booklet folded in half, which he handed to Fred.

"I forgot to put this back into the truck when you bought it."

"What is it?" Fred opened it up and saw it was a road atlas. Donny replied, "It's old, but it got me from here to there."

On the way out after work the woman's voice that he knew from his dreams, and the occasional conversation during his workday, was telling him not to worry. Shaking his head, as if to stop the voice, he went out the side entrance instead of the main door. As the door shut behind him, he started to hear the voices again. It was as if they were in some kind of an argument, but he couldn't really make it out because it was too muffled. As he walked through the parking lot the voices got louder.

Just before he got to the main entrance, out of the corner of his eye, he saw the owner and his wife in a heated discussion. He couldn't make out too much of what was being said, but did see her end the conversation and walk quickly away, getting into her car and slamming the door. She immediately put it in gear and sped off. Fred kept walking, pretending to ignore them.

"Fred, how's it going?" came a shout behind him. He turned and saw Ron, the owner of The Mill, smiling and waving. Waving back at him, Fred yelled out, "I'm doing fine, thanks."

Here I decided to take a break so I could get something to eat, record some of the entries, and smoke a cigarette. As I quickly downed a ham and cheese sandwich and a beer, I mulled over how real Fred's dreams seemed to be. I couldn't wait to see what happened next.

January ended without too many more entries except for the occasional mention of a nighttime walk to The Mill. I couldn't tell if Fred

was getting more secretive or if he was fighting the conflict going on within him. At least I had found out how that picture above Fred's bed had gotten mutilated. The next two weeks' entries were of little substance, mainly talking about his work, and the people he was partying with.

February 15, 1998, was different. Fred seemed to have had a good day at work. He got home and picked up his mail. He had letters from both the Department of Motor Vehicles, and his insurance company. He went into his apartment, opened a beer and sat down in the living room to open his mail. The Registry had sent his registration, and the insurance company a policy covering six months upon getting his license. Fred didn't hesitate. He ran out to his truck, and squatted down to put on his truck's plates. Then he put all the paperwork in the glove compartment. Fred started to walk away, but stopped. He didn't say what made him do it, but he got in, started the truck, and drove off. He knew that he had two weeks or so to go before he could get his license, but it didn't matter. Fred headed toward The Mill. He was just about at the top of the hill when he spotted Kris the owner's wife pulling out again at a pretty good clip. Fred thought to himself that she must have returned to finish the argument. He made a U-turn and followed her onto the interstate.

He stayed back so as not to draw attention to himself, but still close enough to see her. They stayed on the interstate for about thirty minutes. Fred followed her off the interstate, and when he got to the stop sign at the end of the exit he saw a sign saying, "Welcome to Fletcher." Fred couldn't believe that he was in the same town where he had grown up, and where his mother still lived. What was more amazing to him was that he didn't recognize anything on the way, even though he had made the trip numerous times.

Focusing on his driving again, he saw Kris was headed out of town on the main road, so apparently they didn't live in Fletcher. He continued to follow her for about twenty minutes watching her as she pulled into a dirt driveway on the right-hand side of some dirt road in the middle of nowhere. Driving by the place, he observed that they lived in a beautiful cape-style home that had a barn and two out buildings on the property. He continued down the road for another five miles until he finally found a place he could turn around. Stopping long enough to take out his road atlas, he located the roads he took to get there on the map, and marked them.

He arrived back at his apartment without any incident with the law and parked his truck in the back; he locked it up, and went into his apartment.

He turned on his television, put it at a low volume, and went to the kitchen to get the bottle of tequila that was sitting on the counter. Fred got a beer and went back in to sit in front of the television. He got out his pipe,

filled it, and lit it. At about eight o'clock he decided to take a shower. As he started to wash, his mind immediately went to Kris, and he started to get an erection even before he had touched himself. As he worked his way down, soaping his body, the thought of taking a shower to get clean left his mind and became a sexual experience to be satisfied by no one but himself.

Fred had this beautiful picture in his mind of what he thought Kris would look like with no clothes on. When his hands reached his erection he immediately started to pleasure himself. He had done this many times before, but for some reason, he wrote, he felt different when he was thinking of Kris. It wasn't long before he let go with all his glory; standing there he watched it go down the drain. As he dried off, he realized this time he hadn't seen his mother's face. Not only didn't he see his mother's face, but he never thought about it the whole time he was doing it. *Was I finally getting over my problem, or was I just burying it deeper and deeper inside of me,* he wrote. His last entry was to write that he was going to bed.

There was an addition to that entry that went, *The night was a usual night. It wasn't long before I found myself sitting up in bed totally nude. I went into the living room for a drink of tequila, and to finish what was left in my pipe. Returning to my bedroom I started to get dressed. When I started to leave my apartment I remembered to turn around and take my truck keys. I went down to my truck, leaned inside, grabbed the road atlas, and locked the truck back up. I walked down the sidewalk with the booklet in my back pocket. I arrived at the gate to find all my friends outside waiting for me to come unlock the building.*

They greeted him cheerfully, and followed him into The Mill. As they were going toward the door that led to their work area the two little children paused in front of it. The older man and woman also paused, and they turned in the direction Paul was coming from. Paul, not knowing what was going on, said, "What's up? How come you all have stopped?"

One of the little boys took him by the hand leading him back to the lunchroom saying, *"We need to talk Paul."* They all went back to the lunchroom. Paul wrote that it was as if he was going to be interrogated: they all sat on one side of a table, and he was on the other. The woman started off by saying that she thought that he was doing a good job, but that it should progress to the next level. Looking at her somewhat confused, Paul said, "What next level are you talking about?"

The older man said, *"Paul, we have talked about this time and time again. It's time to let go of Fred and start taking care of business, time is running short."*

"How?" Paul asked. "If we are going to do this let's get it over with." They went on to explain to Paul that from this point on he couldn't let Fred make the decisions. If a decision was going to be made it had to be

done by Paul. Fred was going to become totally nonexistent, but only to Fred. If at work Fred was spoken to—Paul would answer, and anything that could come up in Fred's personal life Paul was going to have to deal with. Paul was going to be Fred. The going back and forth was taking too much time. Looking at him they all asked, *"Do you think you're able to do that?"* Paul stood, and paced around for a little bit, then turned to them and said, "I won't let you down." They all stood up in a semicircle, leaned forward and embraced him in a group hug. Paul asked, "If and when I get this done, don't forget me. I don't want to be left behind, alone."

The woman stepped up to him, brushed his face with her open palm and said, *"We'll always be with you, Paul."* With that they all gave him a pat or hug, and went down the stairs to get started doing their work. Paul turned to leave. When he did, the older man noticed something in his pocket and asked, *"What's that?"* Remembering he had the road atlas, he told him he had already mapped out a route.

When he got home, he saw that he was down to his last beer, but there was still some tequila left. Grabbing the bottle, he went to sit down in the living room to ponder the task at hand. Up until this point it had almost been like a game to Paul.

Coming in and out of Fred's dreams as he was, or having conversations with his friends while Fred was on the job, was like playing "peek-a-boo", or "hide-and-go-seek." Looking around at the apartment and seeing where Fred kept everything, he made mental notes so that he would remember when he needed to. That's when he saw Fred's pot pipe and bent over to pick it up; he sat back in his chair checking it out. He took his lighter, put the pipe to his mouth, and lit it. It took a few hits off the pipe before Paul decided that this was one thing of Fred's he wasn't going to give up. Getting up from the chair, he walked over to the kitchen counter where Fred had a calendar hanging up on the wall. Looking to see exactly what day it was, Paul noticed that President's Day was next week, and that Fred had written on it, "Day Off." Finishing his shot of tequila, he headed back for his chair in the living room. Paul picked up a pack of cigarettes to take one out; he noticed that they were Marlboros. They were Fred's, and Paul needed to get rid of Fred, so even though he was curious he crumpled them up in his hands, and threw them basketball-style into the kitchen wastebasket.

He started to panic; maybe he should have made sure that he had some Camels before he threw Fred's away. He remembered that he did have some somewhere in the apartment. He began searching frantically, moving this and that and searching the drawers in the kitchen. Then, going into the bedroom he remembered it was here that he had seen them last. He found what he was looking for on the floor next to his bed. He took one out

and lit it, and lay on the bed to enjoy it. He lay there thinking to himself, "Now it's my time to rule, and make decisions. Poor Fred won't even know what he's missing."

When he got up to use the bathroom, he found the diary. He went into the bathroom to take care of business, returned to the bed, and made sure that the alarm clock on the nightstand was set for him to get up to go to work the next morning before he opened the diary. He started reading from the beginning to get a feel for what type of person Fred was. It didn't take long for him to finish it, because it seemed as though Fred wrote very little of his past and most of it was about his dreams. Paul said, "Heck, I know all that stuff, I was the one doing it all." He thought he'd better do some writing to make sure that someone, after reading this, might understand why he was doing what he was doing. There wasn't much more that Paul entered except, *I'm doing this for all the right reasons, and if they were to really look into it, they might understand.*

Paul closed the diary, laid it beside him on the bed, and fell off to sleep. It didn't take long for his alarm clock to sound off, waking him to the start of his renewed life. He went to the kitchen to get some coffee going, but couldn't figure out how to do it, and instead decided to get dressed, and go to work. Stopping at the door, he went to the calendar, marking the day that Fred had marked as a day off with a big X, and laughed as he went out the door. He stopped at the corner store to get a cup of coffee to wake him up, so he could face his first whole day on the job. He kept wondering if he would be able to do it without anyone noticing. He got to The Mill, went in, and started to go toward the alarm as he usually did every night. He was within a few steps of the box when he heard his friends telling him that he didn't have to do that during the day. Laughing, he turned around and headed down to the heat-treat area to start his day. Punching in at the time clock, he took off his jacket and got started on his days' work. It was at this point that Andy came out to his area and asked, "Dude, How's it going? Are you going to do lunch with us today?"

"I sure am. If I'm running late don't leave without me."

"Sure dude, no problem." It appeared that Andy didn't notice anything different about Paul.

When the lunch buzzer went off, Andy and the rest of the guys came out to see if Paul was ready to leave, saying, "Come on, Fred, let's go, or we won't have enough time."

"I'm on my way, right behind you." As they were getting high at their usual spot Paul brought up the subject of the owner's wife. Only one of the other guys had ever seen or met her besides Paul. They got into a small discussion about how old she was, and how a woman of that age could

look as nice as she does. Finishing their lunchtime smoke-a-thon, they all jumped back into the car and returned to work.

Paul punched in on time and was met by Rob in his area with a list of things he wanted Fred to do. Rob said, "I'm sorry for the last minute list, and not giving you any warning, Fred, but if you don't mind staying over I would certainly appreciate it."

"Sure Rob, anything you need. I don't have much going on anyway."

"Thanks."

Rob left heat-treat to go back upstairs to his office. Paul thought for a moment about staying late with no one there but himself and what he had to remember to do when he left. He continued about his business doing the job to the best of his ability. Right before his second break, Paul felt a hand on his shoulder. Turning around he didn't really see anyone there, but still he felt that there was a hand on his shoulder. Shrugging off the feeling, he continued working, and within the next five minutes or so, he heard the voice of the older man. *"Paul, don't worry about staying here after everyone leaves for the day. All you have to do is make sure that the alarm is set, and the door is locked."* Smiling, Paul decided to take a break.

He went out with the rest of the guys to smoke a cigarette and while standing there talking, he saw someone in his area. He put out his cigarette, and went to see who it was. It was Ron, who had come down with Rob on a walk around to see how everything was going in production. They turned the corner coming in Paul's direction. Paul stood there at first frozen, not knowing what was going to happen, or if he could pull it off. He put a smile on his face and returned to his work. Paul heard Rob's voice first saying, "Hey Fred, Ron wanted to see how things were going down in production, so I figured we would start here. I already explained that you volunteered to stay over to get a little jump on the work for the week. What with the holiday coming up, we all need to push ourselves a little."

That's when Ron asked, "So, Fred, what are you doing on your day off next week?"

"Well, if Rob has his way, I'll be working."

They all laughed, then Ron said, "Don't worry about that. I told Rob that The Mill would be shut down for the day, and that nobody would be working. If I can leave town to enjoy the time off, then everybody else is going to take it off."

"You're leaving town on vacation, sir?"

"No, I'm just going to Montreal to get away for a little bit with my friends. You know, go to the bars, hang out at the strip clubs with my friends, and have no women around to answer to."

"That sounds great—wish it were me. If there is anything you need to know just give a yell. I'll be over here sorting the jobs."

Rob said, "Thanks Fred, but I think I covered everything Ron needs to know about your area."

Ron said, "Keep up the great work, Fred."

The end of the day buzzer went off, and all of Fred's friends came through his area to leave for the day. Some were envious of Fred getting the overtime, while others laughed, calling him a "Kiss Ass." Paul smiled at them all saying good-bye to those he wanted to, and to those who were calling "Kiss Ass", he said, "Fuck you." The last of them finally came through his area to leave. Donny was always one of the last ones to leave because he had to walk around the rest of The Mill to make sure that it was all closed up and shut down. Donny stopped at the door and asked, "So how's your driver's training coming along Fred? Did you get your tags and insurance in the mail yet?"

"Yeah, they came in the other day. As far as my training goes I'm ready to take the test. I already took the truck out for a spin and it runs great."

"Be careful, you don't want to get stopped before you get your license." Paul assured him that he would be careful, and Donny left.

It was about 4:30 PM, when the telephone rang next to the time clock. Picking it up, he heard a voice saying, "Hi, Fred it's me, Pat. I heard that you were working till 5:00 tonight. I thought that you might want to go out driving to get some practice in."

Thinking fast, Paul said, "Sure, I'm not doing anything after work, and I could use the practice."

"I'll meet you at the bottom of the third-floor stairway at 5:00, okay?"

"I'll be there."

Chapter 11

Just as Paul got back to his apartment the phone rang. It was Andy checking to see if he was home, because he and Donny were out cruising and wanted to stop over. Paul said, "Sure, I just got in from driving around with my brother Pat. Oh, by the way, stop and pick up a twelve pack of beer on your way over." As he waited for them to arrive, Paul picked up the diary and wrote down his days' events.

He wrote that he would finish his entry after they left. He got up to put his diary in the bedroom when Andy and Donny arrived. They sat around bullshitting for about two hours, before Donny announced that he had to leave. They finished the pot they were smoking and guzzled their beer as they walked toward the door. Shutting the door behind as they left, Paul turned around and went into his bedroom to change out of his work clothes. Walking through the living room, he took a quick glance around and mumbled, "What a fucking slob." He opened another beer and his bottle of tequila, refilled his pipe, and went to his bedroom. He picked up his diary, opening it to that day's entry; marked February 16, 1998. He briefly read what he had already written, so as not to duplicate anything.

Paul picked up his pen, clicked it with his thumb, and started to finish the entry he had started. *"Well it appears that at least for today I've done it. I don't think that anyone noticed if it was Fred or me."* As he wrote he felt himself starting to doze off. Reaching over to his nightstand, he set the alarm, and wrote one more sentence. *"It will be this Sunday!"*

He woke as Fred did after about two hours sleep, and headed to The Mill. As he walked down the hill he saw that they were all waiting for him. They met him at the gate anxiously waiting to hear how his day had gone.

He told them that nobody knew any different and that they all thought that it was Fred they were dealing with. The two eldest smiled as he spoke, because by the sound of it, their plan was going to work. The two children and the woman started in on their tasks for the night, and Paul turned to the older man before he walked off, and said, "The first will be this Sunday night." Smiling, the older man went on his way to start his work. With that brief explanation they knew that Paul was the right choice of the five. He made it back to his apartment and fell back asleep.

I couldn't wait; I turned the page of the diary, set it down on the bed and ran to the bathroom. I had held off Mother Nature too long not wanting to put it down in the middle of something good. Standing there at the toilet, it sunk in that the last entry wasn't written by Fred, but really by Paul. Going back to the bed, I picked up the diary to compare the two

handwritings from one entry to the other. I couldn't believe it, but they were two different, distinct handwritings that had been produced by the same guy. I turned on my tape recorder and spoke into it, "From the entry on the fourteenth to the entry on the sixteenth there were two distinctly different handwritings. What did he mean by saying this Sunday night will be the first? It appears that Fred has lost all sense of reality, and that this alter ego Paul is now in full control of Fred's mind."

The rest of the week's entries were mainly about his day at the job, and how more and more it was becoming easier to act as Fred. He even stopped mentioning the walks to The Mill. It was as though it was part of his obligation to The Mill to go there and let these people in to work at night. As far as I knew Fred and I were the only ones who knew that these other people existed.

The next entry of any substance was that marked February 19, 1998. Paul got up that day and went into work as usual. Although it was only his first week at sticking to any kind of routine it seemed as though he fell right into it. He got to The Mill that morning and as he walked in through the door he heard Rob's voice asking, "Hey Fred, can I see you for a minute?" Paul stood at the doorway until Rob told him to have a seat, feeling sure that he could handle anything that Rob threw at him. Rob started out saying, "First thing is that after the first of the year you became eligible for a week paid vacation. And second, would you mind working late tonight?"

Paul thought for a minute before he spoke. "No, I don't mind working late tonight. It's not like I have a date or anything like that going on. Let me get this right, you mean to say that I can have a week off with pay?"

Rob said, "Thanks for working, and about that week off; just make sure that you let me know when you want to take it, and we'll schedule it in." Paul got up to leave so that he could punch in on time and start work. He was looking forward to today because when it was over he would have a three-day weekend to himself without having to get up and work.

His day was going along fine. Throughout the day his buddies had all come out to see what he was doing on the weekend, but not wanting to be held down to any plan, Paul was evasive. Andy and Donny came out to see how things were going right before the break buzzer went off. They all stood around talking until it did, making plans to get together that night. When break was over Andy asked, "Dude, are you doing lunch today?"

"I've got too much going on at work, and Rob already asked me to stay till 5:00 tonight."

"Look, dude, you've been working too hard. Everyone needs a break from work. Just tell Rob that you can't work, Fred."

"It's okay. I just have to stay a couple of hours late, and I'll meet you guys at my place by a quarter past five, okay?"

"Sure, Dude."

Paul worked through lunch. He was busy sorting jobs, and going through paperwork when he heard his friend's voices. Turning around in his seat, looking to see if there was anyone else around, he faced the direction that he heard the voices coming from. They were standing there in the corner of his department waiting for him to come over to them. They were interested in whether or not anything had come up to change his plans, and Paul reassured them that everything would be taken care of by Sunday. Paul explained that he had to work late because Fred's asshole boss liked to squeeze every penny he can out of people. The older man looked at him with a slight smile saying, *"I see things haven't changed much over the years."*

Paul agreed with him and turned, saying, "I'll see you tonight."

He worked through the rest of the day without any incidents, or visitors. Rob must be cracking down on everybody to get as much as they can done before the end of the day. He was going about his business when the buzzer for the end of the day sounded. He went outside to take a smoke break. As he stood there he watched as all the others left in their cars to start their long weekend. Finishing his cigarette, he met Donny coming out through his area to leave. As he walked to the door Donny said, "We'll see you at 5:15, big guy." Paul stopped long enough to tell him to make sure that he picked up some beer, and to make a run to the liquor store for a half-gallon of whiskey before they came over. He didn't want to go without this weekend, and not knowing if he would see them he wanted to stock up. "It's all under control, Fred," Donny said. Just as the door shut Andy came running through his department saying, "See you, dude."

Paul finished up and was headed out to clean up when his phone rang. Stopping to answer it, he heard Pat's voice on the other end, calling to remind Fred that he would take him out to practice his driving on Tuesday, and he would also be willing to take him to his driving test. He ended the conversation by saying, "Why don't you stop over if you're not doing anything this weekend?"

"I'll see what's going on, and probably stop by Saturday afternoon."

As he left, he reached into his pocket for his cigarettes, and was surprised to find two large, metal objects. He stopped to pull them out of his jacket. He saw that they were two large anchor bolts with nuts and washers on them. They weren't your typical anchor bolts, but the kind that had a large ring on the end instead of a bolt head. Not really knowing how they got into his pocket he shrugged, and reached into his other pocket to get his

cigarettes. He was running a couple of minutes late and found Andy and Donny waiting out in front of his apartment building.

Sneaking up to the side of the truck where Andy was sitting, he banged on the window with his hand, scaring the shit out of Andy. They got out of the truck holding the bags with the beer and liquor.

As they sat around watching television and getting drunk, Andy said, "What's up Fred? I thought that you liked tequila, and now all you're drinking is this whiskey shit?"

"Everyone needs a change every now and then," Paul shrugged and took the pipe that was being handed to him.

Seven o'clock came very fast. That was the longest that Donny could stay without pissing off his wife. They got up to get their stuff together and leave when Paul said, "Hey Andy, help me out a little, I'm all out of smoke." Andy took his bag of pot out of his pocket and left it on the kitchen counter.

"You owe me, Dude," he said. "You have a good weekend, and I'll try to stop over sometime."

Donny said, "Hey Fred, when are you going to put up some real curtains instead of these blankets? It's so dark in here I can hardly find my way to the door every time I go to leave."

"That's the way I like it, and not only that, but nobody can see in either. I like my privacy."

After they left, Paul went into his bedroom to change out of his work clothes, but he couldn't shrug the feeling of the need to pick up the diary to write about his day.

Finishing as quickly as he could the entry of the nineteenth and getting out of his work clothes, he returned to the living room in a pair of boxer shorts. Before sitting down he went over to his jacket, took the two bolts out of his pocket, and placed them on the counter. Paul realized that he was really high, and reaching down to get his whiskey bottle he accidentally knocked it over. Startled, he quickly grabbed it and sat it upright, putting the cap on it after he poured himself one more shot. He swallowed the shot of whiskey and chased it down with some of his beer, then took a hit off his pipe and reclined in his chair to light a cigarette. It wasn't long before Paul passed out in the chair.

He was awakened a few hours later by a knock on the door. He got up mumbling to himself as he walked over to it. Half awake, he opened the door to find the two little boys from The Mill standing in front of him. They walked into his apartment and sat on the floor. Paul followed them into the living room and sat in his chair. Paul asked, "What's going on, guys?"

The two children looked at him and said, *"You tell us, Paul. You were supposed to let us in The Mill to work, and when you didn't show up they sent us up here to get you."*

"I'm sorry," Paul replied. "Let me get my clothes on and we'll head down." Paul put his jacket on as they left the apartment. When they got to The Mill he found the woman and the older man waiting there patiently.

He let them in, they all walked quietly toward the door that led them down to the heat-treat area. When they got there the two younger ones started to go about their work as usual. The woman and older man told Paul to sit down at the worktable. *"What's going on, Paul?"* they asked.

"Nothing, I just had a little too much to drink. It won't happen again, I promise."

The women replied, *"Paul, this is a very important weekend for us, and you can't screw it up. Do you have what we put in your pocket today?"*

Paul replied, "I was wondering how they got in there and with everything going on I've forgotten what I'm supposed to do with them." Seeing that the children had stopped to listen, the older man told them to continue working and he moved closer to Paul.

The man turned to Paul and said, *"You need to install them in the bed of your truck. One of them at the front end, the other at the tailgate end, and as close to the middle of the bed as possible. Then you need to tie a piece of rope at least two feet long to each one. Make sure your two ends are even, and that you can shut the tailgate. Having this done will make your task on Sunday that much easier. Now go get some rest, and let us do our work."*

"Sure, whatever you say."

With that Paul turned to leave. He had almost reached the door when he heard the woman's voice call to him, *"It will be over soon, Paul, and then we can all be together again. He's right, they have to be made accountable for what they did."*

"I know, but sometimes he makes me feel like I'm nothing. He's not the boss. We're in this together, and I'll do what I have to do, for all of us."

She then leaned forward and kissed him on the cheek. The older man was headed in their direction with an electric drill in his hand. *"You'll need this to put the holes in the truck."* Paul thanked the old man and took the drill. He set the alarm, and left, locking the door as he did.

Back at the apartment, Paul wrote everything down in the diary as Fred had done. Paul found in the diary what Fred had found. It was a way to escape, and to tell how they actually felt. He finished up his entry and went into the bedroom to go to sleep. He stared at the picture above his bed until exhaustion slowly took over, and he was off to sleep.

The next morning he went into his kitchen to make some coffee. Today he had the time to sit and figure things out. He remembered Fred's brother Pat wanted him to stop by the new house where he and his girlfriend were living.

First, he attached the anchor bolts to the bed of his truck. Then he started to make a list of things he needed to buy. On the way back from the hardware store he looked out his side window and saw a McDonalds. He figured, seeing the word hamburgers on the sign, it was a place he could stop to get something to eat. Except for the basics, it appeared that Fred's knowledge or memories had been eliminated from most of Paul's thinking. There were some things he remembered, but most he didn't. He drove over to see if he was right. He parked his truck and went in. After getting his food, he returned to his truck and went home.

He parked in his usual spot in the back parking lot of the building and placed the bag from the store on the tailgate and crawled into the truck. He took the rope out. Holding it in one hand he stretched his arms out to measure it, and then cut two pieces to the right size. Tying one piece to each bolt, he crawled out and locked it back up. On his way to his apartment he stopped by the manager's to pay his rent, and then went inside to eat his food. He watched television as he ate, washing each bite down with a drink of beer. It was almost two o'clock in the afternoon.

Fred had a list of phone numbers on the refrigerator of the people he called the most. Paul ran his finger down the list until he found Pat's number. It took a couple of rings before Pat picked up the phone, but when he did he was pleased to hear that it was Fred. Paul explained that he wanted to come over, but needed a ride. Pat said, "I'll be over in a half an hour or so, okay?"

"That'll be great. I'll be waiting for you."

Paul took a shower, filled his pipe, took a shot of whiskey, and drank a beer. He hadn't even finished what was in his pipe when a knock came at the door. Lighting a cigarette to cover up the smell of the pot, he grabbed his jacket, and went to answer the door. Pat asked, "Are you ready, Freddie?"

"Yeah Pat, I'm ready."

As Paul locked his door he asked if he could drive. Pat handed him the keys. Driving away from his apartment, Pat gave him directions to his house.

When they arrived, Paul saw two little girls come running up to the car as they parked in the driveway. Paul asked, "Who do these two little beauties belong to?"

"They're my girlfriend's daughters and soon to be mine. Come on in and I'll introduce you to Vickie, my girlfriend."

Vickie was out on the deck cooking steaks on the grill. Pat introduced Fred to Vickie, telling her that this was the little brother that he always talked about. Vickie leaned forward, giving him a hug and a kiss on the cheek saying, "It's about time I get to meet you." Paul returned the compliment, and mentioned to her how beautiful he thought the house looked. Pat told him to follow him and he would give him a tour. As they walked through the house, Pat told Fred that he and Vickie were getting married in May. Paul congratulated him and they finished the tour in the kitchen with a beer. At that point Vickie yelled that the steaks were done and supper was ready.

They sat and ate their dinner with very little conversation. After dinner Paul saw the two little girls playing in their bedroom when he went to the bathroom. One of them noticed him in the doorway and said, "It's really nice to meet you, uncle Fred. Are you going to come over again?"

"It was nice meeting you, and yes, I will be back," he answered. When he finished in the bathroom, he went out to the living room and asked Pat if he could give him a ride home. Paul told him that some friends were coming to get him to go to the late movie in Burlington.

Pat said, "Sure, let's go."

Vickie walked them to the front door saying how nice it was to meet him, and that he was welcome over anytime. At the apartment, Paul thanked Pat for everything, and Pat told him to stop by more often.

When Pat was out of sight, Paul lit a cigarette and left to go to The Mill. As he walked, he thought how nice the day had turned out to be. He was able to get everything done that he needed to, and even to fool Pat and his family into thinking he was Fred. At The Mill, Paul told them all what he had accomplished during the day. The older man looked at him as though he was happy with all that he had accomplished, and asked, *"Are you ready for tomorrow?"* Paul nodded yes and left the building.

Back at his apartment, he got the bag of stuff from the store, took out the contents and laid them out to see if everything was there. He noticed one thing was missing. He climbed on his bed and took his knife out of the picture on the ceiling, then took his diary and went out into the living room to put his knife with the other stuff. He sat in the chair writing as he finished his beer with a couple of shots of whiskey for a nightcap. He ended his February 20th entry saying he was going to turn in early because tomorrow he had to get an early start before dawn.

The next morning the anticipation of what was going to happen that day was building up inside of him as he started to write in his diary, drinking his coffee. He finished his cup of coffee and the entry he started, dated February 21st. He knew that he would come back to write about his day when it was over.

As he headed out of his driveway for the interstate, he took the same route he did when he followed Kris two days ago. He arrived at his destination about forty-five minutes later. Going by the house slowly, he noticed that there were no lights on, and there was only one car in the driveway. Beyond the house, he drove to the wooded area that he had found the last time he was there, and pulled far enough off the road to make sure that his truck couldn't be seen from the road. He put on his gloves, put his knife in the sheath on his belt, grabbed his bag, and locked his truck up as he left. He made his way through the woods in the direction of the house, staying far enough off the road so he wouldn't be seen by anyone who might pass by.

At the far end of the yard, he quietly made his way to the barn. He didn't bring a flashlight with him so he was very careful where he stepped. He found a place to wait, inside one of the horse's stalls, and just behind the solid wall that connected to the gate that let the horses out of the stall. He figured that someone would be out to feed them in the morning and while he waited he put on his ski mask.

About an hour and a half went by before a light came on in the barn. He listened to their footsteps as they got closer and closer. The gate started to open.

The person, still unidentified, took a step into the stall. Lunging out of the darkness, he grabbed her by the back of the neck, and slapped a piece of duct tape over her mouth; he brought his knife to her throat. As he did, she dropped the bowl of horse feed on the stall floor. He saw that it was indeed the person he'd come for. Kris's eyes were as big as silver dollars while her head pushed back at his hand behind her neck trying to break free of his hold, trying to scream. The duct tape muffled any of her attempts to be heard, and knowing she was there alone Paul didn't worry. Turning her around, placing her back up against his chest to form a tighter hold on her, he leaned over to pick his bag up off the floor. He started to force her to walk with him through the barn and when they reached the other end Paul turned the light out as they left. When she tried to fight, he pushed his knife into her throat harder and harder, being careful not to cut her.

At the house, he kicked the door open, pushing her inside and onto the floor of the kitchen. He knelt down beside her and pulled the rope from his bag, wrapped it around her wrists and pulled her to her feet again. When she was finally standing, he put her into the hold he had her in when he dragged her from the barn. They proceeded to walk through the house until Paul found a stairway that led to what he hoped to be the bedrooms. At the top of the stairs, he caught her quick glance to the other end of the hallway. She continued to try to fight, scream and resist, but Paul took a chance that the bedroom was in the direction in which she glanced.

He took her down the hall to the first door that they came to. Looking in, Paul saw that it was indeed a bedroom and pushed the door all the way open with his shoulder as they went through it. Dragging her to the side of the bed, he pushed her down on it with him following her. He wasn't about to give her a chance to get up or away. "She was going to feel the pain they all had felt," he thought to himself. He moved her as close to the center of the bed as he could, straddling her, his own weight holding her down.

He placed her arms above her head in the direction of the headboard, untied the rope around her wrist, then maneuvered his knees onto her arms to hold them down. He cut two pieces of rope about two feet long, and tied her wrists together with one—tying it so tight that it cut into her wrists making her bleed. Still holding her arms with his knees, he then took the other piece of rope and tied it to the rope binding her wrists. He pulled on it as hard as he could and tied it to the headboard. Leaning over to the side of the bed, Paul pulled the roll of duct tape from his bag. He pulled a little bit off the roll, sticking it to her mouth, then wrapping it around her head and mouth. He took the rope and carefully measured the next two lengths that he was going to use. She was frantically wiggling around, with her eyes still opened wide, but it appeared to Paul that she was now crying instead of screaming. That was the fear and pain Paul wanted to see.

Getting off her, he pushed her bathrobe up, exposing her knees. Taking one leg at a time, he tied a piece of rope tightly around one knee, then tied it to the headboard corner post. This spread her legs as wide as they could go and raised her pelvic area slightly. He stood there for a moment staring at her lying there in this position. He continued to stare as he leaned over and undid the knot in her bathrobe's tie. He placed his knife tip to one side of the robe moving it slowly to the side to expose her naked breast and the black thong she was wearing. He saw her watching him as he did this, and while he did it to the other side.

Paul's excitement grew having this woman at his total control—a woman he had masturbated to, several times. Taking the knife tip he dragged it slowly over her breast, and down the middle of her torso to the top of her thong. Lifting his knife off her belly, he brought it up to one of her robe's sleeves, slicing it off her body. He repeated this on the other side. He then pulled the robe out from under her, throwing it on the floor. Standing on the side of the bed, Paul cut both of her thong waist straps to expose her naked crotch. He dragged his knife tip one more time from one end of her body to the other, trying hard to keep her fear at its highest level. He started to run his tongue along her body coming to a stop between her parted legs.

Human desire overcame Paul. He pulled off his pants and ripped off his shirt. She watched helplessly as he got on top of her, forcing himself into her as she tried to resist him. Realizing that her efforts did nothing except to help tighten her bindings, she went limp. Paul ejaculated earlier than he wanted to. As he raised himself up off her breasts, he continued to thrust in and out of her, not wanting to stop. Pissed off that it happened so fast he took his anger out on her by slamming his fist into the side of her face, as he called her a bitch and whore. Paul got off of her completely. He went to the headboard and her eyes followed him every step of the way. He untied both of her legs but left her hands bound. Moving back to the foot of the bed, he grabbed her feet and pulled them down to the foot of the bed.

He lit a cigarette while standing at her feet staring at her—smiling the whole time. Grabbing her feet, he flopped her over onto her stomach. Paul went to each side of the bed to take the ropes that were tied to each knee and pulled them as tight as he could—tying them to the headboard corner post again. While he did this he smoked his cigarette, telling her that he was sick of her staring at him, and that there was no need to because she already knew who he was. He got on the bed kneeling between her legs; he grabbed her hair up into a ponytail and pulled her head up. Positioning himself, he pushed his burning cigarette into the small of her back forcing her body to arch back violently from the pain as he made his first thrust into a part of her where no one had ever been before.

It took Paul a lot longer this time to get himself off, but when he did the feeling he had, he would later write in his diary, was unexplainable. Making sure he stayed inside of her until he was finished, he hesitated for a second before getting out from behind her. He went to each side of the bed and untied her legs from the headboard. He took each of her feet and brought them back down to the foot of the bed to flop her back over onto her back. He could see that the fight in her was gone. He took the ropes from her knees, and using one of them, he tied her ankles together as tight as he could.

Looking at the clock on the nightstand to the right of the bed, he saw that it was almost nine o'clock. He went over to the side of the bed and picked his clothes up off the floor, got dressed, and put on his gloves. He lit a cigarette as he moved closer to the bed; leaning over her he brought his face close to hers and kissed her on the cheek. Turning around, he left the bedroom taking his stuff and shutting the door behind him.

Paul went through the house looking for anything that might be used as evidence, then out to the barn. He took the garden rake from the wall, and raked over his footprints. He closed the gate and straightened up the barn to make it look like nothing had happened there at all. He then left the barn dragging the rake behind him to cover up his footprints. He stepped

out onto the grass, and leaned back into the barn replacing the rake up against the wall.

Back in the house, he found her still lying there, limp as a rag doll. He walked up to the side of the bed, leaned over, once more taking one of her nipples into his mouth caressing it for just a moment, and ending again with a kiss to the cheek. He untied her wrists from the headboard, pulled the pillows out from under her head, and put one of the pillowcases over her head. He took the blankets off the foot of the bed where they had been neatly folded and threw them onto the floor into a pile, too. He walked around the bed pulling the sheets loose from the mattress and box spring. Taking the sheet on his side of the bed, he placed it over her, and walking around to the other side he did the same. He took his extra rope and loosely tied it around her knees and around her chest to hold the sheets in place.

He took one more look around on the floor and under the bed to see if there was anything that might incriminate him. Not seeing anything, he picked up his bag with all of his stuff in it and placed her over his shoulder, face down, to carry her to his truck. On his way out of the room he noticed the bathrobe and thong lying on the floor. He bent down to pick them up, stuffing the thong into his pocket. He tossed the robe over his shoulder. As he walked out of the house he glanced at everything to make sure it looked the same as it did when he got there. He watched carefully as he went across the yard walking as fast as he could to the edge of the woods where he'd come from earlier that morning.

Staying out of sight from the dirt road, he made his way to his truck through the woods. Paul took a somewhat different way back, so he wouldn't leave a path that someone might find. He got back to the truck out of breath from carrying the extra hundred or so pounds on his shoulder. He dropped her onto the bed of the truck, and tied her down to the anchor bolts. He backed out onto the road, then parked again along the side of the road. He got out and ran back to where he had been parked to look around for anything that might have been left behind. Paul made sure that he walked over his tire marks the best he could. He drove off, keeping to the speed limit so as not to draw any attention to himself. He got to the interstate without incident and headed south.

On the interstate, Paul sat back in a more relaxed position and lit a cigarette. He tuned his radio to the oldies station. He kept careful watch of his speed and driving the whole way back to Winooski. He didn't get off the interstate at the Winooski exit, but kept driving south until he came to the Richmond exit twenty miles south of Winooski. Getting off there, he heard the radio announcer say that it was 12:30 PM. He drove the back roads to Winooski on his way back to The Mill.

Paul drove around to the back of the building and parked at the door leading into the heat-treat department. He went back up to the front door to let himself in and to turn off the alarm. Then he locked the door, reset the alarm, went down to his area, and went out the door to where the truck was parked. Paul dragged Kris out of the truck and put her over his shoulder to carry her into The Mill. Locking the door behind him, he dropped her in front of the ovens with her head making a loud thump as it hit the cement floor.

It was then he heard voices coming from behind him. Startled, he turned quickly to see who it could be. The voices got louder and within seconds he saw his four friends turning the corner. He turned to continue what he was doing, grabbing the electric hoist control box, and lowering its hook to the floor. Paul bent down and hooked it to the rope in between her wrists. He then pushed the up button on the control box. As the chain raised her arms into the air, he pulled the pillowcase off her head. Her eyes were half shut from the blow he'd given her and the abuse that she had been through. The older man, woman, and the two children watched silently until she was completely off the floor. Paul cut the ropes from around the sheet exposing her totally nude body.

It was then that the older man said, *"Good job, Paul. I didn't think you were going to be able to pull it off."*

"I told you I would take care of it, and I did."

The woman said, *"Paul, she has blood running down her thighs. Did you have sex with her?"*

"Yeah, I did. So what? It was like I had no control over myself. You do remember that Fred had sexual fantasies about this woman, and maybe it was him who was raping her."

He positioned her over the oven and started to lower her into the opening at the top of the oven. Her feet were the first to go into the molten liquid, and when they did her eyes opened so much that they appeared to be popping out of her head. She started to wiggle around to try and stop what was happening to her. Paul kept his thumb on the down button. It wasn't until her knees had disappeared into the oven that the fight left her body. As she was lowered into the oven Paul noticed the other four behind him smiling with their arms around each other.

Paul stood there holding the button on the control box as her breasts went into the liquid, and then finally her head. When he got down to about four inches from the hook, he took a knife from the table and cut her hands from the hook letting them fall into the oven. Moving the hook away from the oven, he picked the sheets and pillowcase off the floor and took them out to his truck. He came back in to tell them that he was going home until tomorrow night, so if they wanted to work they could stay. They decided to

stay; Paul locked the back door, and checked the area as he left. He went upstairs to set the alarm and lock the door. He ran down back, got into his truck and drove to the gate. He got out to unlock it and drove through it; stopping once more to lock it before driving away.

Chapter 12

At his apartment, Paul went into the bedroom and put his tool bag behind the headboard of his bed. He then took the sheets, robe, and the thong from his pocket, over to the corner of the room to put them in the pile with the other clothes. Remembering that Rob told him that he had a week paid vacation due anytime, he marked the week beginning on March 8 on his calendar.

He opened his diary to February 21st, and wrote the details of what he had just done. He took a long pull from the whiskey bottle, and set it back down on the floor.

He noticed a piece of paper lying on the floor crumpled up and out of curiosity he picked it up and straightened it out. It was Fred's paycheck stub. He lit a cigarette and sat back in his chair checking it out. Paul couldn't believe the difference in the amount of money that Fred was paid to do the same work as he had done. But it wasn't the amount of money that intrigued Paul as much as it was the address of the corporate offices printed in the upper right-hand corner.

I had to stop reading for a minute to stretch my legs. Leaning over I turned off the tape recorder and took a cigarette out of the pack. I got up, lighting my cigarette and stepped out onto the porch for some fresh air. I couldn't shed the thought that Fred, I mean Paul, might have killed another person. "It could have just been another dream, heck everything else in this book and the other book was. So why not this?" I thought to myself. I didn't want to call Nick, because he would just make me bring it into the station. I finished my cigarette and went back into the house to take a piss. Getting back onto the bed, I considered the elaborate detail in which Fred / Paul described everything, and decided it couldn't be made up. I turned on the recorder and sat back against the pillows to start reading again. I stopped for a moment to see how close I was to finishing it and saw that I was about a third of the way through it.

The entry continued when Paul came back up from the truck with the road atlas in his hand. He opened another beer, went to the living room and sat down. He leaned forward to turn on the television to the movie channel, sat back into his chair, but wasn't able to get comfortable. He was still a little pumped up from his day, and got his pipe. When he was in his bedroom getting his stuff, he saw that it was 10:00 PM.

He picked up the pay stub again and read the address on it. It was Riverside, Massachusetts. He estimated that it was about a four-hour drive by interstate and maybe five hours by secondary roads. He wrote it down,

then ended his February 21st, entry saying that it was 12:30 AM, and he was turning in for the night.

He woke up in the middle of the night and headed down to The Mill. There he found the people standing outside as usual. When he got up to them, the woman asked, *"I thought we weren't going to see you tonight?"*

"Yeah, then how come you're here waiting?"

The woman replied, *"What else is there for us to do? We don't have any other place to go."* Paul went to the door to let them in. They all walked down to the heat-treat area together and started working where they'd left off. Paul turned and as he went up the stairs, he heard the footsteps of someone following him closely. He continued to the lunchroom before he turned around to see the older man standing behind him. He asked Paul to sit so that they could talk for a bit. Paul sat at the table with the older man sitting down across for him.

Paul asked, "What now?"

The man looked at Paul saying, *"I want you to know that none of us are taking this lightly. These people have to pay and you know it."*

"Yeah, so what? I know they have to pay and they will. I guarantee it."

"Somehow you're going to have to get to Massachusetts. Some of them live there, too." Paul started to laugh.

"What's so funny?"

"I just got done figuring out how far it was to Massachusetts. I did it as soon as I got home this afternoon. At least we're on the same page."

"I guess you are taking this serious. Just follow the same steps that you took the last time."

"Sure, but there's one thing that is different this time. I don't know who I'm looking for."

"Don't worry, you'll get down there and figure it out."

Paul stood up to leave, telling the man good night, and saying, "You got more faith in me than I do." He left the building, locking the door, setting the alarm, and locking the gate behind him.

When he got back to the apartment he sat down in the chair and lit a cigarette. He had left the television on when he went to bed the first time, while he finished his cigarette he watched a late-night, oldie-but-goodie movie. He started to put his cigarette out when he thought that he heard a noise come from his bedroom. He got up from his chair, turned off the television, and went into his bedroom. There was somebody on his bed, a naked body tied to his headboard, face down. He knew this was totally impossible, but he continued to walk closer. He was just about beside the bed when the person turned her head to one side. It looked liked Kris, but how could this be? A little closer and he noticed that instead of a beautiful

woman it was a badly burned one. "It's only a dream", he said out loud. The burned carcass disappeared and Paul lay down to relax with another cigarette. As he lay there he wondered to himself what it was he had just seen. This was no longer one of Fred's dreams, but his reality.

He reached for his diary, and wrote about what he saw and how it had scared him shitless. He also wrote down the discussion he had with the older man. In his diary, he wrote, *"I feel as though I'm in control here but who really knows. Sometimes it feels as if Fred is even telling me what to do. I knew I wasn't supposed to rape Kris and all that, but I did. Fred is the one that had a crush on her not me. It seems to me Fred might be playing with my mind, but it won't work."* He finished his cigarette and his entry.

The next day, Paul had another day off to do what he wanted. By the entry in his diary it appeared all he did was to go out to the corner store for more cigarettes and something to eat. The rest of the day he spent in his apartment getting drunk and high. He finished that day's entry by writing how much he enjoyed his first three-day weekend.

The next morning Paul felt really rested. He got to The Mill with about ten minutes to spare, and took the opportunity to go to Rob's office.

Rob asked, "What can I do for you, Fred?"

Paul replied, "You told me the other day to let you know when I wanted my vacation. Well, if possible, I would like to start it the week of March 8th." Rob looked at the calendar where everyone's vacation schedules were written. Seeing there was only one other person taking a vacation at that time, Rob agreed it would be a good time to take it. Paul got up to leave and thanked him. He was just outside the door when Rob said, "Fred let's try to get as much done before that week as possible, okay? Maybe you can work some overtime to get a little ahead before you go."

"Sure, no problem, Rob", Paul said, as he walked down to his work area.

When he got there Andy was there. He wanted to know how his weekend went and to tell him about some great pot he had scored. Andy said, "It's not really for sale, but if you want some I'll sell you some."

Paul said, "Thanks, Andy. I'm about out of what I got, so let me have what you can." Andy agreed to meet Paul after work at his apartment. Andy went back to his work area and Paul got busy.

He arrived back home beat from the days work. He hadn't even made it to the living room when he heard a knock on the door. He opened it to find Andy standing there. He asked him in and saw that he had brought a twelve-pack of beer with him. Taking two beers out of the box, he handed them to Paul. Andy put the rest of them in the refrigerator and went in to join Paul in the living room.

Andy got his pot out to fill a bowl. He looked in his pockets, but couldn't find his pipe. Andy filled Paul's, and handed it back to him. Andy told him to get an empty baggie so he could split the bag of pot up and give him his half. They sat around for a while getting high and drinking beer.

They pigged out at McDonalds, then smoked another pipe of Andy's pot before Andy left. Paul added to his entry that he actually liked Andy and he thought of him as his only friend. Even though Andy thought it was Fred he was visiting with, Paul liked the situation.

Paul did as Fred did when there wasn't anything special going on in his life. His entries became very short, as if he did nothing during the day. It was almost as if he had stopped going to The Mill, but I knew different. It could have been because when Paul went to The Mill it wasn't a dream like it was when Fred went. In his Friday entry, dated February 26th, 1998, he wrote that Pat took him to the Department of Motor Vehicles to take his driving test. Paul was the one who was behind the wheel that day, not Fred. Starting with Friday's entry, the diary was written with more substance and detail.

Paul wrote, *"I'm going to head down to Riverside, Massachusetts on Saturday. Now that I have a valid license I'm free to go anywhere without worry about getting stopped by the police."* That night consisted of staying in, watching television, and getting drunk. He did mention that he was headed down to The Mill to let them in. Rob told him he didn't have to work that weekend, but would have to work the Saturday prior to his vacation. He got his road atlas out to look at it and to make absolutely sure he had a good idea where he was going. He figured that he could get to Riverside, but finding the exact spot he had to go was another matter. All he had was Fred's old pay stub with the address on it.

It was about midnight when he decided to go to The Mill. He went through the gate and headed over to his friends to explain that he would not be back until late Saturday night, so he wouldn't be down to let them in that night. He told them that he was going to go down to find the place he was looking for and to make sure he knew his way down and back. The woman and older man of the group told him to be careful driving in unfamiliar territory and they would be waiting to see him Sunday night.

Paul left The Mill and returned home. He started to drink more, and picked up his pipe to fill it with some of the stuff that he had gotten from Andy earlier that week. Finishing what he had put into the pipe, he took his last swallow of beer. He went into his bedroom and lay down staring at the picture on the ceiling, remembering Kris. Before he fell to sleep, he leaned over to set his alarm. Paul thought to himself that if some of The Mill's production department was working overtime the plant down in Massachusetts should be working, too.

The next morning, it was about three and a half hours before Paul got to the exit for Riverside, Massachusetts. At the bottom of the exit ramp, he headed toward town where he thought the plant was located. After driving for what seemed like miles Paul finally saw a plant off in the field to the right of the road he was on. He went along until he came to a side road that appeared to go in the direction of the plant he had seen. When he took the corner, the first thing he saw was a little metal sign. It was like a street sign, but this one read, "The Mill, Inc. 5/10 mi." It was then Paul decided never to question his intuition. He had found the place he was looking for, but were they working?

Paul was within eyesight of the plant when he saw a small picnic area on the side of the road. He pulled in and later he wrote that confusion started to overcome him not knowing what exactly to do. He started to walk down the road toward the plant and within minutes was at the entrance gate of the fence that surrounded the plant. He walked through, headed for the plant's front door. Paul saw a lower-level parking lot where numerous cars were parked. They were obviously working overtime in the production department. As Paul continued toward the door he saw a second parking lot off to the side of the building on the upper level. He walked over to the corner of the building to see if there were any cars parked there.

There were five cars parked in the lot. Three of them were parked side by side, two others were parked in spaces marked "Reserved." One of the cars in the reserved parking space was a Toyota Celica, and the other one a Lexus. He left without being seen.

He got back to his truck. Sitting there warming it up, he saw a car coming out of the plant's gate and toward him down the road. It was the Lexus he had seen in the upper parking lot. It pulled up beside him. Paul rolled down his window to see what the man in the Lexus wanted. He explained he was on private property and he would have to leave.

Paul said, "I'm sorry. I got lost and saw the picnic table, so I pulled in to check my map."

They both rolled up their windows and the Lexus took off down the road. Paul put his truck into gear and tried to catch up to it. The Lexus started to slow down when it approached the stop sign at the main road, and Paul could read the license plate clearly: "Mill 2". He followed it, but stayed back as far as he could without losing sight of it.

It wasn't long before he had followed it into a shopping center; he watched it pull into a parking space in front of the grocery store, and he parked so he couldn't be seen. Paul saw the car doors open up, and three people get out, a tall, slender, clean-shaven man out of the driver's side, and a red-headed, nice-looking woman out of the passenger's side. It took a few seconds before the third person got out from the back and walked in front of

the car into Paul's view. It was a young blonde-haired girl who tagged along behind the two adults into the store and Paul assumed it was their daughter. She looked only sixteen or seventeen, if that.

While waiting for them to come out, Paul listened to the radio. He had heard a little bit ago from the radio announcer that the time was four o'clock. As he watched them load the car with the groceries he guessed it must have been a quarter past five. They got into their car and pulled out, and Paul followed from a distance. They turned onto the main road heading for what looked like the downtown area. He thought he had lost them a couple of times when his view was blocked by trucks making deliveries to the local downtown merchants. Cussing at the delivery trucks as he went by, he knew he couldn't afford to take his eyes off his prey.

They continued through town until it appeared to Paul that they were leaving the city limits. Paul was right; he passed a sign telling drivers, "Thanks for Visiting Riverside. Come Again." They turned into a secondary road with very little traffic on it and then he saw them turn onto a road headed for a housing development. He slowed down to put some space between himself and them and as he did, he wrote down the name of the road on the map of Massachusetts in his atlas.

Paul looked ahead and could barely see their car's taillights. They were headed for that housing development and he got worried he might lose them. When he got to where they had pulled off the road, he saw they hadn't pulled into the development, but onto another road. He took the same turn thinking to himself that he had lost them, and wondered if he would ever be able to find them on this little country road. Just as he was going to give up and turn around a little voice in his head told him to continue on.

Paul drove another three miles without seeing a house when he spotted one just off the road sitting behind a group of pine trees. Slowing down, he looked down the driveway, and not knowing if this was their house or not he turned around at the next intersection. On his way back he drove as slow as he could. At their driveway, he saw a mailbox with "Lackly", printed on the side and a floodlight on at the back of the house. He had just about driven by it when he saw the little blonde-haired girl coming around the back corner of the house walking a dog. When he saw her, he knew he had the right house and sped down the road so he wouldn't be seen.

Paul stopped only long enough to get a bite to eat before getting on the interstate to go home. He got off at the Andover exit. He would take the secondary roads back home to Winooski. "I'll be driving at night when I come back the next time, so I better get used to it now," he thought to himself. The ride back took him through many towns and all of them were

small like Winooski. He arrived back at his apartment building's parking lot five hours later.

At home, he wrote down in his diary everything that he had seen and done that day, had a drink and went to bed.

Paul didn't set his alarm when he went to bed, because the next day was Sunday and he didn't have to work. He fell asleep as soon as his head hit the pillow, and woke up the next day around eleven o'clock. Having no food in his place and being hungry, he remembered that Fred's grandfather was a great cook and decided he would go there. He got down to Sam's house within five minutes. Sam was sitting on the front porch.

"So, Fred, things have been going good for you?" Sam asked after he had inspected Fred's truck and they had gone inside for a beer.

"Why do you ask, Sam?"

"I just haven't seen you in a while and I'm concerned about you. That's all."

"Things couldn't be better at the job, or in my life. I have my own place, my own truck, my license, and I'm my own boss at work. No, I don't think that things could get any better." They finished their beers at about the same time and Paul asked Sam if he wanted another one. Sam told him sure and when Paul opened the refrigerator, he saw that there were only two left. He took one and handed one to Sam.

"Hey, Sam, you want to take a ride to the store to get some more beer?"

"Sure."

They sat talking a little bit about everything, catching up on each other's lives. From the job to whether or not he had seen his mother. Paul explained that he was up near Fletcher and thought about stopping in, but didn't. Sam asked him if he wanted to stay for a late lunch and Paul told him sure. Finishing their beers and their meal, they went to the store and Paul asked Sam to pick him up a case of beer, too, while he was in there. Then Paul dropped off Sam, and headed home.

He put his beer in the refrigerator, took one to the living room with him and sat down to write his day's diary entry.

"I find it amazing how nobody notices anything different about me and how they all thought they were talking to Fred. It's great. I can walk around, do anything I want, and everyone thinks it Fred. If only they all knew what was going on, but if they even had the littlest thought that something is different it might make it difficult for me to do what I have to do. All the traveling I've done this weekend has tired me out so I'm going to turn in earlier than normal."

Chapter 13

I thought, "How much stranger can it get?" To have another person inside of you who takes over your whole life has got to be the strangest. I went to the bathroom, and then stepped out on the porch to get a breath of fresh air. Taking in a deep breath, I held it for as long as I could and exhaled. I reached into my pocket for a lighter and lit the cigarette I had brought out with me. I didn't know if I was reading a fabrication of Fred's mind, or if there really was a Paul. Were these murders real or not? I finished my cigarette, and went back to the bed. I looked at the clock to see what time it was. It was late, but I couldn't stop. I made myself comfortable, then opened the diary and started to read again.

Paul started the next entry, March 1, 1998, by recounting his day at work. He wrote he was still working till five o'clock every night, but it didn't really bother him because the money was good. He thought it was funny there wasn't even a rumor going around about Kris being missing, but not many people knew Kris and maybe Ron hadn't said anything to anybody. He went through the gate walking to the end of the road that led to the third level, and decided to take that way for a change. As he approached the front of the owner's car he noticed the license plate. The license plate read, "Mill 1", just as the car's plate down in Massachusetts read, "Mill 2." It was the same family.

March 5th came without incident. His friends decided to stay inside The Mill for the week he was going to be gone, but they really wanted him to come back early if he could. When he got home from work he went to his bedroom to get his bag, diary, and clothes. He got a beer and sat down to write a little before he left. He wrote that he would be back in town no later than Tuesday, March 9. He made sure he had everything he was going to need. He sat down one more time in his chair filling his pipe, and wrote, *"I don't want to smoke any pot while driving my truck. That's all I need—to be pulled over for smoking pot."*

Nevertheless, he took his diary, pot and pipe, and put them into the bag with his clothes.

He got to Riverside around nine o'clock that night and chose a hotel just outside of the town limits that was close to their house. He called the front desk for a wake-up call for 6:30 a.m. He was asleep within minutes.

It seemed he had been asleep only a few minutes before he heard the phone ringing. When he got to the lobby he could smell the aroma of fresh brewed coffee in the air and looking around the lobby he located its source.

He went over to pour himself some and went back to his room, where he finished waking up as he drank his coffee and smoked a little pot.

He drove out to where he'd followed them the previous weekend. Going past their house about a mile, he found a place he could pull far enough off the road so his truck couldn't be seen. He went to the road to check if his truck could be seen. It couldn't, so he headed down the road a ways before going back into the woods. Paul got to the edge of their property, and seeing that the house was dark he sat down in the tall grass to wait. Soon the back door opened and the man took the dog out on a leash. Holding still so the dog wouldn't pick up on his scent, Paul watched as they headed in the opposite direction. The man stayed outside long enough for the dog to do his business and then went back inside. Two hours went by before he saw all three of them come out with the dog on a leash. The adults got into the car as their daughter opened the car's back door to let the dog in first, then followed the dog and shut the door behind her.

When they left Paul came out of hiding and walked over to the house looking for a way to get in. He didn't want to try the front if he didn't have to, in case someone drove by and saw him. He checked all the doors and windows in the back and on the sides of the house. He found nothing unlocked, and bent down to see if he would be able to fit through the little windows that led into the cellar. Guessing he probably would be able to, he pushed on the one in front of him to check if it was locked. It was, so Paul started methodically checking the other six windows. He got to the fourth one before he found one unlocked. Looking around first, to make sure he wouldn't be seen, he held the window with one hand as he slid his body through. He was careful not to break anything on his way in. He landed on the floor, looked around to orient himself and immediately headed for the stairs. He followed them up and found himself in the kitchen.

He started to look the house over, paying special attention not to move or touch anything. As he made his way through their beautiful home he came to a stairway leading to the second floor. Going up the stairs, Paul found the master bedroom at the top; continuing down the hall he saw a bathroom, and right across from it was their daughter's bedroom. Paul went into her room to check everything out and opened her dresser drawers to see what was in them. In one of the smaller drawers he found her bras and panties. He started to get an erection and closed the drawer.

He headed down the hall to look into the master bedroom to see how it was laid out. The last thing Paul noticed leaving the room was a beautiful four-posted brass bed. Smiling, Paul started down the stairs at a brisk pace so he could get out of the house and back to his hiding spot without getting caught. On his way past the kitchen table he grabbed an apple and banana out of the bowl sitting there and proceeded down to the

cellar. He put his fruit outside the window and jumped up to pull himself out. He got out through the window easier than he thought he would and returned to his hiding spot with the fruit in hand. He ate the fruit, then watched all day, until they had returned, eaten supper and retired.

When he got back to his motel it was ten o'clock. He set his alarm clock for 4:00 AM, and dialed the front desk asking for a wake-up call at 4:30 AM. He knew that he would have to get out to his parking spot early enough not to be seen by anyone.

He didn't wake up until the wake-up call came through; he figured he had shut off the alarm without knowing it.

He stopped at a convenience store for coffee and two breakfast sandwiches. As he passed through town he noticed on the bank's clock it was going on 5:15 AM.

Paul drove by the house and made his way down to the spot where he would park his truck. He sat there drinking his coffee and eating his sandwiches. He took the last bite from his sandwich, took a drink from his coffee, and got out of the truck. Reaching into the truck, he put his gloves and full-face ski mask on. He put the knife onto his belt, and checked once more to see if he had everything in his bag. With his bag, he started to make his way to the spot on the edge of the yard where he would sit and wait. Lights came on in the house within half an hour and it wasn't long before the man came out with the dog, taking it to the other side of the house where its run was. Returning, the man reached into the car, and started it before he went back inside.

A short while later the man came back out and threw his briefcase into the front seat of his car. The woman came from the doorway, followed by the young girl to see him off. Both of them gave him a hug and kiss before he got into the car to leave. He backed out of the driveway onto the road and drove down the road until Paul couldn't see his taillights any more. Paul decided to wait for a moment until he was sure that it was okay to leave his secure spot. He heard the back door open again, and the woman and girl went to the garage. The garage door opened, a car backed out, turned around in the driveway and drove out, leaving Paul and the dog the only ones at the house. Paul made his way across the yard to the window he knew was unlocked, held the window open with one hand and slid into the cellar.

He found some unopened mail lying on the counter in the kitchen. Going through it, he saw an envelope addressed to the Lackly family. In the corner of the envelope the return address read "Mom." He found a post-it notepad on the refrigerator, wrote down the address from the envelope, and slipped it into his pocket. He headed into what looked to be a home office for the man to work from. Before he could look around, he heard a car pull

into the driveway. Paul made his way to the kitchen, squatting down behind the counter to wait. He tore a piece of duct tape off the roll big enough to cover anyone's mouth and as he unsnapped his knife he heard the key turn in the lock. With his knife in one hand and the duct tape in the other, he prepared himself for anything.

The doorknob turned and someone entered the house. Her heels clicked on the tiles as her footsteps came closer to where Paul was waiting. He waited until it sounded like the footsteps were right in front of him, then leapt up and lunged toward her. She was a little further away than Paul had thought, and had time to turn and run toward the door. While she struggled with the lock Paul came from behind, grabbing her around the neck with the hand that held the knife, then reaching up with the other hand to slap the duct tape over their mouth. She wrestled with Paul until she felt the knife being put to her throat. She stopped struggling and Paul forced her to the floor onto her back.

He quickly sat down on her belly, and pinned her arms down by putting one under each of his knees. Pulling the rope from his bag, he took the knife away from her neck, placing it beside her within arm's reach, and started to tie the rope around one of her wrists. When he made sure the rope was good and tight on that wrist he wrapped the rope around the other wrist tying it as tight as he could. He got off her, stood up, and yanked her to her feet. He pulled her along as he went toward the stairs leading to the second floor. She resisted him the whole way. Paul started up the stairs ignoring her fight and literally had to drag her up the entire flight of stairs. He reached the landing and pulled her up off the top few stairs standing her on her feet. He stood behind her, put the knife back to her throat, and pushed her down the hall until he got to the master bedroom.

With his excitement level increasing he pushed her down on the bed getting on top of her as he had done downstairs. He tied a piece of rope to the rope between her wrists, cutting it to about two feet long. He leaned forward over her pushing his erect cock into her face as he tied the other end to the headboard. He stood up beside the bed and undid his pant's zipper and snap. He stood there for a moment to give her a good look at what she was going to get. She shook her head from side to side frantically and kicked her legs in an attempt to free herself. Paul grabbed her shirt with both hands, ripped it apart popping the buttons off, and exposed her full breasts. With his knife, he cut her bra shoulder straps and then, placing the knife tip between her breasts with the edge pointing up, he slid it toward her face under the strap between her breasts. The strap stretched as it slid over the knife's edge until it had cut all the way through. He leaned over and started caressing her breasts with his mouth and hands until her nipples became erect.

Paul then got up and unsnapped and unzipped her jeans. Moving to the foot of the bed, he grabbed both of her feet and flipped her over onto her belly. He pulled her pants down to her ankles and then off, leaving her naked except for her sheer, white panties. He tied a rope around each knee, pulled it up as far as he could, and lashed it to the headboard, so that each knee was about up to her waist and her legs spread as much as possible.

He stood back looking at her as she lay there with her buttocks propped up in the air. He got on the bed behind her and with his knife cut her panties' side band allowing them to fall to the bed. Paul couldn't wait any longer. He brought himself up to her backside and thrust it in her as hard as he could. Her head lifted off the pillow and she let out a muffled scream. At the same time the rest of her body went limp. Paul thrust himself in and out of her, concentrating on holding back for as long as possible. It was within minutes from when he had started that he couldn't hold back any longer and as he exploded deep inside of her, he could feel himself throbbing against her inner walls.

He got out from behind her and wiped himself off. He untied her knees and reached for her feet once more. Flipping her over again onto her back, he walked to the side of her, tying her knees back up the same way he had before. He stared at her as she lay there. Her large breasts still had erect nipples. Her flat stomach was just a prelude to what Paul was to find between her legs. He positioned himself in between her legs to get a closer look. Leaning over, he placed his arms around her thighs, bringing his face closer and closer. He couldn't stop himself from kissing her inner thighs and bringing his mouth over her blonde pubic hairs. He caressed her until he felt her getting moist. Straightening himself upright, he thrust himself in her as deep as he could go. He leaned over her grabbing each of her breasts in his hands while he continued to thrust into her. It wasn't long before Paul finished, and, getting off, he untied her knees.

After untying her wrists Paul pulled her up off of the bed and took her into the bathroom. He placed her in the tub, laying her on her back, and tying her ankles together. Searching the shelves and in the medicine cabinet over the sink until he found what he was looking for, he pulled her feet up above her face to expose her front and back openings. He squeezed the douches he had found in the cabinet into her one after another. He pulled them out and stood her on her feet to let the liquid run out of her, and into the tub. When it stopped he laid her back down in the tub and turned the shower on, washing it all down the drain. Paul looked at her saying, "I don't want to leave you all dirty now."

He pulled her to her feet and dragged her back to the bed, where he once again tied her down, but spread-eagled this time. Leaning down to her

from her vagina didn't stop Paul at all and he convinced himself it was just because she was a virgin. Paul wrote he was being driven by something deep inside of him and knew he had to get going and finish what he had came to do, but he just couldn't help himself. He didn't stop his pounding force until he had climaxed once more.

When he had dressed again, he took her to his truck, and tied her into the back. Returning to the house, he went upstairs to get the mother. He started to untie her wrists, but heard a car pulling into the yard. Going to the top of the stairs, he heard the door open and a man's voice yell out, "Honey, I'm home." Paul started to panic, but figured the best place to hide was the same place he had hidden before. He returned to the master bedroom, took a brass candleholder off the dresser and hid behind the door. He heard the man say, "I didn't have to stay overnight, so I thought I would surprise you," as he climbed the stairs. He threw open the door, then rushed to the side of the bed, without knowing Paul was right behind him. Paul with all his might struck the man in the back of the head, and he slumped lifelessly down over his naked wife's body. Paul pushed him to the floor, took off his shoes, pants, shirt, and underwear and then lashed his ankles together and tied his hands together behind him.

He carried mother and father in turn to his truck, and tied them with their daughter.

Going back into the house he went to the bedroom to make sure that he hadn't left anything behind that the police would find. He picked all the clothes up, putting them into one pile; he checked the rest of the room for anything he might have left. He took the clothes and threw them into the back of the truck. Turning back to the house, he took one last look around to make certain there was nothing that could be used as evidence, and went to his truck, shutting the back door to the house behind him.

He took his gloves and ski mask off, put them into his bag, and placed it behind the seat. He started the truck and drove away. On his way through town to the interstate, he wondered if he had gone too far by taking all three of them, but decided that it was too late to change his mind. At the exit just south of Vermont, he left the interstate and took back roads to Winooski.

He arrived in Winooski in just under four and a half hours, going straight to The Mill when he got into town. He unlocked the gate and drove through, then got back out to lock it behind him. Paul drove the truck around to the back door as he had done before and returned by foot to the front door to go in. He turned off the alarm and reset it, leaving the heat-treat area unarmed. Downstairs, Paul encountered his friends. He told them that they were going to be real proud of him this time, but he didn't tell them why as he went outside.

He opened the tailgate and climbed in to undo the restraints so he could bring them inside. He untied the daughter first from her father's neck. As he pulled her out of the truck, her young body slid down the front of her father's naked body. Paul noticed the father had gotten an erection while his daughter lay naked on top of him. Paul said, "Naughty, naughty. This is your daughter, you fucking pervert," then put her over his shoulder, carried her inside and lay her on the floor in front of the ovens.

Going back out, he slid the father out of the truck and onto the ground. Getting a better grip, he proceeded to pull him into the building. Paul didn't lay him on the floor next to his daughter, but instead sat him up against one of the metal poles that supported the hoist, tying him to it by a rope around his neck. He left one more time to get the mother out of the truck. He carried her over his shoulder then placed her on the floor next to her daughter.

Paul locked the back door and went over to the girl. Lowering the hoist hook to her wrists and hooking it to the rope, he pushed the up button on the control box. The older man came up to him and asked, *"Paul how come three? I thought you were only going to bring back one?"*

"I was going to, but then the daughter came home and then the father did so I took them all. Besides that, he is the one we really want." Paul turned to continue what he was doing when he noticed the man was watching him while they were talking. Kicking him in the ribs, Paul asked, "What are you looking at?"

Paul raised the girl until she was high enough to clear the top of the ovens. He was positioning her body over the opening of the ovens when he heard muffled pleas coming from all three of them. He moved his thumb from the up button to the down button, pushing it in and holding it there. Her feet were the first to enter the molten liquid. Looking back at the father, Paul noticed he had shut his eyes to what was happening to his daughter. Paul continued to lower her body into the oven, pausing only for a second to take one last look at her young breasts. The hoist hook was about four inches from the oven when he cut her from it allowing her to fall freely the rest of the way. Pushing the up button until he could safely grab the hook and pulling it in position, he lowered it to the floor once more.

Paul hooked it to the mother's wrists and noticed tears running down the side of her head. Raising her with the hoist until her feet were off the floor, he leaned over to her and whispered, "It's your husband's fault. You only have him to blame for this, and don't worry, you'll be with your daughter soon enough." Paul lowered her as fast as he could into the oven, stopping only to cut the rope from the hook which allowed her to fall the rest of the way.

Paul then brought the hook back down to the father, attached him and maneuvered him over the top of the oven as he had done the other two. Paul looked at him, and said, "I want you to see what is going to happen, because if it weren't for you and the others I wouldn't be here." Paul put his thumb on the down button and held it there until he was completely gone. He returned the hoist to its normal place and took a good look around to make sure everything looked normal. Paul locked the back door, and the older man followed him up to the front door.

"*You done great, Paul. We'll see you tonight,*" he said.

Paul gave a smile, shut off the alarm, reset it for the whole building, and left, locking the front door behind him. He went down back, got into in his truck, and pulled off the property, locking the gate before he left. Driving home, he could hardly stand the thought of what he had just done, but he continued to be aware enough to drive carefully back home, where he parked out back as usual. He gathered all the loose clothes from the back, shut it, and went to his apartment. Once inside he tossed the clothes onto the others in the corner of the living room, went into the kitchen to get a beer, and returned to the living room with his pipe to get comfortably stoned. When he finished smoking, he put the pipe away and noticed that he had calmed down considerably. Picking up the whiskey bottle, he took a couple of pulls on it and put it back on the floor. He was exhausted and ended his entry of March 8th, *"I'm going to bed, good night."*

It wasn't long before Paul rose out of bed as usual to go to The Mill. He walked down to where they were so he could answer any questions they had, and they were all glad to see that he was able to make it that night. Paul told them all about his trip, leaving out all the gory details, what had gone on and how he was able to pull off what needed to be accomplished. The little children went smiling back to their work and the older man and woman followed him upstairs to the lunchroom. They all sat down.

The woman said, *"Paul you had sex with those women, too. I thought we discussed this before."*

"Look, if you think you can do it better, then you do it. Raping them before I take them degrades them that much more. It's like I told you before. I'm not alone here doing this. I have to deal with Fred trying to fight his way back in all the time. I, or should I say we, see these naked women and we can't control ourselves. What's the difference anyway? I'm just going to end up putting them in the oven." The woman got up and went downstairs without saying a word.

Paul turned to the older man to see him sitting there with just a smile on his face. Paul asked, "What are you smiling about?"

"I don't really blame you, son. So far the three women you brought back were really nice-looking and I think I would have a problem not doing

them if I was in the same situation. Paul, how come three, when you were only supposed to bring back one?"

"Well, when I got done with the mother, the little girl came home. I had to take her and when I tied her up I had to have her, too. Then when I was getting ready to take them to my truck, the man came home. But check this out. When I was picking up the clothes his wallet fell to the floor. I picked it up to see who exactly I was dealing with and lo and behold it was one of the Lackly brothers. Not only that, but when I pulled his daughter's body off of him in the truck the fucking pervert had a hard-on. That's how bad these people really are."

The older man looked at Paul, and said, *"You got one of the brothers? That's great, Paul. I'm real proud of you. I couldn't have done any better. You go now and rest."*

"Thanks, I thought I did okay. Sure I'll go home, but I have one or two more to do and I got five more days to do it. You know what they say, no rest for the wicked."

The older man reached out to shake Paul's hand as they parted, then went downstairs to join the rest. Paul went out the front door setting the alarm and locking the door as he did.

Chapter 14

Paul got up the next day and took the diary with him from the bedroom. As soon as the coffee was done, he poured himself a cup, and went into the living room to start the March 9th entry. He wrote that it was a relief that the older man didn't seem to mind what he was doing to the women. It really didn't bother him that the woman didn't approve of his actions. He started to think to himself, as he sat there drinking his coffee, that he really didn't know what had happened to the old man and what could have happened to make him so angry with this family. Paul thought to himself, "I know what happened to the other three—I think I'll ask him tonight."

Paul got the atlas from his truck, sat down in the chair, then took a few drinks of coffee and lit a cigarette. He lay his cigarette in the ashtray and opened the road atlas. He tore the map of Massachusetts out of it and threw it onto the floor as he had done with the map of Vermont. He opened the crumpled piece of paper he had taken out of his pocket; the town he was looking for was a place named Mechanicsville, New York. Paul flipped to the map of New York, and tried to figure out how far Mechanicsville was from Winooski.

Paul went back out to the truck, started it and started out for his next destination. At the New York state line he checked his road atlas to make sure he was headed in the right direction, lit a cigarette and settled in for the rest of his ride to Mechanicsville. He reached into his pocket to get the piece of paper he had written the address on and laid it on his atlas to mark the page he was using.

He started to think about his return and what his friends would say when he brought the mother back with him. At the Mechanicsville exit, Paul stopped at the gas station for directions to Pickett Road. It was exactly where the man at the gas station said it would be. There was a sign at the beginning of the road that read "Dead End", so he knew he couldn't get lost. Paul drove down the road and almost at the end of it he saw a mailbox with the number he was looking for. He went to the end of the road, turned around, and as he approached the driveway again, he saw a car coming out of it.

An older woman was driving the car. It pulled up to the stop sign at the end of the road and then made a right turn, leaving Paul's sight. Figuring it was safe, Paul pulled into the driveway and drove up to the house to see what lay behind the trees that shadowed the property. There were no

lights on inside the little one-story cottage with its white picket fence. Paul turned his truck around and started down the driveway to head back home.

Paul took the interstate heading north to his exit and headed for the Vermont state line. It took another thirty minutes before he turned onto Route 22A north to take him back to Winooski. Paul had forgotten how desolate the road felt when driving it at night and how different a drive it was during the daytime with all of the beautiful views it had along the way.

Paul drove for a few more miles when he saw a car's taillights flashing ahead on his side of the road. He slowed down as he passed the car, and saw it had Pennsylvania license plates. He pulled his truck over ahead of the car and backed up to see if the driver needed help. As he got out of his truck it started to rain and Paul ran back and tapped the window on the driver's side.

The window rolled down and Paul asked, "Is there anything I can do to help you?"

The woman inside answered, "I don't know. I was driving along and it just started to lose power, until it stopped running completely. I've tried it a couple of times, but it won't start."

"Well, I'm no professional," Paul said, "but it sounds like you need a new car. I'll be glad to give you a lift somewhere if you want one."

The woman looked at him and his truck, then she asked, "Where are you headed?"

"I live in Winooski, but I can give you a lift basically anywhere, within reason."

The woman hesitated, as if weighing her options before saying, "Sure, why not? It's not doing any good sitting here and I have a class first thing in the morning. I told my parents before I left that this car was a piece of shit, but do you think they would listen? Do you have any room in the back of your truck for a couple of duffel bags?"

"Sure do. As a matter of fact there isn't anything in there. Your lucky day, huh?"

As she took two big bags out of the car, Paul reached to carry one for her. He unlocked the upper door at the back of his truck, placed the duffel bag he had inside, took the other bag from her and placed it inside, then shut and locked the door.

Paul opened the passenger-side door, gestured to her to get in, and said, "Please excuse the mess."

"Don't worry about it. I'm the same way. I'm just grateful for the lift."

Paul went over to her car and made sure it was all locked up. He returned to the truck, pulled away from the side of the road and headed back to Winooski.

"Oh, by the way, I'm Paul," he said, holding his hand out to shake hers.

"I'm sorry. I didn't even introduce myself. My name is Mandy, short for Amanda. I'm at UVM," as she took his hand to shake. On the way back to Winooski the two of them shared information about their likes and dislikes and got to know one another.

Finally, Paul asked, "Do you smoke pot?"

"Yeah, why?"

"Well if you're interested, we can stop at my place to get stoned before you go home."

"Sure, I don't have anything going on when I get back and besides that it would be a nice way to forget about that stupid car." They continued to chat companionably and before long they were pulling into Fred's driveway.

As they went into the apartment, Paul said, "You're going to have to excuse the mess, I've been gone for a couple of days."

"Don't worry about it. You should see my dorm room," she giggled.

Mandy sat down in the living room chair and Paul got a couple of beers from the refrigerator. He gave a beer to Mandy, and went to his bedroom to get the pot. In his bedroom, Paul noticed his knife in the picture above his bed and removed it. Back in the living room, Paul watched Mandy take a big swallow off the whiskey bottle that was on the floor next to the chair.

"I hope you don't mind," she said.

"Help yourself, that's what it's there for. Here, this will help too, and wait until you taste how good it is."

Paul handed Mandy a full pipe of the pot that Andy had gotten for him. They finished that pipe, and Paul filled it again and handed it back to her to light. When that pipeful was gone Mandy reached down and took another huge swallow from the whiskey bottle and then took one more right behind it. She leaned over to hand Paul the bottle, and as Paul leaned toward her their faces came close. Paul took the bottle from her and Mandy put her other hand behind Paul's neck, pulling him forward to give him a long, wet tongue kiss, catching him off guard. Paul leaned back in surprise and Mandy got down on the floor with him. She then leaned over and as she started to give Paul another kiss, she pushed him down onto the floor, and maneuvered herself on top of him.

They lay there kissing for a few minutes when Paul felt Mandy slowly grinding her crotch against his. Feeling his hard-on, she became excited and started to grind harder and harder. Paul pushed her up by the shoulders, trying to get his hands into her shirt. Mandy leaned to one side

and pulled her shirt off over her head. Soon they both were standing continuing to kiss and removing clothes from themselves and each other as fast as they could.

Back down on the floor totally naked, their excitement for each other grew rapidly. Mandy had Paul's hard-on in her hand rubbing and stroking it so it would get as hard as she could get it. In the meantime, Paul had his hand down between her thighs rubbing her crotch. Mandy stopped kissing Paul, and stood over him—straddling his body, then lowered herself down on him with her back to his face. Mandy leaned over; taking Paul's hard-on in her hands and started giving him oral pleasure. As she did this she positioned her moist crotch over his mouth. Paul was going nuts with what she was doing and started to do the same to her. It seemed like a lifetime to Paul, but within minutes he exploded in her mouth and at the same time, he felt her juices flowing down the sides of his face.

Paul wanted more and took Mandy by the hips and rolled her over onto the floor, placing her on her back, and climbed on top of her. Mandy took his hard-on in her hand and placed it inside her. Paul thrust into her with all his strength and continued doing so until he felt himself approaching an orgasm. But as he leaned his head down to give her a kiss, flashes of Fred's mother appeared in his mind. So vivid were these flashes that Paul couldn't stop them, and opening his eyes to get back to reality, he saw that he was kissing Fred's mother. Paul pulled his face away from hers, but continued to thrust in and out of her.

The images wouldn't stop coming no matter how hard Paul fought to stop them. In a frenzy he seized her throat and squeezed until she started to choke. Her eyes opened wide as she gasped for breath and her body squirmed, trying to get away from him. Paul just continued to thrust himself harder into her. It took only seconds for her eyes to close and her body to go limp and it was at that moment Paul finished his orgasm, staying in her until he was completely done.

Getting off her, he put his hand to her chest and felt a heartbeat under his hand. Without thinking, he instinctively got up, put on his pants, and ran down to the truck to get his bag from behind the seat. Back in his apartment, he thought she was coming back around and worked fast to wrap duct tape around her head and over her mouth, and tie her hand and foot.

When he was finished he was again getting excited. Paul didn't want to look her in the face fearing the images might start again, so he rolled her onto her belly. When Paul drove deep inside of her, she let out a muffled scream and at the same time turned her head to one side. Paul saw Fred's mother's face, and couldn't go any further.

He got up, dressed again and went to the chair to sit down and take a few swallows from the whiskey bottle. He got up once more to get a beer,

watching her the whole time he was up. Back in the chair, he lit his pipe and opened his beer wondering why he was having these images now and not before with the others. Unable to figure it out, he went into the bedroom to get his bedcover.

He wrapped her up so no one would notice that he was carrying a body. It was about 1:30 AM when Paul dumped her body into the back of his truck and closed the tailgates. He headed for The Mill, where his friends were waiting for him. Going through the gate and locking it, he drove his truck to the back entrance. Paul came back around to the front and didn't say much except to greet them as he let them all into The Mill. They all went down to the heat-treat area and Paul went back out to his truck. He didn't waste any time bringing her in and laying her on the floor in front of the oven. He took the bedspread off her and threw it down near the door.

They all stood there looking at the naked, young female body lying lifeless on the floor, wondering who she might be. Paul hooked her to the hoist and started to raise her body off the floor. It was then the woman noticed blood running down the backside of her thighs, and asked, *"This one too, Paul?"*

He ignored her comments and continued the job. He raised her until her feet could clear the oven and then he moved her into position so he could lower her into the oven.

She came to from the intense heat being let off by the oven, and began to squirm and writhe frantically. This had never happened before and Paul started to panic. He grabbed an iron rod from the worktable and knocked her unconscious. It only took minutes before she completely disappeared into the oven with the others.

Paul moved quickly to pick everything up and straighten up the work area the way he had found it. He took the bedspread back out to his truck and threw it into the back with Mandy's two bags, then went back into The Mill to lock up. He knew that someone was following him as he went up the stairs, but waited till he got to the lunchroom before he turned around to see who it was. The older man had followed him, and Paul asked, "What's your problem?"

The older man replied, *"No, what's your problem? We talked about this already and you and me decided that this wouldn't happen any more. Now this."* Paul sat down and started to explain how all he did was to stop and give her a ride.

Paul said, "We ended up at the apartment and started to have a couple of drinks. She came on to me, and we fucked. It would have been all right, but I started seeing Fred's mother and I went nuts. Once I started I couldn't stop. Besides, it's him not me that's having all this sex with them. I just want to get done what I have to and return back here, but he sees these

beautiful women and wants them. Don't get me wrong. I want to have sex with them too, but there's some kind of driving force in me I can't stop. It's as if I have no respect for women at all. This time, though, she turned into an older woman…"

The older man took Paul into his arms, and said, *"Its okay Paul. I understand that it's hard and that you have to concentrate not only on what you're doing, but also on keeping control of Fred's thoughts. There's just one more and we'll be done. You go back home and get some rest. I'll explain to the others."*

Paul left The Mill and went straight to bed after finishing his entry.

He got up early the next morning, without the alarm, got dressed and gathered together what he would need on his next trip. Drinking his coffee in the living room, he noticed Mandy's clothes thrown around, and tossed them into the pile behind his chair. Then he saw Mandy's two bags. He removed anything that had her name on it and threw her clothing onto the pile behind his chair. On the way to the store to stock up on rope and duct tape, he threw her bags in a dumpster.

When Paul returned to his apartment to get his bag, he grabbed the whiskey bottle and swallowed as much as he could. He poured the rest of the coffee into his to-go cup, turned off the coffeemaker, and left to start on his trip. At the Mechanicsville exit, he went to the stop sign at the end of the exit ramp and took a left.

It only took a few moments to get to Pickett Road. Nothing looked abnormal or out of place to him and he turned into the Lacklys' mother's driveway as if he belonged there. He didn't see anyone outside the house or any movement inside. He did, however, notice her car was in the garage. He quickly put on his gloves, took his bag from the seat and headed toward the front door. He knocked.

The door opened wide and the woman standing in the doorway asked, "Fred, what are you doing here?" Startled for a moment, Paul regained his purpose and forced the door all the way open, knocking the woman to the floor. He pulled off one of his gloves to stuff into her mouth until he could get some duct tape to take its place. He sat on top of her and pinned her as he shut the door. He tore off a piece of duct tape long enough to go over her mouth. He couldn't help wondering what the hell she meant when she opened the door to see who it was. "How did she know Fred? I can't remember ever meeting her, even when Fred had control," he thought to himself as he tied her wrists together.

Paul pulled her to her feet and headed through the house looking for her bedroom. He was already excited and, holding her back against him, his knife at her throat, he tore the buttons on her blouse apart, reached into her bra and pulled one of her breasts out to get a good feel of it. It didn't take

long to find her bedroom. He pushed her into the room to the side of the bed and pushed her down onto it.

Straddling her, he lashed her wrists to the headboard. He pushed himself back a little and with his knife cut her sleeves so he could pull her blouse off. Throwing it out of the way, he cut the bra strap between her breasts and then her shoulder straps, exposing her breasts. "For a woman your age," he said, "you sure have some nice tits." He leaned over her putting one of her nipples in his mouth until it became erect, and then did the same to the other.

He stood at the side of the bed and took off his pants. The woman started to thrash about and pull at the rope that tied her to the bed. Paul walked around to the foot of the bed and stood there for a moment looking at her and around the room. Then he reached over the footboard, took the stirrups sewed to her pant legs from the bottom of her feet and pulled her pants completely off. She was wearing lacy black panties, which increased Paul's excitement. He didn't think, he wrote later, that a woman of sixty would have been as nice looking as she was. He went to the side of the bed and leaned over to cut off her panties.

He climbed on the bed and forced her legs open with his own. He drove himself into her as hard as he could, but when he looked down he saw he was on top of Fred's mother. The shock stopped him, and he got off her in horror. He didn't know what to do and wandered aimlessly around the room until he was stopped by a photograph on her bureau. It was a picture of Fred and his older brother Pat.

Paul took the picture to the other room and placed it into his bag to take back with him. Returning to her room, he saw the woman was crying, but it wasn't Fred's mother anymore. Paul decided that if he couldn't see her face he wouldn't see Fred's mom's face. At the foot of the bed, he grabbed her feet and flopped her over onto her belly. Paul got on top of her once more, putting himself into her; he thrust in and out tentatively to see if those images would start again. They didn't, and Paul continued more violently, but then the images started over again. This time he couldn't shake them from his thoughts and got off her, cutting her from the headboard and tying her feet. Angry that he hadn't finished what he wanted to do he threw her into the back of the truck.

He returned to the house, straightened out the bed linen, picked the clothes he had cut off her body up off the floor, then took them out and threw them in the back of the truck with her.

As he drove up the entrance ramp to the interstate, Paul noticed that dusk had fallen on the valley. In Vermont he turned onto Route 22A, for his final leg back to Winooski. He couldn't forget her having called him Fred and the pictures on her bureau. "How were this woman and Fred

connected?" Paul wondered. Paul pulled into Winooski at 8:00 PM, or at least that was the time showing on the clock at the bank.

He drove straight to The Mill. Although it was the earliest Paul had ever gone there, he had to get this woman out of his truck. When he got to the gate he saw all his friends there, as they would have been had he gotten there at the usual time. It was as if they knew everything before it was going to happen. Paul drove through the gate, locked it, and drove around to the back of the building. As he came up around the corner from the back of The Mill, they all crowded around him to see who he had this time. Paul ignored their questions and went into The Mill through the front door with them following him. When they were all inside, Paul locked the door and reset the alarm. He continued to ignore them until he went to the truck, dragged her from it, dropped her to the floor in front of the ovens, letting her body's weight determine how hard she landed.

Paul grabbed the hoist control box and lowered the hook to the floor. As he did this the older man walked around from behind him to get a better look, and said, *"Paul, that's their mother!"*

"Yeah, I thought you would like it, and I didn't touch her. I tried, but I couldn't get the face of Fred's mother out of my mind. It must be her age."

Paul reached down and hooked onto the rope between her wrists and raised her off the floor. Paul later wrote he noticed a look in her eyes—not of fear, but as if she recognized something. He pushed her over the top of the ovens and lowered her slowly. She didn't put up a fight as the others had and when Paul cut her wrists free, he turned to see the older man crying.

Chapter 15

Paul asked the older man to go upstairs with him to the lunchroom under the pretense of asking for his advice. When they got to the lunchroom, Paul noticed the man still had tears in his eyes. Paul reached around him to put his hand on his shoulder, and asked, "What's wrong, old man? Why did that one bother you and not the others?" It was at this point Paul started seeing images in his mind, like movies, like the ones he had the night of the ice storm. During that storm Paul only had images of the two children and the woman's death, but not of the older man or his own.

Paul saw the backyard of The Mill and there was an old station wagon parked in the farthest corner of the lot. As he approached the car, he saw two people, a man undressed down to his boxer shorts and a woman naked except for her panties. They were embraced in a lovers hold, kissing each other passionately. They started to have intercourse—him thrusting in and out vigorously and bringing them both to orgasm at about the same time. Paul thought to himself, *"Boy, can this guy go, and at his age, too."*

Paul realized from the start that the man he was watching and the older man he was talking to were the same person. He heard the back door of The Mill slam shut, and a man walked their way carrying a double-barreled shotgun. Paul didn't know what to do, so he just stood there. The man with the gun walked right in front of Paul as if he wasn't there at all. Apparently no one could see Paul and this was all just an illusion or something.

The man threw open the back door yelling, "Get out of there, woman." He reached in for her, and dragged her naked body onto the dirt lot. She started to plead with him, grabbing at his shirt and pant leg. The man turned just enough to strike his hand across the side of her head, knocking her away from him. He then turned to the man in the car, lifted his gun, and pulled the triggers. The woman was sobbing uncontrollably at his feet while he looked into the car to make sure the other man was dead. Paul heard The Mill's back door open again, this time slamming against the wall, and before Paul could turn to see who it was, the man put two more shells in his gun, lifted it and fired again in the direction of the door.

He couldn't really make out who was lying on the ground from where he was standing, so he walked over to get a better look. When he got close enough to see who it was, he stopped in his tracks and had to put his hand to the wall of the building so he wouldn't fall. It was himself who had come through the door and it was him the man had turned and shot.

Paul walked back over in the direction of the shooter, and saw him grab a clump of hair on the woman's head and lift her to her feet. She was standing there totally naked, crying uncontrollably, not knowing what to do as the man lifted Paul's body, and dragged him over to the car. Standing there, Paul took a good hard look at both of them and realized the woman standing there was actually the woman he had just put in the oven. It was then Paul removed his hand from the older man's shoulder and found himself back in the lunchroom. Paul asked, "Was that how you and I died? Who was that man and was that the woman I just got rid of downstairs?"

The older man answered, *"Yes, Paul, that was the woman that we just got rid of, and the man was her husband and the owner of The Mill at the time we both worked here. You hadn't been working here a week when this happened, and I had been working for nearly ten years."*

"Why didn't you stop me or something?"

"She had to be the one, we had to complete the task we came to do and she was one of the last who had to be dealt with."

"Why did he shoot you? Better yet, why did he shoot me? You could have stopped me."

"He shot me because I was having an affair with his wife and why you, well you were at the wrong place at the wrong time. He had no reason to shoot you and as far as I'm concerned, he didn't have a reason to shoot me. She started seeing me because of his physical abuse and she wanted to get even. What she didn't know was how far she had pushed him, screwing around with one of his employees. She never said anything to anyone and he never got prosecuted for our deaths. He got rid of the car and the bodies so no one would ever find them. If I remember right it was down in Williston at the quarry. The water there is nearly a hundred feet deep and nobody would find it even if they looked for it."

Paul didn't know what to think as he sat down at one of the lunch tables.

The older man sat next to him, and said, *"As far as I'm concerned, we've done what we came to do. It's over now, Paul."*

"Maybe for you, but not for me."

Paul then got up and walked to the front door of The Mill. He set the alarm and locked the door, then walked to the back of The Mill to get his truck. As he turned the corner his thoughts returned to the scene he had just witnessed. He drove through the main gate, locked it, got back into his truck, and drove back to his apartment. He ended the entry as he got stoned smoking his pot and drinking the rest of the whiskey.

Paul wrote in his diary that he stayed inside his apartment until Friday night. On Saturday Andy had come over after work with a new bottle of whiskey to get him to go out and do something. They first went to

get something to eat, but returned to Fred's apartment and sat around getting all messed up on pot and boilermakers until the early hours of the next morning.

After Andy left, Paul wrote that he couldn't figure out how the woman knew Fred and why she had Fred and Pat's picture in her bedroom. He wondered what her relationship to them was. He went down to his truck, figuring the air might clear his head, unlocked the tailgate, and reached in the back taking out all of her clothes. He took them up to his apartment and threw them into the pile with the rest.

Paul sat for a little while in the living room chair staring at the picture he had taken from that woman's bedroom, but he could hardly keep his eyes open. Deciding the picture could wait, he took another swallow of whiskey and went to bed. He sank into a very heavy sleep that would carry through to late the next day. Paul wrote very little about the next day other than he was looking forward to getting back to a routine.

When Paul returned to work everyone stopped by to welcome him back to work and to ask about his vacation. Beyond that note, the length of Paul's entries were like the ones he wrote prior to his vacation. They weren't very interesting and they were very short with no substance. He did mention that he continued to go to The Mill at night to let his friends in, but there wasn't much about what was said or done during those visits.

At this point I felt as though I could put the diary down and take a break to stretch my legs. When I got done doing what I needed to do, I returned to the bed and picked the diary back up hoping I could finish reading it. The entries ran the same up until about the Fourth of July when The Mill had another three-day weekend.

It was on the second of July when Paul wrote that Pat, Fred's brother, had called and asked him over for a cookout on the fourth. He wrote in that day's entry that he was going to bring the photograph he had taken from the woman's home and ask Pat if he knew anything about it. He also wrote he had finally shown his friends the photograph, but they had very little to offer. Paul thought the older man might know something because of the affair he'd had with the woman, but couldn't figure if he did or didn't.

Paul went to Pat's house in the early afternoon on the Fourth of July. The day went along as Pat had planned. The dinner he and his wife served the family and Paul was delicious. Pat and Fred sat on the back deck talking about their jobs and each other's lives before going to watch the fire works in Burlington. It was a very cordial conversation and Paul thought this was a good time to bring out the picture. Paul took the picture out, and asked, "Hey Pat, I found this photograph and was wondering if you knew

anything about it?" Pat took the picture from him and sat back in his chair to study it.

He leaned forward to hand it back to Paul and said, "That's you and me, little brother."

"I know that, Pat, but when was it taken?"

"Well we were both babies, so I presume it was taken shortly after you were born. Where did you get it?"

"I found it going through some of my things, when I was cleaning up." Pat shrugged and said that it was time to go to the fireworks.

As they watched the fireworks with the rest of the family, Paul asked Pat about their father. They both grew up without a father, Pat replied.

"But, look Fred, all I know is that we both have the same father and that he was never around to help us or Mom. Mom told me one time the man who was our father at the time was living two lives; one with his real wife and one with our mother. I haven't ever seen a picture of him nor have I ever seen our birth certificates."

"Our birth certificates? Aren't they at City Hall? You never were curious to who he might be?"

"No, I really don't care. He must be an asshole if he never owned up to two boys as good as us. I suppose they are in the City Hall, but not in Fletcher."

"What do you mean?"

"We were born in the city of Burlington, so I suppose they're there, but like I told you, I never checked."

Paul finished his entry on the Fourth of July all excited that he might be able to figure out why this woman in New York had their baby picture on the bureau in her bedroom. He was going to go to Burlington the next day after work to see if he could get copies of their birth certificates. Maybe he had just uncovered why Fred might have been chosen for Paul to take over.

Paul got up without the aid of his alarm clock. Sitting on the edge of his bed, he thought to himself it was a little dark out to be the right time for work. He took a look at his clock, and saw it was only three o'clock in the morning and remembered he hadn't let his friends into The Mill yet.

When he got to The Mill they all greeted him and asked what took him so long to come down. He ignored their questions while he reset the alarm and locked the door. They all walked together to the heat-treat area in silence. The woman asked about his holiday and his visit with Pat. Paul said he had a good time at Fred's brother's house and no one had yet figured out there was a difference in Fred. The older man and woman followed him upstairs. When they got to the lunchroom, Paul sat down at one of the

tables, and they sat down across from him. They explained to him he wasn't acting himself tonight and wanted to know why.

Paul pulled out the picture of Fred and Pat and explained where he had come across it. He told them about his conversation with Fred's brother, and that he was going to follow up on it. He planned to go the next day to the City Hall to try to find out who this scumbag was who didn't take responsibility for his boys. The older man said, *"Paul, our time is running out. We made a deal and we have to stick to it."*

"I know, but I have a little while to try and figure this out."

The woman then said, *"Paul, you do what you feel you have to, but don't forget what he just told you."*

Paul got up and put the picture in his back pocket as he left.

He got up the next morning to go to work as usual, but it wasn't an ordinary workday. Ever since Paul had taken control of Fred's mind and body his communication with the others was limited to the times when he would let them into The Mill to work. It wasn't even the time for first break when the older man spoke out to Paul. He told Paul that sometimes things are better left unknown. *"Let sleeping dogs lie,"* he said. Paul listened to him, but there was no way he wasn't going to go and check this out. The rest of the day went by fast and in no time he found himself at the doorway of City Hall.

He walked up to the counter in the city clerk's office and was greeted by a nice older woman who clearly had worked there for many years. She asked what he wanted and Paul told her he needed to get a copy of his birth certificate for a new job. He wrote Fred's name and social security number on a small piece of paper and slid it across the counter. It didn't take long for her to return to the counter bringing with her an envelope that contained Fred's birth certificate. He took the envelope, handing her a dollar bill, the required fee, in return. He put the envelope into his back pocket, and thanked her. He drove to his apartment without opening the envelope.

At home, he got a beer and sat in his living room. He just sat there drinking his beer, staring at the envelope, wondering what it might tell him, if anything. Finally, he couldn't wait any longer, and tore it open. At the bottom of the certificate the signatures of the parents were required. He found Fred's mother's signature, then looked to the opposite side of the form. Pat and Fred's father was Ron Lackly, the present owner of The Mill.

Paul dropped the form to the floor, picked up his whiskey bottle and took a large swallow. He picked the certificate back up off the floor and looked again to see if he had misread it. The man, whose wife was the first person he had killed, was, according to this form, Pat and Fred's father. But

how could that be? Not caring anymore whose feelings got hurt, Paul went down to his truck, got in, and headed for the interstate. He was on his way to Fred's mother's house in Fletcher.

At the Fletcher exit, Paul drove through town until he got to the road that led to her house. At the intersection to her road, while waiting to turn, he saw a car coming down her road toward him. As he turned, he was able to see the driver of the other car. It was Ron Lackly. Paul's anger grew as he got closer to her house.

At the house, he sat in his truck for a brief moment to gather his thoughts. He turned off his truck, got out, and knocked on the front door. It took a few moments for Fred's mother to answer his knock. As she opened the door she was tying her bathrobe together. She told him to come in and gave him a hug as he walked by. They went into the living room. She looked at him, and asked, "So what brings you all the way out here after all this time?"

Paul leaned forward and handed her the photograph without saying anything. Looking at the picture, she smiled and asked, "What's going on? Fred, why are you showing me a baby picture of you and your brother?"

Paul took it back from her, and said, "Mom, I got this from a little old woman in New York State I had never met before. So, I started to investigate and guess what I found out? The owner of The Mill Pat and I work for is our father."

"Don't be silly Fred. If I knew your father I would have told you years ago."

"You're lying, mom. Even to my face, you still lie about our father", and as he was saying this he took out the copy of his birth certificate.

Opening it, Paul gave it to her, and said, "The lying has to stop. I want the truth and I'm not leaving until I get it."

"I didn't think you would have ever cared about knowing your father and that's why I never told you or Pat who he was. I was young and had met a man in the bar I used to go to in Burlington. We got drunk together several times before we slept with each other and started a relationship. It wasn't until I got pregnant with Pat that I approached him about committing to each other and starting a serious relationship. That's when he told me that he couldn't because he was already married to another woman.

We didn't see each other for almost a year after Pat was born. He agreed to help me financially with Pat and we started seeing each other again. I got pregnant twice more by him and he lived up to the financial responsibility for you and your sister just as he had with Pat. I knew we could never be a couple, but I wanted to make sure that I had what I needed

to raise you kids. He bought this house for us and sent monthly checks to cover living expenses and we both decided not to tell you kids or anyone. I only see him occasionally and through the years have only given him a few pictures of you children. This must be one of them. The woman you got it from, if I remember rightly, is his mother. When her husband died and The Mill was turned over to him, she moved out of state. Where did you see her?"

"She was at The Mill when I accidentally ran into her. We started talking when she opened her purse to get something out of it. She placed her wallet on the table and it opened to where I could see this picture. I asked her about it and she told me it was of her grandchildren. I took it when she got distracted."

Paul got up and thanked Fred's mother for being honest, but told her he would never forgive her for not telling him. Putting the picture in his back pocket and telling her good-bye, he left. He caught himself crying and thought that Fred might regain control of him. Paul forced himself to think of who his next victim might be and retain his control over Fred's thoughts. When Paul got back to Winooski, he went to Pat's house instead of going home. Pat greeted him at the front door before Paul even had a chance to ring the doorbell. Pat explained he had seen headlights pulling into the driveway and didn't want the doorbell to wake up the girls. Pat asked, "What's up, Fred?"

"I just came from mom's house and showed her this picture along with a copy of my birth certificate. Pat, our father is Ron, the owner of The Mill, but mom said we couldn't have any contact with him about it. They agreed he would take care of her needs as long as there weren't any problems started by her or us."

Pat leaned against the door casing looking at the picture and birth certificate, and said, "I can't believe she knew and she told me nothing about it after all these years. I have always wondered who it might be or what the story really was."

Paul took the stuff back from Pat, and said, "Well, now you know. I'll see you at work. I love you." Paul got into his truck leaving Pat still standing on the porch in disbelief. He got home and drank a beer before settling into his bed to go to sleep.

Paul got up as usual during the night to go down to The Mill. They went to the heat-treat area as usual and the children started to work. Paul stopped the older man and woman from getting started, and said, "Well, I found out why this woman in New York had Fred and Pat's picture. Her son—the owner of The Mill is their father. How do you like them apples?" They looked at each other in near disbelief, but Paul took the time to tell them the whole story.

The older man answered, *"Well now that you figured that out, try to figure out your next step. Time is short."*

"Don't worry. I'm working on it as we speak. If you think about it, Fred even has a motive to want revenge on this family."

The woman asked, *"Haven't we done enough?"*

Paul replied, "No we haven't. I've got one more to do and then I'll be done." Paul returned to his apartment, and finished writing the July 5th, entry.

The entries from this point until the end of May of 2000 didn't have much substance to them at all. They were the typical—got up—went to work—got drunk and stoned—went to sleep, and went to The Mill. Nowhere in these entries did Paul mention any more about Fred's father or what his next step would be. However, he did write about the tension that was growing between himself and the woman. She was telling him that all he wanted was to rape one more and that another one had nothing to do with their purpose. Paul, of course, was saying things differently.

I took this opportunity to stop reading his diary for a moment to get something to drink. I got myself a beer and returned to my bed, setting the beer next to my tape recorder. I noticed the tape was almost finished, so I took the next tape, inserted it, and pushed RECORD.

I leaned against my pillows, smoking a cigarette as I drank my beer and turned to the May 1st, entry. It was here he started to write about his next step. His previous entries didn't give me any clue as to what he was going to do next. One of the things that puzzled me was the length of time that had passed. I remembered reading in his July fourth or fifth entry that the older man told him their time was short and here it was May of the following year. It was his entry on May 25th, which took me by complete surprise.

May 25, 2000. I just came back from The Mill. The children were happy to see me, but I don't think the old man or the woman was. They went in and started working immediately and I returned home. I can't get this man out of my mind. The owner of The Mill was a man who had so much and who had given so little to his own children. Children who were brought up just above the poverty level, children he could have done so much for, but didn't. This man, even though his wife is now gone, has not paid to the level that he must pay. I can't leave until I know I have hurt him as much as he has hurt these children. Knowing how life is so insignificant to all those in his family, I know now who the last two should be. There's nothing that

will change my decision and tomorrow I'll go to Fred's brother's house. I have to go to work now and when my day is over I will start to put an end to all the turmoil this family has created through the years.

It was clear he meant Ron. But who was the other?

The next day at work, the voice of the older man came out of thin air. Paul asked, "What do you want?"

The older man answered, *"It is you who wants something. We did this and were able to hang on for so long because of the injustice done to us. I know what you are thinking and so do the rest of them. We all think it is over and the time to stop is now. If you do this, you will be no better than them. Tonight when you come to let us in, you can join us once more knowing that revenge was ours."*

"I can't. I have to do what I have decided to do. If I don't, I will never be able to go past where I came from. I came to do what we needed to do and after tonight it will be completely done. The Lackly family hasn't paid enough for all they have done. This man had three children he totally ignored and treated as just another bill he had to pay. Believe me, after tonight he will pay."

There was no response. The last entry in Fred's diary was when Paul returned to the apartment from working at The Mill that day. It was added onto the entry he had started when he returned from The Mill earlier that morning. He wrote he had gotten all his stuff together and he was going to finish his beer and head out.

Was he not finished with his entry, or did he just decide not to do anything and call it quits? I didn't know, but I intended to find out! I shut the diary, put it to the side of the bed, and saw that it was 3:00 AM. I got up, went outside and smoked a cigarette. Standing there thinking about everything, I wondered what I was going to say to Nick about the second diary. Putting my cigarette out, I went in to go to bed—figuring I'd call Nick as soon as I woke up.

Chapter 16

Waking up, I glanced at my alarm clock and saw that it was only 7:45 AM. At least I had gotten a catnap. Knowing I needed to call Nick, I got up, collected my cigarettes and lighter, and went out to the kitchen table.

I gave the Winooski Police Department a call. It seemed to ring forever, and just when I thought I might have punched the wrong number, I heard a voice say, "Winooski Police Department, may I help you?" I recognized the voice of Terri the dispatcher.

"Yeah, I need to speak to Nick."

"Who's calling?"

"Its me, Larry."

"One moment please."

Nick picked up his phone and said, "Yeah, Larry what's going on? I haven't heard from you for a couple of days and figured after last weekend you might have taken a vacation. I want to thank you for not saying anything specific in your articles."

I said, "No problem, I gave you my word. Did you happen to take the time to read Fred's diary?"

"No, I haven't. I've been busy trying to figure everything else out in this case. The whole set of circumstances seem weird, plus we're waiting for the rest of the test results to come back from forensics."

I told him it was very important that we get together that day to talk.

Nick didn't really understand the urgency behind my request, and said, "Sure. How about meeting me at the pub at around four o'clock this afternoon." I told him I would be there and hung up.

I returned to my bedroom, set the alarm for 2:30 PM, and crawled back into bed to catch up on some of the sleep I had gone without.

I arrived at the pub a half an hour earlier than we agreed to meet, and immediately ordered a shot of tequila and a beer. Sitting down at the table, I put the other diary on the floor beside my chair. I ordered another round. I had just downed my shot of tequila when I saw Nick entering through the door. I raised my hand, and yelled, "Nick", just in case he didn't see me. I heard him order his shot and beer then change it to two of each, one for himself and one for me. As Nick approached the table I stood up and shook his hand. I waited for Nick to finish his shot before I started.

"Nick, I really think you should read the diary. It might help you figure this all out. When I brought it to you I told you it was really weird."

Nick looked at me, and said, "Don't worry, I took it home, but I just haven't had the time."

I decided it was best to just spit it out and get it over with. I looked at Nick, and said, "Nick, there's something else about the diary."

"What, Larry?"

Leaning to one side of my chair, I picked up the second diary off the floor. "There was a second diary. I didn't say anything, because it didn't seem to matter to you that I took the first one home to read."

Nick took a drink from his beer, and said, "How did you get it?"

"When I asked if I could take the first one we found, I went into the bedroom to get it. I squatted down to get it and thought I saw something else on the other side of the bed. It turned out to be another diary. I figured since you were letting me take the first one another one wouldn't matter. I knew when I was done reading them I would return them to you anyway."

There was a moment of silence as Nick sat there staring at me. I told Nick I was sorry and I knew that I should have said something.

Nick broke the silence by ordering another round for both of us and before it was served I spoke up. "That's why I told you to sit down and read it. The first one was so weird that I couldn't stop reading. I did take enough time to bring you the first one, but I went right back to start the second one. That's where I've been the past three days, and if you think the first one is weird after reading it wait until you read the second one. I swear to you, Nick, no one else knows of the diaries, or their contents." The booze was beginning to make me talkative.

Nick took the second diary from the table and thumbed through it quickly, then finished his beer and stood up. "I'm now going to go home to read these two books as you suggested, but before I leave is there anything else you want to tell me?"

I took the last drink from my glass, and said, "Now that you mention it, there is. I think you should really have a seat though, because you're not going to believe it." Nick looked at me, shook his head, looked at his watch; he nevertheless pulled his chair out, and sat down.

I started to repeat to Nick what I had already told him when I returned the first one to him. When I finished I started to go on about the second one and how it appeared to be a continuation from the first. Fred, I told him, or whoever was writing in these books, was describing some really horrible crimes and deaths. Nick just sat there listening and staring at me. I couldn't really make out if he was listening or just staring off into space, but I was bound and determined to finish my story. I said, "Nick, I think that Fred took part in not just one murder, but several. It sounds weird, but I don't really think that he acted on his own. I'm not saying that there was someone else helping him, but in his diary the name Paul was constantly mentioned. In the first one it was only mentioned occasionally, but in the second one Fred's name was never there, and somebody who called himself

Paul was writing in it talking <u>about</u> Fred. I know this sounds weird, but what I'm trying to tell you is this whole fucking thing is weird."

"Larry you've been watching too many movies. When the test results come back we'll have all we need to put an end to this." I got up as I finished my beer, and said, "Nick you go home, read the diaries, and then call me to let me know if you don't think there is more to this story. It goes deeper than what we know or found at The Mill that day." As I left the pub I heard Nick tell me not to do anything stupid.

I got into my car and sat there letting it warm up. I said out loud, "If I remember right, the first person Fred had a dream of killing was the girl he had met at work. He dated her when he lived at his grandfather's house and supposedly he had met up with her in a dream. That date led to him killing her, but was it a dream or was it real?" Pulling away, I turned down the street where Fred's grandfather lived and that also led to The Mill.

I drove slowly past Fred's grandfather's house and as I continued down the road I came to The Mill. At the top of the hill leading to The Mill there was a sign that read "Canoe Access." I turned down the hill and proceeded to the end of the road where the Winooski River is visible. Pulling over and parking the car, I turned off the engine, pulled out a cigarette and lit it as I got out. I sat there on the hood of my car staring at The Mill and wondering how all of this could have happened without anyone knowing.

As I finished my cigarette and went to flick it onto the road, I noticed the hair on my arm was standing on end. I drove up the hill to head home, and at the next stop sign I found myself at the intersection where Fred's apartment building was located. It wasn't until the sounding of a car horn coming from behind me that I realized I had been sitting there for an indefinite period of time. I pulled away headed for my house.

At home, I took the tapes and my tape player to the kitchen table, sat down, and put the first tape into the player. Pushing the fast forward button and play button alternately, I searched for the spot describing the killing of the girl who was known to me only as Diane.

It was when I got to the November 1st entry that I found what I was looking for. As the tape played I heard my voice reading about the meeting between Fred and a girl named Diane and I let it continue to the part describing the sexual encounter and her death. Stopping the tape, I noticed that I had gotten an erection. I wondered, "What the hell am I doing?"

I sat there wondering whether or not I should continue. Finally the need to get this whole Fred thing out of my mind brought my finger to the play button on the tape player. I got up from the table and as I listened to the tape I went into the bedroom to get the notebook from the nightstand. I returned to the kitchen table just in time to hear the part that described the

disposal of the young girl's body and her car. I wrote down the date and the details of this entry in the notebook. Anything I thought would be helpful in finding this girl I wrote down. When I came to the part where Fred got rid of her car, I continued to write. All that I could get from the tape was that he got rid of her car on a back road somewhere on the outskirts of Winooski.

I got a box of sandwich baggies, got into my car, and left the driveway on my way to try and find something, anything that would prove to me that this wasn't just a fantasy, but a reality. I tried to figure out where Fred had been talking about when he described the location of the place he took her car and set fire to it. I decided that I would start at the supposed scene of the crime—Fred's apartment.

I pulled into the apartment building's back parking lot. I reviewed my notes over and over again, and listened carefully to the tape one more time reviewing my notes at the same time. I still couldn't figure out where the location might be. It had to be somewhere between the Colchester and Winooski town jurisdictions. Where in God's name could he be talking about?

I decided to call it a day. It was close to seven o'clock, darkness was beginning to fall and I had had a lot to drink. I turned onto Malletts Bay Road, the back way to Malletts Bay from Winooski; it took me directly to my house. I turned a bend in the road and out of the corner of my eye I caught a road sign that read Pine Island Road. I slammed on the brakes and pulled over. Could this be the place? It was on the outskirts of Winooski, and it led off into the distance splitting two fields used by the farmer up the road. I turned around and drove back to the entrance of the road. Daylight was running out, but I thought there would be enough for me to see if there was any truth behind these diaries. I said, "Fuck it", and drove down the road.

At a snail's pace, I tried to take in as much as possible on either side. I tried to remember if I had ever seen anyone or even a car on this road the numerous times I had driven by it on my way to town. The road looked like it might be just an access for the farmer whose fields were on both sides of the road, and they had just named it to be funny. I didn't know if I would have time to search as much as I wanted to before dark. At the bend in the road that was beyond eyesight of the main road, I saw an old, run-down farmhouse. All the windows were gone and the main structure of the building didn't look safe. I pulled to the side of the road, put the car in park, and got out, leaving the engine running.

Walking around the outside of the building, I found only bits and pieces of trash. Inside, I walked around the ground floor and found some old, used hypodermic needles that looked as if they had been there for years. The place must have been used as a hangout for junkies or street people. I

didn't trust the second floor, and darkness was coming quick, so I decided to go continue my search down the road.

At least five minutes must have passed since I had left the house and the end of the road was no more than twenty yards ahead of me. I saw absolutely nothing that would confirm what I had read in Fred's diary.

I decided to turn around and return home defeated. Looking in my rearview mirror as I backed the car up, I thought I saw something. I got out and went through the small brush lining the roadside directly behind my car. No more than twenty feet or so from the edge of the road was a burned-out car. If this one was true that meant all the others were probably true, I thought to myself, as I got closer.

I got to the spot and started looking around for anything that I could find, but the night's darkness defeated me. There was a large, black burned area all around the frame of the car, and I decided there was too much to look at. I felt sure that this was the place I had been looking for. Should I call Nick, or find absolute proof first? I decided to go home for the night and return the next day early enough to go carefully through the entire area.

At home, I cooked and ate a hamburger, then sat down with the tapes, the tape player and my notebook. I pushed the play button and listened again to the details of Diane's death. For the past two days or so I had been up late reading Fred's diaries and now I had to sleep.

I woke up around 6:30, and decided to concentrate solely on Diane's murder. If I could prove her death was real, then I would continue to follow up on the other ones. I had a quick breakfast and headed out the door.

At the end of the road, I got out of the car, taking the box of baggies I had remembered to bring from my back seat.

My first impression was I probably wouldn't find anything. I started with the frame of the vehicle first and, as I walked around it, I envisioned the burning of the car and Fred running through the field to get away from it. I arrived back at my starting point without seeing anything of note. I decided that I was going to have to get dirty, and getting down on all fours I started an inch-by-inch search starting from where I placed my notebook on the ground. I worked my way to the frame and then back out to the outside edge of the burned area. I did this for most of the morning, with only a few breaks to smoke a cigarette and drink some coffee, but found nothing.

I was almost done with one side and was about to turn the corner of it where it looked like the remains of an engine sat in the middle of the burned-out frame. As I started down the driver's side of the frame, I noticed that the sun was high in the sky, it was a clear day, and that meant I was in for a hot one. I continued in my search stopping only to wipe the sweat

from my brow. It was during one of my pauses to wipe my sweat that I noticed a shiny piece of metal glittering in the sunlight. It lay inside the frame of the vehicle, on the ground, just behind the engine.

I picked it up, sat back on my haunches and pulled my shirttail out to wipe it off. It appeared to be the vehicle identification tag and most of the numbers were legible, but it was broken on the right-hand end. Marking the spot where I'd left off, I backed out, very careful not to disturb anything around me. Placing the piece of metal into a baggie, I closed it up tightly and put it down next to my notebook. This was the piece of evidence I needed to prove this vehicle was, indeed, the one that belonged to Diane. But I needed the whole tag to be absolutely sure.

Going to the exact spot I had left off, I worked my way around the rest of the burned frame. Nothing. Dusk set in and I was exhausted. I picked up the baggie with the piece of metal in it and the rest of my stuff and returned to my car. Taking the piece of metal out of the baggie to take another look, I was convinced it was what I thought it was. Smiling, I put it back into the baggie, pushed it down into the front pocket of my jeans, and started back down the road.

I looked at my watch. Seven o'clock. I knew Nick left the station to go home at 4:30, and I would have to wait for the next day to see him. I thought when I got home I should record the process I was going through in search of the truth behind these diaries. These kinds of things just don't happen in Vermont and I didn't want to forget anything about my search for the truth, or the process. I pulled into my driveway, tired from my long day in the sun, grabbed everything from the front seat, and went inside.

Dropping everything onto the kitchen table, I went into the bathroom and took a shower. As I dried off, I went to the table next to my bed and picked up a blank tape. I put on a clean pair of boxers and a T-shirt, walked over to the kitchen table and lit a cigarette as I sat down. I put the new tape into the recorder and pushed the record button. I recorded everything I had done up to this point. When I finished, I stared for a moment at the piece of metal, and smiled. I ate a peanut butter sandwich, and went to bed still smiling.

The next morning, after a quick breakfast, I headed into town to see Nick.

When I got to his office, I asked him if he'd had a chance to read the diaries. Nick said, "To tell you the truth, Larry, I did get started on them, but I haven't found anything strange about them yet."

"You must not have read too far into them yet."

"No, I haven't, Larry. But I will. What can I do for you? I know you just didn't come into town to ask me that."

"No, you're right. In the first diary, Fred mentioned a car he had burned up in one of his dreams. I went to see if I could find it."

Nick interrupted, and said, "Larry you just got done saying that he did it in a dream, so why are you wasting your time?"

"Like you said it's my time. I thought about it until I eliminated almost every place and then on the way home I passed Pine Island Road. I took a chance and went down to the end of it. I was just about to leave when I saw something behind the bushes. I walked over to see what it was. It was a burned-out vehicle."

"So, there's a lot of burned out cars all over the place."

"I went back yesterday and searched the whole area. I didn't find much at first, but then when it looked like I had been wasting my time, I found this."

I took the baggie from my pocket and threw it onto Nick's desk. He leaned forward, picked it up and looked at it very carefully. After a few moments, he said, "It looks like a VIN—vehicle's identification number. So what?" Steve came in just then, walked over to Nick's desk and set down some files.

Steve started out again, when Nick asked, "Steve, what do you make of this?" Steve took the baggie from Nick and took a good look at it.

"It looks like a vehicle ID tag. Most of the numbers are clear but the last few are missing." He gave it back to Nick and left.

Nick said, "Well, we all agree what it is Larry, now what?"

"Well I was thinking you could possibly run an inquiry through the Department of Motor Vehicles to see what you come up with."

Nick shook his head and smiled. "If it will stop you from wasting any more time on this wild goose chase, sure, I'll see what I can get for you. I'll give you a call when I get something."

"Thanks Nick, I certainly appreciate it." I stood up to shake Nick's hand. "I'll be waiting to hear from you."

"I should have it no later than the end of the day. Are you sure you only want me to check Vermont registrations?"

I opened the door to leave, and said, "Ha, Ha. Yeah, I'm sure."

I went home from the police station without stopping anywhere along the way. I got my notebook and tape recorder from the kitchen table on my way to the bedroom. The past week had been filled with more excitement than I was used to, and I was tired. I leaned back into my pillows and looked over the notes I had written. My eyes were becoming heavy, and the next thing I knew the phone was ringing. Still half asleep, I thought it was the alarm clock and searched frantically with my hand to turn it off, but then woke up enough to pick up the phone. I said, "Hello, Nick?"

"Hey, Larry, I got what you wanted and you can pick it up if you can get here by four-thirty."

"Okay, Nick. I'll be right in."

I looked at the alarm clock and realized that I had slept through the whole day. It was already four o'clock, and I jumped out of bed, grabbed my cigarettes, and went out to the car. I arrived at the police station with ten minutes to spare.

Following Nick back to his desk, I asked if there was any coffee made up. Nick said, "Sure, if you don't mind the bottom of the pot."

"I'll take anything at this point."

"I told you Larry, you should slow down. But no, you have to do it your way—the hard way."

I poured the coffee and walked over to Nick's desk. I sat down and he handed me a file folder. "Here's what you asked for. There must be close to one thousand entries."

I got up without saying anything, walked over to a table up against the wall, sat down, opened the file up, and started flipping through the pages, running my finger through the names as fast as I could. I turned, and asked, "Nick, do you have a highlighter?" Nick looked in his desk, took one out and tossed it across the room to me.

"Thanks!" It landed on the table, I picked it up and continued checking the list until Nick got up, and said it was time to go home.

"I don't know about you, but I'm starved."

"Thanks for everything, Nick, but I'm going home and finish checking this list." I picked up the file and headed for the door. I returned to the house, but not before stopping a minute to pick up a bite to eat at McDonald's.

Once home, I sat at the kitchen table eating my burger and fries, and continued to go through the file. I separated the pages containing the name I was looking for and continued on. By the time I finished going through the entire list I had come up with four pages, and each one contained a single entry with the name Diane. All of the others I set to one side. Starting with the first page, I began to look at the addresses that were listed for each one. On the third page, I found that this Diane lived in Shelburne, Vermont. The first two Dianes I looked at lived in White River Junction and Brattleboro. Turning to the last page, I saw that one lived in Bennington. The one I thought would be the best to start out with was the Diane Lewis who lived in Shelburne.

I picked up the telephone directory and started to check its listings for Lewis. I finally found a D. Lewis. But in Burlington, not Shelburne. Thinking to myself that she might have moved since the time she registered her car, I picked up the phone, and dialed the number. As the phone rang I

scribbled the number down on the computer sheet that listed her name. The phone rang about seven times before a female voice answered.

"Hello, Diane?"

"No, this isn't Diane. She hasn't lived here for over two years."

"I'm sorry. Do you happen to know where I can find her, or maybe a phone number where I can reach her?"

"Mister, I'll tell you what; if you find her you can give me a call. She left out of here with no notice and not telling me anything. She even owes me three hundred dollars, so please if you find her tell her to call me."

"Sure, no problem. So, let me get this straight. This is Diane Lewis you're talking about, and you said you haven't seen her since 1997?"

"That's right."

"Thank you very much for your time, Miss, and I'll tell her to give you a call if I find her. Good-bye."

A smile came to my face. I circled the girl's name on the list with her phone number and wrote the street address down from the phone directory. I had everything I thought I needed to convince Nick something real had happened.

Chapter 17

I spent the rest of that day at home going through the tapes and my notes to see if there might be anything I had overlooked. At the end of the afternoon, I put all my paperwork to one side and went to the refrigerator to make myself a ham sandwich. With the sandwich, I returned to the kitchen table to continue while I ate. I finished eating, picked up all my stuff and took it to the bedroom. I got onto the bed to mull over Fred and his diaries. I had come to the conclusion that I wouldn't be wasting my time to check out the other stories in Fred's diaries. But, I wasn't so sure I could. I decided it was time to tell Nick everything I had read, whether he had read the diaries or not. I didn't think that it would do any good, but hoped Nick had read them. Pushing it all to one side of the bed, I turned out the light and closed my eyes to go to sleep.

In the morning, I decided to call Nick. The phone only rang twice before the dispatcher picked up. I asked to speak with Nick, and was told to hold on and she would check and see if he was available. I knew what I was going to do, but I also wanted the support of my longtime friendship with Nick.

"Good morning, Larry. You weren't kidding about this Fred character, were you? I finished reading the first diary last night. What a creep!"

I answered, "So you do believe me. That's why I was trying to get you to read the diaries before now. I think they might help you in your investigation."

"At this point, Larry, I'm just saying this Fred guy was really weird and had a strange imagination. I'm really surprised that no one in his life noticed even the littlest bit. He must have put on a good show at his job, because what I've read makes it sound like he's not quite playing with a full deck."

"I'm glad you finally read it. You need to read the second one as soon as you can. This guy totally transforms into an entirely different, weirder individual, who I'm not sure is even him."

"I will, I will, I promise Larry. The first diary took me by surprise, so I'm sure the second one will also."

"Before you hang up Nick, listen to this."

"What's that?"

"You remember that report you got for me from the Department of Motor Vehicles? Well, something showed up on the list. There were four Dianes with VINs matching those numbers from the metal tag I found, all of

whom lived out of town. The closest one was in Shelburne, a Diane Lewis. I looked in the phone book to get her number, but I couldn't find a Diane Lewis living in Shelburne, but I found a D. Lewis in Burlington. Taking a chance, I called the number in the phone book. When the individual answered I asked if it was Diane Lewis. It wasn't, but she did tell me her name was Sue. Come to find out it was Diane's roommate and she went on to tell me that she hadn't seen Diane since Halloween night 1997. She told me Diane went to a party and she never returned. They hadn't been getting along too well and her roommate just figured she skipped without paying her share of the bills. It fits the story in Fred's diary, right down to the date of the entry."

"Larry, slow down for a minute. Are you saying you think that this guy Fred did everything he wrote down in his diary? You read it. It was stuff he had dreams about during the night and when he woke up he would write them down. Now you're saying he's a murderer?"

I started to get irritated. "Why not? With all the evidence pointing in that direction I have to believe he wasn't writing down his dreams—he was writing down what he had really done. I was thinking that his mind probably wouldn't let him believe he could have actually done something like that and he put it off as a dream."

"Aren't you getting a little far-fetched, Larry?"

"Maybe, but I'm going to find out."

Nick reminded me not to do anything stupid as we said our good-byes and hung up. My next step was to follow up on my phone call by paying a visit to Diane's roommate. I had a good idea of how to get there and started on my way.

I wasn't sure if Sue would talk to me, or if she would know anything that could be helpful. It was then I realized I really didn't know what I was looking for. I pulled up in front of the right address. I turned the car off, got out and walked up to the front door. I stood there for just a moment before knocking on the door.

As the door opened a chain lock on the inside of the door stopped it and a woman looked out. Before she could ask who it was, I said, "It's Larry. I'm the man who talked to you yesterday on the phone about your roommate Diane. I thought you might have remembered something else about her leaving, or maybe even have a picture."

The door shut for a moment and reopened. There standing in front of me was probably one of the last two people to see Diane. To make sure this girl didn't feel threatened by me, I backed off to what I thought was a safe distance from her. She said, "What is it you want, mister? I told you everything I know."

"I'm not sure, miss. Like I said, I thought you might have remembered something else that might be helpful in finding her. I remembered I didn't give you my phone number, so if you did remember something you didn't have any way to call me. When I found myself coming into Burlington, I thought I would stop and meet you personally."

"It's nice to meet you, but I haven't remembered anything more because there isn't any more to remember. The only other thing I remembered after you hung up was that her parents lived out of the state. What state or where I'm not sure. If you want you can come in and I'll check to see if I have a picture you can have."

I took just a few steps into the house and left the door open. Sue returned holding something in her hand.

"It's my only picture, but what the hell, you can have it. She's not my friend anymore."

"Thanks, and if I do find her I'll let you know." I backed out the front door as I shook her hand.

Now I had a face to put to the words Fred had written. On my way through Winooski, I had to go by Fred's old apartment. I felt the little hairs standing up on the back of my neck as they always did when I drove by his place.

Sitting back at the kitchen table reviewing the tapes yet once again, I heard a car pull into the driveway. It was Nick and Steve.

"Nick, Steve, to what do I owe the pleasure?"

"Is it okay to come in and talk for a bit Larry?" Stepping out of the entranceway, I motioned for them to come in.

"Have a seat. Can I get you anything to drink?"

"No thanks," they each said in turn. Nick sat across from me so he could look at my face as we talked and Steve sat off to the side. I pushed all of my stuff to one side and out of the way.

Steve asked, "What do you have going on here, Larry?"

"A little research, that's all." Looking around, Nick noticed the picture of Diane I had thumb tacked to the wall. Nick stood up to take a closer look.

"Larry, is this your sister, or a relative?"

"No, it's Diane."

Puzzled only for a moment, but long enough to hesitate before asking his next question, Nick sat down again and leaning over the table toward me, he asked, "Diane who?"

"The Diane from Fred's diary. I took the information from the Department of Motor Vehicles that I told you about and hunted her down. Finding out her roommate hadn't seen her, I took it upon myself to go and

talk to her. She didn't have much to add to our phone conversation, but she did give me this picture so I could put a face to the name."

"Are you serious?"

"Absolutely. I know you think this is about someone's imagination running wild, but there are too many coincidences."

"All right, Larry, just say you're right, what next?"

"You tell me." Nick stood up and walked back over to the picture on the wall. He took a long look at it, as if he was trying to remember what the diary said about this girl.

I saw the puzzled look on Nick's face and asked him to sit back down. I started the tape recorder and went back and forth from play to rewind until I found the spot where Diane was murdered. I turned the volume up and sat back in my chair until it finished. I fancied the look on Steve's face as that of someone listening to the detailed confession of a murderer.

Nick leaned forward to push the stop button. He looked at Steve, and then turned to look at me with a very serious expression. "I told you, Larry, I read the diary. I know you believe this girl was real and I've seen the piece of metal you found. Now I'm telling you, off the record, I think you might be on to something. I just need a little more proof to present it to the chief so I can justify the man power."

"You believe me?" It was a rush. "If you want, I'll take you to where I found the VIN tag."

"Sure Larry, let's go." We all stood up from the table and as I gathered my tape player and notebook, Nick reached for the picture on the wall.

"Hey, Nick that's my picture."

"Look Larry, if you want me to start looking into it seriously I'm going to need this picture to show my superiors. If you want I'll make you a copy."

"Thanks Nick. That'll be great."

Nick and Steve got into the front seat of the cruiser and I got in back.

Nick asked, "Where to?"

"Pine Island Road. When you get there turn onto it and go all the way to the end. The exact spot is somewhat hidden from the road."

As they turned onto Pine Island Road it started to rain and before we could even get halfway down the road it started to pour. Nick pulled over and we sat there in hope that it might be just another spring shower which would pass quickly as they usually did. A half hour passed and there was still no sign of it letting up.

Nick backed the patrol car onto the main road with the car facing in the direction of my house. I leaned forward, and asked, "Where we going?"

"I'm taking you home. We certainly can't see anything out there with all this rain coming down. We'll go out there tomorrow and I'll come and get you on the way."

"Don't forget my copy of her picture."

I ran through the rain to my front porch. Standing there, I watched the car pull out of the driveway. I hoped I wasn't being pushed to the side.

I got a beer out of the refrigerator and headed to my bed. I took off my sneakers, and leaned back into my pillows as if they would take away all my worries and stress. Reaching over to the nightstand, instead of grabbing the tape player, I turned the clock radio on and tuned in the easy-listening station. I finished the beer, and it wasn't long before I drifted off to sleep—still fully dressed.

I seemed to awake in a dark room that was just barely lit by overhead lighting. Looking around to see where I was I determined that I was still in my own bed, but it didn't appear to be my house. I started to become nervous about the uncertainties of my predicament and heard a voice call my name. I looked all around to find the person who was calling me. Not sure, but thinking it sounded like a female, I relaxed. Still searching all around for the individual calling me, I felt a presence straddling me. For some reason, unknown to me, I couldn't resist or ward off this presence. I looked to see who or what might be sitting on top of me. I couldn't make it out until whatever it was seemed to be face to face with me. I realized that it was a young girl. Not having a clear view of her face left me to wonder who it might be, but as I became aroused it really didn't seem to matter.

It was then that I clearly saw a naked, young female and I was going to let her do anything she wanted to. Her breasts were young and firm, and I could see her nipples were erect as she placed them close to my face. As she did this I felt myself getting an erection and, dream or not, I was going to have sex with this girl. She continued on, caressing my neck while at the same time reaching down between our bodies to put me inside of her. It took a lot for me to get off as she moved herself up and down on my erection. Soon it became apparent to me she was starting to have an orgasm and I did all I could to assist her. In the middle of what appeared to be her orgasm the young lady leaned over to my right ear. She started to caress it and said, "Don't forget us. Search and the truth will come to you."

I grabbed her by the shoulders to push her away and as I did, I got a clear look at her face. It was Diane. I sat up in my bed in a cold sweat. With my heart racing, I looked all around the room from my bed to see if what I had just experienced was real or a dream. I didn't see anybody.

Leaning back into the pillows, I lit a cigarette and tried desperately to remember the details of the dream. It was then I noticed I was moist down around my crotch. Pulling my sweat pants away from my body to take a look, I saw I had ejaculated all over myself.

I went to the bathroom to wipe myself off. Shaking from the shock that a dream could do this to me, I returned to bed. The only thing I could come up with was that Diane's spirit had just visited me to tell me to continue on with what I was doing. She told me to continue looking for the truth and I would find it, but what did she mean when she told me not to forget them. Forget who? Was she talking about all the others? I finished my cigarette, put it out, and leaned back into the pillows with a new sense of direction. I vowed to myself I wouldn't give up trying to prove what was in the diaries as fact, and that Fred or somebody really had murdered these people. I closed my eyes, and fell off to sleep uninterrupted by any more dreams until the alarm clock went off at seven o'clock.

The next morning Nick called before I even had my breakfast and told me to meet him and Steve at Pine Island Road in five minutes. I said I'd be there and got dressed, grabbed my coffee cup and car keys from the kitchen table, and set out. As I drove to the road to meet them, I wondered about the dream I'd had. Thoughts of whether it was real or a dream ran over and over through my mind until I just decided to take it for what it was. Maybe it was just my subconscious telling me to go on in my search for the truth about Fred. I pulled up to the side of the cruiser, rolled down my window, and Nick said, "Larry, we'll follow you to the spot where you found the car, okay?"

"Yeah, sure."

It wasn't long before we arrived at the end of the road.

The detectives started to look.

"It's over here behind the bushes," I said.

All three of us walked to the area where I had found the burned wreckage. The two detectives walked around it for a few minutes as I stood out of the way, and after they discussed it between themselves I saw Nick talking into his car radio.

Nick came over to where I was standing as Steve continued to search around the wreckage. "Larry, I let Steve read the first diary the other night as I went on to the second one. After talking to you and seeing the evidence you found, we decided to look into it. I'm not saying the diary is an actual account of what this guy Fred has done, but there are a lot of coincidences that tend to make us believe you may be right. Now, you haven't talked to anyone about this except us, right?"

"Look, Nick," I answered, "You let me read the diaries in confidence didn't you? When I found what I found, I came directly to you."

"Okay, Larry. I just called dispatch to get in touch with the Colchester and State police. I told them I wanted them to meet us out here so they could start a crime scene search, but you're going to have to leave before they arrive."

I looked at Nick in surprise. "Yeah, no problem Nick, but I have one more thing to ask of you first."

"What's that, Larry?"

"I need to find out if there is any missing person report on a Kris Lackly. Is that possible?"

"Sure Larry, but why?"

"She was Fred's second victim."

Nick called his dispatcher to check for a missing person report on Kris Lackly, then turned to me and said, "Give her a few minutes."

I lit a cigarette. After a few minutes Nick's radio crackled back to life and he said, "Sorry, Larry, there isn't anything on a Kris Lackly. You better head out before the rest of them get here. I'll give you a call later."

"Thanks, Nick. I'll be waiting to hear from you."

As I walked back to my car I knew the next one was going to be just as difficult as Diane's was to prove.

At home, I went inside to get my notebook and tape player from the kitchen table. Back out in the car, I pushed the play button to hear how Fred got to Kris's house. As I went down Malletts Bay Road toward Winooski, I saw the crime scene investigation truck pull onto Pine Island Road. Going past Fred's apartment building started to become routine for me and it didn't seem to bother me as it once had. The tape said, "Go to the interstate and get on going north. Then get off at the Fletcher exit. Go through town on the main road and continue out of town for twenty minutes. Pull into a driveway on the left-hand side of a dirt road."

Chapter 18

I remembered I had been here once before when I took Pat from the hospital to his mother's house. As I drove through the main intersection of town, I recognized where I had turned to go to her house, but according to the directions I had to continue straight ahead out of town.

Twenty minutes later I saw a dirt road up on the left and decided it must be the one I was looking for. It didn't take me long to discover I had turned into a farmers' field, and I headed back for the main road. Stopping just short of the main road, I looked to see if I could see another road. I didn't, so I drove along the main road in the same direction I had headed when I decided to turn off. As I went around a bend I saw a road sign coming up on the left-hand side of the road. When I was right on top of it I saw it was indeed a dirt road and probably the one I was looking for.

I turned and drove slowly so I wouldn't miss the house. About three miles along I saw a mailbox on the right-hand side of the road, and a driveway, which I passed, and continued down the road to see if there were any other houses close by. There weren't, but I did notice a spot on the left-hand side of the road which had been used by others to turn around. Pulling into the spot to turn around, I remembered that Fred had pulled into a similar spot to hide his truck.

I put the car into park, turned off the engine, and walked into the woods. I started looking for any signs indicating that someone had been there previously. I must have been fifty feet or so off the road when I noticed tree branches and shrubs that had been broken or bent over. I also noticed what looked like tire tracks, partly smeared, but still recognizable. The spot where Fred parked the truck? I headed back to my car, turned around, and headed back in the direction I had come.

Near the driveway I pulled to the side of the road and parked. I walked over to the mailbox and saw that it read Lackly. As I headed up the driveway I could see that the house sat behind trees and shrubs, making it nearly impossible to see from the road. I got close enough to see that someone was home, and went around behind the house where a car was parked by the back door.

As I reached out to knock on the door the inside door opened. Ron was standing just inside the doorway, and asked, "Can I help you?"

I responded, "Hi, Mr. Lackly. My name is Larry Stone and I'm a local Burlington area reporter looking into the occurrence at your place of business last week. Do you have a few minutes?"

Ron smiled and said, "I sure do, but I want to be honest with you. I don't know too much about what went on. My manager probably knows more than I do." Ron offered me a drink, but I refused it and followed him to the living room.

Not sure how to question Ron about his wife and wondering if she was even missing, let alone dead, I asked vaguely what he knew about the incident at The Mill. He told me everything he had been told by his manager and the police. Sitting there talking with Ron, I listened for any noise or commotion that would tell me somebody else was in the house. I heard nothing.

"So, Ron how's your wife Kris doing?"

I immediately regretted this fumbling approach, but after a moment, with no quiver in his voice, he said, "Kris no longer lives here. We're getting divorced."

"You are?"

"Yeah, she left me last February on President's Day weekend. I left to go to Montreal and when I came back she was gone. We were having problems long before that, though."

"I'm sorry to hear that. I want to thank you for taking the time to answer my questions. Whatever went on at The Mill was weird and I'm just trying to figure out what really happened."

"It sure is weird. Why anyone would want to do something like that in my building is beyond me."

I shook Ron's hand, thanking him again for his time. He followed me to the door to let me out.

A few yards away from the end of the driveway there was a barn. "Nice barn," I said.

Ron smiled, and said, "It sure is."

"What kind of livestock do you keep?"

Laughing again, he said, "It's not really livestock. I have a couple of horses I keep in there."

"Would it be all right to take a look at them? Because I sure would like to."

"Sure."

What Fred had written in his diary started to flood my mind. Ron opened the door and reached in to the right side of the doorway and turned on the lights. We first stopped at the stall on the right-hand side of the barn, and Ron told me about the horse that was stabled there. On the opposite side, we came to the second stall. The stable door, the location in the barn, and the distance from the house was exactly as Fred had said. On my way back to my car I actually counted the steps to the house. As I thanked Ron

for showing me his horses, I couldn't believe it really was approximately seventy-five feet from the barn to the back door.

As I headed toward the main road and town, I picked up the tape player, pushed the play button—listened to my recorded voice read the pages containing the description of Kris Lackly's murder. I turned off the machine and put it back on the passenger's seat with a smile on my face. I was confident I had been in the house and barn Fred had described, but there was one question on my mind: Why didn't Ron seem concerned about his wife's whereabouts? The only thing I could figure out was they must have had some truly bad marital problems and Ron just said, "Fuck it."

It was getting dark out as I drove down the interstate headed for the Winooski exit. As I came to the stop sign at the end of the ramp, the McDonald's sign lit the sky and sent a hunger signal to my belly. I turned off the exit, pulled up to the drive-thru window and ordered my dinner. Within minutes I had the gourmet meal in a brown paper bag lying on the front seat next to me.

Coming up to Pine Island Road, I saw police crime scene tape across the access to the road and wooden roadblocks up, preventing anyone access.

At home, I took a couple of bites of my gourmet meal while I dialed Nick's house number and waited patiently for him to pick up his phone. I got no answer. I decided to call the station even though it was after hours. Maybe something else was found at the scene of the burned-out car I had missed. The phone rang only a couple of times before the dispatcher answered it and I asked her if Nick was still there. "Yes, Nick is still here, but he's in a meeting. Can I give him a message?"

"Please tell him to give Larry a call at home before he leaves."

The dispatcher asked if Nick had my number and told me she would give him the message as soon as she saw him. I thanked her and hung up.

Ten minutes later Nick called back.

"Larry, I've been trying to get in touch with you since earlier this afternoon. Where've you been?"

"Why? I've been out of town for the day, and on my way home I saw Pine Island Road all roped off. What's up?"

"Well, after looking around for a little bit I decided to call the state police crime scene team in. As they were looking around I remembered Fred said he took the plates off and destroyed all other paperwork that could connect Diane with the car."

"Yeah, so…"

"I suggested to the leader of the crime scene team that they perform an informal grid search of the surrounding area. They were at it a couple of hours when one of the officers shouted that he had found a license plate.

Larry, it was no more than a hundred feet from the wreckage, in the direction of Winooski."

"Are you kidding?"

"No, and when we got back to the office and ran the plate through the Department of Motor Vehicles it checked out as registered to a Diane Lewis. I immediately radioed the search team to rope off the area and to continue their search."

"I told you, Nick. These stories aren't a fabrication of anyone's mind. They're the real things. Now what?"

"Like I said, we are going to continue searching the area. And you and I need to get together to talk this out. Steve thinks it's just a coincidence and doesn't believe the diaries have any basis."

"And what do you think, Nick?"

There was a small moment of silence, and then, "I think you were right the whole time."

"Well, Nick, the story doesn't just end there. I did some more checking into the diaries and I was going to ask you over tonight to tell you about it."

"I'll be over as soon as I can finish up here. I'll probably leave around eight o'clock."

"I'll be waiting for you."

I hung up the phone, got all my information out, laid it on the table, and made notes of everything I'd seen that day.

Sitting at the kitchen table, I glanced at the clock on the wall. It was five of eight and I began to get anxious for Nick's arrival. At that same moment there was a knock at the door.

"Hi, Nick, come on in."

"Thanks Larry. Isn't this some shit we got ourselves into?" He sat at the kitchen table and I walked over to pour some coffee for both of us. "I don't need any of that stuff. I'm already wound up tight as a ten day clock."

"When you get done hearing what I have to tell you, you'll need it. You think your day is almost over, but just wait until you hear what I have to tell you."

Nick picked up his coffee, took a sip, and asked, "What do you mean?"

I told Nick that since I had convinced him of the first murder, I figured it would be easy to convince him of the second one.

"The second one?"

"Yeah, the death of The Mill's owner's wife. In the diary Fred called her Kris." I went on to explain that I had driven up to Fletcher to try and find the scene of the next murder based on what was written in Fred's diary. I told him that I had, indeed, found the road described in the diary

and the spot where Fred had actually parked the truck. "There were some tire tracks still up there. Most of them were brushed over or destroyed, but there were some that were pretty clear."

"Speaking of trucks, we got lucky and found Fred's truck. An officer on routine patrol spotted it, and when he called in the plates he was told the truck was registered to Fred. We have it in the police garage, taped up."

"Where did you find it? Was there anything in it?"

"About three blocks from his brother's house, brought it to the station, and started looking for any kind of evidence. We didn't come up with anything that would help us determine what happened at The Mill yet, and now I feel we need to go through again because of what we know about Diane."

I started to pace the floor trying to remember the spot where Fred wrote he had left his truck when he went to Pat's house. I sat back down and said that the tire tracks weren't the only thing I had found while I was up there.

"I found Ron and Kris Lackly's house on that same road. The tracks were within walking distance of their house, just as he described in his diary. I took a chance and knocked on the door. Ron was there and told me his wife had left him. The funny thing is that it was around the same time Fred said he had gone up there to rape and kill her President's Day. When he returned from his weekend trip she was gone with no indication why or where she went. Ron explained they were having serious marital problems and believing she'd left him, he filed for a divorce rather than a missing person report."

Our conversation went back and forth for a while and finally Nick said, "Well, Larry, obviously there is more to the diaries than I thought. I haven't figured out who this Paul character is or what he has to do with the whole picture, but if we continue to look I'm sure we will find out."

Nick stood up from the kitchen table, stretched and reminded me that none of what we discussed could be released yet. I reassured him that the confidentiality we had as professionals and friends would stand as far as I was concerned.

On his way to the door, Nick turned to me and said, "I guess I better head up to Fletcher tomorrow and see if I can find out anything about Ron's missing wife."

"I'll talk to you tomorrow, Nick. Have a good night and thanks for stopping."

"Night, Larry. Thanks for your help with all of this. If it hadn't been for your persistence I don't know if I would have followed up on it."

I chuckled smugly, and said, "That's what friends are for, Nick."

I went back to the kitchen table after getting myself a beer from the refrigerator. I fast-forwarded the tape to find the section that detailed the rapes and murders of the family in Massachusetts. The weird thing was that these entries were written by "Paul." Who was he? Paul was also an important character in the disappearance of Kris Lackly, but in that portion of the diary the story went back and forth between Fred and Paul so much that it was hard to keep up. I believed Diane Lewis was killed out of Fred's anger and delusions about his mother. With the disappearance of Kris Lackly, though, I couldn't really figure out who was doing what, or why.

My attention was drawn back to the tape as it played on to the part that described entering the house and rendering the woman helpless. The details of this situation had so many similarities to the one that involved Kris Lackly that it started to give me the chills. There was one difference though. This time he involved the whole family. I felt myself getting aroused as the rapes unfolded, but feeling a little disgusted at being aroused by the plight of these women, I started to take notes on the clues given in the diary about the location of the next abduction. I knew it was in Riverside, Massachusetts, but pinpointing the exact location was going to prove to be a problem.

I did the same as I had with the other two abductions. I stayed up to the early morning hours, playing the tape over and over again to get whatever information I could. I never made it to my bed that night, but instead fell fast asleep at the kitchen table with pencil in hand. I woke up to the phone ringing, and looked at the clock on the kitchen wall to see what time it was. It was 12:30 in the afternoon. I shook my head and picked up the phone.

"Yeah, hello." Nick's voice came through the receiver bringing me to my senses very quickly.

"Larry, are you sleeping? Listen, I went up to the Lackly's house early in order not to miss him. He gave me the same story and when I asked why he didn't file a missing person report he changed the subject to the validity of my jurisdiction in the matter."

"What did you tell him?"

"Nothing that would give away my investigation, but I explained to him what had happened at The Mill might have involved Fred. I needed to talk to everyone and anyone who had any contact with Fred, that's all. You're right though; it fits the description in the diary. Steve and I are going back up there to pour some plaster into those tracks you found."

"Is there enough there to match it to anything?"

"There sure is. We'll get a good impression. Give us a few hours and when we get back we'll make a comparison to Fred's truck and I'll give you a call."

"Okay, I'll be waiting."

Hanging up the phone, I knew what they were going to find out from that plaster cast. Was it Fred, or was it this other person Paul who was driving? Could we be dealing with a possession, or a case of multiple personality disorder? No sane person would be going out and committing these violent acts, so it had to be one of the two, but which one? Or something else? Rereading my notes and listening again to the recording of the diary gave me evidence of both, if that's possible. I figured the only way I would get any answers to these kinds of questions would be to contact professionals. The University of Vermont has a large medical program, so I figured Burlington would be a good place to start my quest.

I got out the phone book and checked the yellow pages. After several phone calls I finally found two individuals who might be helpful. I tried a paranormal psychologist first. I got through and briefly explained that I was doing some research for an article I was writing on possession and its effects. He agreed to see me at 5:00 that afternoon. So far, so good.

The second doctor I called was a clinical psychologist who had a very busy schedule, but I wouldn't take no for an answer. I had to understand multiple personalities and wasn't going to hang up without an appointment. He finally agreed to see me first thing the next morning. He said he would be able to give me a half hour or so prior to his first appointment.

Chapter 19

On my way to Burlington's Medical Center, as I drove past Pine Island Road, I noticed the roadblocks were still up and there was a policeman still positioned at the end of the road. I thought to myself, Nick was really starting to take this seriously, but would he if he found out it was a possession? I was ready for anything, but was Nick?

I found the experimental psychology department on the top floor. The woman behind the reception desk asked if she could help me and started to hand me forms necessary for new patients to fill out before being seen. I said, "I'm the person who called to see if it would be possible to ask Dr. Bloomberg a few questions about the subject I'm writing a paper on. He told me he would be able to give me a few moments of his time."

She answered, "Oh, yeah, now I remember. I'll give him a call and let him know you're here. You can have a seat over there while you wait."

"Thank you."

It didn't take long for the doctor to come out to the reception area to get me. I followed him back to his office where I took a seat in front of his desk. The doctor sat down behind his desk and leaned back as if he was also using this time to relax from a busy day. "I'm writing a paper on the subject of possession. I need to know specifically if it can actually happen and if it has ever been documented."

The doctor explained that there had been numerous cases of demonic possession documented throughout the years by reputable people with incontrovertible evidence on which they based their conclusions. He continued on about various individual cases.

I asked if it would be possible for the thing possessing the person to take total control over that individual. Again the doctor started to recite case after case of incidents that had occurred in the past, and told me about the most recent case he was aware of which had occurred no more than two years ago. As I finished writing, I looked up, and asked, "How is one to know whether or not it is a possession or a split personality?"

The doctor thought for a few seconds about the question, and answered, "It can sometimes be really tough and requires extensive examination before something like that can be determined. Sometimes a person who has been diagnosed with a split personality adopts this personality, letting it possess every aspect of their life, so in a sense it should be considered a possession. Whereas a demonic or spiritual possession—which is to say that a being from another plane of reality, such as a ghost or the soul of someone who has died, takes complete control over

a individual's life—is different. It wouldn't be gradual as in a split personality, but rather a change that occurred all at once. One would see drastic and uncontrollable deviations in the individual's life. That is not to say that a possession of this type might not happen gradually, but it is highly unlikely." Looking at his watch, the doctor explained that this was all the time he could afford to give me, and said, "If you need additional information feel free to call again."

I got up, reached over the desk to shake the doctor's hand, and thanked him for his time. By the time I arrived at my car, I still was unsure of what might have been going on with Fred at the time the diaries were written. Driving home past Fred's apartment and Pine Island Road, I had almost convinced myself Fred might actually have been demonically or spiritually possessed. I thought that maybe I was getting a handle on what might have happened to Fred, but why?

I went inside and threw the keys along with my cigarettes onto the table. I started a small pot of coffee so I would be able to keep awake. No more than ten minutes had gone by before the telephone rang.

Nick said, "Hey Larry, I thought you might like to know the cast we took from the wooded area up near the Lacklys' home matched Fred's truck front passenger-side tire. Unfortunately this is not really solid proof Fred was the only person who was up there."

"Then I guess we still don't have any real proof?"

"Well, we do sort of, because it does match in every detail, and we still don't have any valid reason from Ron Lackly as to why he never filed a missing person report. Whether or not Ron Lackly cared where the hell his wife had disappeared to, doesn't mean that we aren't curious. He could actually believe that she just up and left; not considering that anyone would do what is written in the pages of Fred's diary."

I didn't mention the appointment I had that day. I wanted to gather all the information I could before broaching the subject. I really didn't think Nick would believe that Fred was possessed as easily as he would believe he had a split personality. I wanted to review the diaries as I gathered the knowledge of both possibilities and come to a conclusion myself before trying to convince Nick to see it one way or another. I hung up the phone and returned my attention to the tapes. But the coffee I had made was not doing its job. Finally, I went to bed. As I lay there quietly everything ran through my mind and before going off to sleep I had convinced myself Fred was possessed.

The next morning, I realized that I actually came to the conclusion that Fred was possessed days ago after the experience I had while I slept. The sexual encounter with the girl who looked like Diane from the diary was as real as it gets. Having actually had an orgasm along with her telling

me not to forget them was enough for me to believe. Nobody, but nobody would ever be able to convince me it was anything else.

I took my keys and cigarettes from the table as I ran out the front door, jumped into my car and took off for my morning appointment with the second psychologist. I knew exactly where to go because I had seen the doctor's name on the sign in the lobby when I was there the day before.

At the nurse's station on the second floor, a nurse asked if she could help me and I informed her I had an appointment to see the doctor. She asked my name and told me that she would let the doctor know I was here waiting to see him. I thanked her for all her help and took a seat in the waiting area.

I had just barely opened a magazine when the doctor came out to get me. We introduced ourselves to each other and as we did I thanked him for seeing me on such short notice. The doctor told me that it was no real problem as long as we were done before his first appointment came in. I followed him to his office explaining that I only had a few questions that I needed answers to. The doctor held his office door for me to enter as he told me to have a seat. I kiddingly asked, "Not the couch, I hope?"

"Not unless you have something you want to discuss other than your essay."

He began by asking me to explain what I was going to do with the information gained from this interview. I told him I was simply writing a paper on the adverse effects of someone having a split personality. How it affected their life and the lives of those around them. I went on to explain that I didn't need any detailed specifics about any one case study and that I only needed general answers to a few questions I had. I took my notebook from my side and opened it.

I asked, "Does a split personality develop all of a sudden, or is it something that comes over someone gradually?"

"Split personalities are something that develop over many years and generally develop due to some kind of trauma in the individual's life."

"Trauma?"

"Something in their life they saw or experienced that they wish to forget."

"Is this condition something that can take over and control an individual's life?"

"Yes, but it is very rare that the other personality dominates the individual. Usually the other personality takes over when confronted by something that resembles the trauma that caused it. It can also take over when faced with the same level of stress created by the first traumatic experience."

"So then, the other personality, as you call it, could never control an individual in their everyday activities for an extended period of time?"

"I have heard of such things, but there is no documentation supporting such a finding. If it happens it is very rare."

I thought a moment, trying to formulate another question, when the doctor looked at his watch and stood up. Explaining that he was sorry, he said the time was getting close to his first patient's appointment. I told him I understood and greatly appreciated the time he took. The doctor said, "I hope I was able to give some insight on the subject, and if you need more time, please feel free to call and set another appointment. I'll be glad to help all that I can."

I left his office and as I headed to the elevators to leave I was more than certain now that Fred was possessed. The only problem I faced was to get Nick to believe it.

At home, I noticed the light blinking on the answering machine. I pushed the play button and heard Nick's voice asking me to give him a call at the station as soon as possible.

I picked up the phone and dialed Nick's number. It didn't take long for Nick to pick his phone up. "Hey Larry, what have you been up to?"

"Not much, how about yourself?"

"Well if it would be all right, Steve and I would like to come out to visit for a while."

"Sure, I plan on being here the rest of the day."

"We're on our way."

Twenty minutes later Steve and Nick were standing on the porch. Asking them to come in, I offered them a seat at the kitchen table and pushed everything to one side to get it out of their way. "It sure looks like you've been busy," Nick said.

"Yeah, but I'm sure you have, too. Have you figured anything out yet?"

"Yeah, we sure have." Steve said, "This Fred character is a real nut case and may have murdered three people and himself with no apparent reason."

Nick took a notebook from his shirt pocket. "We know that it was Fred's hand at The Mill; the burned out car was right where he described it would be; the girl called Diane is missing; the tire prints by Ron Lackly's house were the same as Fred's truck, and Ron's wife is missing."

Nick went on to explain he and Steve went back up to Ron Lackly's house to further explore the possibility that she didn't run off with someone else. They explained to Ron that after talking to all of her friends and family they discovered that she was having an affair. After finding out who it was and after talking to him, they dropped the possibility that she ran off

with him. "We ended up finally convincing Ron there was something strange about his wife's disappearance and advised him to file a missing person report. Is there anything new with our newest police investigator?"

I answered, "Look, I'm just trying to help. If you don't want my help, Nick, then I'll stop and let you all figure it out."

Steve said, "Larry, don't get all upset. Nick was just kidding with you. We hope you realize that we are very thankful for all your help."

"All right, if I tell you what I've been trying to figure out you have to promise to listen to it all before you come to any conclusions."

"We give you our word that we won't interrupt or comment until you are through. Right, Steve?"

"Yeah, sure. Why not."

"I had the weirdest dream, a dream like I never had before. While I slept that night after taking you both to Diane's car I was visited by what I believe to be the spirit or ghost, or whatever you want to call it, of the girl described as Diane. She was naked on top of me and after she had gotten me and herself off sexually, she leaned over whispering in my ear not to forget her and the others. I went to the bathroom and found out that I actually did get off in my sleep. I know by looking at your faces you don't believe me and that I just probably had a wet dream, but let me finish. That next day I went up to the Lackly's and found what I told you I found. It was all falling into place as it was written in the diaries. No, we don't have any solid proof, but everything else I've found out is true to the words he wrote. It was after you told me that the tire tracks matched Fred's truck it seemed to be all coming together. So I made two appointments with two different doctors to find out what I could about split personalities and possession. After talking with them I have come up with the only explanation of this person Paul showing up in the diary. The spirit or ghost of a person by the name of Paul had possessed Fred. Why, I don't know. That is all I have up to this point, but I will tell you as I find out more."

Steve and Nick took a long look at each other before either one of them said anything. Nick asked, "Larry, you want us to believe this guy named Fred was possessed by a ghost by the name of Paul? If it were true, why him? That dream you told us about, we all have had them at one point or another in our lives, or at least most men have. There has got to be a more reasonable explanation to all the things that we have been coming across. I can't go to my superiors and tell that we need a cross and silver bullets to solve this case. They'll laugh me out of the station."

"Look, Nick, I'm just telling you what I've come up with and where I'm going. If you don't want to believe me that's your decision, but I've got to go with my gut feeling. There is no way Fred was normal like you and me. The doctors I spoke to—without breaking our confidentiality, by the

way—led me to believe that if he had a split personality, it wouldn't have been Paul who was writing all the time in the diary. The other personality doesn't take over total control of the individual as it does with a possession."

There was silence. Nick stood up and then Steve stood up, rubbing their heads as if they didn't know how to respond to what I said. As they walked toward the door, Nick turned around, and said, "Look, Larry, tomorrow I'm getting a warrant to search the Lackly's house and property. I don't believe the story that this woman just walked away from it all. All the people I talked to say she isn't like that."

"I never believed that story myself, but why Ron wasn't more concerned I still can't figure out. While you're doing that I think I'm going to look into the other murders." Steve had gone out to the car while Nick and I talked on the front porch.

"Larry, those other murders happened in two other states—supposedly. I won't be able to do anything for you."

"If I find anything, I'll let you know and then you can notify the authorities." Nick stepped off the porch and walked to the car shaking his head.

"Good luck, Nick."

Nick opened the door and before he got in, he said, "Yeah, buddy. You too."

I spent the rest of the day checking over the tapes and my notes to make sure I knew where to go and what to look for. Actually I already knew what had to be done, but I hadn't decided to put my heart and soul into it until I heard once more the grisly details that involved that young girl. I went to bed knowing I wasn't sure I was ready for what the future had in store for me, but I was determined to get to the bottom of all this.

Chapter 20

I felt as though I had been revived or reborn. It seemed as if it had been weeks since I had been able to get a good night's sleep without being disturbed.

I packed a bag with at least two weeks' worth of clothes and all my notes and tapes along with the tape recorder. Just as I was about leave, I went back into the house and got my camera. As I left my driveway, I started to get excited about what I was on my way to do.

I drove the familiar route to the interstate Fred had taken to get to Riverside, Massachusetts and Fletcher. At Pine Island Road I felt something change inside me. I no longer felt my hair standing up, as if I was getting used to all of this. The police tape had been taken down and there was no longer a policeman standing guard at the end of the road. On my way through Winooski I wondered if I should be doing all this on my own. As I got closer to the interstate, I began to lose my nerve, but the last opportunity to chicken out had gone by and I soon found myself on the interstate, headed south to Massachusetts. Before I realized it I was crossing the state line between Vermont and Massachusetts and started to become more confident with what I was doing. About thirty minutes or so later, I came to the Riverside exit. Exactly as Paul had written, the hotel he stayed at was just before you got into the downtown section.

As I entered the lobby of the hotel, I looked around and, seeing the resemblance to what Paul had written, I knew I was at the right place. I asked for a room for two nights and the clerk told me I was lucky because there was only one room left. I could have it if I didn't mind it being the smallest room in the place. I told her that would be okay. I also told her that I really wanted to stay here because a friend had told me it was the cleanest place he had ever stayed.

Handing me the key, she said, "Why thank you. We try real hard to please our customers. With all the larger motels and hotels nowadays it's hard to stay in business, and we have been real fortunate. Word of mouth has kept us alive." I took the key from her, turned around, and headed back to get my things from the car.

Opening the door to the room, I took a quick glance around; she wasn't kidding about it being small. I unpacked my files and tapes, spread them out on a little table in one corner, and got to work. The details were still unclear to me as to why this family. Even more disturbing was why Fred had included a child this time. All the other murders, even ones I hadn't investigated, involved only adults. The second thing that concerned

me was that if this family disappeared all at once, why is it that nobody had called the law? At least, I thought, other family members would be asking questions, filing reports…

I closed the file, pushed it to the side, and sat there mulling it all over. Could Paul have just wanted to kill time while waiting for his victim? I remembered the woman at The Mill say that he wasn't there for sex. Why would he do this then? It was then that I felt the hair on my arm rise. Did this episode of the diary show the two sides of Fred; Paul who went there to get his next victim and Fred who only wanted to have sex? Paul knew from conversations with his friends at The Mill that he needed to tend to business, but he had also explained to them how hard it was to completely control Fred's desires that were inside of him.

I listened to the whole story of Paul's trip here again and how he found his way around. I listened to the part telling about his arrival here at the hotel. March 6th was the date Paul started on his trip here.

On a hunch, I called the front desk. The same girl who checked me in came on the phone. "May I help you?"

"I told you my friend had stayed here. I need to know if I have the date right of his stay. Would you mind checking to see if on March 6th of last year a Fred Lamperee checked in?"

She told him that it would take a few moments for her computer to come up.

After what seemed an interminable pause, she said, "Sir, the computer is up. What is the person's name that you were looking for?"

"Fred Lamperee on March 6th. He might have used his middle name, Paul."

She replied, "That's what he did. There was a Paul Lamperee here on March 6th. He checked in around seven o'clock and…"

She hesitated for just a second when I asked, "And what?"

"I was just getting ready to say what room he stayed in. Isn't this a coincidence? He stayed in the same room that you are in now."

"The same room?"

"He sure did. Is there anything else I can help you with?"

"Yes there is. I would like a wake-up call for six o'clock."

I played the tape and found out I had taken good notes on how to find the company Paul went to and the house where the family lived. It was getting late and I knew I was going to have an early day tomorrow. I planned on going to the company first thing in the morning to see if it was really where it should be, according to the diary. I got up and went to the bed. I unknowingly had set myself up for a very restless night's sleep.

The moment my eyes closed, my subconscious kicked in and placed me at the murders I had been studying. I wasn't just going over the facts,

but I was actually there watching them as they took place. I tried to move closer to each bed, but I found I couldn't move. It was as if my feet had been glued to the floor. These flashes lasted for as long as the sex did. Each dream episode ended the same way. Paul would be in the process of raping them and as he finished he would turn to look at me and smile. These dreams continued throughout the night, constantly repeating and never changing except for one time. I jolted up in my bed in a severe sweat. I sat on the edge of the bed smoking a cigarette. The dream was the same as the others except this time he raped the young girl. She must have been seventeen or so. It looked as though the man raping these women was Fred, but I knew it was Paul and as he finished the last one, he turned to me and said, "See you soon, Larry."

I walked over to the table and sat down. I figured the dreams were a result of my being overtired and because of the fact that I was staying in the same room as Fred had came as a shock. The last part of my dream when Paul turned and said what he said stumped me. Since it was almost five o'clock I decided to stay up.

Listening once again to the tape, I went to the part in which the diary described the rape of the young girl. I went over it time and time again as I sat there waiting for my wake-up call. I couldn't find anywhere in my notes or from listening to the tape where it described the little girl in detail except for her breasts and the color of her hair. In the dream I saw every detail of her so vividly, as if it was a photograph. How could that be?

I went into the bathroom and took a shower. My day was just getting started a little earlier than I had planned. I turned off the shower and as I got out I heard the phone ring—my wake up call. After getting dressed I picked up my notebook and tape player, and took them out to the car. The lobby lights were on, so I went in to see if they had any coffee. When I walked through the door the smell of fresh brewed coffee filled my nostrils.

As I poured myself a cup of coffee, I heard a girl's voice saying good morning. I went over to the desk and with a smile told her good morning. She asked me if I would be staying another night. I told her I would probably be staying another couple of nights and by the time we had finished talking my coffee cup was almost empty. I took the last swallow and went over to the coffee pot to pour myself another one. On my way out I told the girl to have a good day and that I would probably see her later. This ordinary exchange cheered me considerably after my nightmare.

I got into my car and headed back toward the interstate where Paul said he turned down a side road leading to The Mill's corporate office. I drove all the way back to the interstate, and continued past it until I could safely turn around. The diary said he drove toward town until he saw a plant that was set off the road. It wasn't long before I could see it. Slowing

down, I started to look for the side road that would bring me to it. Sure enough, it was only seconds before I came to a road I thought was the one Paul was talking about. "THE MILL, INC. 5/10 MI." Said the sign. In the parking lot I sat a moment trying to figure out how to approach the situation.

I got out of the car and straightened my clothing to make myself look just a little bit more presentable. I headed to the door still trying to figure out what to say. A young woman behind a reception desk greeted me. She smiled politely, and asked, "Can I help you?"

I walked up to the desk with a smile on my face, and replied, "Yes, I would like to speak to the owner please."

She asked, "And you are?"

I told her who I was and that I just needed a few questions answered about their business for an article I was writing. The woman picked up her phone and told someone on the other end there was someone here to see them. Hanging up the phone, she said, "You can wait over there, if you want. Someone will be right out to talk with you."

I sat there for about five minutes or so wondering if I had made a mistake. I had asked for the owner and that, of course, was the person I had figured was Paul's third victim. Just as I finished my thought, a man came through the door from behind the receptionist's desk. I sized him up, looking at his features to determine if he looked similar to Ron, but he didn't. He approached me with his hand extended. "I'm very sorry, but Mr. Lackly is unavailable. I'm Alan Shackle, the vice president of the company."

Shaking his hand, I said, "Well that's okay. I can come back later. When would be a good time to come back so I could meet with him?"

Alan then told me that Mr. Lackly and his family went on an extended vacation as a graduation gift to his daughter and would not return until the end of summer. He went on to say that he would be more than glad to help me and answer any questions I had about the company. Caught off guard by his response, I told him I had to run out to my car to get my pad, going on to explain stumblingly that I really hadn't anticipated being able to see the owner until I'd made an appointment. "Back in a moment," I said.

Sitting back down in the chair I had just got up from, I pulled my pen out of my shirt pocket. I asked a lot of generic questions about their operation, size, and the number of employees they had. Thirty minutes or so went by and we seemed to be finishing up when I asked one more question.

"Out of curiosity, when did the Lackly family start in this business?"

"The family has been operating this business since 1917, in one form or another."

Thanking him for his time, I got up and started to leave. Alan said, "Here's my card if you need any more information. I'll be glad to answer what I can. I'm sorry Mr. Lackly wasn't here to meet with you."

"Thank you. I'll do that, and that's okay, it was just bad timing on my part. I got all the information I needed from you." I went out the door and got in my car.

As I drove from the parking lot and through the gate I couldn't help thinking this was why nobody knew what Paul had done. Or maybe he hadn't done anything; maybe he had just fantasized about doing it because of what he had already done. The only way I figured I was going to find out was to go out to where he said the house was to see if it was really there. If it was, there would be only one way Paul would know it and that would be because he had gone there. I knew Fred could have gotten the location of the office building easily by asking around at The Mill. I stopped just short of the main road and consulted my notebook.

Thumbing through it, I found the page where the directions to the family's house were. Within thirty minutes I found a house that was located in the general area Paul said it was but I wasn't going to let myself get excited just yet. I turned into the driveway and followed it around to the back of the house. There in front of me was a Lexus with the license plate, "Mill 2".

Nobody came out to greet me, but that wasn't odd if they were actually on vacation. I walked up to the back door and knocked. When no one came to the door I opened the screen door and knocked on the main door as loud as I could. On my last knock the door opened slightly. I stood there for a moment deciding what to do. I kept extra napkins from fast-food places in the car in case I would ever need one. I grabbed a couple of them, to avoid leaving any fingerprints, and my camera so I could take pictures of everything I found.

Returning to the house, I pushed the door open and went in slowly. I stood at the end of the kitchen's breakfast bar where Paul had overpowered the wife. Not noticing anything of much interest except what looked like scuff marks across the linoleum, I continued to walk carefully through the house. When I got to the stairway leading to the second floor I noticed there were two shoes on it, one was at the bottom and the other one on the fourth step. I continued up the stairway being careful not to step on the shoes. I came to a hallway at the top of the stairs. It was in the first room I came to that I found what I was looking for—the brass bed. I stepped into the bedroom. The first thing I noticed was that the bed was not made. This would stand to reason because Paul wrote he had taken all the linen when he left.

I found a family picture on one of the bureaus, put it in my back pocket and continued my search. Not really knowing what I was looking for, I did know I had better leave as soon as possible in case someone had seen me pull into the driveway. I walked around to the side of the bed. There was a slight stain on the mattress and I wondered if it might be a bloodstain. I took a quick look into the bathroom where he had supposedly cleaned the wife off, but found nothing. There was no clothing on the floor, no sheets, and only that slight stain on the mattress.

I decided I had better take pictures of everything as I found it. When I finished with that, I returned to the kitchen and found an envelope with a New York return address on it and the name Lackly. I took a Post-it and wrote it down, just as Paul had. Putting the paper into my pocket, I left the house, shutting the door just as I found it. I knew Paul had been there, because of all the details he wrote about—everything was the same as it was in his diary.

When I got back to town I pulled into a diner to get something to eat. I ordered lunch and went over in my mind all the things I had just seen. How would I convince Nick that these people were dead? I had taken pictures of everything inside and outside the house, which would at least show that somehow Fred or Paul knew exactly what he was talking about with respect to the details of the house and surrounding area. The man's coworkers thought they were on vacation, his brother Ron didn't mention anything, and the police were not yet involved. I ate as much as I could, paid for my meal, and got into my car to head back to the hotel.

When I arrived back at the room, I read everything I had written and then played the tape yet again. It was like being in the house I had just come from; every detail was exact. Instead of listening to the rapes again I fast-forwarded the tape to the part that gave the next address where Fred went. The tape told about a girl that was broken down on the side of the road that he stopped to help, but the next victim with an address lived in Mechanicsville, New York. Pulling the address from my pocket, I confirmed it was, indeed, the same address I had written down.

I planned to drive to New York and look up the woman Paul had written about, but I decided to stay until morning and get an early start.

I reviewed the part of the tape recounting Paul's trip to New York. I took very detailed notes about how to find this town and the woman's house. I also wrote down every detail about what her house looked like. When I felt as though I had all the information I would need, I turned the tape player off and closed my notebook. I lit a cigarette and tried to relax. I'd had a very stressful day, which included breaking and entering and confirming three murders. At least they were confirmed in my mind. Now I had to convince Nick.

I also remembered the dream that woke me up. Every little detail about the Lackly family murders I had seen as if I was there in the same room. I thought the dream could have risen from all the knowledge I had gained from the diaries, but when Paul turned and said, "See you soon Larry," I was stymied. Was it because of the room I was sleeping in, or all the other things I was going through, or was Paul sending me a message? Trying to figure all this out was also starting to exhaust me. I took a long walk around the town to clear my mind, had an early dinner and went to bed.

That night my mind played tricks with me once more, but instead of the murders I saw Fred talking to some people I didn't recognize. I was in a haze, and really couldn't make the individuals out. All I really knew was that there were two children standing with what looked like a man and a woman. I heard their voices as they talked and they seemed not to have realized I was there. I started to approach them from behind, but no matter how close I got I could not make out who they were. I decided to take a chance by getting a little closer, and as I did Fred turned his head. I stopped in my tracks and Fred laughingly said, "You think you know everything, don't you, Larry?"

I woke up and leaned over to see what time it was. It was only three o'clock in the morning but I decided to get up and smoke a cigarette. When I finished, I started to put out my cigarette in the ashtray. There were also two Camel non-filter cigarettes stubbed out in it. Paul's brand.

I threw the ashtray across the room. Trying to analyze the situation I paced the room back and forth. Should I try to go back to sleep or should I leave? I remembered something I had seen on a television show a couple of weeks ago. It was a show about forensic science and they said DNA could be retrieved from virtually anything.

I found the butts in the corner of the room lying on the floor and, using my pen, I pushed them into the cellophane wrapper I had taken off my cigarette pack. Were they actual proof that Fred was here? Maybe they belonged to the person who cleaned the room and that I hadn't noticed them when I got back. I returned to bed to try and get a few more hours sleep.

The morning came quickly. I threw my suitcase in the back seat of my car and put my notebook and tape player in the front. I then went into the lobby to return the key and sign the receipt. The girl behind the desk asked me if everything was okay with my stay and I told her everything was just fine. As I looked the bill over I told her I had found some cigarette butts in my ashtray that didn't belong to me. She looked puzzled, and said, "I'm sorry. I know we had a cleaning woman that was known to do that occasionally, but she quit six or seven months ago."

"It's no big deal. Thanks for everything."
She in turn replied, "Thank you and drive carefully."

Chapter 21

I stopped at a fast-food joint to grab a bite to eat, and sat in the car studying the road atlas to determine the most direct route to Mechanicsville, New York. I found my route and finished my breakfast. I couldn't figure out why I was having the dreams I was having. Maybe Paul was trying to tell me something. But, to look at it from Nick's perspective, it was probably just my over-active imagination. How would I convince Nick this family had fallen victim to Fred and then have it turn out that it actually wasn't Fred but Paul? I set out for the interstate and concentrated on my driving.

Across the state of Massachusetts, northbound on Interstate 87 past Albany, I started to see signs telling me how far I was from Mechanicsville. It was closer than I thought and before I knew it my exit was in front of me. I needed to look at my notes, and at the end of the exit ramp I saw a gas station and pulled in.

According to my notes, I needed to go back under the interstate and take the first right, and then the first left. I found Pickett Road exactly where the directions indicated. What I would do when I arrived at the woman's house never entered my mind, at least not until I turned the corner onto her street. I saw the same "DEAD END" sign that Paul did and figured I had better come up with something real quick. I pulled into the driveway, and saw a car parked near the house. I parked off to the side, and before I got out I wrote the license plate number down in my notebook.

I walked as casually as I could up to the front door and knocked, then waited there patiently and when no one came to the door I knocked again. Still no one answered and I started to look around the front of the house checking for broken windows or anything that might look out of the ordinary. Nothing looked out of place in the front of the house, and I started around back. Still I didn't see anything out of the ordinary and returned to the front of the house to knock once more. No answer. What should I do next? I didn't want to leave until I had a chance to look inside. How could I get in? I was just about to check under the welcome mat and flowerpot for an extra key when I saw an older man coming up the driveway.

I waited until he got closer. The man greeted me and asked, "Can I help you, sonny?"

"I don't know. I was traveling through and wanted to stop in to visit my grandmother, but it looks like she's not here. I started to leave when I figured I had better use her bathroom. She usually keeps a spare key under the mat."

Looking me in the eye as he spoke, the man said, "I'm Elroy. I'm your grandmother's neighbor and when I saw you drive in, I figured I'd better check who it was. You see, the misses and me watch the place for her when she's out of town. Funny thing is she didn't mention she was leaving this time and usually she does. The misses came over a while ago and saw her car, but didn't get no answer at the door or on the phone so we just figured she went someplace."

"Glad to meet you. My name is Fred and I'm from Winooski, Vermont. I'm sure glad that grandma has someone watching out for her."

I bent over to look under the mat for a spare key, but didn't find one. Standing back up, I said, "I guess grandma changed her hiding spot."

Elroy smiled, and said, "Oh, that key. She gave that one to ma and me so in case we needed to get in for something. Here it is. I keep it on my key chain all the time."

He handed me the key. I opened the door and gave the key back to him. "Thank you so much, Elroy," I said, sincerely meaning it.

"Don't mention it, I'm always pleased to help when I can. When you get done taking care of your business you're more than welcome to stop over for some coffee, if you'd like."

Smiling, I said, "Thanks, but no thanks. Since grandma isn't here, I'll just use the bathroom, leave her a note, and head back home. It was a real pleasure meeting you, Elroy, and thanks again."

"Not a problem, son. Drive careful." As the last of his words came out of his mouth, Elroy turned and headed back down the driveway. I remained standing on the porch in the open doorway still not believing how easy it was to convince him.

I thought to myself that I had better make it quick just in case he got suspicious and came back. It was then that I remembered I had left my camera in the car and ran back out to get it. I had sixteen shots left, and back in the house I started to take pictures of everything. I could take my time at home reviewing them.

I soon found the woman's bedroom. There were no sheets or blankets on the bed and the pillows were on the floor. Compared to how neat the rest of the house was, this didn't fall into place. Carefully stepping into the room I started to take pictures. I hadn't gone more than a foot into the room when I noticed brown spots on the side of the dresser. Thinking it might be blood, I took a close-up picture. I also noticed the same kind of spots on the hardwood floor. Click. Another picture. I stood up and looked at the top of the dresser I'd found the spots on. There were many small-framed photographs on it and some were standing upright and others had been knocked over. I thought to myself that this was probably where the picture had been that Paul took.

I was getting nervous, so I finished up the roll of film and headed out to leave. As I reached for the doorknob I stopped, pulled out my shirttail, and wiped the doorknob off in case I'd left any fingerprints. I wiped the outside doorknob the same way, shut the door behind me—locking the house.

As I drove away I looked to see if anyone was watching me as I drove down the road. I didn't see anyone, not even Elroy. At the stop sign I turned right and headed back for the interstate. It wasn't until I had actually gotten on the interstate that I started to relax.

About three hours later, about 15 miles south of Vergennes, I was cruising at a safe speed up Route 22A, listening to the radio when I heard a voice softly say, "You forgot one." I looked in my rear-view mirror to see if someone was in the back seat. I assumed I must be hearing things, and continued down the road. Ten minutes later, while a different song played, I heard the same voice repeating the message. I looked into the back seat again through the rear-view mirror. Shaking my head, I told myself that I must be going nuts. I made it back to my home in Malletts Bay safely at about 9:15 that evening.

I had gone too many days without a good night's sleep and decided it was time to have one. Setting the alarm clock was the last thing I could do before passing out completely dressed.

The next morning, I noticed the message light on my answering machine was blinking. Why I hadn't noticed it last night I wrote off to being mentally and physically exhausted from my trip.

I pushed the message button. The first one was a hang up, the second one was a telemarketing call, and the third call was from Nick. "Hi Larry. I had hoped that I would find you at home, but I guess you're not back yet. Call me when you get back, I got some news for you."

I reached down and pushed the erase button. "You've got some news?" I thought. "Wait until you hear what I've got."

While I showered I ran through everything I had come across on my trip and how I was going to present it to Nick. I knew I had to tell Nick everything, even my dreams. The murders were going to be hard to prove to Nick.

The first thing I did was take my film to a one-hour photo shop. I told the clerk I wanted two sets of prints and the man told me I was welcome to wait or come back for them in an hour. I saw a pay phone a few feet from the store and decided to call Nick. The dispatcher told me he hadn't arrived yet, but asked if I wanted to leave a message on his voice mail. I told her sure and left a message for Nick to meet me at my house as soon as he could, but not before ten. I then went into a bakery in the same shopping center to wait out the hour.

I finished eating and walked back to the photo shop. The man told me it would be a couple more minutes to finish printing the second set. I asked if I could see the first set while I waited, and he handed them to me. I started to thumb through them. They had all come out as I hoped. I hadn't finished looking at them all when the man came over and handed me the second set. I paid him, thanked him for printing them as fast as he did and returned to my house.

I took one set of prints to the kitchen table, where I sorted them into two piles, one for each crime scene, so when Nick got there it wouldn't confuse him.

Nick and Steve got there a little later. I told them to have a seat at the table and asked if there was anything I could get them. Both of the detectives declined anything and asked how my trip went. I sat across the table from them, and said, "No way, you first. You called me and said you had something to tell me."

Nick replied, "Well, after you left we went back up to Ron Lackly's house with a warrant to take a look around. We didn't find anything in the house; it was clean. Going out to the barn, it appeared to be the same way until we got to the stable where Fred supposedly waited to attack. There we found two clean prints and two smeared ones. Apparently, according to the diaries, he wore gloves, but must have taken them off for one reason or another. The prints matched Fred's fingerprints. I don't know about this Paul person, but we do know that Fred was at the Lacklys'. Then yesterday out of nowhere the manager at The Mill called our office and told me one of his workers had found a satchel or bag of sorts. Going down there, we found it matched the one described in the diaries that Fred used when he committed these crimes. How the crime-scene people missed it, I don't know. They must have assumed it was something that they used at The Mill. I still don't know about this Paul character, though. I ran the whole story by Steve the other day so he would be able to help me work this out in my mind. With all the information you got about split personalities and possessions I'm finding it hard to sort out."

I looked at Steve and then back at Nick, and asked, "So what did you all come up with?"

Steve stood at this point and leaned against the counter. Standing there, he lit a cigarette and said, "Well, Larry, it's a little hard to believe that Fred was possessed, but maybe he had a split personality. One way or another with all we have right now the only thing that is for sure is that we're dealing with a serial killer. So far all our victims have only one thing in common. They're connected to The Mill."

"And Fred knew all of them."

Nick in turn asked, "So did you find anything on your trip?"

I sat there for a second before I spoke, to gather my thoughts. "I started out by following the directions that were written in the diaries to the towns that were mentioned. Before I forget, Nick, I want to give you a license plate number you might want to check out. A Massachusetts plate labeled, "Mill 2".

"Mill 2?"

"Yeah, Mill 2."

Nick wrote it down and handed that piece of notepaper to Steve. "Steve, will you go out to the car and run that while we go on here?"

"Sure, I'll be right back."

I went on, "After arriving in Riverside, I went to a hotel and checked in. From there I followed the notes I took from the diary on how to find The Mill's corporate offices. I followed the directions and had no problem locating the office building. When I said I wanted to speak to the owner/president, I was informed that he and his family were on an extended vacation. I spoke with the vice-president under the pretense of writing an article about their company."

"What exactly were you looking for, Larry?"

"I don't know, anything I guess. From there I started to follow the directions to the house of the family that Paul supposedly murdered. I was thinking that anyone could get the directions to the office building, but not to any one individual's house. Following my notes, I was once more surprised to find the house exactly where Fred wrote it was and that's where I found the car he described with the license plate number I just gave you. I went to the door and didn't get any answer. Killing time, I grabbed my camera from the car and went back to the door to try knocking again. It was then…"

At this moment Steve returned to tell us the license plate belonged to a gold 1999 Lexus owned by Don Lackly. Nick just looked at Steve for a moment and then turned to me. As far as I was concerned everything was falling into place, as I wanted it to. I wanted them to see the evidence for themselves. Steve sat down at the table and I cleared my throat to continue.

"Like I was saying, after getting my camera I went back to the door and knocked again. This time I must have knocked too hard because the door opened slightly. I waited there to see if anyone would answer and no one did. I wondered about the dog he wrote about and where it might be. I walked over to the side of the house where I thought it should be according to the diary and saw that it had chewed through its lead. So I went back over to the house and pushed the door open. I went in and took pictures of the entire place. I knew right where everything was from reading the diary. I continued up the stairway as did Paul and went to the bedroom where everything supposedly happened. I want to tell you two, this house was

clean and in order, all except the bedroom where he said he raped the mother and daughter."

"You went into someone else's house without them being there? Anything you have for evidence can't be used in court."

"I sure did. But you aren't going to court. Everyone is dead."

I put the photos in front of them.

"Other than the bedroom being all messed up there wasn't much more out of place, as you can see."

Leaning over and pointing to something on one of the pictures, Steve said, "That's a bloodstain." Nick looked up over the top of the pictures at me to find me smiling.

"Okay smart ass, what else do you have?"

"First things first. I want you to know that I didn't take anything or touch anything. I even went so far as to put a tissue over my hand when I opened and shut the door—with the sole purpose of not destroying any of the evidence."

Nick shook his head. "So far, you've kept the knowledge of the second diary from us and now you've broken into somebody's home. Is there anything else?"

"Now that you mention it there is. I left there and went back to my hotel room and gathered my stuff. The next morning I headed to New York State where Fred went for the next victim. I got to the Mechanicsville exit, pulled into the first gas station I found, and read the notes I took down about this one."

Interrupting, Nick asked, "Let me guess. You found this place, too?"

"Yep. And it too was exactly where Paul wrote it would be. This was different though, because I didn't know how I was going to approach this one. I ended up just driving right into the driveway and knocking on the door."

Steve just sat there in total amazement. "Larry, never in my seventeen years as a police officer have I ever come across anyone like you."

"Well, I couldn't wait on you two. You guys are still debating whether or not he was possessed or just had a split personality."

Nick said, "Just finish your story, Larry."

"Like I was saying, I pulled into the driveway and parked on the lawn off to the side of it. I got out and wrote down the license plate number of the vehicle parked in the driveway as I did the other." I tore it out of my notebook and handed it to Steve.

Nick looked at Steve as if he wanted to say something and at the same time Steve started to get out of his chair saying, "I'll be right back, Nick."

"When I walked up to the door this time nobody answered, and, of course, the door was locked. I didn't see anyone inside, so I walked around to the back of the house. Returning to the front of the house, I was met by one of the neighbors. He introduced himself and I in turn introduced myself as Fred Lamperee."

Nick's head hit the table in disbelief. "I told him I was passing through and wanted to visit my grandmother. He said she must have left for a vacation as she usually does around this time of year. So I started to leave, but figured I would take a quick glance under the welcome mat for a spare key. That's when the man informed me she had given it to him and his wife so they could watch the place. Explaining that I really needed to use the bathroom and seeing I knew where she kept her spare key, he unlocked the door without me asking him to. I couldn't believe it. After he opened the door he turned to leave, offering me coffee for my ride home."

Steve came back inside from the patrol car and told Nick the car belonged to an Eve Lackly who lived in Mechanicsville, New York.

"So, like the other place, I didn't touch anything and if I did I wiped it off not to leave any prints. I took pictures of the entire inside of the house."

Nick held his hand out motioning me to give him the pictures. Nick and Steve went through the entire pile without a word.

I was disappointed they showed no reaction. I asked, "Did you see anything unusual?"

"Nothing more than a few drops of blood and a messed up bedroom, like the one at the other Lackly home. Is that everything, Larry? I mean you didn't leave out anything else this time like you did with the extra diary?"

I sensed the sarcasm in his voice, and said, "Look, Nick, maybe I didn't do what was right, but I did what I felt was right. I didn't ruin anything and I actually gave you some useful information that you can follow up on. There are a couple of other things, but they're personal. If you want to hear them I'll tell you."

Nick looked at Steve, and said, "Sure, Larry, why not. It can't possibly top what we've heard so far."

I leaned forward and rested my arms on the table. "Since you put it that way. The hotel I stayed in when I was in Massachusetts was the exact same one that Paul stayed in and wrote about. When I checked at the front desk and asked if there was a Paul who stayed there on March 6th, they told me that there was someone there on that day by the name of Paul Lamperee.

As I slept that next night after going to the house and before I left, I was woken up by the dreams I was having. In the first one I was in the same room as the Lackly's daughter as she was being raped while tied to her mother. The thing that woke me was that the person raping her turned to me and said, "See you soon, Larry."

Nick and Steve both started to stand up when I said, "Wait, there's more. The next night I was woken up the same way, but this time I saw the same person talking to four other people and in my dream I walked up behind them. Before I was able to get too close that same person turned, and said, "You think you know everything." Both times it looked like Fred in every way, but when he faced me and spoke to me it wasn't Fred. It was someone altogether different. Someone I didn't recognize."

Nick got up and then Steve followed him toward the door. I said, "I know it sounds weird, but you asked. Don't forget in the diary Paul wrote that when he raped that young girl he caused her to bleed and in New York—Paul wrote he tied her wrists so tight they started to bleed. Everything written in these diaries is true, Nick. You've got to believe me."

Stopping in the doorway Nick turned and said, "I do believe you. But it is a little bit hard to swallow and how do you think I'm going to convince anyone else?"

"Wait a minute. When I woke from the second dream I found these two Camel non-filter cigarette butts in the ashtray. I didn't put them there and no one from the cleaning crew at the hotel did, either. They're the same brand Paul wrote in the diary that he smoked. I saved them to see if you might want them."

Steve walked over to me and reached out to take the small package from me. They then both walked out to the car and I followed them to the porch. Before getting into the car, Nick said, "Larry, you've given us a very big egg to swallow. Give me some time and I'll let you know what we come up with."

I stood there and watched them leave. I knew that they didn't want to take me seriously, but they did have the pictures. Shaking my head, I went back inside, lit a cigarette, and grabbed the last beer from the refrigerator.

Chapter 22

As I drank my last beer I decided to play the tapes once more, but this time I wanted to listen to them from the beginning. I thought there might be a chance I had missed something and wanted to make sure that I hadn't. I started listening to the first tape hoping to find something to show Nick and Steve that I wasn't going crazy. That, indeed, Fred had been possessed or overpowered by a force from outside of him and that it wasn't Fred who was committing the murders. I knew it was Fred physically doing the killing, but it wasn't Fred mentally plotting and committing these crimes.

I replayed the first tape without finding anything I hadn't already hit on and had checked out. I started the second tape, sat back in the chair and lit another cigarette. I came up to the part where Mandy was being murdered after the section in the tape describing Paul going to Eve Lackly's house the first time. She was a University of Vermont student who had broken down on the side of Route 22A. There wasn't much about her other than the fact that she was another one of Paul's victims.

I hadn't started a file on her for the simple reason that the others were much easier for me to follow up on. I listened, writing down the few facts I had available to me. She was a University student, she lived in the dorms, and she was around twenty years old. One thing she did have in common with the others, or at least two of them, was that while having sex with her, Paul started to have flashes again of Fred's mother's face.

I stopped the tape for a second to try to find a reason why Fred had these flashes. The only thing that came to mind was the incident in the first tape where Fred's mother ripped the curtain open as he showered and stood totally nude watching him. Had this been the start of Fred's psychological problems with women? Or was it one of the numerous times he had to put her to bed and she would grab his jeans rubbing his dick that did it? Is that why maybe he saw his mother's face? A pretty good reason for Fred to have problems with women. When Paul saw these flashes it was during the rapes and Fred's thoughts of his mother were stronger than whatever Paul was thinking, and came through as if it were Fred having sex. Most of the time Paul could suppress Fred's thought patterns and when they started to slip it wasn't long before Paul regained control and finished what he needed to do. Except during sex acts, apparently.

I continued to listen to the details that went on after Mandy's murder. He again took his victim to the oven located on the bottom floor of The Mill and disposed of her body. As I listened to it this time I picked up

on the fact that the woman who was a part of the group of spirits Paul was with expressed her disgust each time Paul raped these women. She said things like, "that is not our purpose", and "that isn't what we talked about." Again she expressed it more angrily when Paul brought Mandy's body to The Mill. Then another thing struck me. After each rape and murder, Paul wrote that he took the personal clothing of his victims and threw them in a pile in Fred's living room behind the chair. I tried to remember whether or not I had seen clothing piled up in Fred's apartment. I thought I did, but none of us really checked it out, thinking it was just a pile of his dirty clothing. I realized then this might be something that would further prove the truth of the diaries as well as give Nick and Steve something they would be able to see and feel for themselves.

I wrote down in my notebook, "Call UVM", and underlined it. Underneath that I wrote a note to myself to call Nick and Steve. I pushed the play button and continued listening to how Fred left his apartment headed for his brother's house. That's where the diary ended. Something must have gone wrong at The Mill on his last trip there, but what? No matter how many times I listened I couldn't figure out what had happened, or how the remains of Fred's hand ended up on the floor in front of the oven.

I decided to go to the University to try and find out something about this girl named Mandy. I began by calling the University Police Department and asking how I could find out about an individual who was attending their school. I was told I needed to call admissions to find out whether or not the individual was a student there. I called admissions and told them I needed to find out the correct mailing address of one of their students. The person on the other end asked what the student's name was and I realized I didn't have her full name. I thanked the person I was talking to and hung up the phone. Calling the University police again, I asked how I would be able to review a list of reported missing students from their school. The dispatcher who answered the phone told me that I was more than welcome to come to their office and go through the list of students who had been reported missing. I got the directions to the office from the person on the phone and thanking them very much for their help, I hung up.

I knew this one individual wouldn't make or break the case, but it was just one of the loose ends that needed to be investigated. It took me about twenty minutes to get to the offices of the University police. I was greeted by the individual I talked to on the phone. I explained that I was checking up on an individual whose family was concerned as to why they hadn't heard from their daughter. The dispatcher pointed to the wall that was to the right of him and explained that any student who was reported missing by family or friends was put on the clipboard. He also explained it

may not necessarily be updated. They get reported, but if whoever is looking for them finds them, they don't always notify us. I thanked him and went to the clipboard.

Unable to remove it from the wall, I was forced to stand there as I thumbed through hundreds of names. On these reports were the student identification picture they were all required to have taken and their physical descriptions. Not knowing Mandy's last name, I figured with my luck it would probably be the last name in the batch. I made it to the last names beginning with "L", and decided to take a cigarette break.

When I finished, I returned to the diligent work of thumbing through each report. I had been there almost two hours, and was about halfway through the "P's", when I came across a Mandy Pinsoe. I found one more Mandy, but she was an African American woman, and I told myself that I would have remembered if Paul wrote that she was an African American. I went through the rest of the reports, without finding the first name Amanda or Mandy. I opened the clips on the clipboard and removed the report of Mandy Pinsoe from it. I asked the dispatcher if it would be possible to get a copy of it. "No problem," he said, and ran it through the copier.

I thanked the dispatcher for all his help and left to try and piece together Mandy's murder now that I had a face to put to the story. I fast-forwarded the tape to the part that described Paul's first trip to Mechanicsville, New York, and on to the part in which he started to strangle her as he saw Fred's mother's face in hers.

I suddenly realized I had never mentioned Mandy's murder to Nick and Steve. I dialed the number for the police station, and the dispatcher immediately put me through to Nick as if she already had orders to do so, when and if I called. "Larry, I'm glad you called. I was just thinking of calling you. What's up?"

"I just wanted to tell you and Steve that I think that I have located a picture of the girl named Mandy from the diary. Supposedly, Paul picked her up on the side of the road and ended up killing her. This happened in between Paul's two trips to New York. I went to the University police department and went through their missing person files. There were two Mandys reported missing. One was an African American, which, of course, eliminated her. What were you going to call about?"

"After going through all the pictures you took and the information you compared and found to be true, Steve and I decided to take another trip to Fred's apartment."

"Why?"

"Well we haven't got much to go on from our standpoint. We're in Vermont and these other two murders happened in two other states. There has to be something there we missed."

"I remember there was a pile of dirty clothes in the corner of the living room. Do you think that it might be the same pile he mentioned in his diaries?"

"You're right. I forgot all about that pile of clothes—it could be. This might be the way we can tie Fred to all of this. We don't have Fred and we don't have anybody who seems to be looking for these women. If the pile of clothing is the clothing mentioned in the diaries we can have tests done on every piece in hopes of identifying the owner."

"I want to be there when you go in. I deserve to be there. If this is the pile of clothing we will have everything we need."

"I'm sorry, Larry, but I'm going to call in the State Police crime lab so that no evidence is sacrificed. They're the best crime scene forensic unit we have in the state. I'll let you know what we find out, buddy."

I hung up the phone without saying good-bye, feeling as though I was being left out of the most important step that might prove everything I had been working on. I wasn't about to let this happen again and went back to listening to the tapes.

I got to the story about how the owner, who was actually Ron's grandfather, had caught the older man in the back seat of his car screwing his wife. It continued to tell how Paul, hearing the noise outside, stepped out through the back door and found the owner just after shooting the older man. The owner couldn't afford any witnesses and out of blind rage turned the gun on Paul as he stood there. Paul was then gunned down for being in the wrong place at the wrong time. The owner then drove the car to the Williston stone quarry. Rigging the gas pedal and putting it into gear sent the car speeding forward and over the edge of the cliff. If this car could be found it would be just as important as the pile of clothes in validating these diaries. I stopped the tape and wrote down some notes about what I had just heard so I wouldn't have to play the tapes again.

How could I go about proving this part of the tape? It must have happened over fifty years ago. To be able to prove the existence of Paul and the older man would be awesome. Especially if I could prove there was a Paul, who had supposedly taken over Fred's actions and life. It would once and for all show that Fred was possessed and did not commit these acts.

The quarry still existed except that it had been closed for years to the public. The owner didn't want to have the liability in case someone got hurt. The quarry couldn't be more than fifty to seventy-five feet deep and, if I could get permission from the owner, maybe I could use my scuba

equipment to find the car. Figuring I had nothing but time to lose, I decided this was what I was going to do next.

I went to the closet and pulled out all of my diving equipment. Sitting on the bed, I took an inventory of everything and performed an operational check of every piece. Finding I still had everything, even though it had been a couple of years since I had actually dived, brought a smile to my face. I knew I would need a few practice dives before I actually attempted to dive that deep. I had made several dives of one hundred feet or more when I was actively diving. I didn't know if maybe I should call a few of my ex-diving buddies to join me in this dive. Who would believe I was actually looking for a car that had two dead bodies in it?

I put everything into the trunk of the car, closed the trunk and went to the nearest convenience store to pick up a six-pack of beer. When I returned to the house, I lit a cigarette and opened a beer, pondering what I was going to do. By the time I finished the first beer I had decided to go the next morning for my first attempt at diving.

I was awakened by the telephone ringing the next morning. I had fallen asleep without setting the alarm clock and as I leaned over to answer the phone I looked at the clock to see that it was 10:00 AM. I picked up the phone. Nick was on the other end. "What's going on, Nick?"

"I just wanted to let you know that the boys from the crime scene unit just finished up in Fred's apartment."

"Yeah? Was our hunch right?"

"All I can really say for sure is that they found at least six different pairs of women's underwear of various sizes, a pair of men's underwear, numerous articles of clothing, and numerous bed sheets. They found some with what looked like bloodstains on them and they also found numerous hair samples on each piece of the underwear. Whether or not they were Fred's I couldn't tell, but I'm pretty sure the woman's underwear weren't."

"Yeah, but nowadays who really knows?"

"You got that right. This whole case is the strangest I've ever been involved in, so I don't discount anything until it's proven one way or the other."

As I listened to Nick explain the whole process of DNA testing, I contemplated telling him what I was about to do, then Nick said the DNA profiling would take at least two weeks to get any results. When I heard this I decided it would be best not to say anything about what I was about to do. Nick said he just wanted to let me know what had been found and that it was starting to look like I was right about Fred and these victims. "I have to go now, Larry, but I wanted you to know Steve and I are going through with the investigation. We will be contacting the officials in the other states so they can start looking into the possibility of these murders. Along with that

we will be asking for DNA samples or profiles of each person considered to be a victim."

"I certainly appreciate it very much Nick. Let me know how it all turns out. I'll call you later. Bye."

"Later, Larry. Bye."

It was finally coming together and Nick and Steve were finally seeing that everything I told them wasn't just my imagination running away. They had gathered the evidence from where Diane's car had been burned and now they possibly had the clothing from all the victims.

I knew this was coming to an end, but I still felt as though I needed to find this car. After breakfast I went to the dive shop in Burlington to have my tanks serviced. I figured I had about an hour of dive time with my tank setup at the depths I was planning to go. After filling my set of tanks, I went into the front of the store and bought a set of the next size larger tanks, and got them filled also. I told myself I had better keep the extra set on the bank where I entered the water so they would be close by when I needed them. At the mouth of the Winooski River I parked as close as I could to the bank without getting stuck.

I had left in such a hurry I had forgotten to put on my diving shorts, so, after a quick look around to make sure no one was watching, I pulled my pants off, and quickly pulled on the shorts. I headed down the slight bank to the side of the river with all my gear and laid my extra set of tanks there. Sitting on a rock, I put my fins on and made one final check of my breathing equipment. I pulled my mask into place and, leaving my second stage regulator hanging below my mouth, I walked slowly into the river. The river wasn't as deep as I needed it to be, but it was only a few hundred yards to where the river met the lake and it was at least fifty feet deep there.

I got to a point where I figured I was at a good depth to start diving and went down for my first dive. I came to the surface after ten minutes realizing it was just like riding a bike. Once you learn you never forget. I stayed there making a few more dives for as long as the air in the tanks lasted. When my air supply was getting low, I made one more dive and it was on this dive that I reached the depth of sixty feet. While I was down there I also discovered the diving light I owned was okay for recreational use, but it wouldn't be bright enough to perform a search at that depth. Returning to the surface, I headed back to the bank where I had entered the water.

I quickly changed tank setups and went back out. I returned to the general area I had been diving to continue and to see if I could reduce my breathing in order to stay down longer. I dove to the seventy-five foot mark three times before my air supply was too low to reach that level again and decided to call it a day. Sitting back on the same rock taking my fins off, I

assured myself that there was no reason I couldn't make the dive at the quarry. Even as I reassured myself of my ability there was one side of my brain telling me that the quarry was full of obstacles where the lake was wide open.

I parked in the side parking lot of the dive shop and followed the signs directing me to where to get the tanks filled. After they were filled I took them back out and placed them in the trunk. I remembered that I was going to need a different light and went into the shop.

When I explained what I needed, the salesperson told me I was looking for a commercial lighting apparatus. I followed her over to the opposite side of the shop where there were four lighting units displayed. All of them looked too big except one. It was lightweight and the label on the side said it had ten thousand candle power. The salesperson told me I was holding the newest and best available, but wasn't sure I wanted to know the price.

"How much?"

"Five hundred, but I'll give you ten percent off if you want it and pay by check or cash."

Handing it to her, I said, "I'll take it, and thanks for the discount. Oh, I'm also going to need a complete set of breathing apparatus."

"Your total is eight hundred ninety-two, fifty, tax included."

I wasn't made of money, but had been living very modestly for the past ten years and had been able to save quite a bit. She rang it up and subtracted the discount as I started to fill out my check. I handed it to her and she checked to see if all the information was correct as she handed me my new underwater light and breathing equipment. She thanked me as I started to walk out of the shop, and I thanked her for all her help. I placed my new equipment on the back seat and drove home.

I pulled into the driveway as close to the house as possible. I got the light from the back seat and brought it to the kitchen table where I read the instructions that came with it. I had been shown by the salesperson the basic operation of it, but I figured I had better make sure I knew what I was doing. I went through everything, including the battery removal and installation. I wanted to know that no matter what, I would be able to understand what was going on when I went to use it at the quarry.

I took a beer from the refrigerator and put two McDonald's hamburgers I had bought the day before into the microwave, then went into the bedroom to watch the six o'clock news. I watched the news and ate my dinner. I reached over to the alarm clock and set it to wake me up at 4:30 AM. I wanted to get as early a start as possible in order to get into the water before daylight. It was a good thing I had set the alarm because I ended up dozing off shortly after setting it and way before I had finished my beer. It

seemed the mental strain and the long hours of the previous days had caught up with me.

I woke up at the first sound of the alarm going off. It wasn't long before I got into the car and drove off, headed for the same spot as the day before.

I entered the water shortly after and congratulated myself on how quickly I was able to get into the water. I felt confident it had all come back to me. Pulling the light along, I headed out as deep as I had been the day before. Knowing I had at least one good hour of diving time with each tank set and wanting to stay at the bottom as long as possible using the new light, I waited till the last minute to dive. The light lit the bottom of the lake up as if I was at the surface with the sun shining. I could see everything for what I figured was a hundred feet. I was able to stay at that depth for about forty-five minutes before I saw that my first set of tanks was almost empty. I switched tanks and returned to the bottom to practice using the light and breathing. Each time I returned to the bottom I seemed to be getting better and more used to it.

By the time I got into the car it was almost eleven o'clock and I headed for the dive shop to fill the tanks. At the shop, I found I would have to wait a while. Apparently everyone else had the same idea. I decided to go into the shop to look around for anything else I might need.

Nothing seemed to jump off the shelf at me and as I started back out to see how long the line was, out of the corner of my eye I saw something that caught my attention. They were floating markers that were used by divers when they came across something underwater and wanted to relocate it later. They attached to the item or something near the item below the water surface and had a flotation device with a fluorescent flag attached.

I got the tanks filled without much more delay, and left on my way to find the owner of the land in which the quarry was located. It took me about thirty minutes to get to Williston and the road which I remembered the quarry was on. I thought about the times my friends and I had gone there as high school kids to swim. I also remembered the quarry hadn't always been shut off to the public until the year a boy dove off and hit a rock ledge that was under the surface of the water, killing himself. After that, the town told the owner that he would have to block the road off to the public. Driving by the road that led to the quarry, I saw that the blocks were still in place. I continued down the road to the first house I came to. I knocked on the door, and waited until someone came to answer it. The door opened and standing there was a woman who appeared to be in her eighties. I asked, "Sorry to bother you ma'am, but do you know who the owner of the quarry down the road might be?"

The woman thought for a second or two before she answered, "It used to be my father's land, but then he sold it. Come to think of it I'm not quite sure who does own it now."

I thanked her and went back to my car.

I decided the easiest way for me to find out who owned it was to go to the town clerk's office. They would have all the records of the sales and ownership in their files. I went to the town office building but as I approached the counter I couldn't see anyone behind it. I rang the bell for service and a man appeared from behind a shelf where it appeared the records were kept.

"Can I help you?"

I explained that I was interested in learning who now owned the land where the quarry was. "I'm not sure if I'm at the right place or not, but figured you would be able to tell me who I needed to speak with."

"Well you're at he right place and, yes, I can get that information for you, but it will take a few minutes."

"Take your time. Thanks."

Ten minutes passed. The man returned to the counter and told me the property still belonged to the Wilken's farm. The man asked, "Do you know how to get there?"

"What? The quarry or the Wilken's farm? I know where the quarry is, but I'm not sure how to find their farm."

The man explained that I needed to go on the same road as the quarry was and continue past it. He then said I would see a house on the same side of the road a ways down from the quarry.

"There's a road about a half a mile down from the house and you'll want to take that right. Go down the road for about a mile and then take another right. The Wilken's farm will be on the right-hand side of the road."

"So the owner lives on the backside of the property the quarry is on?"

"Yep, their farm is about a mile away from the quarry. The quarry is actually on the far end of their property line." I thanked him for all his help and left.

Chapter 23

Following the directions that had been given to me, I got to the Wilken's farm in twenty minutes. I stepped up onto the porch and knocked on the screen door. I heard a man's voice from behind me ask, "Can I help you?"

Turning around, I said, "Yes, I mean, I hope you can. I am looking for Mr. Wilken." I noticed the man was dressed in overalls and had dust and dirt all over him. He looked as if he had been working in fields all day.

He brushed off his hands and extended one toward me. "I'm Mr. Paul Wilken. What can I do for you?"

"My name is Larry Stone. I'm a freelance writer for the Colchester and Burlington newspapers. I'm sorry for bothering you like this."

"It's no bother, I needed a break or I was going to go nuts. I've been working on that broken down tractor of mine most of the day and it's still not running right. If I didn't walk away from it soon I was going to shoot it. How can I help you, Larry?" I explained that during my research I came across some information that led me to believe that a car had been dumped in the quarry fifty or so years ago.

Pulling out my wallet and opening it to show him that I was a certified diver, I said, "I would like your permission to dive for a day or two at my own risk to actually see if it's in there. I'll be willing to sign any release form you wish me to in order to be allowed to do this."

Rubbing his face as he thought about it, the man asked, "There's a ton of vehicles dumped in there—most of them without any permission. What's so important about that car?"

I thought for a minute, then said "To tell the truth, there might be two dead bodies in it, but I don't want to get the police involved until I know for a fact."

The man said, "My insurance man told me not to let anyone in there, but since you're being truthful about it I'll let you and only you. When do you want to do this?"

"Thank you very much, Mr. Wilken. And don't worry, I won't bring anyone with me. Please don't mention this to anyone, or at least not until I know one way or another. How's tomorrow first thing in the morning?" He agreed, and I extended my hand to thank Mr. Wilken again before leaving.

As I walked to my car, Mr. Wilken said, "Don't you worry about that. I'll be here, but I don't get up and started much before five."

Laughing, I said, "Don't worry about me. I won't be out here until seven or so and I'll check in with you before I go to the quarry." I waved to him as I pulled out of the driveway.

I got home around 6:00 PM, and found a message on the answering machine. It was from a solicitation company. I got a beer out of the refrigerator, and sat at the table with my notebook opened to take one more look at the information about the car being dumped in the quarry. I listened to the tape again and found I had written down everything regarding the location. I sat back in the chair and realized I might need more than a couple of days. Then the phone rang.

Nick was on the other end.

"Hey Larry, how you doing? I just thought I'd give you a call and let you know that we contacted the other two states. We also got Mr. Lackly to file a missing person report."

"That's great, Nick. What was the other police departments' response?"

"Well, at first they were a little suspicious, but when I began to tell them about the evidence we had, they started to listen. They also told us they would get back to us after their investigation. I just wanted to thank you again for all your help and I also wanted to tell you that we probably wouldn't even have looked into it if it wasn't for you."

"That's what friends are for, Nick. I gotta go because I'm getting up early for an appointment tomorrow. Let me know if you come up with anything else."

The next morning, I began to worry about what I might run into while I was diving. I wasn't scared or anything like that, but knew I was going to run into things I hadn't seen in the lake.

The water there at the quarry was mainly rainwater. Yes, there were some fish in it, but mainly it had bugs, leaches, spiders, and snakes. I decided to wear my wet suit instead of the shorts.

It wasn't long before I was pulling into the Wilken's farm driveway. Before I had even gotten out of the car I saw the farmer coming from the barn.

"Good Morning, sir," I said.

Mr. Wilken returned the greeting, and asked, "How do you plan on getting over there?"

"I don't know. I figured you could tell me."

"I don't think you really want to take your car through the fields and the road from the main road is blocked. I do have a little four wheel RV you could use."

"I have two tank setups to take with me and a diving light. Will I be able to carry it all with me or will I have to make two trips?"

"I have a little trailer that hooks to the back end. It should be able to haul all that."

"That's great, Mr. Wilken. I don't know how I'm ever going to repay you for all your help."

"There's no need for that. I don't get many visitors out here anymore since the children left and it's pretty nice just having a different face around." Mr. Wilken turned to go into the barn to get his four-wheeler and I started to get my stuff out of the car.

Mr. Wilken pulled the little rig alongside my car. I smiled and said, "That's perfect."

Mr. Wilken left it running, got off and told me to get on.

"It's pretty easy to drive. It's like driving a car without a body on it and if you take your time you won't have any problems," he said.

He explained how to operate it and I took few turns around in the driveway.

I stopped and turned it off so I could load up the trailer with my equipment and asked, "Which is the quickest and easiest way to get there?"

"You see that big tree out in the middle of that field standing by itself? Well, it's about three-quarter of a mile from that tree. You can't miss it because you will be approaching from the low side of the quarry."

I started it and told Mr. Wilken thanks as I headed for the tree he had pointed toward. At the edge of the driveway, I turned, and said, "Oh, by the way, if I'm not back by four…"

"I'll come looking for you, and don't you worry." Again I told Mr. Wilken thanks and continued on my way.

I had been driving for about fifteen minutes when I saw the white rock cliffs of the quarry in the near distance. I drove around to the right of it to where I could see the road that people had used to get to it, figuring it would be the best place to start. I pulled to an open space where it looked like a beach entrance. Turning off the RV, I walked to the edge and saw that there was no beach, but instead a tremendous drop-off.

Walking around three quarters of it, I saw that the whole outer edge was a cliff and decided to go in where I had parked the RV. I thought that if I had a problem, it would act as a marker to someone who was looking for me. I put on my gear and placed the diving light at the edge of the quarry.

I eased myself into the water. Where I had entered must have been a good ten feet deep or so. I put on my mask, my regulator in my mouth, and grabbed my light, turning it on before I actually removed it from the bank. I first wanted to see how deep I could go and headed for the bottom of the quarry.

With the light in front of me I could see everything I wanted. It wasn't long before I could make out what I thought was the bottom. Checking my gauge I saw that I was only at sixty feet. I had some diving weights on my ankles which seemed to be enough to keep me at the bottom if that was where I wanted to be. Taking the light, I started to turn in a circle to see if there were any vehicles nearby. I dropped one of the floating markers onto the bottom surface where I stood, released it and let it float to the surface.

I decided I would go about thirty feet from my marker, but I couldn't find any vehicles at the bottom of the quarry. I went back to my marker. I scouted the same way in three other directions, but only saw a few pieces of old machinery. My time was running out with the first set of air tanks so I returned to the surface, switched tanks and returned to the bottom of the quarry at a point about thirty feet from my first dive. I repeated my routine of swimming in every direction for about thirty feet.

Disappointed again, I went in the opposite direction. I was on my final attempt at locating anything that would bring hope that I wasn't wasting my time when I saw what appeared to be four wheels of a vehicle. Swimming over to it, I found an old four-door sedan lying upside down on its roof and attached my marker. It clearly wasn't the vehicle I was looking for, so I returned to the surface. This was going to take a little longer than I had anticipated. I decided to leave my marker in the water so I would know where I had left off.

I returned to the farmhouse and was greeted by Mr. Wilken. I shut the RV off, and said, "That quarry is bigger than I thought."

"It sure is big. It's a big useless hole in the ground. Did you have any luck?"

I told him where I had gone in and that I hadn't found anything except a few pieces of machinery and one car, but not the one I was looking for.

"If you don't mind, Mr. Wilken, I'll come out tomorrow and search again. It might take more than the two days I had anticipated, though."

He told me I was more than welcome to take as long as I needed. I finished putting my stuff into the car and told him I would see him at the same time the next day.

I arrived at the dive shop with just ten minutes to spare before they closed at five, and got both sets of tanks filled.

I stopped on the way home to get a sub for supper and a six-pack of beer. As I ate I drew a crude picture of the quarry in my notebook. I marked out the area I had searched that day. After looking at it for a while I closed the notebook, set up the coffeemaker and alarm, and went to bed.

The next day I arrived at the farm about the same time I had the day before, but this time the RV was already out of the barn and waiting for me. But I didn't see Mr. Wilken anywhere. I thought I'd better leave my keys in the ignition just in case I'd parked in Mr. Wilken's way. It was the least I could do in return for his hospitality and help. After putting the keys in the ignition, I went over to the RV to get on my way. Not until I was actually beside it did I notice the note that Mr. Wilken had left for me. It didn't say much except that he was sorry that he couldn't wait for me, but he had work to do in the fields. I took off through the field toward the quarry.

At the quarry, I saw my floating marker was still in place. I lit a cigarette as I looked around and sat at the edge of the water wondering how someone would dump a vehicle into the quarry from the high cliff side. Putting out my cigarette, I got up, tossed the cigarette butt on the ground, and headed back to the RV to put on my gear. Seeing how dry the grass was around the quarry, I decided I had better pick up my cigarette butt just in case it might start a fire. As I picked up the butt I noticed something. It appeared that there used to be a road along the side of the quarry. Exactly how old this road was I would have to ask Mr. Wilken when I got back. Following it, I found that it went all the way around to the backside of the quarry, putting me directly on top of the high cliffs. Whether or not this meant anything I decided to ask when I got back.

I made my way back to the RV and got my gear on to start diving. I made up my mind I would continue my way toward the cliffs in the same direction the road followed. I dove on the car I had gone to the day before, and disconnected my marker from it. I came across more and more debris as I moved closer to the cliffs. I made two thirty-foot moves to my right before I noticed my air was running out. I set my marker again.

Shining the light again to my right I couldn't believe my eyes. No more than twenty feet from me there was a large piece of construction equipment sitting on the bottom. I swam over to it and saw that there was a lot more equipment near it and a pick-up truck that I determined had to be at least a 1950s model.

I went back to the surface with five minutes of air left and changed my tanks.

I jumped back in, swam to the marker to follow its rope back down to the bottom and continued to look in all directions from where I had placed the marker. There was a lot to look at, but not what I was looking for. I swam to the left of the marker and came across more debris than before and even an old rusted-out motorcycle. I didn't really know what all the debris was and didn't waste time looking it over. I thought to myself as I looked around that all the vehicles I had come across were intact, though

severely rusted, but I knew I would be able to distinguish a station wagon from a sedan if I came across one.

I continued to swim to the right of the marker when out of the corner of my eye, on the edge of the light beam, I thought I saw something. I turned toward the object, and shone my light directly on it. About fifty feet away lay a station wagon upside down on it roof. Not knowing what I would find in it when I got closer, I approached it very slowly. The roof was slightly crushed from the impact of landing on the bottom, but other than that it looked in good condition. I was about three feet from it when I thought I saw something shining from it like maybe a piece of jewelry.

Inching my way forward, I saw that the door was ajar and tried opening it. On my second try the door came open and a large water snake lunged out at me from the darkness. I jumped back and swam as fast as I could in the opposite direction.

Getting back to the marker, I looked at my air gauge and saw I was about to run out. I'd had enough excitement for one day. Back on the shore, I took off my tank, and reached for my cigarettes. I smoked my cigarette as I finished sketching the debris and vehicles on the bottom. I convinced myself the station wagon I found was too new-looking to be the one I wanted, but wrote a note to check it tomorrow when I first went in. I had just enough time to get back to the farmhouse before Mr. Wilken would start to worry, and drove as fast as I could to make it back by four.

Mr. Wilken was just coming out the front door. "You had me starting to worry, son. What kept you? Did you find something?"

"I'm sorry, sir. I sure did find something. It was about three- to four-feet long and it scared the shit out of me. That's why I'm a little late getting back; I had to calm down. I found one other thing, though, and that was what appeared to be an old unused road. Was there a road that went up to the back side of the quarry, or was that road made by people who had come up to swim and party?"

"I tried to warn you about those snakes. They'll catch you off guard most of the time, but they're basically harmless. As far as I know there was a road that went back there when the quarry was open; now whether or not any of those kids used it, I couldn't tell you. Did you find the car you were looking for?"

"No, not yet, but I'm finding a lot more junk. It's just taking a little more time than I expected. Do you mind if I continue looking? I'll pay you for the use of your RV, it's been a big help."

"Don't worry about the money and you just keep looking for what you're looking for at least until you find it or satisfy yourself that it's not there.

"Smiling and shaking Mr. Wilken's hand, I said, "Thank you so much, sir. I really do appreciate it."

I headed back to the dive shop.

This routine went on for a week and still I hadn't found anything even resembling the vehicle I was looking for, except for the one with the snake. My days were long and my nights were short, but I was determined to prove I was right. Every day I woke up and headed to the quarry telling myself that this station wagon did exist and I would find it that day. I was never disappointed to the point of giving up, but went home some nights wondering whether I should go on. Those thoughts never stopped me from waking up the next day to continue.

On the eighth day, the vehicles on the bottom of the quarry appeared to be piled up on top of each other. This told me I was in the right place for dumping. It also meant I had to take more time searching a smaller area in order to be sure I hadn't missed the one I was looking for. I was exhausted that night when I returned home and took very little time to eat before going to bed. That night I had a visitor in my sleep. During a dream I had a problem making out where I was, but did realize that there was a man's voice talking to me. It wasn't the voice I had heard in my previous dreams. Walking closer and closer in the direction I thought it was coming from, an older man stepped out from behind me. I knew it was an older man by the sound of his voice. He said, "Don't turn around and don't stop looking. We need you, Ruth."

I was scared out of my wits and didn't say anything but I spun around to see who it was. There was no one there. I didn't have any more dreams that night that I could remember, but when I woke up the next morning I wrote down what I could remember about the one I did have. The last note that I wrote and underlined to myself read, "RUTH?" This delayed me only a few minutes on my way to the quarry.

The dive that day went along about the same as the day before. I found myself searching through a pile of crushed and rusted-out vehicles. They weren't all cars and trucks; there were machinery debris and construction vehicles as well. My marker still floated above the area I had just checked out and I was thinking to myself I would have to move it when I was done for the day. I still had at least fifteen minutes' of air. As I headed back to the marker, I fanned my light back and forth so I wouldn't miss anything or possibly run into something. I went around the backside of a pile of what looked like scrap-metal made from everything but the kitchen sink. I was just about around it with my marker in sight when the light illuminated something to my left.

I shone the light full on it, and saw that it was a car turned on its side. I couldn't really tell what kind of car it was because the bottom was facing me. I racked my brain trying to remember whether or not I had already looked at it. It was getting so it was hard for me to remember all the vehicles I had checked out, but I also remembered going around the front of this pile when I returned from changing my tanks. I decided I had enough air for a quick look.

The license plates were still on it. I moved to the front of the car to check the condition of the license plate, and saw that it was, indeed, a station wagon, but was it the one I was looking for? I took my diving knife out of its sheath and attempted to remove the screws that held the license plate. The corrosion was too much and held the screws tightly to it. I only had a few minutes left before my air ran out and returned to the surface.

Pissed about not finding this car earlier, I swam to the shore to call it a day. I got in my car and said good-bye to Mr. Wilken as I left to get my tanks filled, perhaps for the last time.

I went to bed knowing I was going to find something on my next dive.

I got up the next morning, got my shit together, including this time a small pry bar and a couple of screwdrivers, as soon as I could and left the house drinking my first cup of coffee from my to-go cup on my way to the Wilken's farm. I met Mr. Wilken as he was bringing his RV out from the barn. I drove out across the field headed to the quarry.

At the quarry, I swam out to my marker and headed for the bottom. I found that I had remembered exactly where the car was. I swam over to the front end of it and pulled out one of my screwdrivers. Working for a few minutes with my first choice I found it didn't work and tried the other one. Neither one of the screwdrivers would turn the screws that held the license plate to the car. I had to go back for the pry bar, which I stupidly had left ashore. I chose to swim over the top of it instead of going around as I had done the other times. I cleared the body of the car and felt my left foot catch onto something. I turned to see what it might be but it all of a sudden became free, and I continued my ascent.

Not wanting to waste any time I quickly switched tanks, pulled the two screwdrivers from my dive belt, and replaced them with the pry bar. I was soon in front of the car I had just left.

I set the light down on the bottom and arranged it so it illuminated my work area. It didn't take long to pry the license plate from the car. It floated to the bottom and landed close to my light. I picked up the light and the plate at the same time. I didn't want to take the chance of losing it and decided to take it to shore. I started to swim to the surface and as before my left foot got caught on something. Without turning around to see what it

was I jerked my foot up and down to free it. With one more try I used all my strength to pull it free at about the same time I turned to see what it was I had been caught on. There was nothing there except the open windshield of the car. I swam to the shore figuring I had been hung up on the vehicle itself.

The swim to the shore seemed to take a little longer than normal. My foot hurt and I figured I would check it when I got there. At the shore, I got myself out of the water, and took a good look at the license plate. I saw that it was a Vermont license plate, dated 1938. Was this the car? Was my search almost over? I could hardly wait to go back and see, but I had to see how badly I had hurt my foot.

As I brought it to my right knee to lay it on I saw that my ankle had four bleeding tears in it. I decided I had come this far and I wasn't going to let a few cuts stop me. Sure, I was in pain, but all I had left to do was to go down there to take a look into the car to see if in fact this was the one from the diary. If it was, I told myself, it would contain the skeletons of Paul and the older man who was shot by The Mill's owner.

Chapter 24

I put my mask over my eyes and jumped back into the quarry for my last dive. I followed the marker's line to the bottom and coiled it up to move it over to where the car was. I turned on my light and swung it from side to side to see if there was going to be anything in my way before I headed over to the car. This time I went to the middle of the car. I was going to get up on top of it. As I pulled myself up along the undercarriage it suddenly started to shift toward me. Thinking that it was going to fall on me, I backed off. But it had only shifted a little as the weight of my body caused it to settle a bit more into the bottom surface. This time I put my new light on the bottom surface in a position that illuminated as much of the car as possible, then used my old waterproof flashlight, which I carried on every dive as a back up, to look into the car.

I swam back over to the car and used the hand holding the flashlight to help pull myself up onto the car's front door. Carefully, I turned toward the back of the car and turned on the flashlight so I could look down into the back seat.

As I shone my light down into the back seat, two grossly decomposed bodies came up from the guts of the car with their arms reaching out. I didn't waste any time getting off the car and swimming toward the surface of the water. Looking back for a split second, I saw the two bodies reaching out from the back seat window, their faces distorted into horrifying images and strips of flesh hanging off their arms. I finally came to the surface and in no time to the shore. I pulled myself up on the bank and ripped off my gear, throwing everything onto the trailer of the RV. I grabbed a cigarette, and my hand was shaking so hard I couldn't light it. I gave up and wasted no time getting back to the farmhouse. Pulling up alongside my car, I opened the trunk and tossed everything into it including the license plate. I looked around everywhere for Mr. Wilken, frantically searching the barn and the grounds, but found no sign of him. On the porch of the house, I yelled his name as loud as I could.

The front door opened and Mr. Wilken stepped out onto the porch wondering what all the commotion was about. Seeing the look in my eyes and trying to make sense out of what I was trying to say to him, Mr. Wilken went back into the house for some water. I took the glass from him and drank almost all of it without stopping. When I put the glass down on the handrail of the porch I started from the beginning, but this time I was calmed down enough so that Mr. Wilken could understand. Mr. Wilken

asked, "You mean to tell me that you found that car you were looking for with the bodies?"

"Not only did I find the car with the bodies in it, but they came after me as if they were trying to grab me."

Laughing, Mr. Wilken said, "Son, if those bodies were in that car they weren't coming after you. Maybe stuff shifted enough to loosen them and they floated toward you and you just thought they were coming after you." I told Mr. Wilken that he was probably right, though I didn't believe it. Mr. Wilken said, "I guess you better notify the police, hadn't you?"

"That's where I'm headed. Please don't go near the quarry or tell anyone." I got into my car and left the driveway in such a hurry I almost lost control of it.

I came to the main intersection before the interstate and pulled into the state liquor store. I didn't take long picking out what I wanted—I put a fifth of tequila and a six-pack of beer on the counter. As the salesgirl rang it up, I asked for a pack of cigarettes. I put the booze into the back seat and noticed that I didn't have my diving light with me. I had left the bottom of the quarry in such a hurry I didn't take the time to grab it. I slammed the door—hard. Five hundred dollars down the drain!

At home I grabbed the tequila bottle, opened it, and guzzled as much as I could in the first swallow. It burned my throat as it went down and I chased it with a large swallow of cold beer. I had drunk at least a third of the tequila and three beers before I was calm enough to think of what I was going to tell Nick and Steve.

It was almost 5:30 PM, and if I was going to talk to Nick I had better call soon. I went to the car and retrieved the license plate from the trunk. Back at the table, my hand was steady enough to light a cigarette and dial the police station's number. Nick answered his phone before I had even heard it ring. "Nick, I need you and Steve to stop by my house after work. Okay?"

"Hey, buddy, long time no hear. What's going on?"

"I just need to speak to both of you."

"Okay, okay. We'll be by in less than an hour." I hung up and took another large swallow from the tequila bottle and one from my beer. I lit another cigarette and waited at the table sipping the beer until they arrived.

I had left the inside door open so they just let themselves in through the screen door. I was almost half in the bag sitting at the kitchen table. I told them to have a seat. They both sat down across from me and assessed my condition. Nick asked, "What's going on, Larry?"

"I'll tell you what's going on, Nick. For the past week I've been diving in the Williston quarry looking for the car the owner of The Mill had dumped in there."

Steve asked, "What car are you talking about, Larry?"

"The car that Paul/Fred wrote about in the diary. The one that the older man had been shot in and Paul had been put in after being shot. The diary said after shooting them the owner of The Mill drove it to the quarry and dumped it. So while you went and did your thing, I went to look for this car."

"Well, did you find anything?" I finished my beer, lit a cigarette and took several deep breaths.

"Yesterday I thought I had found the car, but I ran out of air. It was the only car or vehicle that had a license plate on it, it was a station wagon, and it looked as if it came from the same year as what was described in the diary. Going back today I was able to pull the license plate off it." I reached down to the floor, picked up the license plate and handed it to them. As Nick took it from me, he looked over at Steve in amazement.

I got another beer from the refrigerator and asked if either one of them wanted one. Nick and Steve both told me no thanks and I returned to the table. I started to lift the tequila bottle to my mouth, when Nick asked, "Haven't you had enough, Larry?" I finished taking a swallow from the bottle, put it back on the table, and leaned back in my chair.

"Let me finish my story before you judge whether or not I've had enough."

"Okay," Steve said, "go ahead and tell us the rest of it."

"After I took the license plate to the shore to put it with my gear for safekeeping I returned to the bottom of the quarry. Getting up onto the side of the car to take a look into the back seat area was when I saw…I saw…"

"Saw what, Larry?"

"I saw two badly decomposed bodies coming up out of the backseat area toward me with their arms stretched as if they were trying to grab me."

Nick asked, "Are you sure you saw these bodies?"

"Yeah, I'm sure."

Nick sat back in his chair and looked at Steve for a moment. "Larry, does anyone else know that you were diving there and what you found?"

"Just the farm owner where the quarry is. I had to get his permission to dive there, but I told him not to say anything until I could talk to you."

Leaning over onto the table, Steve said, "Larry if those bodies were in there for that long they would be skeletal without any flesh and they certainly wouldn't be grabbing at you."

I leaned back in my chair and lifted my left leg up onto the table and said, "Oh yeah, then what are these?"

Nick saw the four streaked cuts on my ankle, and said, "Good God, Larry what the hell did you do to your ankle?"

"They tried to keep me down there with them, but I pulled free."

"Give me a break," Steve said.

"You don't believe anything about what I've been telling you. The dreams, the voices, this has all been a big joke to you. Well I'm telling you this happened and they are down there just like what the diary said. Haven't you two heard and seen enough to believe those diaries? Those bodies down there not only had skin on them—or the remains of skin—but they also had hair. One had short gray hair and the other one had shoulder length brown hair. How can I be making all this up, you assholes? Check out the license plate if you don't believe me."

Nick told me to calm down and relax for a minute. I lit a cigarette, and sat quietly, occasionally taking a sip from my beer. Nick broke the silence.

"Well it's not that we don't believe you, but it's a little hard to swallow. Tomorrow we'll come out and pick you up and you can take us to the quarry. While you were diving we requested from the other police departments involved everything and anything that they could supply us to get a DNA report on all the missing people. We have received hair samples from the three victims in Massachusetts and are waiting on the other one from New York. While we were waiting for that we got hair samples from Ron Lackly's wife's hairbrush. We have all the DNA reports back from the clothing found in his apartment. We also put a rush on Mrs. Lackly's hair sample. I was going to call you tonight to let you know that we actually have a match. The sample taken from her home and a pubic hair removed from one of the woman's underwear matched perfectly. I'm telling you this because we do believe you, but some of this stuff is very, very weird."

I replied, "I'm sorry, Steve. Nick, you know me. It just has been a long day and a lot of crazy shit is happening to me and I can't figure out why."

Nick said, "Well, we feel as though we have figured out the events from May 27. Fred went to his brother's that day knowing that Pat was out of town on business and he also knew he would have easy access to the house from Pat's wife. Once in the house he overpowered her, tied the children up, and before leaving the house raped her in the same manner he did the others. Taking her to The Mill and dumping her naked body off in the heat-treat area, he returned her car to their house. He walked back to The Mill, let himself in, then finished her off as he did the rest of his victims. After disposing of her body in the oven something happened to Fred. We aren't sure if it was suicide or what, but his charred hand was on the floor and his blood was found on the hook of the hoist.

We actually have another good match from the pile of clothing from the victim named Diane Lewis. The one problem we're having is the connection of the victims. Why these people?"

I answered, "The only thing I came up with comes from the diaries. They're all from the Lackly family, or at least worked for them. All except Mandy who he found on Route 22A on his way home from New York. Ron Lackly's grandfather killing that older man and Paul must have something to do with it and as far as the others go, I haven't figured it out yet. I always thought that this kind of anger and lust for revenge died with the person."

Steve asked, "So you believe spirits from another time actually came back and killed these people?"

"Who said they came back? I don't think they ever left. Two of them have been trapped at the bottom of the quarry for all these years and the others I don't know."

Nick said, "Wait a minute Larry. We don't even know who or what you found at the bottom of the quarry. So let's call it a night and we'll be out first thing in the morning to go to the quarry."

"I'll be waiting for you."

Nick and Steve said their good-byes and left.

Knowing that I probably wouldn't be getting up on my own because of the amount of tequila I consumed, Nick gave me a call before coming over to pick me up. Nick let the phone ring for several minutes to no avail. He decided to come to my house before picking Steve up in case it took a while to get me out of bed. He started banging on the front door to no effect. He then went to the bedroom window and started to bang on it. After the third or fourth try, he finally got me to wake up. I went from the bedroom to the bathroom before going to the door to let Nick in.

Nick greeted me with a smile as he opened the door and handed a coffee to me that he had picked up on his way over. I thanked him, sat down at the kitchen table and cradled my head in my hands for a minute, hoping to ease the throbbing. I then lit a cigarette and said, "I know now why I don't drink like that anymore."

"Come on Larry, you have to get your shit together so we can go and pick Steve up. I came here first because I knew you were going to have problems getting out of bed." I heaved myself up and managed to get dressed. Then we left to go and pick up Steve.

I gave them directions to the Wilken's farm. When we arrived Mr. Wilken greeted us as we got out of the truck. I introduced everybody and explained why we were there. Mr. Wilken told Nick and Steve that he was expecting them and if there was anything he could do, just to let him know. I explained where the quarry was in relation to where we were and

suggested we take Nick's 4x4 to get to it. At the quarry I showed him where the marker was. Nick radioed for the state police to send a diving team out to their location with a 4x4 vehicle. All three of us got back into Nick's truck and drove back to the farmhouse to wait for them. We explained to Mr. Wilken that we were going to have to open up the other road to get some heavy equipment in. Mr. Wilken told them that it would be all right as long as we agreed to close it up when we were through.

It took about a half an hour for the state police dive team to get there. Nick explained the situation and told them he wanted to verify what he had been told. He added that if there was a vehicle down there with two bodies in it, they were going to have to pull it out. The team followed us to the quarry and we showed them the marker. It didn't take long for them to enter the water and resurface with their findings. They confirmed that the car was there, but said it only contained two skeletal remains in it. I looked at Nick, and said, "That can't be. I know what I saw.

"The officer in charge of the dive team called in for the equipment they were going to need and told Nick that they would notify him when they brought it up. Nick told Steve and me that we were done there for the moment and we left.

They told me as soon as they found anything out they would give me a call. Steve would check out the license plate I had given them yesterday, and he was going to follow up with the other police departments to see when they could expect to get their DNA results. I got out of the car and as I made my way morosely to the front porch I told them I'd be waiting to hear from them.

I was exhausted and hung over. It seemed as though the past few weeks had caught up to me and all I wanted to do was to lie down and go to sleep. I threw my keys on the table and soon found myself on my bed lying there in my boxer shorts smoking a cigarette. I fought to keep my eyelids open so I could finish it without falling asleep, and I remember rolling over and putting it out in the ashtray on the nightstand. The next thing I knew I was standing in the back office at the Winooski Police station.

I stood there for a moment wondering what the hell was going on as I watched Nick and Steve sit at their desks talking on their telephones. It was crazy, as if I was there and I wasn't. It also seemed as though someone had turned on a cheap dry ice machine like a local rock band would have at a bar to fill the room with a low-grade fog. It wasn't a real fog or one that was very thick, but there was this thin haze pervading the entire office. I could see and hear everything that was going on, but it was as if no one could see me. I tried talking to them, but they couldn't hear me, either. What was even stranger was that no matter what they did or where they

went I always seemed to be only a few feet away, but I couldn't get any closer or farther away.

Throughout the day I watched Steve on the phone and running here and there. Finally the Department of Motor Vehicles called him back with a name they had pulled from their archives. The person their records showed as owner of the license plate in 1938 was an individual by the name of Alfred Cook. They also said it was registered to a 1936 station wagon. Steve went upstairs to search through Winooski's clerk's office for any records of death for an Alfred Cook. Unable to find any, Steve went to The Mill on a hunch.

When Steve arrived at The Mill, I was there waiting for him and that haze seemed to follow. He went to the reception area and asked to speak to Rob. Steve explained to Rob that he needed to look into the employment of an individual who supposedly worked there. Rob was more than willing to assist the police any way he could, and asked, "Who are you looking for?"

"The man's name is Alfred Cook."

"Doesn't sound familiar to me, but let's see what our personnel manager says."

"Thanks."

Going to the personnel office, Rob introduced Steve to Nicole, the personnel manager for The Mill. As Rob left the office, he said, "Nicole, take some time and see if you can help him out, because I can't."

"How can I help you?"

"Well, let's hope you can. I'm wondering if you have any record of an Alfred Cook working at The Mill."

"Do you have any idea when he supposedly worked here?"

"Yeah, sometime around 1936 or 1938."

"Our computer records only go back ten years, but there might be something up in the warehouse on the hill. Back then I was told they kept everything in ledgers. I'll take you up there if you want."

"If you don't mind?"

"Rob told me to help you if I could. Let's go."

Steve followed Nicole up to a building on the hill. It didn't take long for Nicole to locate where the ledgers from the past were kept.

"What year did you say?"

"Let's try 1937."

Nicole found the ledger for 1937 and found Alfred Cook with no trouble. Steve asked Nicole if it would be possible to look at the following years to see when his employment terminated. They looked in the 1938 ledger and found his name. His name wasn't registered in 1939, however,

and there was no explanation as to why. "Would it be possible to get copies of those pages from all three years?" Steve asked.

"Sure if you want to help me carry them down to my office."

Nicole made the copies and asked, "Is there anything else?"

"There is one more thing. I'm wondering now if I could sit here and go through them all one more time?"

"You're more than welcome, and if there's anything else, just ask." Steve started with the 1937 ledger and wrote down all the entries that had the first name of Paul. There were four in 1938. But in the 1939 ledger, he found only three Pauls. Circling one of the names on his list, he closed the last ledger, got up, gathered his copies, and thanked Nicole. At the station, he met Nick on his way out the door. "Nick, you're not going to believe what I just found."

Nick replied, "You can tell me on the way over to the quarry. They just pulled the car out and won't move it until we get there."

Chapter 25

They headed for the quarry and I found myself in the back seat of their car. On their way, Steve explained that, working on a hunch, he had gone to The Mill to go through their old employment records. He found that there was an Alfred Cook working there in 1937, and 1938, but not in 1939. He told Nick he had checked for anybody by the name of Paul, too. Steve told him that there were four Pauls who worked there during the years 1937, and 1938, but in 1939 there were only three. One of them started in 1939 and after one week's entry, disappeared, as did Alfred Cook. Nick said, "Then this Paul person who wrote in the diaries might have actually existed, along with the older gentleman who was mentioned? Is that what you're saying?"

"That's not all. Check out his last name."

Steve held out his notebook to show Nick the name he had written down. Even though I could see and hear everything they were saying and doing, no matter how hard I tried I could not read the name that he had written down. Steve asked, "You don't think he might be a relative, do you?"

"Nothing will surprise me at this point, but I can't actually say."

At the quarry, Steve followed Nick to the side of the station wagon's back doors. There were two nearly complete skeletons. Nick pointed to one of them as if showing Steve something. Nick turned to the officer in charge and asked him to call for the coroner to come and move the remains. Nick also told him to impound the car at their garage so they could go over it.

Nick and Steve got into their car and left. Nick told Steve to follow up with the coroner and the state police. Steve asked, "What do you make of that guy's chest?"

"I'm no professional, but if you ask me it looks like it had been blasted in or out by something."

Nick and Steve went back to the station. Nick saw that the information from Massachusetts had arrived. In the envelope was a picture of the family, the three sources of hair that were used for DNA sampling, and a letter explaining what they had found out about this family up till now. Looking over his shoulder I saw the letter contained mostly information we already knew, but also they looked into the family's travel arrangements and found that their tickets had gone unused, and that one of the DNA samples was taken from a bloodstain found on a mattress. Nick mumbled to himself, "How could an entire family disappear without anyone knowing?"

Nick asked Steve to run the new DNA samples from Massachusetts over to the lab so that they could compare them. He also told him to tell them to do it ASAP. Just as Steve got up to leave Nick told him to tell them that he would pick up the results in the morning on his way into the station.

Nick sat at his desk thinking. At length, he heaved a sigh of frustration and said to the wall, "How did Larry know about everything? All he had were the two diaries to go by. Everything about the murders was described in them, but he seemed to believe them from the get-go. And what was this shit about Fred being possessed? Shit like that just doesn't happen in the real world." He emphasized the point by pounding a fist on the desk.

Nick left a note on Steve's desk telling him he had decided to go and talk to me man-to-man. Nick knocked several times before he finally gave up and turned to go back to his car. When he was about halfway there, I found myself on the front porch in my boxer shorts. He turned around and headed back to the porch. What was strangest of all was that this time he could hear and see me, and yet the low-grade haze still existed. "So, you were sleeping," he said.

I held the door open allowing him to enter. I followed him in and went to the bathroom. He sat at the kitchen table waiting for me to finish. I came out of the bathroom and set up my coffeemaker blearily and turned it on before I joined him.

"So what's up?"

Nick leaned forward to grab the tequila bottle and poured himself a shot, which he downed in one gulp. He set the glass back on the table, and said, "I'm sick of this shit. All this spirit bullshit, rapes, murders, and you seem to know everything before anyone else does. You tell me what's up."

"Calm down, Nick. I don't know what your problem is, but I don't think tequila is going to help. I find the facts because I look for them. You as a police officer have rules that govern you and how you must get the evidence. I don't have those rules. I make my own. If I had waited for you and the other police to get the facts this whole thing might have been played out as two unsolved murders and five missing people."

"So why the hell didn't you say anything about your relative who worked at The Mill?"

"Relative?"

"Yeah, relative. Like maybe a Paul Stone. He's the only Paul who worked at The Mill at the same time that an Alfred Cook did who owned the car in the quarry. They also both seemed to stop working at The Mill the same year. You never mentioned that, how come?"

I thought for a minute about what Nick was asking. Then I got up from the table and went into my bedroom. Nick took another drink, and asked, “Where do you think you’re going?”

“I want to show you something. I’ll be right back.”

It was at this point I started watching everything go on again as I did before Nick saw me on the porch. In a few minutes I saw myself return from the bedroom holding a pistol pointed at Nick. Nick didn’t notice at first because he was focused on pouring himself another shot, but as he placed the bottle down on the table he looked up. The haze seemed to thicken to the point it was difficult to see. Then Nick’s voice broke through the haze, and asked, “Now what the fuck are you doing? Don’t you know it’s dangerous to point things like that at other people? Why don’t you just put that down and we can finish talking.”

In a strange whispery woman’s voice, I heard myself say, “Larry took a vacation and don’t you worry, we’re going to finish talking all right. You see with all your technology and all your resources if it wasn’t for my help you would have never looked into it. What you didn’t seem to find out was that Paul had an older sister by the name of Ruth who also worked at The Mill. If you actually read the diaries, there was an older man, a woman, two children, and Paul at The Mill every night. Well, you know who Paul was and we know who the older man was, but who was this mystery woman? That’s right, Paul’s older sister, Ruth. I had to put an end to our purpose, but it was taking you all too long to do things. I got to give it to you, though, eventually you got around to figuring things out.”

Something was definitely bizarre here. It was me I was seeing, but it wasn’t my voice coming from my mouth. I watched as I paced back and forth and this voice told the story of how a machine was being moved when it fell from the lift and crushed her. The Mill contacted her family and made no offer to compensate them or even to help with expenses, even though it was their company’s fault. She told Nick she ended up being buried in the town’s pauper’s cemetery in an unmarked grave.

Her voice rising in anger, she said, “And if you think I’m going to lie around and let these people get away with doing that, you’re dead wrong. A couple of years went by and then that bastard shot Alfred and my youngest brother, Paul. It wasn’t long before we found each other. We all wanted revenge and we all couldn’t rest until we got it. The children were just too young at their death to really know what revenge was all about. They were buried next to me in that graveyard in an unmarked grave, too. Stuck like the rest of us with no one knowing what exactly had happened at that sweatshop everyone calls The Mill.

“That’s when we decided to wait for the right opportunity and the right person. Fred seemed to have all the qualities we were looking for. He

was something short in the brain department from the mental abuse his mother had put him through over the years. He was a loner, a relative of the Lackly family—Ron's son, if you remember—and because of his alcohol and drug use he didn't even realize what was going on." She—I—stopped pacing and stared at Nick; who just shook his head.

"How come Larry?" he finally asked.

Still speaking angrily, Ruth said, "Because he had the friends like you who would check out the leads that he found from reading the diaries. We didn't always use him. He was necessary to put a stop to Paul, though, and you would have found that out sooner or later. Plus we like to keep things in the family, if you know what I mean."

"How?"

"You would have found his fingerprints where they shouldn't have been. Like I said, eventually."

Nick poured himself another. He swallowed his shot of tequila, put his glass down very deliberately, and asked, "So you killed Fred? Why?"

"I didn't kill Fred. I killed Paul. He was raping and sodomizing all those women and that wasn't what he was supposed to be doing. That girl he found broken down on the side of the road had nothing to do with this. That's when I decided I had to do something. Paul had conned Alfred into believing that it was none of his doing, that Fred was in some kind of control at times, but I knew different. Paul was always a womanizer and this was a way he could get away with it. He was supposed to get Pat—Ron's other son—but Fred was still strong enough in him to prevent him killing his brother. He settled for Vicki. Before he left his apartment for Pat's house I had Larry follow him as well as when he unlocked The Mill to bring her in. I saw that he had done the same to her as he did the others and after he disposed of her body I made my move.

With Larry's strength I overpowered him and lifted him off the floor. I saw that the hoist hook was directly behind his head and slammed his body toward the floor. As I did, the hook went into the back of his neck. I raised his kicking body over the top of the oven and lowered him into it. He continued to fling his arms around until the very end. That's how one of his hands ended up on the floor. All we wanted to do…"

Interrupting, Nick said, "All you wanted to do was to kill these innocent people and ruin the lives of others."

"Ruin the lives of others? That fucking family ruined the lives of many and they still are. We just found a way to pay them back."

"What about the dreams and images of Fred's mother during some of the sexual assaults? What about the girl who supposedly screwed Larry as he slept, and the dreams of the older man and Paul when Larry was in Massachusetts?"

"Those dreams were my attempts to convince Larry to go on and as far as that girl who fucked him as he slept, I just made myself appear to look like that girl named Diane. I created those dreams for Larry, so he would continue. Fred's horrors about his mother were too strong for me. Paul couldn't keep them from emerging when his body got excited. Just like it was me who convinced Larry to go diving in the quarry, but it was Larry who did the actual diving. It was the only way I could convince you that the car containing the remains of Paul and Alfred were there. In order for them to pass on they needed to be found and their story needed to be told."

"What about the children and you?"

"The children have been satisfied, also. As for me…"

They both heard a noise outside. It was Steve coming to join Nick. He saw me pacing back and forth holding a pistol, and heard a woman's voice coming from my mouth telling the gruesome story we all had been investigating. Not sure of what he was listening to, he pulled his revolver out of its holster, and shouted, "Freeze!" She or I turned toward the door and pointed the pistol at him. In that split second Steve decided to shoot before he was shot. He hit my body in my right shoulder. My body fell to the floor and the pistol flew out of my hand and slid across the floor. Steve shouted, "Nick, are you okay? What the hell is going on?"

Nick got up from the table and went over to where I lay on the floor. Softly the woman's voice said, "Thank you. I'm glad you didn't kill Larry. All I wanted to do was to tell you our story and explain that Fred and Larry had nothing to do with it. We were just using them the whole time and…"

The next thing I knew I was staring up at Nick as he stood above me on the phone calling for an ambulance and then seeing the haze disappear before passing out. I woke up to someone grabbing both my hands. Not knowing if it was still part of my dream or what was going on I jerked my hands away. It took a moment, but I soon realized Nick was on one side of the bed I was lying in and Steve was on the other. As I started to regain my bearings, I tried to sit up and felt a sharp pain in my right shoulder. There were IV lines going into my arms.

I realized that I must be in a hospital, but didn't really know for what reason. The last thing I knew I was having a terrible dream and before that I was at home in bed going to sleep. They both told me to stay still and to calm down.

"Calm down! I go to sleep, have one of the weirdest dreams I've ever had and the next thing I know I wake up in a hospital. Yeah, sure I'll calm down. When you tell me what's going on."

"Larry, you've been shot, but the doctors say you'll be up in a day or so. They also said it wasn't anything serious and that you got lucky."

"Lucky. I've been shot! How?"

"Steve shot you at your house when he thought that you were going to shoot him and me."

"You got to be kidding. That was all a dream. I wouldn't ever do anything like that."

"I didn't mean to," Steve protested, "but you or whoever had a gun pointed at Nick and then turned it on me."

"Nick, what is he talking about? Me or whoever."

"Well, at the time I was talking to you, but it wasn't you. There was this person by the name of Ruth Stone inside of you. She said she was one of the spirits that was at The Mill with Paul and the others. She told me the whole story and was getting angrier by the minute. That's when Steve walked in."

"Ruth?"

"Yes, Ruth."

All this time I had worried whether or not Nick believed me and finally the tables had turned.

"Then it wasn't a dream? Are you telling me Ruth possessed me?"

"I'm afraid so, and that's why we need to get your fingerprints. We want to compare them to the ones we got to verify what she told me."

I just lay there in silence. After a minute or two, I lifted both of my hands so that they could fingerprint me. Steve kept apologizing and explaining that there wasn't anything else he could do. I looked at him and told him I knew and not to worry about it.

Nick placed the sheets of paper with my prints into an envelope and told Steve that he wanted the State Boys to run my prints against all those they found at The Mill.

Nick told me he had to get going, and they both left, leaving me to puzzle over this grotesque situation. Then a nurse came in to give me a sedative, and I was out like a light.

The next morning I felt a lot better.

I was just starting my breakfast when Nick and Steve appeared. Nick explained that they had gotten most of the forensic results back and thought that I might want to hear them. He pulled a sheet of paper from a folder. Pausing to read it first, he then told Steve and me that the examiner determined that there were significant matches of the three people from Massachusetts and Pat's wife. Steve said, "Well that takes care of five victims and Fred, but what about Fred's other victim, Mandy?"

Nick replied, "Well, the only thing we can do about Mandy is to get blood samples from her parents. As for the woman in New York, we're still waiting."

Still wondering about the night before, Steve asked, "What the hell did I walk into last night?"

Nick scratched his head and hesitated for a moment. "Well, apparently the woman mentioned in the diaries was Paul's older sister Ruth who worked at The Mill. Seeing what Paul was doing to all of his victims she got a little pissed off and wanted to stop him. She said that they only wanted to get revenge from the family that owned The Mill. The only way she could get Paul to stop was to kill Fred, so she took over Larry in order to do that. Then she influenced his thoughts and actions so that all this would be brought out in the open. The only way that their spirits would be able to move on was for the bodies of Paul and Alfred to be found, getting even with the family for the deaths of the others, and for someone to be told why it was being done. That's when you came in and shot him."

Steve raised his eyebrows as far as they would go. "You mean to tell me that all these murders were committed by the spirits of other people from another time?"

"Yeah, if you can believe it."

Nick's cell phone rang. It was the state police fingerprint expert telling him that my prints did match a set taken from the hoist control box at The Mill. They now had all the pieces.

In the days to follow my gunshot wound healed pretty fast. The rest of the reports on Mandy and from New York, proved that everything written in the diaries was fact. It also proved that all of these people did die at the hands of Fred. Or Paul. They decided that there wasn't any evidence to prosecute me, but they did have enough evidence to go public with the facts of Fred's murderous rampage.

I was at the police station when they wrote their reports. They knew they couldn't tell the truth—who would believe them?—so they filled their paperwork out as if Fred had done it all, then committed suicide. As he signed his report, Steve asked, "You know if anyone was to really hear or see the true facts behind this case they would consider us all crazy, don't you?"

Nick slammed his folder shut and said, "Yeah, I know. I'm just thinking that if it happened this time, it can happen again."

"Not in our lifetime, I hope," I piped up. "C'mon, I'll buy you a drink. The paper paid for my story on delivery."

About the Author

Tracy Lamphere was born and raised in Vermont. He takes basic human needs and desires, and adds them to his twisted imagination to tell his stories about his home state and other places he has traveled. The Mill is just the first story he has to tell about Vermont. He has always believed that if one dies unexpectedly—their soul remains trapped until their issues can be resolved. Through his writing, Tracy explores this possibility and shows what the result can be. He also wants everyone to know that Vermont is not just known for its' maple syrup and ice cream, but that every picturesque town in Vermont's countryside has a story to be told.

Printed in the United States
1429400007B/7-51